Readers love

Amy Lane

Keeping Promise Rock

Keeping Promise Rock probably has a flaw somewhere. I was just too busy falling in love with the characters to notice.

—Rainbow Reviews

You know how you can tell when someone is a great author? It's when that person writes a book filled with such heart wrenching emotion that the reader can't stop crying, either tears of sorrow or of happiness. That's what author Amy Lane has accomplished with *Keeping Promise Rock*.

—Fallen Angel Reviews Recommended Read

If I Must

This short story is delightful, entertaining, and thoroughly fabulous.

—Whipped Cream Reviews

http://www.dreamspinnerpress.com

Making Promises

Amy Lane

Dreamspinner Press

Published by
Dreamspinner Press
4760 Preston Road
Suite 244-149
Frisco, TX 75034
http://www.dreamspinnerpress.com/

Making Promises

Cover Art by Paul Richmond   http://www.paulrichmondstudio.com

ISBN: 978-1-61581-461-9

Printed in the United States of America
First Edition
July, 2010

eBook edition available
eBook ISBN: 978-1-61581-462-6

Dedicated to moms and their boys.
Trystan, Kewyn, you are my boys,
I am your mom, and
that will never, ever change.

Acknowledgments

Back about a thousand years ago, after I got my teacher's credential, my stepmother took me shopping for an outfit in which to interview. I came out of the dressing room at one point, and the next thing I knew, Janis, my stepmom, was adjusting my bra, pulling up my socks and generally straightening my clothing, while I sat passively in daughterly mortification. After a moment, Janis realized what she was doing—and that I was twenty-three and not eight—and said, "I'm sorry—you realize that when you're sixty and I'm eighty, I'm still going to be adjusting your socks."

My stepmother has become the guardian of the elderly in our home. An ICU nurse, she has taken over the last affairs and the medical needs of my father's mother, her ex-husband's mother, and her own mother. She has been there in their final moments.

She is nothing short of a miracle.

She has taught me everything I believe about life, death, kindness, and dignity in all of it. If there is anything about Mikhail and Ylena's relationship that touches you at all, you may thank her.

It's about time I did.

Thank you, Janis. Brother, did I luck out.

Prologue

Just when you think you got it down...

    "Promises in the Dark"—Pat Benatar

SHANE PERKINS had never had a male lover before. He didn't know protocol, but he was pretty sure that two beat cops boning each other in the locker room of an L.A. precinct violated a whole bunch of it.

"No," he said firmly, when his partner—still fully clothed—wrapped his arms around Shane's naked, burly chest.

"No?" Brandon Ashford looked more like a calendar pinup than a cop. He was tall, built like a willow tree with deeply defined muscles in his chest. He also had dark blond hair, blue eyes, grooves in the side of his mouth, and a pair of dimples that men and women had probably been falling into since the day he was born.

"No" was not a word Brandon heard very often.

"We'll get caught. Don't like Top Ramen. Would rather eat hamburger."

Shane heard the puzzled draw of breath behind him and sighed. Once again, whatever came out of his mouth had jumped two sentences down in the conversation. It had made sense in his head—they get caught, they get fired. They get fired, they don't have any money. They don't have any money, they end up eating Top Ramen instead of at their favorite hamburger stand in the Barrio.

He felt Brandon's frustrated shake of his head. "Yeah—whatever, Shane." Brandon's hands came up to his shoulders and he fitted his lean form against Shane's back. "I'm not talking about *lunch*, man, I'm talking about, you know…." Brandon lowered his mouth to Shane's ear, and Shane *loved* it when someone whispered in his ear. It was, in fact, how Brandon had coaxed him into bed the first time—what had started as casual, harmless banter had gone up six notches when Brandon had whispered it in Shane's ear.

"*Lunch…*," Brandon whispered, and Shane sprung a boner that could have dented the locker in front of him.

"Someone's going to…," Shane whispered back helplessly. What he really wanted to do was bend over. He wasn't hung up on being a top or a bottom—it was just that Brandon was behind him, and that was easier.

"No one's going to," Brandon said, grinning. He'd won—he knew it. His hands fumbled at Shane's towel, and the thing dropped, revealing Shane's thick, blocky body. The only time in his life Shane had ever felt graceful and fine-boned had been in Brandon's bed, under the magic of his hands. Those hands were traveling the fronts of his thighs now, tickling the thick brown hair that grew at Shane's groin.

"You ever think about waxing?" Brandon purred, and Shane's head tilted back onto Brandon's shoulder.

"No," he muttered, but whether it was to the waxing question or to the "should we do this at work" question, even he couldn't tell.

"Better access." Brandon placed a gentle kiss at Shane's neck and then one on his collarbone and then one at his spine where his short, curly hair was shaved at the back of his neck. That one brought out little sharp teeth to nibble, and Shane tilted his head forward again, feeling helpless. It wasn't fair. Brandon could do this to him, and as far as he could tell, nothing he said to Brandon had any effect at all.

"Access is fine," Shane grunted, and Brandon reached around him to take hold of his cock, which was growing stiff with or without his approval, thank you very much. "It's—" His voice trailed off because Brandon had just stroked and squeezed, and his teeny-tiny brain had all but exploded. "Appro… appropria… fuck." Shane grabbed hold of his common sense and self-respect with both hands and jerked away, turning to tell Brandon he would just have to put his porn-dog on hold.

Which meant that when their captain walked in, Shane was the naked one sporting wood, and Brandon was the fully clothed one who looked like he was being sexually harassed.

Brandon smiled that winning grin and held out his hands. "Hey, there partner—nice of you to think of me, but you know I don't swing that way!"

Of course, when Shane thought back on it, all he had to do was say something witty, something that made the whole situation so wildly unlikely that the captain would just roll his eyes and assume that they were just horsing around, being buddies, whatever.

But Shane wasn't glib. He wasn't witty. Brandon had the words. Shane had an inconvenient brain that frog-jumped over the details and stuck on concepts that needed a master's thesis to explain. A wicked blush swept his body, even as his damned prick withered and drooped, and he looked up at the captain in completely helpless misery.

"*Titanic*," he blurted. A truer word was never spoken.

The captain just looked at them before turning and walking out of the locker room without a word. Brandon turned away in disgust, chuffing out air like a scolding parent.

"Jesus, Shane—just once could you not be such a psychopath?"

"*Titanic*," Shane muttered again, because sure enough, that one moment had sunk them both.

He was wrong, though. It didn't sink them both. It dragged Shane down to hell, but Brandon got off scot-free.

Shane should have guessed as soon as Brandon got reassigned. He wasn't sure if it was the captain's idea or Brandon's, but since Brand had been refusing to talk to him in the squad room or the locker room or on the phone, he assumed it was Brandon's. He spent a horrible week waiting for a call from Internal Affairs but the night he was sent out to the area surrounding USC all by himself, he realized the call would never come.

So, before getting out of the cherry top in the city's worst neighborhood by himself, with gunfire echoing between the darkened streets under shattered street lights, he placed a call to IA himself, along with the time he'd asked for backup.

Then he placed a call to his answering machine at home for double assurance.

Then he got out of the car alone, loudly identified himself and ducked behind the door to the car, and prayed.

A month later he was almost recovered from the severe internal injuries that occurred when too many bullets hit a Kevlar vest at close range. As his lawyer was wheeling him out of the hospital his friendly IA agent was there with a check to keep him quiet.

Shane looked at the check and wondered if it was his imagination or were all those zeros covered in blood?

"So what are you going to do?" Brandon asked him over the phone that night. Brand hadn't come to see him in the hospital. Shane had hated himself for hoping that he would. Nope—just this one awkward, pathetic phone call, and Shane wanted it over more than he wanted more pain meds for the surgery stitches.

"Go far away," Shane said softly. "And find someplace they'll let me be a cop again."

Brandon had been a fourth-generation cop but had always thought of the job as beneath him. He knew he was pretty, and he lived in L.A.—he had better things to do with his time. At Shane's words, he snorted with disgust. "Only you, Shane. You've got enough money there to go anywhere in the world. *Do* anything in the world! Have some imagination, why don't you?"

Shane had a vivid memory, one that had flashed in front of his eyes when he'd enrolled in the academy, one that had sustained him in the long hours of studying and working to make a minimum rent and buy Top Ramen on the way through. It had greeted him when he'd graduated and made the whole thing worthwhile.

He'd been eight years old, and he and his father had been in the back of the Town Car. His father had been busy working on documents, and they'd been driving through the neighborhood where Shane had gotten shot, actually. His father was president of the university at that time—it hadn't made him any more or less busy or any more or less distant, but it had made the ride to drop him off before school a little more interesting.

They were there at a stoplight when Shane saw two cops run down a guy with a gun. The guy had been hauling ass, nervous, twitchy, wearing a thousand layers of clothing. (When Shane grew up and walked the same beat, he recognized crack addiction, although by the time he came into the job, meth was the drug of choice.)

The policemen had been... extraordinary.

Shane had watched, wide-eyed, as they'd blasted through the street, not with their guns but with their commitment. The cop in front had made a solid tackle, landing on the bad guy (as Shane had thought of him then) and cuffing him efficiently and without violence. As the two cops pulled themselves up off the dirty ground and stalked away, their prisoner in their charge, Shane had been awestruck.

They had done something *real*.

Shane was mostly a quiet, chubby kid. He liked living in his own head, in a place of knights and dragons and absolute good and absolute evil. He liked ideals. His mother was on the other side of the world, his father was distant, and his twin sister was so devoted to the world of dance that it was like they didn't even live in the same house. Those books had raised him—had, in fact, instilled within his heart every hard-earned value he possessed.

And there they were. Real life knights in shining armor, doing real live acts of bravery to slay crack-addicted dragons and save trick-turning princesses.

More than anything, Shane wanted to be one.

And now, ten years out of the academy and technically just months away from getting his detective's shield, that hadn't changed. He was still weird. He still lived more up in his head than down here on earth. He had learned that the line between good guys and bad guys was less than absolute—many of the "bad guys" were simply lost, addicted, and hungry. He had learned that many of the "good guys" were bullies, excited about using their power simply because they could.

But the basic principle was still there, clean, unsullied, and beautiful. He was a good guy. He could make a difference. All of the fanciful crap in his head could be real when he was on the streets helping people.

"It's the only thing I've ever wanted to do, Brandon," he said, now in the darkened confines of his sterile apartment. He should have something, he thought idly. If he was going to go far away, maybe he could buy a house, get a dog or something. He'd been gone for a month and hadn't had so much as a goldfish to go belly up without him.

Brandon gave a short laugh. "Only you, Shane. Let me know where you end up."

"I don't think so," Shane replied. "In fact, I'm thinking you're my object lesson for who I *don't* want to let into my life."

He hung up on that one. It was the best line he'd ever had.

Chapter 1

And if I build this fortress around your heart…

"Fortress Around Your Heart"—Sting

BENNY FRANCIS might have had a toddler of her own, but in this moment she was all bright eyes and excited child herself.

"You're going to the autumn Renaissance Faire? Really? Ooooooohhh…. I *loved* the Ren Faire… the summer one in Fair Oaks!" She turned to Andrew, the young private that her brother Crick had met in Iraq. Andrew worked for her brother's boyfriend, Deacon, on their Levee Oaks horse ranch now and was as much a part of the family as Benny or her daughter or any of the other folks who revolved around The Pulpit like planets around the sun. "Drew—you remember! You took me there in June?"

Andrew nodded soberly, only an act of will keeping his blinding white grin from erupting in his dark-skinned face. Obviously he remembered something funny about the incident that Benny wouldn't think funny at all.

Shane nodded at Benny over his slice of chocolate cream pie and tried not to be weird. He wanted to say, *Oh dost thou, Lady Faire, tell tales of knights in days of yore!*, complete with a hokey British accent and everything, but he enjoyed his Sunday nights here at The Pulpit and really didn't want Deacon or Crick or Benny or any of the people who gathered here for dinner once a week to look at him the way Brandon had looked at him that day in the locker room. He was sincerely trying to not be too much of a psychopath.

"Oh tell me, Lady Faire, do you swoon over knights on prancing steeds?"

The words—so close to the ones in Shane's head—were uttered in an *atrocious* British accent, and Shane tried not to glare at Jeff, Crick's best friend.

Jeff was so gay he made an Easter Parade look like a funeral for straight people—but he was also glib and witty and funny, and he could pull off the Lady-Faire schtick where with Shane it would merely be dumb or odd or socially backward. As badly as Shane yearned to belong here at this big, battered wooden table in this old ranch-style home, it was just not any goddamned fair at all.

Benny rolled her eyes at Jeff and said, "If I wanted a knight in shining armor, oh court jester thou, I've got Deacon or Jon or Shane here to fit the bill."

Jeff was slender and almost comically graceful. He was the kind of guy who could mince when he stepped and trill when he talked and then get totally goddamned serious, and people would take him seriously. His hair was the same lustrous dark brown as Shane's, and Shane suspected it had the same unruly curl, but Jeff's had a sophisticated cut to it and some sort of amazing hair glue that made it sit down and behave.

Jeff could get any set of friends he wanted. It just seemed unfair that he should want the same set of friends that Shane wanted, because Shane didn't have a whole lot of luck in the social department. Or the friend department. Or the family department.

But wait a second. "I'd be a knight in shining armor?" he asked Benny, and she grinned at him from around the fuzzy brown head of the toddler in her lap. The little girl was eating her mother's pie with a single-minded glee that Shane admired. He'd never seen anyone suck whipped cream out of their own tangled hair before.

"Of course you would, Shane! Look at you—you drive a muscle car for a prancing steed, you perform good deeds as a matter of course, and not a soul on the planet could doubt your good intentions. Yup," Benny finished happily, taking the second-to-last bite of pie on the plate from her daughter. "Definitely a knight in shining armor!"

"What does that make me?" Andrew asked, a little real hurt mixed in with the mock outrage. Even Shane could see that in spite of the age difference, Andrew wanted to be Benny's knight in shining armor all by himself.

Benny's grin at Andrew changed temperature and wattage, and Andrew's hurt seemed to disappear. "You're a squire—you're like a knight in training. You'll be knighted eventually."

"Will you be my Lady Faire?" Andrew asked, and Benny went from charmed girl to age-old-temptress in a heartbeat.

"Maybe," she teased and then turned to Shane before she could see Andrew put a hand to the imaginary shaft in his heart. "So, are you going to buy a costume?"

"A costume?" he said blankly, and she nodded—and Andrew rolled his eyes.

"Yeah—you know. Everyone's in costume. The actual knight costumes are usually reserved for the guys on horseback, but there are some great peasant costumes and merchant costumes and…." She looked fondly at her little girl. "We bought the basic dresses, but there were wings and hats and stuff."

She didn't say anything else, but her eyes darted to where her brother, Crick, and his boyfriend were washing dishes. Deacon—the boyfriend—actually owned the horse ranch, and Shane knew the place was in trouble. Deacon had been outed in a spectacular fashion that involved being beaten by a local police officer and a rather dramatic court case. The fallout had resulted in a loss of a lot of the ranch's local business. When Crick had returned from Iraq in May—injured and unable to go out and earn any extra income—keeping the ranch had been an iffy proposition at best.

Something had happened to give them some time. Shane knew it had something to do with Crick's decision not to go to college after his return (a thing that hurt Deacon deeply but didn't seem to bother Crick at all) but whatever had happened didn't change the fact that finances were still touch-and-go. Once a month the family—and that included Shane now, much to his honor—had a meeting where Deacon showed them how much money they had lost and how much they still had in capital and what sort of spread that could afford them in another part of the state or even the country. They all knew it would kill him to give up The Pulpit. His father had started the ranch from scratch, and Deacon loved it only slightly less than he loved Crick. But Deacon was adamant—the family came first.

Benny and little Parry Angel would have the best education and the best circumstances money could buy, and if that meant moving the ranch before they lost it, that's what it meant.

That didn't mean everybody's heart didn't stop during the monthly family meetings while they waited to see if they had just a few more months for the ranch to start making money again. It didn't mean that Deacon wasn't thin and transparent from stress—his best friend Jon had instituted a "Deacon weigh-in" during the family meetings so the family could keep an eye on Deacon's health. Shane looked unhappily to where Deacon stood, his six-foot frame made to look short by Crick's extra four inches. At the last weigh-in, he'd been one-sixty. It was better than when Shane had gotten there—called out because Crick and Benny's crazy-assed family had decided it was time to share the crazy and take the baby from her young mother—but it was still not enough to make him look strong and healthy, and Shane needed him to be strong and healthy.

Shane was working for the local police force these days. He should have been the enemy after what Deacon had been through, but they'd invited him into their family as a friend. His entire life, Shane had never had a family with that much warmth. He needed the ranch to be here in Levee Oaks. He needed this family to be all right.

Shane looked thoughtfully to where Deacon was shooing Crick off from resting a pointed chin in his shoulder to try and get him to eat a slice of pie. He was six feet of scrawny, determined alpha male hidden behind a shy smile and a blush. Deacon himself wouldn't have denied Benny or Parry Angel anything. If Benny had held off on a Renaissance Faire shopping spree, she had probably not spent the money voluntarily, to do her part toward keeping The Pulpit right where it was.

Shane looked back at Benny. Her hair was bright orange this month, and her eyes—a pretty blue but still the same shape as Crick's—were wistful and dreamy. Benny could be the closest thing to a damsel in distress that Shane ever got to rescue.

"What did you want to get?" he asked, inviting conversation. He set his detective's brain on "record" then, and it was a good thing too. It turned out a sixteen-year-old girl with a beloved baby on her arm could dream a whole lot of princess after one trip to the Faire.

A few minutes later, Benny carted the baby off to her bath—which turned out to be a community event, since Deacon's friends, Jon and Amy, were there, and they decided that four-month-old Lila Lisa needed a little bathwater on her bottom as well. When the community baby-bathing event had sucked half the people out of the room, Deacon asked who wanted to bring the table scraps out to the potbellied pigs. Shane practically knocked his chair over in an effort to volunteer.

The pigpen was in the dark behind the stable, but Shane didn't mind the walk. The early October night was still warm enough for cargo shorts and a T-shirt, and the breeze that blew off the delta and through the valley was crisp enough to suggest November was coming. It was a pleasant night to be out, and that was good, because he had something to do while he was there under the stars.

He rounded the corner to the barn on the way back, found the stack of hay bales under the soda light suspended from the barn, pulled his little notepad and pen out of his pocket, and started writing. He was so intent on his task that after he got all of Benny's fanciful wishes from the Renaissance Faire down on paper, he was surprised to see Jeff had come out on the porch of the house and was standing there smoking a cigarette.

Shane put the paper and pen in his pocket, grabbed the empty plastic bowl that had held the scraps, and tried to walk back into the house like he hadn't been doing anything that needed talking about.

Jeff wouldn't let it slide.

"Did you remember the scent of the hand lotion she wanted?" he asked as Shane came up the steps.

Shane flushed. "Chamomile-lavender, with a little bit of vanilla," he said quietly, and Jeff raised his eyebrows on the inhale. "Those are bad for you," he said, trying to just go past that other thing.

"Which is why I only get one a day," Jeff said primly, blowing smoke. "The military might have paid for Andrew's new, spiffy race-specific prosthetic eventually."

Shane tried for innocence. "Why would you think they didn't?" *Don't blush don't blush don't blush don't blush.*

"For one thing, Benny only spent a day on the phone trying to clear up the insurance—we all know *that's* a children's fairy tale in itself, don't we?"

"What makes you think it was anything else?" Shane kept his face as neutral as possible.

Jeff looked sadly at the end of his cigarette and stubbed it out on the bottom of his shoe. "Mmmm... I don't know. Maybe the office buzz about the 'big hulking cop' who came in and paid for Andrew's new, spiffy black-skinned leg and asked billing to keep it hush-hush? That's always a big hint something else happened, you think? I work in the VA hospital, Shane—did you think it was going to be a secret?"

Shane grew extremely uncomfortable, and, yes, the dreaded blush swamped his fair skin. "Please don't tell them," he begged at last. "People have their pride, you know?"

"I'm not going to ask you why you're doing it," Jeff said after a moment, "because we both know it would take months the other way, and I'd probably do it too—but I don't have the money."

Shane looked down, and the silence stretched long enough for Jeff to trot down the stairs and throw the butt-end away in one of the trash cans at the end of the house. He came back, squirting alcohol on his hand from a bottle he kept in his pocket.

"You ready to tell me yet?" he asked, rubbing his hands crisply together, and Shane shrugged. "Look, big guy, I'll keep your secret, but only if I know you're not out on the streets turning tricks for the green, okay?"

Shane actually managed a chuckle on that. "Funny."

Jeff shrugged. "Yeah, I've got a mouth."

"Not your mouth—the idea that anybody would want me. They'd probably be afraid of weirdness, like some sort of STD."

Jeff pulled in a breath and peered at him in the dark. "This family loves you, Shane. In fact, I think they worry about you. If you're weird it's because you're too much in your own head, and you only have to look at Deacon to see how that can hurt a guy. Now are you going to tell me where you're getting the cash, or am I going to have to blab about your Secret Santa routine?"

Ouch. Shane glared at Jeff. "You don't even like me." It was true— Jeff had been the master of the catty epithet since he'd arrived. "Big guy" was an improvement over "Yeti," "Sasquatch," and (after he'd outed himself at the dinner table) "Shane the hairy Hoover."

"That's not true," Jeff protested without even flinching. "I like you fine. I was *jealous* of you, but I think you're an okay sort."

"Jealous." Blink. "Of me?"

Jeff shrugged. "You walk in to answer a call, and they invite you to dinner? Hell—I had to work Crick's arm like Christ himself with the healing touch to get that invite!"

"Jon invited me," Shane mumbled. "He was kind of a dick to me when he got here. He felt bad."

"Really?" Jeff perked right up. "So it was a pity thing? Excellent. No hard feelings, right big guy?"

Why would there be? Jeff was the one who had offered the olive branch. Shane shrugged. "Nope."

"Good, then tell me where you got the money, I can tell Deacon to stop worrying, and it can be our little secret."

Shane scowled, feeling like shit. "Deacon put you up to this?"

Jeff waved his hand. "No—he was going to do it himself. The thought of the two of you out here *not* talking was enough to give even the baby a case of the squirmies. So spill or this goes public to the family. They *are* our family, right?"

Shit. Yeah. "L.A.P.D. let me walk into an ambush. When I didn't get my queer ass blown to hell, they gave me some cash to take away the sting."

Jeff opened his eyes large and pushed theatrically on his swinging jaw. "Are you *shitting* me?"

Shane rubbed at his chest, where he could still feel his scars from the surgeries under his shirt. "Naw. You know, when your ribs puncture your lungs through your vest and they have to take out your spleen and shit, I guess a little joke's gone too far."

He was unprepared for Jeff's slug to his jaw—both for the connect and for it to hurt so much. He landed on his ass and looked up at Jeff with absolute amazement in his eyes.

"What in the fuck...?" He was just that befuddled.

"You still *work* that job!" Jeff said, upset. He was shaking out his hand—and he should have been, dammit; that *hurt*.

"So...." Shane blinked hard. "Can I repeat? What in the fuck?"

"You *asshole!*" Jeff growled, and Deacon came out just then and took stock.

"What in the fuck?" Deacon stretched his hand out with the question, and Shane took it, still looking puzzled.

"Deacon, he *hit* me!"

And Jeff was furious at *him.* "Deacon—you want to know where his money comes from?"

"You promised not to tell!" There was something about this conversation that sounded… unfamiliar and familiar at once. Shane couldn't put his finger on it, but it made the moment even more surreal.

"That was before I found out you were attempting suicide-by-cop!" Jeff snarled, and Shane let go of Deacon's hand and sat down hard on the porch again.

"I'm what?"

"You get *shot* in L.A. because you're a big stupid queer-ass bastard, and then you come *here* where even the civilians get beaten for it! And you don't tell anybody here…. You just show up to Sunday dinner like you're going to be around for a while and not a soul here knows you're a walking fucking target!"

"I'm not a walking target," Shane said, coming heavily to his knees and once again taking Deacon's patiently offered hand. "And I only wish I was fucking. Something. At all."

Deacon Winters had an extraordinarily pretty face, shaped like a squarish oval with a square jaw and chin and an angel's mouth and lovely, dark-fringed green eyes. At the moment, those pretty eyes were looking at both of them like Shane had seen him look at Crick and Benny when they argued, and that's when it hit him.

He and Jeff were arguing like brothers. He looked at Jeff again. The guy was examining the manicure on the hand that had bruised Shane's jaw as though it was something precious. Okay—they'd been arguing like a brother and sister. Whatever. Siblings.

Shane flushed and spoke the truth because he owed the guy that. "It's nice of you to worry," he said quietly, and Deacon arched an eyebrow at him, as though he had more to say. "Seriously?" Shane asked Deacon, responding to the unvoiced question, and Deacon nodded.

"Fucking seriously."

Shane blew out a breath. "Okay. Fine. I'm sorry I didn't tell you all there might be a problem that way. I just didn't think it was worth your time, okay?"

"No," Deacon said judiciously. "Jeff, how bout you go inside and have Benny or Crick look at your hand. Shane and I need to have a talk out here."

"Yeah," Jeff muttered.

"Jeff?" Man, Deacon had that note of command in his voice. Shane would give his left nut to sound like that.

Shane was thirty-one, Jeff was his age or older, and Deacon was younger than both of them. Jeff turned to Deacon like a little boy would turn to his father. "Yes, Deacon?" he asked sweetly, batting the dark fringe of his brown eyes at the man.

Deacon looked blandly back. "I do believe Shane apologized."

"Fi-ine." He said it complete with rolled eyes too. "Fine. I'm sorry I hit you, you big stupid cop. Please try not to get your dumb fat ass shot off before next Sunday, okay?"

"I promise," Shane said sincerely, looking at the man in surprise. He took an awkward step in, and Jeff sneered at him. It was Shane's turn to roll *his* eyes. "Thanks, Jeff, for giving a shit."

"Yeah, what-the-fuck-ever." Jeff snorted and walked back in to the house, leaving Shane alone with Deacon.

He was unaccountably nervous.

Deacon looked at him for a second and touched his jaw with soft fingers, then grunted. He walked to the door and shouted, "Crick, get me some fucking ice!"

"Stop swearing in front of the baby, asshole!" came the reply through the door, but Shane had no doubt that Crick was doing what Deacon had asked.

Deacon walked to the porch rail and leaned his weight on it, just like Jeff had been doing earlier. "You got shot?" he asked mildly, and Shane shrugged.

"I… I was sent into a dangerous situation without backup," he said carefully. "The Kevlar, you know… doesn't protect you from the impact."

"No. No, it doesn't. Was Jeff right? Were you out to your department?"

Shane turned a deeper red, if that was even possible. "Not on purpose," he mumbled, and Deacon turned to him with eyebrows raised to his hairline.

"Do I want to know?"

Oh God. Anything but tell this story to Deacon. Shane honestly thought he'd rather tell his father, were the fucker still alive, than Deacon, who actually sort of liked and respected him.

"Do I have to tell you?"

Deacon looked at him gently. "Look, Shane, I can't make you. But…." The man looked embarrassed, but since he often looked embarrassed, it suited him. "Look. You go ahead and keep that locked in your chest, that's fine. But I'm the poster child for repression, and I gotta tell you, you need to tell someone. What we're worried about right now is exactly what Jeff said. Does *this* department know about you, and are you in danger? Because if you've got other backup out there, you haven't told us about it. And if we're it, we need to know, right?"

Shane swallowed. "I'm going to be gone next weekend. Would you feed my animals on Saturday?"

Deacon didn't even look surprised at the abrupt change of subject. "So we know to go get them if anything happens to you, right?"

"Yeah—Angel Marie eats a lot."

Deacon raised his eyebrows. "Angel Marie?"

Shrug. "If I'd known Parry Angel when I named him, I would have found another name. Anyway, I'm afraid if I don't get to him in a day or two, he'll eat a cat." Oh Christ. That came out weird. He knew it did, but he couldn't help it. Angel Marie wouldn't eat Orlando Bloom or the others on *purpose*, but the ginormous doofus wasn't exactly discriminating in his taste, and he weighed over a hundred and fifty pounds himself. So far, Shane counted himself lucky that the Great Dane cross hadn't eaten *Shane* for breakfast.

But Deacon didn't bat an eyelash at that, either. Shane felt a sudden surge of out and out love for the guy. It had nothing to do with how pretty he was or that he fed Shane once a week and invited him in on the family meetings. It had to do with the fact that he never ever made Shane feel weird.

"Okay, so you show us where you live and how to feed your animals, and in return, you promise us that if things go hinky, you'll give us a call. If you think you're going somewhere without backup, we'll give Jon a call and show up, simple as that."

"Deacon, you guys aren't cops!"

"Nope. But this is a small town. We know most of the local troublemakers, same as you. Shane, Parry Angel in there calls you her 'Unca Shaney'—you're not going anywhere without backup!"

Shane made his face as stern as he could. "Citizen," he said meaningfully, "you do not put yourself in danger—"

"Shove it, Perkins. We're all licensed to carry—"

"Vigilante-ism is a crime."

"So is discrimination. I want your word on this, Shane."

How had this spiraled out of his control like this? Shane had been in charge of his own destiny since… since… since he'd seen a bad guy taken down when he was a small child!

"Deacon! Look, this isn't safe. You have got to know the many, many things wrong with—"

"With sending a brother into danger?" Deacon looked at him with measured eyes, and Shane had to concede. There was something in Deacon Winters—some measure of fineness, of self-possession—that made it impossible to go up against him when he was like this.

Shane grunted. Great. He finally had a family, and his big brother thought he couldn't take care of himself. "Does Crick ever win an argument?" he asked bitterly and knew the sound of Deacon's laugh before he made it.

"All the goddamned time. Irritating asshole."

"Who just brought you ice!" Crick protested, shouldering his tall, broad-chested frame through the screen door. Shane wondered how long he'd been listening before he took his cue line, and then he dropped the ice pack in his hand with an oath and Shane stopped wondering.

"Did you get some for yourself?" Deacon asked, picking the pack up off the ground and taking Crick's hand in his own. Crick had come back from a two-year tour of the Gulf with souvenirs that made Shane's surgery scars look like skinned knees from childhood. The boy—he was twenty-three, maybe—rarely complained.

"It's numb enough," Crick muttered. "Don't mind me, Deacon. Ice his jaw before it swells."

Deacon raised Crick's twisted, scarred hand to his lips in a brief, tender show of affection that brought a lump to Shane's throat. It was like anything, any amount of happiness, was possible in a world where that gesture could happen.

Shane stood still as Deacon applied the ice gingerly to his jaw. He knew both lovers had been EMTs at one time, and Deacon had the professional touch to prove it.

"So where are you going?" Deacon asked quietly. "When we watch your animals, where will you be?"

"Gilroy," Shane told him. He didn't mention the Renaissance Faire—if Deacon didn't know he was going, he couldn't offer money to buy Benny the stuff that Shane had planned to buy.

Deacon looked up with a wrinkled nose and a shrug, inviting more input. Gilroy was sort of a big ol' nowhere—lots of farmland, lots of ranches, a few suburbs.

"My sister's going to be there," Shane told him.

"You have a sister?" Crick asked, plopping his ass down on the garden seat that rested against the wall. "Wow, you think you know a guy."

Shane raised a sardonic eyebrow. Fact was, he spoke less than Deacon—they all knew it. "Haven't seen her in years," he said quietly. Not since their father's funeral, actually, but they'd kept in touch once or twice a year since. She'd sent him flowers when he'd been in the hospital, along with a letter. *Dammit, Shaney—find another job or learn to duck. I'm way too self-involved to get all tangled up in this grief bullshit, so you're just going to have to live.* He'd gotten cards and the occasional calls since then, and he'd called back. She'd wanted him to come see her perform for the last year, and he had some time off. He figured it was time.

"What's she doing in Gilroy?" Deacon asked. Gilroy was a good three-hour drive into, literally, the middle of Bumfuck Nowhere and Left Ass Cheek of Yemen.

Shane had to smile though, because the answer was so unlikely. "Would you believe dancing?"

He couldn't wait to see her in action—she'd always been beautiful when she danced.

Chapter 2

And so they linked their hands and danced, Round in circles and in rows...
"The Mummers' Dance"—Loreena McKennitt

SHANE had always liked driving. It was one of the reasons he'd bought the GTO. Being in his own head, blasting rock music as loud as he wanted, feeling the power of the automobile under his hands and the way it purred over the road—it was meditation, pure and simple.

Part of the journey was on a two-lane highway that wound around the brown hills that bordered the coastlands. He'd left early, so traffic was moderate, and the rumble of the pavement under the deep-grooved posi-traction wheels was soothing. Between that and Springsteen on the stereo, Shane was in his happy place by the time he pulled off at what was essentially a roadside attraction.

Casa de Fruta used to be merely a fruit stand in the middle of nowhere, but the founders had added a restaurant and some novelty shops, and the effect was charming, like finding Tom Bombadil's house in the middle of a hazardous journey. For the last few years, the adjoining property had housed the Renaissance Faire for eight weeks in the fall, and as Shane pulled up into the dusty gravel (he paid the extra five-spot for the VIP lot) he thought again of Tom Bombadil's house and *The Lord of the Rings*.

Because Gilroy after a long, hot, summer was a dusty, dry, graceless hunk of land, but the Renaissance Faire turned it into a storybook with the boundless magic of humanity's capacity for whimsy.

Shane was wearing jeans and a *The Who* T-shirt (the old bands were coming back—he'd always known they would!), but as he parked the car and made his way through the parking lot, he felt supremely self-conscious. Almost everyone else was in costume.

The costumes for the men ranged from leather pantaloons tucked into knee-high boots with a leather over-vest and a linen undershirt to basic cotton trousers (loose and floppy with a drawstring waist and ankles) and a large, blousy, big-sleeved tunic, usually with a V or tied neck. Most men had a vest on over their tunics, and *everybody* had some sort of hat—leather, raffia, corduroy, linen. The variety of headgear materials alone was impressive, and that didn't even include the styles. The colors ranged from loud to bright with a dash of understated and the occasional neutral, and the assortment of pieces to any given ensemble was as varied as the men themselves.

And that was just the men.

The women did all of that with a combination of skirts and laced bodices—usually with bosoms flapping out of the bodices and sometimes even with thighs showing from hoisted, banded skirts. Shane had to admit he had always enjoyed looking at a nice bosom, and at this point his dry spell had been long enough that he didn't care which team he was batting for, he just wanted to *play*. The squishy handfuls of boobage being pushed into touchability were just as enticing as the occasional glimpse of bare chest that he saw from the young men. Anything, dammit—*anything* just as long as he knew he had the option of human touch sometime in the near future.

A happy family passed him: mom, dad, teenagers—a boy and a girl—all dressed to the nines. The more-than-plump mother was holding two grade-schoolers by the hand—also in costume. Mom's floppy bosoms were not as graceful as those of the college-aged girls whom Shane had passed on the way from the car, but her adoring husband still made her stop so he could "fluff" them anyway.

Shane was glad his sunglasses hid his rather wistful look at Happy Ren Faire Family. He liked them—by the end of the day, the little ones would probably be exhausted and whiny, but as he watched the older boy swing his little sister in the "princess dress" up into his arms, Shane couldn't help but think of Deacon's little family back at home. He was part of that, he thought resolutely. He was buying his princesses—both Benny and Parry Angel and even little baby Lila—a truckload of princess crap. Hell, he'd even spring for one of those Robin Hood hats for Drew. He was going to be the indulgent uncle in that happy family if he had to spend all of that useless fucking money sitting in the bank on the Renaissance Faire alone.

His state of being perpetually horny faded, and he remembered why he was here.

He was here because he had family, and he wanted more.

He got his ticket from the will-call booth and ventured under the wooden archway, taking a program from the gleeful young women calling greetings in affected Olde Englyshe accents that were no more authentic than Shane's jeans and T-shirt but no less charming for all of that.

It took him less than a minute to scan the program and make an abrupt left into the food court. His sister would be performing in fifteen minutes.

First he got himself a soda and something called a toad-in-a-hole (it turned out to be a sort of meat pie), and then he sat himself down on a hay bale to people-watch while he was waiting. It was worth his time.

"That's a nice costume, isn't it?"

Shane turned and found the mother whose family he'd been admiring grinning at him as she sat what looked to be a preschooler on her lap. Shane looked back to where he'd been focused—on a giant of a man wearing what looked to be leather armor, complete with silver (or stainless steel?) buckles and belt rings and a gigantic sword.

It helped the guy's image that he was well over six-foot-four and had long black hair down to his waist.

Shane had, oddly enough, actually been focused on the costume.

"It's amazing," he said to the nice woman. "Where does someone get something like that?" He gave a look to her many colored—and many layered—skirts and her flowered bodice (which in no way color coordinated with anything else in her outfit).

"You'll see—after you eat lunch, just follow that path down there. Most of the vendors are selling *something* that will help you make your costume. You get here an ordinary wank in a T-shirt, but you can leave like a knight in shining armor if you like."

The little girl in her lap took a drink of mom's soda and pushed a mop of the brightest red hair out of her face. "I don't wanna be a knight. I wanna be a princess!"

"Absolutely, baby," Mom said dryly. "You can be nothing other than a princess." She met Shane's eyes. "And you can be a princess too," she told him soberly, and he laughed outright, because she was friendly and because, like Deacon, she made him feel welcome.

"Probably somewhere in between," he said with a wink, and she laughed. Her husband met her then with a handful of food balanced in his arms, and the illusion that he was part of a happy family vanished. The music started then, right there in the middle of the food square. Shane stood up with his food and moved with the edges of the crowd who were gathered to see his sister dance.

Kimmy had grown in her senior year of high school, and it had almost broken her heart when she'd reached five feet, seven inches tall. The fact was dancers needed to be tiny—the better for their partners to hoist them over their heads or whip them around like ribbons made of muscle and grit. It also kept the amount of weight pounding down on delicate joints and tender cartilage bearable—but still, Kimmy had kept dancing.

She had danced through injury, through demotion from one of L.A.'s premiere dance troupes to finding work where she could get it. It had been ten years since she'd discovered the Faire circuit—performers who were booked in Faires (and there were Renaissance, Celtic, Tudor, Viking, Dickens, or some other old European events happening all over the country on nearly every weekend of the year) made their living doing something they loved. As Kimmy had been telling Shane for ten years, what was valued on the Faire circuit was showmanship, craft, and true athleticism—not who had the youthful body capable of doing the move of the week.

The woman who stepped into the ring sinuously, dressed as Titania, possessed all of those qualities—showmanship, craft, and a truly gifted grace and athleticism. She also had some meat and muscle on her bones— a thing for which Shane was grateful. Her bulimic days to keep a dancer's weight were obviously over, and he thought she was beautiful. She was wearing a green unitard and tights, and her long, blond-streaked brown hair hung in waves down her back. Her brown eyes slanted mysteriously at the crowd as she stopped as though listening and then grabbed the strong drapery suspended from a hard-bolted scaffold, erected directly above the dancing square.

As she climbed, a costumed man appeared—shirtless, but with a hairy pair of trousers on. Truly hairy—he also had pointed ears, long hair, and eyebrows colored in to wickedly arch. He began the narration as Puck, telling the story of Titania's seduction by Oberon, and Shane was lost. He still saw small things—the bandages wrapped around Kimmy's feet and knees were worn threadbare and showed him that she was still plagued by injuries, but the way her body moved like silk in water showed him that she was doing what she loved, and it was worth it. The way Kimmy's mysterious smile never wavered even as she worked her dancer's body around the hanging draperies, seeming to fly above the ground, told him that her heart was still in this hard, difficult work—and the way her hair clung to her face with sweat told him that she'd learned that nothing you really loved came without its price.

Shane was so proud of her he actually felt his chest swell. His whole life, he'd wanted to be lovely and graceful, he'd wanted to move like his heart moved, and here was his twin sister, doing just that, and she was beautiful.

And then Oberon entered, and Shane's brain took a vacation.

Oberon was supposed to be dancing in the forest before he caught sight of Titania's loveliness and became enchanted. Shane was completely enchanted by Oberon.

He was small—maybe an inch or so shorter than Shane's sister—and slightly built. His hair was blond, tightly curled, and came to a point on his forehead above almond-shaped gray eyes. He was… delicate. Pretty. He had high, Slavic cheekbones and pouty lips and a little diamond of a chin, complete with a dimple, and Shane's heart tripped over itself and fell in a puddle as he began to move.

He moved like poetry, like music, like song. Birds were clumsier, cats more awkward, snakes less sinuous. The music was slow—it was time for a power exhibition—and Oberon performed. He was not dancing on a floor in toe-shoes; he was dancing barefoot, his feet wrapped like Kimmy's, indicating injury or pain, and still he moved as though his body was pure power, and not flesh and bone at all.

 Slowly he extended his foot, his leg parallel to the ground in front of him. Just as slowly, he raised his foot, then grasped it, holding his leg nearly flush with his side before he left his toes pointing to the blue sky and bent backward, taking his weight on his hands and making a graceful extension under the golden October sunshine.

His other foot came off the ground, and he held the pose until Kimmy swirled the sturdy draperies around his feet. He tangled himself in them, and then—as the narrator told of Titania taking a fancy to the dancing faerie king—used the draperies and his amazing body to haul himself upward to join Kimmy for acrobatics in the air.

Please God, let him like guys.

Shane was half ashamed of the thought. It wasn't like he had a chance—even a chance of a chance—with such a person. The man clasped hands with Kimmy, and the two started a slow spin, hands clasped, legs extended in the draperies, bodies stretched out over the ground.

Oh God. It almost seemed impossible that Shane was breathing the same dust.

It was just, Shane thought, his eyes hopelessly glued to that lithe body rippling with lean, corded muscle, that it would be nice to dream. It was like when a middle-aged woman, happily married, found out that her favorite movie star was gay. It broke her heart a little just to know that there wasn't a chance even in fantasyland for the two of them to ever touch.

Shane just wanted to know that there was a chance of touching. Just to know it, he thought with a painfully thudding heart, just to know there was a chance.... It might make celibacy worth it just to know someone that beautiful might ever touch him.

The dance continued and time stopped. When it was over, Shane clapped with the rest of the patrons in the food court, and the three performers stood together, bowed, and set up the tip basket. Shane waited until the crowds had cleared out and walked over and dropped a twenty in the basket Kimmy was holding, and she looked up at him in surprise.

When she saw who it was, she passed the basket off to Oberon and squealed, launching herself at Shane with enough enthusiasm to make the three-hour trip to Gilroy completely worth it.

"You *came*! Oh God, Shaney, you *came*!"

Shane laughed and hugged her, picking her up and swinging her around. "How many sisters you think I've got, sweetheart?" he asked as he put her down. (*Three*, he answered himself, if he counted Benny and Amy, which he did.)

"Did you see? Did you like?" Kimmy asked excitedly, bouncing up and down, and then she stopped and flushed. "I'm sorry—I've been trying to be less about Kimmy and more about the rest of the world." She paused like a schoolgirl remembering her times tables. "How was your trip? Do you like the Faire? Will you be staying long?"

"I'm here for the rest of the day, Kim. I've got a hotel room, but I need to leave early in the morning. I was hoping we could go out for dinner or something—even if it's with your friends and all." He took a chance and swung his chin around to indicate Oberon and Puck, both of whom were hanging out like friends to see who the behemoth hugging their Titania might be.

Kimmy's face lit up, and Shane forgot her pretty companion for a moment. His sister was honestly happy to see him.

"You'll stay?" she asked again hesitantly, and Shane smiled, feeling very happy he'd come.

"Yeah—how many more performances you got?"

"What, Mikhail—three today?" She grabbed Shane's hand and looked behind her at Oberon, who was showing no signs of bugging off into the dusty wonder of the Faire.

"You have three," he replied in voice that held a slight accent. "I have only one more."

"Oh yeah," Kimmy said, frowning in thought. "I'd forgotten. Mikhail isn't a regular member of the troupe—he's taking some of the slack off Kurt while he's healing up." She pitched her voice conspicuously over her shoulder. "Although we'd *love* for him to join us on a permanent basis, wouldn't we, Brett?"

"I'm all for it!" Brett muttered with a lewd and playful waggle of his eyebrows, and Mikhail cast a furtive look at Shane and blushed.

Shane tried very hard to keep walking and not just turn around and stare. Did that blush mean what he thought it did? He dismissed the idea of what Brett might be to Mikhail—why would he blush?

"I have things to do this season," Mikhail was saying softly. "If there's still room in the troupe when those things are done, I'd be happy to join, Kim—you know that."

Kim's face softened. "Yeah, I know."

"Where we going?" Shane asked. He was being dragged past myriad vendors, all of them in costume and calling raucously to the passers-by to come see the wares set up in a variety of tents.

"Well, I'm going to do my next costume change!" Kimmy laughed as she dragged Shane behind what looked like the Faire proper to a set of smaller tents behind the vendor's tents. "And then I think we're going to go get you some clothes. You're sticking out like a sore thumb, Shane. Was that really the effect you wanted?"

Shane cast a sideways look at Mikhail and knew he turned red. "No," he said thickly. "Sore thumbs hurt." Christ. Did he really say that? *Jesus, Shane, try not to be such a psychopath, would ya? Thanks, Brandon, you big fucking prick—by all means take up residence in my head-space right now.*

But Mikhail looked up at him with a smile. "Da," he said, his accent even stronger. "Then we must bandage this one in fine Faire clothes—is your wallet thick enough for good healing?"

Shane grinned. "Consider it a 'green-thumb' kind of hospital," he said happily, and although Mikhail was laughing, he realized that Kim was looking at him with something like pity.

"Still talking in code, huh, Shaney?"

Shane let out a big heaving sigh. "Yeah, Kimmy, sorry 'bout that. But I'd love to go shopping. And maybe while we're at it, you could help me find this shit too?" He pulled out his carefully made list and gave it to his sister, who gave it to Mikhail.

"You have a girlfriend?" Mikhail asked, and dammit, there could be no mistaking the disappointment in his voice.

"More like a little sister and a niece," Shane corrected hastily, and Kimmy said, "Hey!"

Shane shrugged, turning his attention back to Kim. "Sorry, sweetheart, but it's true. I've sort of got... I don't know. A family at home. Brothers—one of them a real pain in the ass, but I think he loves me like a brother anyway. A sister—two, actually—and they've got babies. It's...." He grimaced, remembering the day he'd met Deacon and Crick and their motley crowd in Deacon's kitchen. Motley, oddly assorted, with complicated stories, but still family.

"It's complicated," he said at last lamely. "But mostly it's family. I love 'em."

"And I am?" Kimmy asked, her face set in stony lines. Kimmy never had liked not being the center of attention.

"Always invited for holidays," Shane told her gravely, and her face relaxed a little.

"Well, I guess it's good you've got someone the other three-hundred-and-sixty-four days of the year," she said grudgingly. "Wait here. I'll go change." She'd stopped in front of a tent big enough to sleep maybe four people and ducked inside.

She left Shane looking awkwardly at her two companions, trying to reconcile "Brett" to "Puck" and "Mikhail" to "Oberon."

"So," Shane said, wishing he could think of some way to be smooth, "you, uhm, don't do the Faire circuit full time?"

Mikhail looked at him hopefully, and Brett grunted, "I'm out of here," and socked Mikhail on the arm. "Remember, we've got a show at two o'clock—try not to be jerking off before curtain." And with that, the guy with the long hair and hairy pants stalked off.

"Asshole," Mikhail muttered sourly at his back. "And no," he continued, turning to Shane with a slight smile, "I don't do the Faire circuit full time. It's sort of my...." He paused, searching for a word. "Mad money. I teach dance during the week. I'm saving for something, and that's where this"—he indicated the tip bucket—"usually goes. And that reminds me...."

With that the little dancer stuck his head into the tent and said, "Kimmy—don't you usually keep this for us?"

"Jesus, Mikhail, give a girl a little warning!" Kimmy's voice was muffled through the tent and what sounded like clothing.

"Like I care about your breasts. Here—I don't need any more temptation to spend my money, right?"

"Yeah, I hear you. I'll put it here, and Kurt will make it safe when he gets here. Now move! This fucking thing's a bitch to lace up, and queer or not, I don't want witnesses."

Shane's heart did a fantastically orchestrated happy dance, complete with acrobatics and costume. When Mikhail popped back out of the tent wearing a long turquoise colored vest over his bare chest, it was all Shane could do to not babble like a moron.

"So, um…." His tongue froze in the back of his throat, and it occurred to him that there were worse things than babbling.

"You are Kimmy's older brother?" Mikhail asked after an awkward pause.

"Twin," Shane told him, wondering if he should be affronted.

Mikhail blinked and looked at him as though he hadn't actually seen him the first time. "You two are nothing alike," he decided with a sniff, and Shane knew his cheeks grew pink.

"She's always been real graceful." He had to look away. "Clothes. What sort of clothes should I buy?"

"You are graceful!" Mikhail said, surprising the hell out of him. "But you move like you have somewhere to go. She moves like the world will come to her."

"I heard that!" Kimmy shouted from the tent, and Mikhail rolled his eyes.

"I hope you did!" he called back. "Your brother is here, and he wishes to go shopping, and you are wasting your break trying to make your breasts look bigger. They're small. Be happy. They do not get in the way."

"Look, you queer Ruskie bastard, I've got forty minutes until my next gig, and I have to look like a fucking peasant, so would you cut me a fucking break?"

"If you have to look like a fucking peasant, I suggest you call Kurt over here, because the only part you are going to get right is the fucking. Now get your ass out here, you silly girl, and greet your family." Mikhail gave the tent an ill-tempered look. "It's inexcusable. She's spent weeks talking about nothing but seeing you, and now she's hiding in there like a frightened child…"

"I'm not hiding!" Kimmy snapped, coming out of the tent and tying the front of her bodice, but she gave Shane a sidelong look, the kind he recognized from childhood that said she was only telling half the truth.

"Not anymore," Mikhail said, his sulky little mouth curving up on one side smugly.

Shane had to laugh. "You've worked with her before?"

Mikhail shrugged. "I have subbed in her troupe many times. She's very sisterly—I think she needs a real brother to squander some of that attention on."

Kimmy flushed and then took Shane's arm. "Well, then, let me get to it," she said brusquely, but she wasn't meeting Shane's eyes, either.

"You want to come along?" Holy cats. Shane couldn't believe he actually said that. It was almost... smooth or something, like he was a whole other person. Almost like he was talking to Deacon or Crick.

Mikhail looked like he was on the verge of saying "No," and Kimmy said, "Please, Mikhail—you never wander the Faire. You just hang out in the tent listening to music!"

Shane heard Mikhail's little sigh as he came alongside. "I have no money for the Faire," he muttered, then he brightened. "But I am not spending my money, am I?" He turned a blinding grin to Shane. "I am spending *yours.* Excellent—this should be very fun!"

Shane had to laugh. "Glad to oblige." He let Kimmy lead him past the tents that housed the performers (fairly close to the bathrooms, he noticed with a grimace) and into the Faire proper. He got his bearings quickly—it was laid out on a simple loop, with the food court forming a cul de sac off to one side and the jousting area off to the other.

"Keeps the horse shit well and good away from the food," Shane observed thoughtfully, and Mikhail smiled.

"You know something about horses? Here—let's go in here."

Shane allowed himself to be led into a vast tent full of what appeared to be machine-sewn cotton clothing and hustled into a corner and told to stay put. Kimmy and Mikhail whirled around the store, coming to him with trousers—both fitted and loose—and shirts in a variety of colors.

"White!" he said at one point. "I know there are six zillion colors for the shirts—"

"Tunics," Mikhail supplied blandly.

"Whatever—but I want white."

"Gold would look very good with your complexion," the little dancer said, holding up a bright gold shirt... *tunic*... judiciously under Shane's chin.

"But white would look better with a black leather overshirt!" Shane said firmly, and the way Mikhail's eyes lit up made his vision swim for a minute.

"You want a leather jerkin? Like a constable or a rowdy?"

"A constable?" Shane said, trying to remember what that was. "Yeah—I'm a cop. I can be a constable—but I need a white shirt underneath the... jerkin? Really? Is that the word?" Because it sounded like something completely dirty, and he wanted to make sure he'd heard right.

"Da," Mikhail nodded sincerely—but his gray eyes were twinkling, and Shane grimaced. Little bastard knew exactly what Shane was trying not to say. He tried and failed to come up with a smart comeback—anything but imagining Mikhail um...er... *jerkin'*, and then Kimmy's brain caught up with her ears.

"You're a what?" she asked, horrified.

"A policeman—I told you that, Kim. That's why I moved to Levee Oaks—to take a job."

"You fucker," she said, her voice lost and a little empty.

"Kimmy!" Mikhail protested—because unlike their banter previously, she sounded like she really meant it as an insult this time.

"Are you trying to get shot again?" Shane heard the quaver in her voice and felt bad.

"Not really, Kim. Wasn't trying to get shot the last time, if I recall."

"You were shot? I thought you said you dealt with horses!" And to his credit, Mikhail sounded concerned as well.

"My friends deal with horses. And I wasn't really shot," Shane said to both of them. "You're not shot if the Kevlar holds—mostly you're *shot at*, right?"

Kimmy put her hand on her stomach, which was cinched pretty tight with a leather thong through a red-flowered bodice. "That's not funny, asshole. You were in the hospital for a month—"

"A month? And you were not shot?"

Shane shrugged and rolled his eyes—he hadn't wanted to talk about this, not today. "Yeah, well, who needs a spleen, right? From what I understand, they're sort of redundant. Mikhail, did you want a shirt?" He held up a black shirt with ties coming from a V-necked collar—and Mikhail took it numbly.

"It's very nice—they took out your spleen?"

Oh God. Shane had been there during dinners when Deacon had been cornered about his weight or working too hard or taking too much on. He'd seen the guy turn red and try to blow off any and all attempts to make his own health serious, and it had pissed him off.

Now he knew how Deacon felt.

"Look," he said quietly, so they knew he'd been hearing their concern and not their sharp words, "I'm fine. I'm working in a quiet little suburb of a place about a twentieth the size of Los Angeles. It's like going from Interpol to mall cop—I'm seriously taking it easy, so don't sweat it, okay?"

"Don't sweat it?" Kimmy asked bitterly. "When I sent you flowers, they were seriously doubting whether or not you'd survive, dammit!"

"You didn't go visit him?" Mikhail asked sharply, and Kimmy snapped, "I was in rehab, okay?"

Shane blinked. "Rehab?"

And now Kimmy flushed and threw a pair of trousers at him with undue force. Shane dimly realized that their little corner of the store had cleared out pretty damned quickly, and he felt bad. "Which is what I was going to tell you about when you got here—but then you had to go and tell me that you're trying to kill yourself without the high!"

"Don't be dramatic, darlin'." Shane put an armload of clothes down and took both her hands in his. "Look—how 'bout you calm down and let me change, and sometime when we don't have an audience, we can talk about this, okay?"

Kimmy looked around and laughed shakily. "Sorry—I know how you don't like scenes. I just…." And now she looked away, embarrassed. "I wanted to explain, you know? Part of coming clean is explaining to people you wronged, and… I didn't come to visit."

Shane shrugged, honestly surprised. "No worries, Kim. You sent the only flowers in the damned room. It's all good. Now can I go try this shit on? I want to find the place that sells leather!"

"Yeah, fine," Kimmy sniffed, looking over her shoulder. She wanted out of this scene, too, it was clear as day. "Here—let me go find some girl shit for you—some of that stuff on your list was here."

"I like leather," Mikhail said when she was gone. He had a sly little smile on his sulky mouth, and now Shane blushed.

"Chafes," he muttered, remembering an experience with an old girlfriend.

"Not if you don't wear it for long," Mikhail said gaily, and Shane had to laugh.

"Try on that shirt," he said earnestly, and Mikhail looked at it judiciously.

"It is a small—I know it will fit," he said with confidence. "But I have no money."

"Do you at least like the color?" Shane asked with some exasperation.

"It matches my jerkin and trousers very well," he conceded, and Shane rolled his eyes. Geez… try to do something nice for someone. Okay—that wasn't entirely true. The truth was Shane really wanted to see him in the shirt. He looked at Mikhail awkwardly for a moment and flushed. Not that seeing him without it wasn't a treat too.

Mikhail caught that look and the blush, too, and smiled, arching his eyebrows and looking very gamine. "If you would like to see it on me, I will try it on."

"Thank you," Shane muttered, and then he disappeared into his dressing room. The dressing rooms were hardly more than curtained cubicles, and he knew he could hardly keep his big, awkward body from challenging the edges of his space. When he and Mikhail bumped bottoms through the curtain, and his body—so long denied any contact at all—began to wake up and show a little interest, Shane knew he had to make some conversation.

"Uhm, this Kurt that Kimmy keeps mentioning—is he a nice guy?"

"No," said Mikhail shortly. "He hasn't stopped using for one thing, and he treats your sister like shit for another. Did you really get shot?"

"He what?" Shane whirled around and pulled the curtain aside, and then slammed it shut again. "You didn't tell me you were going to try on pants too," he mumbled, backing up against the plywood partition that marked the solid side of the cubicle. The guy had also not mentioned that he was going commando.

"You didn't ask," came the mild reply. "You act as though you have not seen another man naked. I take it that's not true?"

"One," Shane blurted, looking fiercely at the curtain and wishing he could get rid of the mental image of Mikhail—all smooth, tanned skin and pale blond hair at his groin and the center of his chest. That picture in his head was making him stupid. "And that's not the point. My sister—you're saying this thing with Kurt isn't a good idea?"

"He also shortchanges me on the tips," Mikhail muttered, and then, more brightly, "but that's okay—I flushed half his stash and replaced it with baking soda. Jerkoff."

"Jesus," Shane mumbled. "She was so proud she had it all together."

"And she did not visit you in the hospital." Mikhail was still talking—almost to himself, it sounded like. "Why was it your fault you got shot?"

"It wasn't." Shane had a sudden understanding. Talking to this man was like following a kitten with a ball of yarn. That thing was going to take him a lot of different, tangled places before he unraveled it and put it in order. "Stop chasing worsted," he muttered, "and let's keep talking about Kimmy."

"Your sister loves you," Mikhail said, and there was some shifting as he moved out of the dressing room. "Now I am not naked—would you care to see me?"

"I'm not even dressed yet! Gimme a moment!" Shane shut up for a moment—Mikhail was distracting him entirely—and worked at getting his trousers and tunic on. He came out of the dressing room and stopped.

Mikhail was wearing the black shirt with a turquoise huntsman and new black trousers and he looked....

"Handsome as a cat," Shane said without meaning to, and then he wanted to smack his head against the four-by-four post holding the entire tent up.

"One that chases worsted balls of words," Mikhail finished for him, looking pleased. "And your sister—she is proud of her life here. Kurt is...

he is not a good part of it, but he is only a part. She wants you to see that she's happy. That is all—you don't need to love the only addiction she still has, yes?"

"I still haven't met the guy," Shane said, looking around. The entire tent—every wall—was filled with clothes neatly hung on dowels suspended on the support bars. All those clothes and not one damned leather jerkin.

"We need to go somewhere else for trousers," Mikhail said judiciously, and Shane looked down at the loose-fitting pair he'd just pulled up.

"What's wrong with these?"

"They are baggy."

"They're comfy," Shane said, shifting his hips inside the roominess and deciding that this could be a very nice way to be costumed.

Mikhail scowled at him and pulled at the sides of fabric at Shane's hips, making the pants taut around his crotch. He looked up at Shane and smirked.

"There is another style that is fitted—you will look very good in them."

"I don't like to flash that around," Shane grunted, jerking the loose fabric out of Mikhail's hands, and Mikhail grinned at him.

"I should think not, if you've only had one lover." He grinned then with all his teeth, and Shane rolled his eyes.

"One *man*," he said with emphasis. "I've had women too."

Mikhail's eyes narrowed as though he didn't like the thought of competition. "Did you like them?" he asked tauntingly, and Shane felt the need to clarify a few very personal things about his life.

"I liked them fine," he said firmly. "I've just got an equal opportunity pecker, that's all."

One corner of that sulky little mouth came up in a pure sneer of scorn. "Then why so few lovers?"

Shane grimaced. "Because I've got a one-chance heart, okay? Now let me go put on my jeans, and I'll buy our clothes."

Mikhail opened his mouth in surprise and then something like outrage. "I'm not going to sleep with your 'equal opportunity pecker' just because you buy me clothes!" he protested, and Shane rolled his eyes.

"I'd be disappointed if you did. I just feel like being nice. Now shut up or that urge will pass right quick." And with that he stalked into the stall to change.

By the time he'd gotten situated with the clothes (kept the tunic on, took the trousers off, put the jeans on, folded the T-shirt) several things had settled themselves in his mind.

One thing was that Kimmy needed him. She might not have admitted it—and she might not even be prepared to act on it—but he knew without a doubt that she needed him. He was her only family, and there was a reason she'd started keeping contact and a reason she hadn't asked for help when she'd had a tough time, and he needed to be there for her just like Deacon and Crick were there for him.

Another thing was that he was way out of his league with Mikhail. The man was... beautiful, and quick, and funny, and very, very full of himself. How he could make arrogance appealing was beyond Shane, but Shane liked it very, very much.

And the third thing—the thing that didn't occur to him until he was approaching his sister and Mikhail as they held up the faerie wings and little girl dresses and big girl dresses that he wanted to buy for Parry Angel and Benny—was that Mikhail knew exactly what Shane had meant when he was thinking kittens and yarn.

He wondered if he could clone that quality and inject it into someone who was not so beautiful it made his breath stop in his chest.

Chapter 3

She don't lie, she don't lie, she don't lie…
    "Cocaine"—Eric Clapton

"SO," SHANE said meaningfully when they were on their way again. The vendor was holding his enormous bag of purchases for Benny and Parry Angel, and he had to admit that if he didn't have a lifetime whack of mad money, he'd be eating Top Ramen for a year. It was okay though—he had a shirt, he was on his way to get some more really expensive shit that would help him fit in here, and even though it had been messy, he and Kimmy had held their first real conversation since her argument with their parents. (Shane had not needed to argue with his parents. He had simply signed up for the academy and moved out of the house. Kimmy had needed their money to push her through dance—it made a difference.)

"So?" Kimmy was holding on to his arm and she was leading him somewhere specific. He didn't know how she and Mikhail could keep track of all of the different clothing vendors and what they sold, but he'd heard the hurried conversation between them as he'd been paying for his purchases. *Do we go to X? No, they don't have this, this, or this. How about Y? Yeah, but he's a total asshole. How about Z? Perfect. And then we can go to X-sub-1 for this and this. Excellent. We have a plan.*

Shane was content to allow himself to be led about the Faire, surrounded by people in full dress trying gamely to talk in fake Olde Englyshe and happy to be somewhere, anywhere, besides their ordinary, everyday lives.

"There was something you wanted to tell me, Kim?" he probed gently, and she sighed.

"Yeah. The coke got pretty bad. I've been clean since rehab—but...." She shrugged. "I started when I was really young, you know? It keeps you awake, keeps you thin—sort of a win/win situation, until you figure out you've spent all your tip money on it and you don't have anywhere to sleep. I hit Mom up for the cash so I could go in style—one of those real swank joints that give you the 'poor-pitiful-you' song and dance—but mostly?"

"Yeah?" Shane asked, dodging a couple of children chasing their parents. The little girl had on a dress way too big for her and had hauled the train of the thing through the neck of it, exposing a chunky bottom in Tinkerbelle underwear. Shane thought of Parry Angel and went *awwwwww.*

"Mostly I just felt alone. Really alone."

Shane turned toward her and remembered when they were kids. Their house had been cold and lonely, and they had, at the end of the day, each retreated to their own rooms. Shane went to his books and his stories, and Kimmy went to her dance, and they forged alien personal worlds where pain was distant and they could each be the heroes of their own stories.

Shane had a sudden memory. "I came home from the hospital," he said, "and went to my apartment, and it was... four white walls and a couple of concert posters. I decided that whatever I did with myself, the next time I got shot, I wanted someone to miss me."

"I'd miss you, Shaney," Kimmy told him earnestly, and Shane smiled at her, and they both knew it to be the lost, lonely smile of their childhood.

"I've *missed* you, Kimmy," he said truthfully, and her lower lip quivered.

"I used to be so mean to you," she mumbled. "I called you all those horrible names and made fun of you, but I was in rehab and you were... in surgery, and I just kept thinking that you were my only family, and you didn't even know I gave a shit, and that wasn't right."

Shane looked away for a moment and realized that Mikhail was standing idly in front of another clothier's, waiting patiently for them to finish their personal bullshit. Shane watched him perk up and cock his head as though listening, and then swear, trotting over to them reluctantly.

"Kimmy, *lubime*, you are going to be late, and then your asshole boyfriend will come yell at me! You need to run!"

Kimmy dashed her cheeks and grimaced. "Look, Shaney—you don't want to come to this one—it's an ensemble and…. Okay, I'm not going to be the center of attention, so you have my permission to skip it, okay? Go shopping with Mikhail here and meet us at the jousting in an hour—"

"Not long enough, *lubime*," Mikhail said decisively. "We'll meet you before curtain."

"Mikhail!" she protested laughingly. "He's *my* guest!"

"And I want to keep him for an hour or two. Give over, cow-woman, and go dance.'"

"Bastard," she muttered sourly, but she grimaced again, gave Shane a quick peck on the cheek, and called "Don't be late!" before vanishing into the crowd.

Mikhail watched her go with a combination of amusement and satisfaction, then turned to Shane, grabbed his hand, and said, "The time is ours, Kimmy's brother. Let us go spend your money frivolously and talk some more like kittens and yarn."

Shane looked bemusedly at their twined hands in the thick, gold October light. "Pretty day, but not a season," he said, wondering if Mikhail would follow him this time too.

Mikhail tugged at his hand imperiously, and Shane met a pair of speculative gray eyes. "No seasons. Only days." His voice was clipped and short—he wanted Shane to understand, and Shane did—but he wasn't necessarily going to just fall in line.

"I don't do single nights," he said, narrowing his eyes. "One-chance heart, remember?"

Mikhail pursed that sulky mouth and blew out a frustrated breath. Then he smiled smugly. "Pretty day," he said simply. "I will hold hands with a pretty man on a pretty day, and we will enjoy the Faire. Agreed?"

Shane smiled, and although he'd never have called himself the kind of man who kept secrets, there must have been *something* enigmatic about his expression, because Mikhail's eyes narrowed. "Come on, Mickey,"

Shane said, enjoying that imperious glare immensely. He *never* had the upper hand. "We have shopping to do."

"I am not a cartoon mouse," Mikhail said disdainfully as they started for the shade inside of the booth.

Shane laughed and started singing to an old pop standard, clearing things up a little. *"Oh, Mickey, you so fine, you so fine you blow my mind, hey Mick-ey! Hey, Mickey!"*

Mikhail gave a disdainful little sniff, curled that upper lip, and shrugged. Shane knew he was pleased.

"So," Mikhail asked while Shane was in another dressing room, fiddling with the hooks on the side of the *very* fitted trousers.

"So what?" Fuck. He was going to need a larger size. He hooked them anyway and started with the jerkins. *Yeah, buddy, you know what you'd like to be jerkin'. Shut up—I'm trying not to be a complete spazzmonkey.*

"So how did you get shot at?" Mikhail's voice was muffled as he searched through rack upon rack of clothes for just the perfect set of trousers and jerkin or huntsman to make Shane's outfit complete (Shane realized that he was going to have to start visiting the faires on a regular basis just so he didn't feel like an idiot to be owning all these clothes.)

"Same way most people are—someone aims a gun at them and pulls the trigger." With that vague answer, he looked in the mirror and took a gander. Ewww—some parts of his body just did *not* need that much definition. Shane sighed and stuck his head out of the dressing room. "I'm too fat for this stuff, Mickey—could you start picking a size extra-large?"

He was greeted by a pair of icy gray eyes. "I don't know which is more irritating. The way you won't answer this question or the fact that you think you are fat." Boldly, Mikhail reached out and pinched at the flesh of Shane's stomach. Shane yelped and threw himself backward, clothes jumping off the hangers as he knocked into them, and Mikhail still glowered, apparently not giving a shit.

"That's not fat, that's skin. You are a big man, but you are not fat. Now take off those clothes and give me a straight answer, you obnoxious man—I just want to know if you are going to be dying anytime soon."

Shane rolled his eyes and tried to bend over in the over-tight pants to pick up the clothes. He stood up before the pants could rip, and Mikhail rolled his eyes and shooed him back in the booth, bending to pick up the dropped clothing with the same preternatural grace he showed in everything else he did. "Don't try to change the subject—now change!"

"Bossy little prick, ain't ya?" Shane muttered, but he was charmed just the same.

"I'm going to leave you in there naked unless you start talking," Mickey's voice was set on "saccharine" and Shane sighed.

"You know that 'blue wall' you always hear about when people talk about the police force?" Shane asked, pulling the laces out of the jerkin and then pulling the thing over his head.

"Da," Mikhail muttered. Shane could hear the clinking of hangers as he set things to rights.

"Well, let's just say it's not really pleased when there's a pink brick in it."

There was a digestive silence. "Are you sure you're not a purple brick?" Mikhail asked, with just enough of a bitchy edge to make Shane poke his head out quizzically.

"That really bothers you, doesn't it?"

Mikhail looked sideways and shooed him back inside. "Hurry and give me those clothes, so I can give you something that fits. And yes. It bothers me. Too many stupid men saying 'bend over, boy, and give me that—but I'm not a faggot, I have a wife!'"

Shane took off both his garments and put them on hangers in the silence that followed, and then stuck his head out of the booth, holding out the hangers. When Mikhail reached for them, Shane grabbed his hands and made sure he had the man's complete attention.

"I like women too," he said quietly. "They're soft, they have breasts, they smell good—what's not to like? But that doesn't make me any less in bed with a man when I'm there. It doesn't mean that bodies together aren't bodies together—and hearts together aren't hearts. I'm not going to apologize for what I am any more than you should."

"Hearts and hearts," Mikhail sniffed, as though the idea were too fantastic to contemplate. "Here, try these on. And you still haven't answered my question."

"The thing with a lot of cops," Shane said, putting his jerkin on and wondering when he was going to lose this guy by over-explaining things like he tended to do, "is that they like to see things in black and white—or blue and pink. There is no purple. A whore is a whore—she's never a teenager, trying to support a baby. A gang-banger is a gang-banger—he's never a guy trying to keep a family together. A junkie is a junkie—he's never a lost kid who just needs a little help to get his shit together, you know? So... I'm a pink brick. I'm not a purple brick that can sort of fade into the wall, I'm an abomination, and I need to be lured into a back alley so the real bad guys can shoot at me." Shane sighed. The other side of the curtain was horribly silent. He'd lost the guy—his trademark weirdness had done him in. "You know—because a cop's a cop, he's never a redneck homophobic bully with an axe to grind."

Shane opened the curtain, ready to concede that the clothes he'd put on weren't going to rip off his body if he bent over, and was surprised to see Mikhail staring at him with wide, shiny eyes.

"You believe that?"

"Which part? The real part or the sarcastic part?"

"The real part—where people on the street are people and not... garbage. You believe that?" Mikhail's clipped, accented voice had become thicker, and the arrogant edge was completely dulled and soft. His sulky lip almost trembled.

Shane was surprised. "Well, yeah. Some of the kindest people I've ever seen have been on the street. Some of the most"—Shane moved his hands; God, he sucked at words—"tender things I've ever seen have been between people who had nothing to lose, so they hung on to each other."

Mikhail looked away, and it wasn't Shane's imagination—his chin was trembling. "You believed that, and you were a pink brick, so they tried to smash you. Bastards."

Shane reached out a clumsy hand—to cup Mikhail's cheek, to clasp his shoulder—he wasn't sure which, but it didn't matter. The dancer stepped back, pursed his lips, and was suddenly the perverse little flirt who had claimed that the day was only going to be a day at the Faire in the company of a pretty man.

"The size is good, but the color is for shit. Take it off. I have a whole other look for you."

"Mikhail...."

"Did I say I was going to spill out my life's story for you? I am not that man. Now move!"

Shane did as he was ordered—and refrained from pointing out that spilling his life's story was exactly what Mikhail had demanded Shane do for him. An hour later they were pelting their way through the crowd, trying not to be late, and Shane's estimation of how much mad money he could spend had risen considerably.

He was wearing fitted black trousers that hooked from a flap over his crotch on either side of his hips, with his prized white shirt over it and a leather jerkin over that. Mikhail had discouraged the idea of black, and the laced over-vest with the little sleeve caps was a naturally shaded gold with green patches at the shoulders. The whole works were bound by a studded brown belt with a little leather pouch to hold his wallet jouncing from the side of it. He had on a green leather hat *exactly* like the kind he always imagined Robin Hood wearing and a pair of soft leather boots that came up to his calves.

The pile of stuff he had just locked in the trunk of his car would humble the tickle trunk of an affluent pre-school.

It had actually been the dragon that had nearly made them late.

They were just getting ready to go pick up the bags they had left at various vendors—many of them with dresses, yarn, soap, perfume, CDs, and paintings for Benny and Parry Angel, as well as a rather spectacular piece of stained glass packaged for Shane himself—when they passed the large corner booth with the stuffed puppets, and Shane fell in love.

"The three-headed red dragon," he said before he could stop himself. And since he was spending money... "And the blue one too. And the set of finger puppets with the little animals... and the angels!" They were perfect. They had curly brown hair and blue eyes, just like Parry Angel and Lila, Jon and Amy's baby.

Shane had forked over his credit card and turned to find Mikhail's amused eyes on him, his arms crossed in front of his chest and his hip cocked to the side.

"You are striving for some sort of award?" he'd asked, and Shane flushed.

"Sometimes the only thing that gets you through being a kid is a different world where you can be a kid," he muttered, taking the giant paper bags filled with expensive toys from the delighted shopkeeper.

He turned back to Mikhail and was unprepared for the soft look again and that sudden vulnerability that he'd seen inside the clothier's. "For me, it was dance," he said softly, and Shane smiled.

"You're a beautiful dancer," he told Mikhail, his sincerity resonating through his toes. If anything, Mikhail's high-cheekboned face became both more remote and far more fragile.

"That is kind to say," he said, half-embarrassed. "Come, we are late."

So here they were, running and late, and Shane had to wonder. What was that sharp little triangle of a face hiding when Mikhail looked like a thin pane of glass ready to shatter?

Mikhail and Kimmy's second performance was no less amazing than the first. In fact, as Shane stood in the sunshine and watched Mikhail extend his amazing body and use the suspended props hanging from the archway to swim in the air as a fish might swim in water, he was even more beautiful.

It dawned on Shane that he had held this man's hand for the better part of an hour, and his palms started to sweat, and his breath hammered in his chest, and spots started dancing in front of his eyes.

Best. Day. Ever.

And Shane even knew where he worked—and it wasn't far from Levee Oaks.

"Citrus Heights?" Shane had asked over a tiny spoonful of limeade-flavored ice. "Where in Citrus Heights?"

"The corner of Greenback and Sylvan," Mikhail had told him. Shane had bought him his own ice. Mikhail's was lemon, but he kept using his spoon to steal bites of Shane's. Shane let him.

"I know the place—The Car Czar, right?"

Mikhail smiled. "Da—it's mostly Russian-owned. There is a dance studio along the back of the strip. I teach there four nights a week."

"And you work the faires for…?"

Mikhail had shrugged, shades of darkness in his eyes. "I am saving for something. Besides—this is real performance. People are glad to be here, and I make them happy. What's not to like?"

So he might be at the faires on some weekends, but most nights a week he was right where Shane knew to find him.

Shane watched him now with sweating palms and breath panting shallowly in his chest. That was assuming he wanted Shane to find him. The thought was fantastic—amazing, breathtaking, and absurd.

But that didn't stop Shane from feeling the imprint of that fine-boned, lean hand in his own for most of the rest of the day.

The performance ended, and Shane whistled enthusiastically. Kimmy waved at him from her place in the front, and Mikhail raised an ironic blond eyebrow and tilted his head as though allowing Shane to idolize him. Shane rolled his eyes and did just that.

Eventually the tippers cleared out, and Shane walked forward to Kimmy's enthusiastic viewing of his new look.

"Very nice, brother—and I have to say, Robin Hood fits you better than Sheriff of Nottingham, right? You may want to think about that...." She trailed off meaningfully, and Shane shook his head.

"You think of anything else I can be, and I'll think about it," he told her, and Brett, who had once again reprised his roll of Puck, said, "Some sort of hairy-pelted animal?"

Shane blushed—his chest hair was peeking out of his V-necked shirt, and it was dark and curly and....

And Mikhail kicked the guy in the shin.

"Better a bear than a ferret," he snapped, and Shane and Kimmy looked at them both in surprise.

"Lover's quarrel," Kimmy said apologetically, and Mikhail shook his head and stalked forward.

"Nyet. I would have to love him, and I never have. Come—let's go see the horses before you have to perform with your asshole boyfriend," he called over his shoulder.

"Mikhail!" Kimmy sounded legitimately shocked—and hurt—and she looked at Shane as though he could come up with an answer.

Shane shrugged and stayed shoulder to shoulder with her as they followed the guy through the dust and the throngs, trotting to keep up.

Mikhail slowed down as they passed a booth that Shane hadn't seen yet, one with tiny glass vials of scented oils. He must have had a fondness for scent, because it was almost like someone threw a rope around his neck and pulled him toward the shelf. He wrinkled his nose—it was a tiny booth off in its own corner—and the oils were high enough to make him stand on tiptoe.

Kimmy glared at him, and Shane looked at her and sighed. It was his job, he guessed, as designated "pretty man" of the day.

"Do they have 'cranky Russian bastard'?" Shane asked, wrinkling his nose at the variety. There were little glass vials set up in a board to support them, and each vial had a glass wand inside to sample the scent. Shane picked up a glass wand experimentally and brought it to his nose. "Ewwww."

Mikhail looked up as Shane replaced the wand and smiled faintly. "Brown sugar. Too sweet for you. You need something bolder."

"Vampyre?" Shane asked, bemused. That's what the glass tube said, sweartagod.

Mikhail waved him off. "No—it is dry and dusty. And dead. You are very much alive."

"I'm also very confused."

"Here—cedar wood. This smells like you." Mikhail held up the wand and Shane took a delicate sniff.

"If you say so."

"I'm embarrassed," Mikhail said suddenly and grabbed Shane's wrist, swabbing a little bit of oil on it and then replacing the glass wand in its vial. He pulled one from a vial marked "chamomile" and swabbed it along the same patch of skin, then held Shane's wrist to his nose and inhaled, closing his eyes slightly.

"That's it." He looked up at the shop proprietor, an older woman with her hair up in a costume hair net and a rather serene expression. "Two vials—the clear kind. Three parts cedar, one part chamomile. No, no," this to Shane who was pulling out his wallet, "this is my purchase."

Shane raised his eyebrows but kept to the subject. "Didja lose your pants in public?"

The reluctance with which Mikhail faintly lifted his sulky mouth made his smile that much prettier. "I am embarrassed because he is an ass, and because I have slept with him, and because he doesn't deserve to breathe your air. Are you satisfied now? Should we put on make-up now and hug?"

Shane's eyebrows hit his hairline, and he blinked. "Apparently we're sticking to perfume," he said after a moment, when the proprietor had handed Mikhail the two plain vials of scented oil on leather cords. Mikhail handed one to Shane.

"It smells like you. It smells better on you. Now put it over your head and wear it, dammit, and let's go see the horses."

Shane complied and looked at Kimmy as Mikhail grabbed his hand. She raised her eyebrows and shrugged and caught up with them as he was dragged through the dusty, thronging crowd.

The jousting area was set up in its own cul de sac away from the food and the vendors. There were temporary stalls set up with the horses at rest and the name of the stables emblazoned on a carved wooden sign attached to the front of every pipe-constructed stall. Shane approached the horses and laughed a little.

"They're smaller than I thought they'd be," he said to Kimmy, who agreed. She'd been the one to get riding lessons when they were younger.

"They're stockier," she said thoughtfully. "More like ponies but a little taller."

"The ones in the ring are bigger," Mikhail said, nodding toward the jousting ring. There were stands on one side complete with tarps overhead to keep out the sun and what looked to be a royal family seated in the center getting ready to watch the spectacle. "They have to be bred sturdy to hold the big men wearing the metal, but they have to be bred sweet-tempered...."

"Because that's a whole lot of freak-out for a skittish horse," Shane agreed, looking at the crowd and the men with weapons and all of the things that Deacon and Crick would have said were dangerous to have around a horse in the first place. "Deacon's horse, Shooting Star, would have killed someone by now."

Mikhail shuddered. "I don't see how they do it," he confessed. He was standing a good five feet behind Shane and Kimmy as they stood near the stall, checking out the animals. "They are already too big."

"I'll have to introduce you to Angel Marie," Shane said with a laugh. The horse near him looked like she was going to eat his fingers as they hung on the metal bar above her head so he reclaimed them and moved away. Together, the three of them started wandering toward the stands on the far side. They were early—maybe they could claim a seat out of the sun, which was pretty damned relentless at three in the afternoon.

"Angel Marie?" Kimmy asked, laughing, and Shane shrugged.

"I've got, like, six dogs—he's the biggest."

"You named a boy dog 'Angel Marie'?" Mikhail sounded bemused, and Shane looked away, embarrassed.

"You have to see him—he's like a cross between a Great Dane, a Bull Mastiff, and a Newfoundland. It's like someone went to a dog show and made a 'big dog DNA milkshake', and Angel Marie is what popped out. I figured it was either Big Fat Bug-Faced Baby-Eating O'Brian or Angel Marie. I picked Angel Marie."

Mikhail blinked for a moment and then smiled. It was a whole smile, not tainted by irony or coquettishness or his perpetual sneer, and if Shane hadn't been mostly in love as it was, the smile would have done him in.

"I have seen that movie—right after we arrived here in this country. It was very funny." With that he took Shane's hand again and led them to the bleachers, where they spent the next hour watching men control horses while wearing armor.

Shane couldn't stop talking about it as they walked back to watch Kimmy do her last dance—where he would finally meet the elusive Kurt and take them both to dinner.

"Deacon would have loved that," he was saying as they approached the stage, and Kimmy ran around the hay bales set in rows for the audience so she could get ready for the performance. "He's really good at breaking horses, and he always loves a challenge!"

"If you know nothing about breaking horses, how do you know he's good at it?" Mikhail demanded, and Shane found himself a hay bale and sat down before he answered.

"You have to see him in the ring. The horses practically read his mind. You barely hear any commands or see him do anything—I've never even seen him use the whip or anything. And Shooting Star is supposed to be the meanest, orneriest bitch to ever bear a saddle—I've heard people who haven't been on the ranch in years talk about that horse. And Deacon rides her. She thinks he invented hay. He's just good at his job, that's all—and so's Crick, but Crick likes to talk to people. Deacon puts all that into horses."

"Enough!" Mikhail grunted sourly. "I'm sorry I asked. I don't want to hear about Deacon, god of horses, any longer. Keep talking about Shane, stupid cop with the insane number of dogs."

"And cats."

"Cats?"

"I've got six of them too."

"Whatever. Tell me about the man who would do that." Mikhail's impatience was getting hard to tell from his gentleness, and Shane smiled a little. It was fun getting him riled. But it was hard answering that question.

Shane sighed and leaned forward and rested his elbows on his knees, looking around to see which of the people at the Faire that he'd seen during the day would be watching this performance. The family he'd first seen—the one with the teenagers and the small children and the over-plump mother and long-suffering father—was huddled in the corner. The children were munching moodily on some pretzels, and they looked exhausted. So did mom and dad, in a good-natured way. The older children were still talking excitedly, and mom smiled up at her ginormous son and handed him a wrinkled set of bills with a wave of her hand. Another parental resolve not to spoil offspring gone with the resolve not to eat another cookie.

It was a good family, Shane thought, loving these complete strangers with all of his heart.

"Shane, stupid cop with an insane number of stray animals, is not that interesting a person," he said after a moment. "Uncle Shane, indulgent spoiler of children—he's got potential to be someone."

Mikhail leaned forward, matching his pose. He didn't say anything, but he leaned slightly so that their upper arms were touching, as were their thighs. He had taken his shirt off for the performance, and it was hot, so he was simply wearing the little turquoise vest. Shane was acutely aware of this smooth-skinned, tanned, muscular body, hot and smelling like sweat and work and cedar and chamomile, seeping heat into Shane's skin through his new clothes.

He had to sit up straight after a moment of doing that, because his lower body woke up with a happy heart and an eager look to a new adventure that Shane was pretty sure wasn't going to happen that day, and he looked fondly at his "date for the Faire."

To his surprise, Mikhail spoke first.

"You will go out to eat with your sister after this, da?"

"Yeah."

"You will take her and her asshole boyfriend, and then drop them back off?"

"Yeah."

"I will be here—I'll be staying in the tents behind the Faire. Some of us sleep here, if we don't have a hotel room. You will come say hello?"

"Yeah." Shane blushed and looked at his hands. "I'd like that. But I'm not sleeping with you tonight."

He heard the disgusted sniff and slanted his eyes sideways to catch the pout on that sulky little mouth. "No one asked you to," Mikhail said loftily. "But I will be here if you want to say hello."

"I'll look for you to say hello," Shane told him. Carefully, as natural as the rising sun, he moved his hand to Mikhail's knee and turned it palm up.

Mikhail put his hand in it, palm down, and then the music started and they both turned their attention to the stage.

Chapter 4

Now they call you Prince Charming...
"That Smell"—Lynyrd Skynyrd

SHANE was grateful Kimmy only made him see her second show the one time. He could never really get into clogging. About halfway through the show, he heard Mikhail's soft laughter next to him, and he turned stern eyes to his companion for the day.

"I'm sorry," Mikhail whispered, "but if you could only see your face! I would never doubt where I was with you, Shane-the-stupid-cop, because if you ever wore that expression, I would know I had crossed the line."

"Like now?" Shane muttered dryly, and Mikhail burst into another paroxysm of laughter—this one muffled against Shane's bicep.

Shane ignored him and dutifully watched as his sister finished up her number—but not before she cast Mikhail a glare that could have seared meat, right from the stage. Of course that set him off again.

Finally, finally, the program ended, and Mikhail stood, his fingers still linked with Shane's, and with surprising strength he hauled Shane to his feet.

"Remind me not to piss you off," Shane told him, impressed, and together they waited patiently until the tipping queue had cleared out (Ren Faire Mom gave the smallest child a dollar to put in the basket) and then joined Kimmy and the extremely pretty man next to her.

"Shaney!" Kim cried, and Shane wondered how long it would take for that name to start grating on his ears like it had when they were kids. "Here…. Come here. I want you to meet Kurt. He's the leader of our troupe, right? But he strained his shoulder, which is why Mikhail got to come sub—anyway, we're living together in a little apartment in Monterey. That's where your Christmas cards have been going, right? So, uhm…." She paused in the awkward silence. "Shane, this is Kurt. Kurt, this is Shane."

"The one with all the money, right, Kimmy?" He was dressed in a troubadour's outfit, complete with cape. He had a narrow face with high cheekbones, dark blond hair in a stringy ponytail, and a light blond growth of stubble on his cheeks and chin, and Shane disliked him on sight.

To her credit, Kimmy blushed. "I don't know how much," she mumbled, "and I don't care."

"Oh, c'mon, Kim—I was only kidding!"

Kimmy's look, sideways and quick, could only be described as "hunted." Shane met Mikhail's eyes, and the dancer arched his eyebrows. *No. I was not exaggerating.*

Mikhail chuffed out a breath, and Kurt held out the hand that wasn't wrapped tight around Kimmy's shoulders. "Hey, little man, I hear you did a top-notch job filling in my shoes. Well done!"

Mikhail gave the hand a perfunctory shake and said, "I counted the tips Kimmy had you put in the safe. I will expect my full cut tomorrow. Please don't 'miscount' it like you did last week. I need that money."

Kurt waved him off. "No worries, little dude—that was a mistake last time. Won't happen again."

Mikhail smiled thinly. "See that it doesn't." Then he turned to Shane and took their twined hands and pulled them to his lips, kissing the back of Shane's wrist with a flirty little smile. "And you—by all means say 'hello' should you have a moment. And I suggest you all leave now, or you'll get caught in the traffic either in the park or outside."

He let go of Shane's hand just slowly enough to be reluctant, and then stepped back, took a little bow, and turned and trotted through the crowd.

"He's right," Kimmy murmured. "We should go. If we're here at close, our job is to run through the Faire and herd people out. Let's try and get out ahead of the chaos, shall we?"

They took Shane's car. Kimmy sat in back because Kurt held the seat of the two-door forward for her and said, "Here ya go, babe." Then he refused to wear a seat belt because it might crush his cape.

If it hadn't meant hurting his baby, Shane might have hit a tree as they were driving (providing he could find one in Gilroy) just to watch the guy go flying through the window.

The questions about money were incessant—how much he'd gotten from the settlement, where he kept it. His response of "in a bundle in my sock drawer" made Kimmy giggle, and Kurt ended up telling her to cut it out, the men were talking. Shane started wondering about how much bodywork would really cost. He was, as Kurt kept pointing out, financially loaded.

When he found Shane unresponsive about the money, Kurt started talking shit about Mikhail, and Shane actually had to watch his breathing as red spots danced in front of his eyes.

"I didn't know you were queer, bro—if I had, I would have warned you off the little dude. He's sort of a man-slut, you know? Never met a Faire hook-up he didn't like?"

I don't do seasons, only days. Yeah, Shane knew. He also knew—with a cop's bone-deep instinct—that there was a reason for that, but he wasn't going to discuss Mikhail's sex life with this guy.

"You know, I think you only get to use the word 'queer' if you actually swing that way," was what he did say. "Or if a queer person likes you as a friend."

Kurt had laughed. "Well, it's a good thing you and me are tight, my man, am I right?"

"No."

Kurt laughed some more, and Shane patted his steering wheel sadly. He really did like this car. And Kimmy might get hurt in the accident as well. But it was oh-so-tempting.

"Shane's bi," Kimmy said unexpectedly from the back, and Shane caught her eyes in the mirror and smiled.

"This is true," he said, as though encouraging a child. The Kimmy who had squealed that morning when she saw him seemed to be in hiding. So was the brutally honest Kimmy who had talked about being an addict and wanting a family. This Kimmy was a frightened Kimmy, and she was huddling in the back of the car as though saying "boo" was going to get her kicked onto the pavement and into the middle of nowhere. (Was this really the main road to Gilroy proper? Shane had seen more metropolitan thoroughfares in the middle of the Canadian wilderness.)

"I thought you were really brave, Shaney," she said now, casting a furtive glance at Kurt. "You took a chance on someone. Even if it didn't pay off, you... you know. You can find someone who won't be a cowardly weasel...."

"Oh come off it, Kim!" Kurt said dismissively. "The guy was only being smart. You've got to look out for yourself, right—shit! Why'd you do that?"

"Squirrel," Shane said with a straight face. Kurt had slid across the seat and smacked his head on the window when Shane swerved, and now he was putting his seat belt on with something approaching zeal.

"I saw it too," Kimmy said seriously, but she met Shane's dry glance in the rearview with twinkling eyes.

Shane had directions—and dinner reservations—for a local steakhouse in Gilroy, and he pulled into the parking lot with a certain feeling of relief. At least dinner would give Kurt something to do with his insipid mouth besides annoy the hell out of Shane.

It was a typical steakhouse, dark tables, dark wood paneling, big rough wood timber four-by-fours in strategic places. They didn't get as many odd looks for their Faire attire as Shane expected when they were led to their table—of course, they weren't the only ones there in costume. Shane figured it must be a regular occurrence at this place. He was actually staying at the motel across the street; both steakhouse and hotel had come recommended when he'd bought his ticket online.

Kurt ordered the most expensive thing on the menu. Shane had expected it, and he'd ordered his own T-bone steak as well, wrinkling his nose when Kimmy ordered a chicken salad.

"Sorry, big brother," she said with a grimace. "Since I'm not a coke-whore anymore, I've got to keep my weight down the old-fashioned way."

"It's not working," Kurt said critically. "You can really pack it in on your thighs, Kim."

"You look beautiful," Shane snapped, sincerely. "In fact, that's one of the first things I thought when I saw you. You look strong and healthy—good for you."

Kimmy smiled radiantly at him, and then Kurt opened his mouth up about how she'd never be model weight again, and the smile went away.

"Don't like models," Shane grunted. "Don't like thirteen-year-old boys, either."

"Ewww...," Kurt said, looking at him in horror. "What does that have to do with anything?"

"Same goddamned chest, moron."

And then the waitress arrived with food, and that was the best news Shane had heard since Mikhail had gone trotting off into the Faire.

He ate steadily, enjoying his food and giving off his best "don't bother me, I'm eating" vibe. Kimmy ate the same way—it was probably a throwback to their childhood, when they were both to be seen and not heard at the table, but it was also, Shane suspected, Kurt's oppressive presence.

Halfway through the meal, when Kurt excused himself to the bathroom, both of them heaved a sigh of relief.

"I'm sorry," Kimmy mumbled, showing eloquent eyes over her half-eaten salad. "I... he's...."

"If you say 'he's nice to me-ee,' I'm going to toss my dinner right here, Kim. You are so much better than that."

Kimmy looked up, sad and naked. "What do you want me to say, Shane? I needed someone. He was there. I settled. That doesn't mean it's all bad, you know?"

Shane looked down at his hands, thought of holding Mikhail's in his own for the whole day, and then reached across the table and took his sister's hands. In spite of the weight she'd gained and her obvious strength as a gymnast, her hands were fine-boned and felt fragile under his big, hammy paws, and he smiled a little.

"I'm not a chubby kid anymore, Kim. I could protect you. You could come and stay with me and get your shit together and never have to depend on an asshole like him again."

Kimmy swallowed and refused to meet his eyes. "I'll work it out," she said gruffly. "I'll… I want to do it myself."

Shane thought of The Pulpit, of the interdependence of people that made up that family, and stroked the back of her hands sadly. "No one can do it themselves, sweetheart."

She sighed—it was an old sound—and pulled one hand out and patted his knuckles like he was a small child. "Let me try, okay?"

"Just know—know. You have my number. You—and I mean you alone, that asshole's not invited—you, Kimmy, are always invited to my home."

Her hand disappeared from his vision. When it came back it was wet and smeared with mascara. "I'll hold you to that."

There was a heavy moment, and then she sighed in annoyance. "Christ—Shane, could you go check on him? He's been gone a hell of a long time."

Shane had a bad feeling just walking into the bathroom. It was your basic four-stall, two-urinal set-up, but the sounds coming from the end stall did not bode well. It sounded like someone sucking in a whole lot of nasal spray. Shane took a minute and got a hold of his temper, then angled his vision through the crack in the end stall.

And watched Kurt do another line.

He didn't make another sound. Just turned his big body around and started fumbling with the wallet in his little leather pouch. When he got back to the table he lucked out: their waitress was right there, refilling Kimmy's soda. He took out a handful of bills and put them in the girl's hand.

"We're going to have to leave," he said amicably. "Could you tell the guy who was here that he needs to find his own way back?" The surprised woman took the money even as he held out his hand and said, "C'mon, Kim!"

"Shane!"

"He's not getting back into my car—if you want a ride back, you need to come with me now."

Kimmy hopped up and hurried after him, and Shane roared out of the parking lot as though he was being chased by the hounds of cocaine hell.

They were silent for a few moments in the purring car as Shane tried to get them off of the main drag of Gilroy, and then he said, "Shit. Christ. I'm still hungry. You up for an ice cream or something, Kim?"

He heard her half-laugh, and then, "Yeah. Why the fuck not?"

They stopped at a frostie—the old-fashioned kind run by mom and pop or whoever—and Shane got some fries to make up for the potato he hadn't had a chance to finish, and Kimmy got an ice cream, and they sat together on the rough wooden bench and ate in bemused silence.

"I'm going to have to go back and get him," she said after a moment.

"Yeah—but not in my car. If he gets busted with that shit in my car, Kim, there goes my career—such as it is. And honestly, I just don't want him near me. I'm sorry…."

"Don't be," she interrupted. "He's an asshole. But he's my asshole. I'll come back and deal with him, and we'll probably make up because we're in the middle of Faire season, but…." Her voice trailed off, and he hated the hopeless note that had entered it. She took a deep breath and forced some optimism. "In the meantime, now that you're done with your fries, how 'bout you go get a banana split, Shaney. Just because you're not fat anymore doesn't mean you don't get some empty calories after you've lived through a day like this."

Shane smiled at her. "With the exception of the waste of skin doing lines in the bathroom, my day was actually pretty damned good."

Kimmy smiled back. "Kurt's an asshole—"

"We've covered that."

"What I'm trying to say is don't listen to him about Mikhail. Mik's good at the fair hook-up—that's true. But he's a really good guy. I think he's just lonely, you know? He doesn't know how to ask for more, so he settles for what he can get."

Shane looked at her pointedly. "No wonder you two are such good friends."

Kimmy's grimace was eloquent, and Shane took that chance to go get the banana split. Kim helped him eat it.

They got into the GTO again, and the atmosphere was almost lighter somehow.

"Nice car," Kimmy said, running her hands over the leather. "Did you fix it up?"

Shane nodded. After he'd gotten the new job, he'd settled down to find some new interests to help define the new Shane. Working on the car was one of them, and the animals were another.

"Why don't you find something on the iPod," he said, pulling out of the narrow parking lot onto the main drag again. "It's a good night to roll down the windows and crank up the volume."

"Good," Kimmy said with some humor. "The better to let the garlic seep through our clothes."

Well, Gilroy did hold the title of "Garlic Capitol of the World." Why not?

"Any preferences?" Kim asked, after scrolling through the menu for a few moments. "Gimme a clue or something here, Shaney—you've got what? Ten thousand songs on this thing?"

"Eleven thousand, six hundred, and twenty-three," Shane corrected. Indulging in music had been one of the perks he'd given himself with his blood money. "But there's some duplicates, so that's probably not exactly right."

Kimmy laughed and decided on a choice. "Bruce. He seems to be something in common—anything special?"

"Have you heard the *Magic* CD?"

Kimmy made an approving sound, and the first strains of "I'll Work For Your Love" started to rumble through the car. They rolled down their windows in tandem and let the music move through them. One more thing, Shane thought with a little bit of optimism. One more thing that bound them together like family.

The Faire lost some of its glamour without the enthusiastic crowds. As Shane drove up around the fairgrounds to the employee parking lot in the back, it looked dusty and peaceful but no longer the place where dreams of an innocent, exciting past could come true. For the first time,

Shane thought longingly of his jeans—if for no other reason than because they were comfortable and his.

But as Shane dropped Kimmy off by the RV that she and Kurt traveled in, he saw Mikhail lounging shirtless on a hay bale, ear buds in his ears and a thoughtful look on his pretty face, and suddenly the place looked a whole lot brighter.

Kimmy looked in Mikhail's direction and gave a short laugh. "He's going to be all casual, right? But his little tent is way off on the other side of the lot—and if you look, there's plenty of hay bales there too."

Shane couldn't help his sweet, hopeful smile. "I'm not going to be another Faire hook-up," he said, meaning it. "Not tonight." But he got out of the car anyway. He could talk to the guy—really, wasn't it worth getting out of the car to talk to someone who got his jokes?

Kimmy came around and gave him a hug—the kind of hug where she buried her face in his neck and stayed for longer than she had to.

"I'm so glad you came, Shane," she said softly. "As fucked up as I am...." Her voice threatened to break, and he shh'd her and rocked her and kissed her hair as it rested under his chin.

"Kim, we're family. Just tell me you won't forget that I'm your family again, okay? You don't need to be in rehab to call. It doesn't need to be Christmas. I'm...." He blushed and looked yearningly at Mikhail, as much of a long-shot as that seemed. "I'm getting into family now. Now that I have one... you can be a part of it. That would be nice, Kim. They'd like you."

Kimmy wiped her face on his shoulder. "I need to be a better me first."

"Kim...."

But she was gone, running for the RV and pulling her keys out of her own leather pouch at her waist as she ran. She was still in her faire clothes, her ankles flashing in her dancing boots under a skirt the color of ripe pomegranates and her brown wavy hair falling to her waist as she ran. She was beautiful and fey....

And she made him want to cry. The RV roared to life and lumbered off, leaving a hurricane of dust in its wake. Shane watched her go and then turned around toward the hay bales and the shade to find Mikhail.

The other man had started walking, bare feet, bare chest, and all. He was almost to the GTO, and Shane was both surprised and pleased.

"So," Mikhail said, casting a disgusted gray-eyed glance to the departing RV, "I take it the asshole boyfriend got left behind?"

"He was doing lines in the bathroom," Shane said with a sigh. He leaned his ass against the hood of the GTO and expected Mikhail to do the same. He was surprised—shocked, stunned, breathless—when Mikhail leaned forward instead of backward and rested the front of his body on Shane.

Shane's hands came up to the man's muscular biceps and he closed his eyes for a moment as he felt the smooth skin under his palms. Mikhail was short enough that, half-sitting as Shane was, their groins were right. Up. Against. Each other.

Shane groaned and leaned his forehead against Mikhail's and said it again. "I'm not going to sleep with you, dammit. I'm going to *court* you!"

Mikhail grunted, and the sound conveyed a world of cynicism in one syllable. "Men don't court me, pretty man. They fuck me. I'm a sure thing. Can't you just take a sure thing? You are pretty, I am available?" His shoulders moved in a shrug, and Shane's hands slid to his elbows. Absently Shane rubbed his thumbs over the tender skin on the inside of Mikhail's elbows, and he heard Mikhail's breath catch and shudder in his chest.

"You are pretty," Shane whispered. He leaned his head back and saw the thick golden light hitting that blond hair and turning it almost transparent. "And you are the only person I've ever met who speaks 'Shane Perkins'." He caressed that vulnerable skin again just to watch Mikhail shudder.

"You are a hope," Shane continued, leaning his head forward and touching his cheek to Mikhail's temple. "We go into your tent and do whatever tonight, and tomorrow you'll be gone. No hope. We leave it good tonight, and I court you, and you'll be a hope." He could feel the tight wire of reluctance as the other man leaned into him, and then, perversely, Mikhail ground his groin—swollen and aroused—up against Shane, and he groaned.

"You can do that until I come in my pants, you little bastard, but that's not going to keep me from thinking you're worth the wait."

Mikhail went limp against him—it was a surprise. "You did not look this stubborn this morning," he said softly, peering up from his chest, and Shane rubbed that sensitive, tender skin again. There was a roughness under his thumbs, irregular bumps, scars, under each thumb, and as he glanced down Mikhail stiffened and started to pull away.

"I didn't know you yet," Shane replied absently. "Now that I know what you're worth... hey. Don't pull away. Let me see?"

Mikhail had taken a step back and was standing, fists balled at his sides, with a miserable, defensive expression on his face.

"You want to see? You stupid, stubborn man—you want to see? What a prize I am? What sort of hope I am? Here. Come look—you will see." And with that he turned his arms out, so Shane could see the soft white skin he'd been stroking. Under the tan and the dust from the fair were the terrible ravages of a catastrophic love affair with needles and death.

All sorts of things fell into place, and Shane's expression softened. Mikhail looked away from him. "Don't pity me," he bit out, sniffing to hide the fact that he was near tears.

"Don't insult *me*!" Shane snapped back. Did Mikhail think his words in the dressing room were just that? Pretty words with no heart? "Those are really old, aren't they?"

Mikhail glanced at him—an improvement over the knot he'd tied his face in—and then looked away. "Da. Ten... no, eleven years."

"What are you? Twenty-five? Twenty-six?"

"Twenty-five."

Shane took a chance and took a step forward. He missed the closeness, the warmth. He needed to be back to that place between them before he left. "You were a baby," he said softly. "How did you get out?"

Mikhail shrugged, and Shane inched forward again. They were standing a foot or two apart, and Shane just watched Mikhail's expressive face—his defensiveness would slip, and he would be naked, and then he'd pull it up again, and he would be angry. So much emotion bottled up in a compact, cynical, muscular body.

"My mother," Mikhail said, after his anger dropped and he was... just bare and vulnerable. "She... she was nurse." His accent was much thicker. "She brought me clean needles, condoms…." He shrugged and almost made it look insouciant. "I was the only disease-free junkie in St. Petersburg, da?"

"Good to hear. She got you into rehab?"

Mikhail gave a humorless laugh. "After she got me stoned and into an airplane for the Promised Land, yes."

Shane nodded neutrally. "I bet it was horrible."

"I don't remember," Mikhail lied thickly. He looked away like he was pretending they weren't standing close enough to feel the other one breathing.

"How did you start?" Shane cupped his elbow gently and brought up his arm for a closer inspection. Yes, the veins had been ravaged—they were pitted and had probably nearly collapsed. But the skin was unblemished around them now.

"I was dancer. It… it is common, in dance. You get hurt, you get rid of hurt so you can dance some more. One day, you can no longer dance because the thing you did to dance has ruined you." Another one of those lying shrugs. "And then you are turning tricks in alleys so you can do the thing that ruined you and so your mother does not starve."

Shane met his eyes and nodded so Mikhail would know it was understood. He'd been a junkie and a prostitute, and there was no glossing over that. And then, while Mikhail was glaring at him, daring him to show compassion or pity or anger or disgust, Shane brought that tender flesh up to his mouth and kissed it.

The sound Mikhail made was beyond pain, so Shane kept kissing the scarred, once-ravaged skin, running his tongue over the line of abused vein and then bending, moving his mouth up that strong bicep, up to Mikhail's smooth shoulder, up to his neck and the strong, clean line of his jaw. He stopped when he got to the ear and used his nose to brush some straying curls back. Then he put his lips there in the hollow and whispered, "You are still my hope, and now, I'm your promise."

"Don't promise things," Mikhail whispered back in the broken voice of a lost child. "It's not nice."

Shane pulled back and captured that pointed chin in his fingers. "It's only not nice when you don't keep it." He closed the distance between them again and gave a brief, hard kiss against the sulky, lush mouth, and just when Mikhail relaxed enough to open up and give him access, Shane pulled back and started rooting through the pouch at his side.

While Mikhail stared at him in outrage—and disappointment— Shane wrote hurriedly on a receipt he didn't care about and then thrust the paper into Mikhail's unresisting hand.

"That's my cell number. And my home number. And you'll probably throw it away—but that's not the point. The point is, I'm going to leave before I end up doing you in the back of the damned GTO, but you can call me and bitch me out about it if you're so inclined. The point is, I'll be seeing you—if not this week, next week. You think that"—he nodded toward Mikhail's arm, resting at his side now—"is going to make me want you any less—or think any less of you—then you're as deluded as you think *I* am. Now give me a kiss goodbye and let me know you'll miss me, and I'm going to get in the car and go to my hotel like a good knight in shining armor, okay?"

He was half expecting the crack of the hand across his cheek—and he enjoyed it more than he thought he would.

"I'll *eat* that number before I use it!" Mikhail said, putting it into his own belt pouch with more care than Shane thought he knew.

"I'm sure you will," Shane replied mildly, wincing as he rubbed the bruise forming on his cheek.

"And if you think I'm just going back to my tent to moon over you, you're insane!"

"I'm sure that's true," Shane said, nodding. Oh, God he was beautiful. His eyes were sparkling, and his cheeks were blotchy with anger—and he wasn't defensive or miserable or sad. He wasn't expecting to be rejected or offering to settle for a night or a minute or a quickie in the back of the car. He was absolutely possessed with his own worth, and that's exactly how Shane wanted him.

"I'm going to fuck some stranger!" he threatened, and Shane had to gasp for a moment before he conceded to himself that this was a valid threat—and a valid consequence when courting someone with Mikhail's damage. He'd have to deal with the possibility, that was all there was to it. Mikhail must have heard the intake of breath because he looked up into Shane's eyes and said, "I'll fuck ten of them!" spitefully, and with a little bit of wildness, and Shane's eyes narrowed.

"You do that," he growled, and then he grabbed Mikhail's shoulders and turned him back against the car. "You fuck as many random strangers as you need to and get that all out of your system." And then he mashed his mouth against Mikhail's, and Mickey opened for him immediately—angry, aroused, passionate—and Shane plundered. He held his palms against the smooth skin of Mikhail's shoulders and trapped him there firmly, making no bones about the fact that he was bigger and stronger, and for all Mikhail's quickness, Shane could outpower him in a heartbeat.

But he didn't have to, because Mickey's mouth was open and wet, and he was whimpering in the back of his throat and pulling unhappily at the leather jerkin and the oddly fastened pants and trying to get access to the skin of Shane's back. For his part, Shane raised his hands to frame Mickey's cheeks and was stroking his thumbs along that sharp, vulpine jawline.

He wanted a cape and tights and a big "S" on his chest for pulling away.

Mikhail actually whined as he did it, and Shane gave a panting, breathless smile. "You do that," he gasped, his chest heaving with hunger. "You do whatever and whoever you have to do—but you just remember: you'll be thinking of me the whole time, and I'll be back for you. On a day when you're Mikhail and not Oberon and I'm Shane and not Robin Hood, I'll be back, and we're going to start this again."

With that he put Mikhail firmly away from the car, got in, and turned over the engine. He pulled away in a cloud of red dust, "I Came For You" blaring defiantly from the stereo.

Chapter 5

Even if we're just dancing in the dark...

"Dancing in the Dark"—Bruce Springsteen

MIKHAIL watched the car peel out and fought the urge to stomp his foot like a child. He had been so close... oh God.... He had tasted *so* good.

"Courtship," he muttered to himself, standing under the twilight sky with his hands on his hips. "Courtship? Who do you think I am? I am no damsel in distress. *Fuck* damsels in distress. Fuck you for that matter. Big stupid cop—think you are all that, don't you? I'll think you are all that while I'm getting laid, yes. That's when I'll think of you."

Jesus. Didn't he get it? Everything was all right for those moments of sex. The world was golden, rosy promise, warm human feeling, and kindness when bodies were touching. It was all one could count on—it was all a man needed.

Bitterly disappointed, Mikhail stalked toward his tent. He had sandwiches in a cooler there and soda. Shane had bought him a late lunch, but he burned calories very quickly, especially on days like this when he danced and when he was *looking forward to sex all day*. Bastard.

You are my hope, and I am your promise.

Bullshit.

He got to his tent and sat down on his little fold-out stool propped up in the front. He'd been subbing for troupes at the faires for a couple of years and had managed to do without the hotel room and live in relative comfort just the same. Everything in the tent could be folded up and put in a camper's backpack, and he was proud of that. It was self-sufficient, and

Mikhail enjoyed being self-sufficient. Too many painful things could happen when you depended on someone to be waiting for you with comfort. Self-sufficiency was a virtue.

With a practiced motion he put his ear-buds in and hit play on his iPod. He liked music. All music—classical, jazz, old rock, new rock, rap, pop, metal, strings, brass, and the didgeridoo. He had earned enough money for a laptop when he'd been twenty years old, and his next purchase had been the iPod. It was old, and it couldn't hold as many songs as he'd like, but he could spend hours picking out what would go on it, and that was something.

Moodily he leaned back against the canvas back of the stool and peered up at the stars. His fingers went to the little pouch, and he pulled out the number and looked at it.

It looked legitimate. Go figure. He knew people—he should give someone those numbers and make the stupid cop a prime victim of identity theft. He reached into the pouch again and pulled out his little vial of oil and pulled off the cork, inhaling lightly.

Involuntarily his eyes closed. He could still smell the oil on the big stupid cop's skin, under his leather jerkin. He could see his broad, friendly face splitting into a grin—a shy grin—under the autumn sun. He could hear his voice telling him... miracles, if truth be known. A man who would spend a fortune on children who were not his because he wanted to see them smile. A man who would come to a world he didn't understand and buy clothes to match in order to impress a sister he hadn't seen in years. A man who would look at him, track marks and all, and call him, Mikhail, a hope.

Stupid man.

Carefully Mikhail put a little bit of scented oil on the receipt in his hand and then replaced the cork and put the vial and the phone numbers back in his pouch. He had a box at home for such things. Then he resumed his contemplation of the sky. The stars were coming out, and since Gilroy was mostly rural farmland, that meant something. It was getting a little bit cool—sometimes an ocean breeze made its way in from the coast—and Mikhail reached inside the tent for the shirt Shane had bought him.

It fit very well, and Mikhail took out a little bit of oil and daubed it on the shirt too. The promise was a lie, of course, but it would be nice, sometime in the future, to remember the lie and pretend it might someday be real.

He put the oil back and was prepared to tip his face to the sky and enjoy his music (Coldplay was the band today—"Kingdom Come" was a favorite song, as was "Clocks") when a silhouette interrupted his view.

"Go away," Mikhail said sourly. "I do not wish to speak to you tonight."

Brett leaned forward and tried to touch lips with him, and Mikhail rolled off the chair, onto his knees in the dust, and came up furious.

"I said go away! You think I want to touch you now? After what you said to that nice man?"

Brett rolled his eyes and shrugged. "It was a Faire hook-up, Mikhail—you have them all the time. And then we have them, and then we have next weekend, right?"

"Nyet." But it was true, he thought, not liking the way it sounded when Brett said it.

Brett smiled and moved behind him, trying to wrap his arms around Mikhail's chest. "C'mon, Oberon... let's you and Puck go make a little music, right?" Mikhail shrugged him off and turned around.

"I don't think so," he said. He was going to add, "Not tonight," but he remembered the way Shane had flushed in embarrassment, had called himself fat, had generally made very little of himself with all of his kindness and his quick words and his beautiful smile. "Not again," was what he said instead, and he kept his face carefully cold as Brett jerked back, hurt.

"Mikhail...."

"No. You were possessive. You do not say mean things like that unless you think a hook-up is a lover, or a boyfriend or...or...." Or a promise. "I do not feel any of those things for you, and you will only be hurt if we keep doing this."

Fuck. The look on Brett's face was enough to confirm that line of reasoning. Damn. This was why it was important not to get attached, not to make promises. Even if you didn't make promises, people relied on you, and you let them down. Mikhail sighed and looked away.

"I have hurt you. It was not...." Fuck. "It was not intended."

Brett wiped his cheek on his shoulder, trying to be manly and unaffected. His pointed ear came off, and he tried a sloppy laugh to prove that Mikhail was wrong, he was all fine and good.

Mikhail sighed and moved forward, pulling the ear point gently out of Brett's hair and working the glue out of the long, coarse strands. Brett smelled like sweat and earth and a little like patchouli. These smells did not move him.

"I've seen you bend over behind a tent between sets, take it in the ass, and then show up at my van at the end of close," Brett muttered, his voice muffled. His narrow, Puck-ish face was dirty with dust and make-up, and the tears he'd pretended not to shed were cutting tracks through the brown and leaving pale skin in their wake. "I've never seen you look at anyone the way you looked at that guy today."

"He started it," Mikhail muttered, feeling unreasonably like he might—just possibly might—owe this man a little honesty for kicking him out of bed for good.

"Yeah, Ice-Man, how's that?" The sad thing was, the epithet wasn't bitter. They'd been calling him Ice-Man since the incident Brett had just mentioned. It had been his first day working the circuit, and he'd been giddy and excited—and horny. It had been the beginning of his reputation of a man who would be fucked by anything with a prick and who would never look back.

"He looked at me," Mikhail said reluctantly, hating the dichotomy, "as if I were a god." Silly, deluded man.

"Yeah?" Brett muttered, looking sideways at him like Mikhail would reach out a quick, hard foot and kick his orphaned puppy or something. "What's that like?"

"I'll let you know when the madness of it has faded," Mikhail said heavily. Then, feeling foolish because it seemed to mean something to him after all, he seized Brett's hand and gave it a gallant farewell kiss on the knuckles. "We have been good friends, have we not?"

"We've been fuck buddies, apparently," Brett said bitterly, but he didn't jerk his hand away either.

"That too. Without the fucking, I would still like the buddy?" He thought about Shane, who would laugh when he said this because it was cleverly worded. Most people thought it was simply his accent getting in the way.

Brett sighed and pulled his hand reluctantly away. "Whatever, man. If you still want some when you get your sanity back, you know where I'll be."

"A generous offer," Mikhail said, meaning it, "but unnecessary. Have a good night."

He sat in silence for what must have been an hour, in the stillness of his music and the purple diamond sky. He contemplated going to bed. He contemplated jerking off. And then a part of him lost its mind. It's the only way he could explain finding his cell phone in his hand or the way his heart beat when a man's voice answered.

"I am being fucked silly by ten man-gods. Don't you wish you were here?"

Shane's low chuckle in his ear was... magic. Hot chocolate with cinnamon and whipped cream and caramel on the coldest day of the year. "Nope. If you're being fucked silly, I want to be the only one in the room."

"You could have been." His irritation flooded back, and he couldn't help his disgusted sniff. "Stupid, foolish man."

"Yup."

"What are you doing?" He was honestly curious. Something about Shane's voice suggested a darkened room.

"Watching *Kung Fu Panda* in the dark."

"I love that movie!" He couldn't keep the delight out of his voice. Children's movies fascinated him. He had been in dance since he was very small, and there had been no time for movies. In the rehab clinic in New York, their only entertainment had been paperback books in a language he did not yet speak and shelves upon shelves of movies he had never seen.

"Me too," Shane said, his voice soft. He probably really was in the dark. Mikhail, who did not consider himself an imaginative man, suddenly pictured Shane wearing an old T-shirt (green—it should be green) and a pair of sleep shorts, stretched out on a hotel bed in the dark. It was a comforting picture—Mikhail decided that was the man he was talking to as he sat on his camp stool under the stars.

"Yeah," that warm, dry voice said in Mikhail's ear, "I sort of identify with that damned panda, you know?"

"You are not fat." Stupid man. He was big, warm, and solid. Mikhail had enough of whip-thin dancers, lean, hungry poets, or cold, substantial men who denied who they were.

"I'm not you," Shane said, and his admiration was so honest and frank that Mikhail found himself humbled. Irritating man.

"Yes, well," he sniffed, "who could be?"

Shane's low rumble of laughter in his ear was comforting. It said that somehow Shane heard what he was thinking as opposed to the spew of arrogance that came out of his mouth.

"So what's your favorite?" Shane asked, and Mikhail had to pull himself back into the moment.

"My favorite what?"

"Your favorite movie?"

Mikhail was stumped. "No one has ever asked me… it is like music. I love it all, not just one kind."

"That's sort of depressing from my end," Shane said thoughtfully. "Are you sure you can't think of a favorite?"

Mikhail couldn't think of why that would depress him, so he turned the question about instead. "You think of one, and I'll see."

"*WALL•E*," Shane said with satisfaction. "Hands down, that little robot 'bout broke my heart."

Mikhail found himself laughing in spite of himself. "How very appropriate." And it was. WALL•E—the hapless knight in rusted armor. Except WALL•E had eventually been *very* important to the object of his affection, hadn't he?

"So what's your favorite?" Shane asked with some insistence, and Mikhail sighed because he suddenly knew exactly which cartoon was his favorite. He shouldn't say—it was almost too personal.

"*Lilo and Stitch*," he said facetiously.

"*Lilo and Stitch*?" It was clear Shane was waiting for an explanation.

"'For such a small person'," Mikhail quoted, "'you have an unusual level of badness in you.'"

Shane laughed obligingly and then said, "Now tell me your real favorite."

Mikhail flushed. "No," he rasped, unable to suddenly brush off the question, to give another facetious answer.

"I've asked a personal question."

"Da… *shit*!" Because his phone just beeped—the battery was low.

"Battery?"

"Da, I mean yes. And I need to make another call tonight." Shit. He… he had been enjoying the conversation. "Well, I must go, stupid cop. It was a good day."

"I'll see you later…."

"Nyet… I mean I doubt it. I shall…."

"I don't make promises I can't keep."

"Goodbye." Mikhail couldn't say all he wanted to say, so he figured it would just be better to end the conversation entirely. His phone snicked shut, and he sat for a moment and started to shiver. Cold. He'd put on his shirt—maybe it was time to go in his tent while he was letting his phone rest up before his call.

The tent itself had a foam pad and a flashlight, a sleeping bag, and a pillow. The much laundered, all-cotton clothes worn at the Faire tended to shake out well in the morning. Mikhail took off his jerkin and his pants and rustled up some underwear from his knapsack (in case, well, whatever called him out of his tent in the middle of the night.) The shivers were still there. Common sense told him that it was still seventy degrees outside, but he wanted the comfort of his sleeping bag, so he sought it.

When he was situated, he pulled out the phone again and dialed. The voice on the other end was old and female, hoarse and ragged and much, much beloved.

"Hello, *malenkiy mal'chik*… was your day good?" Ah, Mutti—she'd started learning English the second they stepped off the plane, but endearments and greetings were hard to kick. Besides, as she frequently told him, he'd never stop being her little boy.

"Hello, Mutts," he said quietly. Something about speaking in a tent—it made him quiet. "How was your day?"

"It was good. The girl came, she hooked up my medication. I feel better." Mutti always said she felt better—but she was dying. How much better could she feel?

"Did you eat?"

"Da—she warmed the food in the refrigerator after she gave me a bath."

"Is that part of the service now?" The insurance was through his mother's work—she had been a nurse in Russia and had earned the degree again in America. The insurance was good, but they were Mutti's details, not his.

"I do not think so—but she is a very nice girl. She is single—maybe you should meet?"

Mikhail's smile, had he known it, was bitter. "No, Mutti, I do not think so. We should run away together, yes, and then where would you be when you need a nurse?"

"When I'm gone, perhaps," his mother said, as though this answer satisfied her very much.

"When you are gone, I shall be too broken-hearted to care," he replied, making his voice light and frivolous when, with the surprising exception of much of what he'd said to Shane, this was one of the most serious truths he uttered in a day.

"Phfaw!" his mother laughed. "When I am gone, you shall be partying on my grave, Mikhail Vasilyovitch, and I know this because I have put it in my will."

"You contrary old woman, you probably have, too!" Mikhail had to laugh—there was no choice. His mother... oh God. His mother. She had uprooted her life to put him in dance academy, and when he'd been injured, he'd addicted himself to make that gamble pay off. She'd taken his trick money and given him clean condoms and clean needles, and the whole time she had been squirreling away cash under her mattress for their visas and plane tickets so that when he needed her—had *truly* needed to get away from Saint Petersburg or die—she had been there.

She'd pumped him full of enough heroin to keep him high for three days. It had been a gamble. He could still remember the shaking of her hands on the needle and the band around his arm and the way she'd done the math on paper instead of in her head so she could check the figures three times and make sure she was not setting him up for an overdose instead of saving his life.

But she had done it. She had cracked wry, shrewish jokes the entire time. *We're in a plane,* lubime—*if you look down from your high, maybe you can see us down below. You need to relieve yourself,* mal'chik? *Try hard not to piss away too much of that heroin, you're going to need it before I get you to the clinic. Stop ogling the pretty men,* mal'chik—*what, you think you are still on the streets?*

So yes, Ylena Vasilyovna Bayul, who had given him her father's name when his father had not stepped up, probably had the strength and grit to put such a clause in her will, insisting that Mikhail dance upon her grave. Knowing Ylena, she would have specified the music and the choreographer as well.

"To Tchaikovsky, of course," his mother said now with mock dignity, making him smile again.

"*March Slav* or *Nutcracker Suite*?" he asked dubiously.

"Go with the crowd pleasers, *lubime*—*1812 Overture*, of course."

"Ayee! Mama—could you at least pick something that is *supposed* to be danced to?" The thought of choreographing to *1812* made his head hurt.

"Nyet," Ylena said imperiously. "For all our time together, I want my overture, and I insist upon you dancing like an angel. Don't even think of letting me down, *lubime*, or I shall be a very obnoxious ghost."

"So noted." His phone beeped at him and he sighed. "My phone is dying, Mama—I will be home tomorrow, late. My people will drop me off as usual." Mikhail did not drive. In New York they had not needed to, and in California, it had given him perverse satisfaction to milk the shitty public transportation for all it was not worth. Self-sufficiency—it was his motto, creed, and faith.

"Be safe, Mikhail Vasilyovitch—dance beautifully. I know you will."

"For you, Mama, I will dance like angel, yes?" Always, for his mother, he would dance his best. A sudden image in his mind: the look in Shane Perkins's eyes that morning as he had begun to dance as Oberon. *I'm not you.* Yes, well, thank God for that. Perhaps, tomorrow, Mikhail would dance for that look in warm brown eyes too.

"You are my angel, *lubime*. My bones hurt—it is getting cold here at night." Perhaps the high sixties. For a woman who had lived her life in a frigid place with soul-stopping snows, Ylena had immediately taken to Northern California's temperate winters. Of course, the cancer didn't help.

"I promise, Mutti—we shall have Christmas in the sun. It will warm your bones and seep into your icy heart."

Ylena's laughter was warm and sweet, as Mikhail was sure his would never be. "It is a good promise. For my part, I promise to live that long. Good night, *mal'chik*."

"Good night, Mutti."

Mikhail hung up the phone and turned it off to save power in case he needed it. While he'd been speaking, his body had warmed in the sleeping bag, the soft heat releasing the scent of the oil he'd put on the shirt he still wore. Shane. He closed his eyes then, moved his hands under his shirt and over his chest, not thinking about masturbation, just thinking about the pressure of Shane's hard warmth against his narrow body.

Stupid man, making stupid promises. A day at the Faire was a moment, that was all. It was nothing to base promises on.

Mikhail closed his eyes, breathed in that scent, and pretended that Shane's warmth was his. He would dream, he thought rather self-indulgently. He would close his eyes and dream that Shane had stayed, kept him warm in his tent for a night. He would dream, maybe, of dancing again and seeing that look again on a solid, handsome face with a pair of warm brown eyes.

A man could not be held accountable for dreams, could he? The gods would surely give him those.

THE next day, he and Kimmy danced beautifully. Kimmy felt it too—a sort of electricity, the kind of thing that made the audience's hair stand on end and the whole world hold its breath as they performed each move, shushing appreciatively in awe.

As they took their final bow and the last tipper toddled away (the children who wanted to tip always charmed them, without exception),

Kimmy looked at him through slanted eyes. "My brother should visit more often," she murmured, conscious of Brett's stony silence behind them.

"I'm sure I don't know what you are talking about," Mikhail said blandly, and Kimmy took his arm, pulling him away from Brett's glower and dodging Kurt's smarmy wooing of the crowd.

She pulled him quickly behind a bank of vendor's tents and demanded, "Tell me you're going to be good to him!"

Mikhail couldn't meet her eyes. "We are not dating," he said to the dirty canvas behind her. "It was simply a wonderful day."

Kimmy's fingers—strong, like any dancer's—caught him under the chin and jerked his eyes to meet hers. "Don't bullshit me, Mikhail. You two really had something. My brother doesn't just have *days*—not with his girlfriends, not with that fucker who got him shot—"

"I'm sorry?" This hadn't been mentioned.

"His old partner—the guy who outed him in front of his department and then just walked away to let him get ambushed—"

"*Mudak!*" Mikhail felt his chest freeze. Oh, and here he was, thinking he had the secrets, he had the pain—how could he not have learned that everybody had secrets and pain? Kimmy was looking at him in surprise—he did not often let his Russian slip when he was not talking to his mother. Mikhail looked away again, trying to get his emotions into control.

"He talked of pink bricks," he said, almost to himself. "Pink bricks and blue bricks, but not about"—his mind fought for the word— "...betrayal...." Mikhail did everything but stamp his foot. Oh, what an *irritating* man. "Of course not. Why would he tell me?"

"Because he doesn't talk about it," Kimmy said sternly. "Just like there's shit that you don't talk about to anyone but me, right, Mikhail?"

Mikhail scowled at her. "Of course he didn't tell me!" he snapped, not sure who had pissed him off more. "Why would he tell me that? We knew each other for a day...."

Kimmy laughed softly, interrupting him before he could continue. "Okay, okay...look. He'll find you, trust me. And when he does, I'll let *him* tell you that story. But... right now? Just promise me...." She looked away. "Man, just promise me you'll take him seriously, okay? Shane...

he's so earnest. People don't take that seriously these days. They laugh at it...."

"Your brother isn't a joke," Mikhail said, part angry and part bitter. The man had certainly carved a damage path through *his* complacency, hadn't he?

Kimmy nodded and patted Mikhail's cheek a little, some sisterly tenderness escaping her stern expression. "He got to you, didn't he?"

"You should go live with him," Mikhail told her seriously, taking that hand and kissing it. "He wants to be your family."

A shrug, a self-sufficient firming up of all of her resolutions—Mikhail knew what she was doing just by watching her body language. If he'd had a mirror that morning, he would have seen the self-same gestures. "I want to be a better sister for him. But I'm glad he has you."

Mikhail was opening his mouth to say, "He *doesn't* have me, dammit!" when they heard Kurt calling for the both of them, and what came out instead was, "Can we see your asshole boyfriend doesn't cheat me out of my tips this time?"

Kimmy nodded soberly. "I swear he won't."

She kept that promise, actually—but it was close.

"This is not enough," Mikhail said mutinously as Kurt was handing him his pay envelope, and Kurt shrugged.

"It's what I counted, little man!"

"Bullshit," Kimmy said, surprising them both. "You promised him an equal share—that's not what I got, that's not what Brett got, so that's not equal."

Kurt rolled his eyes. "It's a few dollars, babe...."

"Don't 'babe' me—Mikhail needs that money, and you *don't* need more coke, so cough up his share before I call my brother down here to make you!"

Kurt's face grew hard and furious at the mention of Shane, but he reached into his own pocket and produced another sixty dollars. "Look, bitch—don't make me get all hard-ass with you."

Kimmy looked at Mikhail to see that he was okay. Mikhail nodded, and Kimmy gave a smile—a losing smile, a conceding smile—that made Mikhail's stomach churn.

"No worries, sweetheart," she said sincerely. "I'm just looking out for my guy, 'kay?"

"Yeah, we'll see if it's okay if I leave you here tonight." The threat sounded half serious, and Kimmy closed her eyes as though putting on her armor and then walked a sinuous hand down the back of her boyfriend's neck.

"C'mon, baby—don't be that way. We don't get good dancers if we don't treat them right, mmm?"

Simpering, begging, she took up Kurt's attention, and Mikhail slipped out of their battered RV, where the money transaction had taken place.

He wanted the right to go in there and slug the guy and throw Shane's sister over his shoulder and take her away from Kurt. The desire made him shake with the violence of it. Kimmy didn't deserve that... that... *mudak*, and for a minute he felt the absurd compulsion to go fight for her honor as she had fought for his paycheck. His steps were slow enough as he walked away that he was still there when Kurt popped his head out.

"Hey, little man—you still on for next weekend?" His hair was out of its queue and his jerkin was half unlaced, and Mikhail made himself wonder what Kimmy had said to prompt the worry at this point in her seduction.

Mikhail met Kurt's eyes with undisguised contempt—for himself or for Kurt, he was not sure which. "Yes. I'll be here."

He turned to leave again, his leather boots making soft puffs in dust over the gravel, and there was a murmur from the RV before Kurt called out again. "Hey! Kimmy says to tell her ass-fucking brother 'hi' for her!" Then he turned back inside, snarling, "You owe me for that, bitch," and slamming the door behind him.

Mikhail scrubbed at his face with his hands. *Damn you, cow-woman—damn you!* That was a sacrifice is what that was. Kimmy knew what a sacrifice would mean to Mikhail—she knew it was the one thing that would make him keep a promise.

Fine. Fine, big heifer cow. If your stupid brother comes to see me, I won't tell him to fuck off, how is that?

With a sniff and a great deal of acting squandered on dust and sunshine, Mikhail went to find his ride.

Mikhail didn't like horses, but Rose and Arlen MacAvoy came down from Grass Valley with the horses for jousting, and they had been nice enough to give him a ride when he subbed in Gilroy. He always considered himself supremely fortunate that they didn't make him ride in one of the trailers in the convoy, the ones with the gigantic animals, letting him crouch in the backseat of the extra cab instead.

This evening he stowed his pack in the adjoining jump seat and belted himself in behind the passenger seat, pulling out his iPod and getting ready to be in his own head for the trip. He had no idea what made him sit, poised, earbuds in hand, and wait for the older couple to situate themselves in the front until the truck's diesel engine was ready to start.

Rosie looked back at him quizzically, and he caught the significant look between her and Arlen and hated himself for not just putting his earbuds in and pouting until they forgot it and left him alone.

"Did you have a good run, Mikhail?" Rosie asked after a moment, taking off her battered felt hat and smoothing her graying hair back into a fuzzy bun. She was a thin, wiry woman with a pleasant, round face. Mikhail had often wished that he was better at introductions—Ylena would like her. "I saw you walk by the horses with a nice looking young man—a new friend?"

"He knows horses," Mikhail said, feeling awkward. "I do not know horses, but he is unafraid."

Arlen chuckled a little. "That's key when working with horses—don't be skittish, and odds are they won't be."

Mikhail nodded. That suited Shane. His presence was... soothing. "I...." God, why was he saying this? He couldn't. He couldn't confide in these people, no matter how well-meaning. "He has friends who deal in horses. He seems to admire them a great deal."

"Anyone we'd know?" Arlen asked curiously. "We know most of the names in northern California."

Mikhail frowned. "He talks a great deal about a man named Deacon, and a place called The Pulpit. The place is in trouble. They are like family.

He worries." *Excellent, Mikhail—you can't give your own confidences, so you blather someone else's into the ether. What a prize you are—so much incentive for the man to return.*

Rosie furrowed her brow. "Seems to me I've heard of the place—Deacon Winters, right? Some sort of scandal with the police—always seemed they got a bad deal, but I'm not good with the details. You say they're friends of your friend?"

Mikhail nodded and struggled gamely onward. "Yes. He... I get rides from you all the time. I know nothing about horses. Will you tell me?"

He felt like a first class asshole, but it seemed to work. Rosie and Arlen spent the next three hours telling him about horses—that it was hard on the body but good on the soul and how much they loved the big animals and what made a good horse and what made a skittish horse and what made a right old bitch that should be shot for dog food.

"Just like people," Arlen said pragmatically. "Some of 'em are sweet, and some of 'em are sour, and some of 'em are just plain evil. But the ratio is skewed, to my way of thinking."

"Yeah!" Rosie laughed. "There are a lot less plain old evil motherfuckers in the horse world than there are in the human world, that's for damned sure."

Arlen nodded in agreement and started talking about studs and mares, and Mikhail's eyes glazed over a little. But he had time to reflect that they did that a lot, spoke off the other. Two people who had been together so very long that they were confident the other would be there in as much as a heartbeat. The ultimate promise. Then something Arlen said brought him back from his musings.

"Yeah... I sure am going to hate to leave it!"

"Leave it?" Mikhail asked, a little panicked. Where would he get his rides now? "When?"

Arlen laughed as though he could read Mikhail's mind. "Not this season, Mikhail—maybe not even next season—but Rosie and I are getting on in years. It's time to sell the business and retire with a couple of easy-going pasture horses, take it easy for a bit, you know?"

Mikhail nodded. "Yes," he said, thinking about his mother, who had worked until the cancer made it impossible. "It is good to enjoy life while it is yours." He would be sorry to see Arlen and Rosie pass out of his life, he thought with a little melancholy. They were nice people—they had been good to him.

The trip back went much faster than it usually did, and Mikhail felt bad. He so rarely made an effort to involve himself with the people around him—his mother, Kimmy, Anna his boss at the dance studio—these were the extent of his human contacts, his friends. And here Arlen and Rosie had been ready to be friends, and he had thought of them only as a ride home.

They pulled into Citrus Heights around eight o'clock, and Mikhail started to get his gear ready as they neared the first bus stop—it was where they usually dropped him off, and he was surprised when Arlen didn't slow down.

"Since we're on Greenback, Mickey, show us where you live—we can drop you off there."

Mikhail didn't seem to know how to refuse the offer without being offensive. With some embarrassment, he found himself directing Arlen down Greenback then left on Sylvan. It was a tetchy little neighborhood, although the apartment complex on Sylvan was respectable enough. As Mikhail hopped out of the little side door of the extra cab and stood on the step-side to pull out his camper's backpack, he looked shyly at Arlen and Rosie for judgment in their eyes for the quality of the neighborhood or the smallness of the apartments inside their little box-like buildings.

There was none, and Rosie hopped out of the truck (with some spryness, for a woman who claimed to be on the verge of retirement) and gave him a hug.

"It was a good trip home, Mikhail—we'll see you next week. Don't forget our number between times, okay?"

Mikhail nodded, feeling awkward, but she had been kind. "I do not usually talk much," he said apologetically, and Rosie laughed—she and Arlen laughed a lot, he thought.

"Oh honey, we know that. We're just glad you gave us a chance tonight." With a little more creaking, Rosie released him and climbed back into the truck, and Mikhail waved as the truck (and its big, smelly burden of terrifying animals) disappeared out the driveway and onto busy Sylvan Road, turning toward Auburn and the freeway.

He trotted through the complex and up the stairs to his second-floor apartment, letting himself in quietly in case his mother was napping. He should have known better.

"You are home, *mal'chik*?" Her voice was raspy from illness, from bad lungs, from many years of smoking thick Russian cigarettes with no filters. She once told him that it was easy to forgive him his addiction to drugs—she had possessed her own.

"Da, Mutti," he murmured. "Was a good take," he said, coming into the living room. His mother loved children's movies as much as he did— she was watching *The Iron Giant* on their DVD player. It always surprised him to see her so gaunt, wearing a brightly flowered turban to hide the spotted, bald skin of her scalp. Her hair had once been ash blonde—from a bottle as she aged, yes, but he had seen pictures. When she had been young, it had been thick and healthy and very pretty. So had she. Now, not so much—she was merely a bag of bones hiding under the afghan she had crocheted herself. She had once had the sort of energy that would fill a room.

"That is good," she said tiredly. "One more weekend closer to Mexico, da?"

Oh God, he fervently hoped so. He hadn't had the nerve to count the money he hid in his sock drawer after his work at the Renaissance Faires. It would be such a near thing.

"Of course, Mutti," he said out loud. He had called the travel agency and spoken to her doctors. Everybody had okayed the trip; all he needed was the money. "You just need to live that long—the doctors said it should not be a problem for a tough old cat-woman like you. Listen to them. They are very wise."

"Phfaw!" Ylena pushed away the notion with her withered hand, the gesture giving a hint to the elegance she had once possessed. "I will live until you have found a woman to care for you. Get off your fat lazy ass and start looking, *mal'chik*. I will be a medical miracle at the rate at which you are doing it, and that could be exhausting."

"I think I shall remain a lover of men," Mikhail said archly, coming to give her a kiss on the cheek. "If it will keep you alive, it will be well worth it."

"I do not mind the men in your bed," Ylena said with a sigh, accepting his kiss. "But they will not care for you. Could you not at least pretend to like a pretty girl, so she could cook for you?"

"If it will make you happy, Mama, I will look, just for you," he murmured, kissing her cheek again and hugging her frail shoulders with as much strength as he dared. It was an empty promise; they both knew it. Ylena fretted, though, that he would be alone when she was gone. She had invested so much of her life into him—she wanted to know he was cared for when it was no longer her task. Mikhail no longer had the strength to argue with her about whether he liked men or women. His mother would always love him, but believing he would someday marry and be cared for eased her mind, and that was what he cared for now.

"Pfaw!" she exclaimed again. "You smell, *mal'chik*. Go shower, then come eat the food the girl left. She was a very nice girl. You should see her."

Mikhail laughed tiredly. "Yes, Mutti. I'll think about that." With that, he took his pack into his bedroom and emptied out his clothes into the hamper. His regular Faire clothes would wash just fine with the rest of his laundry, but the new black shirt would need to be soaked in the sink with some vinegar or it would stain all his other clothes.

Without thinking, Mikhail took it from the pile and held it to his nose. The scented oil was still there, but it smelled like him now and not Shane. Regretfully he set it back down next to the hamper to wash. Then he rummaged in his camping pack and came up with the leather pouch from his belt. Carefully he pulled out the vial of scented oil and the little scrap of paper with Shane's numbers on it. The numbers were in his phone now—he could throw the paper away.

With fingers that were calm and still, he opened the plain cedar box on his dresser—one of the few adornments in the room, which mostly featured his laptop and a number of posters of his favorite musicians. Inside it were inconsequential things, things he rarely ran his fingers over or thought of. It was like the box inside his heart, only real, and he rarely opened that one, either.

With reverence, he placed the glass vial in one of the little alcoves at the top—for a woman, it would be for earrings, and since his ear was pierced, he had a few of those too. But this one was bigger, and it fit the vial very well. The number he kept folded and simply laid on top so it would be there when the box was opened. He looked at the inside of the box for a moment and then pulled the vial out, uncorked the tiny stopper, and spread a little bit of oil on the velveteen. When that was done, he lowered his head, closed his eyes, and inhaled gently.

Shane. Yes. There he was, inside the cedar box.

Keeping his mind carefully clear of betraying words, Mikhail replaced the vial to its place of honor, made sure a fold of the paper was weighted by an earring post so it would not fly away, and closed the lid.

He moved slowly as he went to wash that smell off his skin.

Chapter 6

What others may want for free… I'll work for your love
"I'll Work For Your Love"—Bruce Springsteen

SHANE'S first thought on Monday was that he absolutely could *not* call Mikhail immediately, or he would scare the man screaming back to Russia with his neediness and devotion.

His second thought was to wonder who in the hell was pounding his door down at six- thirty in the morning when he didn't have to go in until ten and why the damned dogs weren't throwing themselves at the door threatening to eat the fucker.

He stumbled out of bed in his sleep shorts and not much else, throwing off cats with the covers, and waded through furry bodies, tripping over the little one on the end before throwing open the door. Deacon was standing on his porch in sweats and a T-shirt and running shoes. The guy took one look at Shane's gooey eyes and bare feet and said, "You forgot, didn't you."

Oh yeah. Shane closed his eyes and said, "*Fuuuuuuuccccckkkkk…* shit, Deacon—come in, have some water or something. Let me put on my running gear, and I'll be out in a minute."

"No worries." Deacon followed him in and while Shane disappeared down the hall, made himself busy by rubbing silky ears and being licked to death by the fearless warriors who had apparently decided he was their god.

Deacon had that effect on people.

As Shane threw on his clothes, the dinner conversation from the night before ran through his brain. *A little late to remember this now, you think? Quit bitching and find your fucking running shorts, asshole.*

Deacon had been the one to suggest it. When he'd come out to get Shane's key (which he now had a copy of) and to learn about the animals, he'd noted that if they cut through the fields behind their properties, Shane's house was less than a mile away.

Shane hadn't thought about it, really—by road they were nearly five miles apart, and he sat on about six acres of spread-out land. Apparently Deacon *had* thought about it—he had a riding mower and had spent a part of his weekend carving a nice little path through the tall grasses between the two houses. After dinner, Deacon asked Shane if he wanted to go running in the mornings, since he could warm up on the way to Shane's and Shane could cool down on the way back from Deacon's.

"All the better for him to torture someone else," Crick had said sourly, passing behind Deacon on his way to the sink with dishes. Deacon had reached a casual hand behind him and brushed Crick's thigh as he passed, limping slightly on his bad leg and balancing the dishes on his good arm. A light bulb had popped up in Shane's head.

Crick wouldn't be up to running after his injuries. He had gotten back up on a horse over the summer and could spend some time riding them, but he was still struggling to work them with his body not up to one hundred percent.

"I'll still be torturing you," Deacon said mildly. "But this way I won't get fat while I'm doing it."

Crick dropped the dishes in the sink with a clatter, walked deliberately up to Deacon, and swatted him in the back of the head.

"*That* is the most piss stupid thing I've ever heard anyone say ever." He stalked away, grumbling, and Deacon looked at Shane a little sheepishly.

"Don't look at me," Shane said, holding up his hands. "I happen to agree with him!" Deacon had put on weight since Shane had first arrived, it was true, but fat was at least sixty pounds away.

"Does that mean you don't want to go running?" Deacon asked, blushing.

"Didn't say that!" Shane usually went running on the high school track a couple of times a week. It was lonely and it was boring, but it let him eat chicken-cheese-mayonnaise casserole (which is what Benny had cooked that night) with impunity. Having a running buddy on the country back roads sounded like a definite improvement over lonely and boring any day.

"Good. I'll see you at six thirty sharp," Deacon told him, standing up from the table. "Now I gotta go make nice with Crick."

"Making nice" had taken about fifteen minutes, and when he came back, Shane and Jeff had managed the dishes, and Deacon confirmed their running time. He'd asked Jeff if he wanted to join them, but Jeff had held up his hands in horror.

"Oh honey, no! I do what all metropolitan gay men do—I go to the gym!"

And that had been that.

Shane had come home, fed the dogs, coddled the cats, and fought for sleep for over an hour, trying to figure out the best way to approach Mikhail without scaring him off. He was obviously afraid of big animals—Shane had to try to be the bull in the china shop of the man's sensibilities, and that's all there was to it.

And now here he was, pulling his running gear out of his ass and hopping into his shoes as he hobbled down the hall. Deacon looked up from his position on the floor. He was seriously in danger of being loved to death by the dogs, who hardly noticed when Shane skidded in.

"I told you, no worries," Deacon said, squinting. "We've got time."

Shane flushed. "Yeah, but I forgot, and I feel like an asshole. Why don't you have a dog?"

Deacon shrugged and stood with a reluctant tug on Sophie's ears. (Sophie was a Labradoodle—her ears were pretty addictive as fondling material, Shane had to admit.)

"Too many horses. Wouldn't mind a dog—they're reliable. Remind me of Crick."

Shane had to smile as he tied his shoe in a double knot. Of course, for Deacon, all good things came back to Crick.

"How'd you two make nice last night?" he asked awkwardly, and then could have kicked himself when Deacon looked at him sideways and smirked.

"Didn't figure you for the type to want details."

Shane grimaced and turned red, and Deacon smirked some more—and turned red too. "I was just wondering, you know…."

"I told him that I liked to run," Deacon said, turning away and trotting out the entryway. By some miracle, the dogs stayed put, and Shane thought seriously about asking Crick if Deacon would want a puppy for Christmas. The shelter knew him on a first-name basis by now, and it seemed a shame to waste all that mojo on Shane's dogs alone.

"And…?" Shane stopped at the rail to stretch. He wasn't twenty anymore, or even twenty-seven. He would, in fact, be thirty-two this coming year—and he needed to catch up to where Deacon was, warm-up wise.

Deacon looked at him patiently and did his own warm-up stretches, just to keep him company, Shane was sure—the guy had already done a mile just to get there.

"And Crick is always telling me I should want things for myself. You ready to go?"

"Which way we goin'?" Shane asked, bemused.

"This way," Deacon said, going right on the battered road from his driveway. "Jon only lives about a half a mile this way, and with any luck, we won't have to roust him out of bed."

Jon, Deacon's best friend, was, in fact, waiting for them as they rounded the corner. Jon and his wife Amy were lawyers, so their house was bigger and newer on the inside, with less acreage of land on the outside. Jon was stretching his movie-star body along his white picket fence as they neared.

In spite of being sort of a prick to Shane when they'd first met, Jon had turned into a decent person. In appearance, he looked like Brandon—a dimple in his chin, movie-star blue eyes, streaky blond hair. In personality, he was loyal, brave, and faithful—both to his wife and to his best friend for life, Deacon. So basically, Jon was the anti-Brandon, and that made Shane like him in spite of the bad introduction.

Together, the three men started running, following Deacon's lead and listening to Jon's mindless banter. Shane could see that Deacon and Jon had run together before—they fell almost naturally in stride. But they were both conscious of Shane on the other side of Deacon, and they adjusted, and Shane wasn't a slacker, and he was sort of proud of the way he kept up with them. The morning was crisp but not cold, and the roads were near to empty in the gray-to-golden light. Even the horses ignored them as they trotted past, using the dirt and grass stubble margins between the fences and road to spare their joints.

An hour later, he was proud of the way he didn't pass out as they slowed in front of his house to drop him off.

"A... little... farther... than I'm used to...," he gasped as he clutched the porch rail and watched black spots dance in front of his eyes.

Jon patted him on the back. "Yeah, Deacon could run five miles a day when he had mono—his dad damned near had to tie him to the bed to keep him off the roads." Jon had the decency to sweat when he said it and to sound a little winded himself.

"I like running," Deacon said mildly, and Jon did the mature thing and stuck out his tongue.

"What he's not saying," Jon panted in a mock-confidential tone, "is that he runs just as well emotionally as physically. And he wants us to be his enablers. Can I hit you up for some water, big guy?"

"Yeah," Shane panted, pulling his house key out of the Velcro pouch on his wrist and gasping a few more times as Jon took it. "Just don't let out the—" There was a sudden ruckus and a howl and Jon saying, "Holy shit!"

"Oh. Fuck. Dogs." Shane defied his own predictions of never moving again and sprinted to the gate of the fence that stretched around his property, slamming it shut before the damn critters could scatter across the county.

So the dogs got let out early, and Deacon damned near had to scrape Jon off the floor, he was laughing so hard. "Jesus...," Jon giggled as Deacon hauled him up by his armpits into the house. "I swear two of those were Deacon's yearlings. Holy shit, Perkins—did you put out an ad for furry freeloaders?"

And at that point the cats—from Orlando Bloom to Judi Dench—all came trotting out because the dogs were gone and that was the cue for chow time, and Jon started laughing again, and this time Deacon let him just flop ass-first in the hallway as he went in to get his own water.

"You like animals," Deacon said quietly as Shane poured out kibble and started opening cans of soft food. Dame Judi Dench had a hair-trigger stomach—she didn't do kibble anymore, not at her age.

"They don't think I'm weird," Shane told him with a sigh, realizing not for the first time that having a dozen or more creatures flopping in what should be his dining room sort of put him in the "weird" category permanently.

"You're not weird," Deacon said surprisingly. "What are their names?" He had learned the names of the dogs when he'd come to feed.

Shane knelt down and started scratching ears and necks of loudly chomping felines. "This one's Orlando Bloom," he said, rubbing the big tortoiseshell with the white socks behind the ears. "This is Kirsten Dunst," the delicate white one with the blue eyes, "Robert Downey Junior," a battered gray bruiser with torn ears, "Jensen Ackles," a very handsome dappled brown cat with hazel eyes, "Maura Tierney," a feisty looking long haired Himalayan mix, "and Judi Dench," an aged yet dignified gray striped cat with a delicate nose.

Jon had recovered and was helping himself to a glass of water, but as Shane continued with the list of names, he set the glass down carefully on the counter and pinched the bridge of his nose. "Okay... at the risk of going off again, I've got to ask...."

Shane grinned at him. "The names?"

"Oh yeah," Jon said. Deacon, who was looking a little wide-eyed himself, just nodded.

"I figured the damned things sleep with me anyway, I might as well dream!"

Deacon laughed—it was a quiet, hearty sound, and it made Shane proud to have caused it. It was Jon who made the connection and said, "Judi Dench?"

Shane ducked his head. "She's an old cat," he muttered. "And I like dry, sarcastic people."

And then they both laughed, but they clapped him on the back and grinned at him as they did, and he realized that he'd impressed them. It was a sort of warm feeling, knowing you had friends that not even your most eccentric behavior could frighten away.

It wasn't until the guys left that it occurred to Shane that, in spite of telling them about his sister and her asshole boyfriend and the Renaissance Faire and the trip to the beach he'd taken Sunday before he got to Deacon's in time for dinner, he hadn't once mentioned Mikhail.

It just seemed too perfect, he thought. Like talking about it would ruin it—sort of like cutting wild flowers for a vase.

Of course talking about it wasn't the only thing that would ruin it.

"You signed us up for what?" he asked Calvin again.

Calvin Armbruster was his partner—sort of. Most of the time, the local patrolmen rode in their own squad cars alone. Sometimes, when the municipality was expecting a lot of traffic—or needed everybody on duty—they would pair up. When they did, Shane ended up with Calvin.

Today they were paired because Calvin's car was in for maintenance, and he was talking up a storm. Calvin was one of those whip-skinny blond kids who would probably get beefy when he passed thirty but for the moment had shoulder blades like coat hangers. He was twenty-four, which was older than Crick, but he didn't seem older, needy wife, wide-eyed children, and all.

Calvin liked to talk, and he seemed to like Shane fine because Shane didn't often talk in front of strangers, and they got along all right.

Today, he was talking about signing Shane up for shit duty.

"We're working *what*?" Shane asked in horror.

Calvin was nonplussed. "You know—Homecoming. The whole town shows up. You and I are part of the unit that hangs out on the field, keeps folks from getting rowdy. It'll be fun! We'll be up close and personal and see the game—the Levee Oaks Trojans may get picked to go to State this year! It'll be awesome!"

Shane looked at Calvin, just looked at him for the duration of the red light, a little pucker woven between his eyebrows. When the light turned green, he looked back at the road and stepped on the gas, just shaking his head.

"Why? What's wrong with working Homecoming?"

Shane grimaced. He'd done the math. Monday was too soon. So were Tuesday and Wednesday—but Thursday was just about right. And as far as he knew, Mikhail didn't work Friday night, and he obviously would be in Gilroy on the weekend, and Shane's whole "I'm not stalking you, but I'm stalking you" plan *depended* on finding him at work. And being there for Homecoming meant being there for the frosh *and* the JV and varsity games, and that meant Thursday.

And it's not like he could tell Calvin any of that.

Shit.

Shane sighed and shook his head again. "Calvin, has it occurred to you that I might possibly have plans on Thursday or Friday? Man, the least you could have done was consulted me…."

"Well, do you have plans?" Calvin wanted to know. He'd been nosy beyond nosy into Shane's personal life, and Shane had to breathe slowly for patience.

"I might have, but it's more than that."

Calvin sent him an eloquent look and Shane sighed again.

"Man—what in anything we've said to each other in the last six months has made you think I'd be excited about high school football?"

Calvin blinked. "Wasn't everyone? I was on the team—hell, I was first string, wide receiver. How about you?"

"I was in the band, fucktard. I played the goddamned clarinet, and I did a damned fine job of it. And no, I'm not all that excited about the football team. Some of those kids are punks, we roust them every weekend, and the only reason they haven't had some damned nasty consequences is because they're on the team. I don't get why they get a free pass, but the kids with the eyeliner end up in juvie lock-up every damned time. It's not fair, and I'm not in the mood to celebrate it with the rest of this cold-assed town!"

The silence on Calvin's side of the car was both digestive and a little defensive. "You know," he said after a minute, "if you wanted the town to be nicer to you, maybe you better spend a little less time out at Deacon Winters' place. People talk."

Shane jammed on the brakes and swerved onto the road shoulder, which was right in front of the supermarket parking lot entrance, and he could give a shit. "You need to find another goddamned partner." His voice had never been colder.

Calvin's mouth dropped open. "Jesus, Perkins...."

"I'm not shitting around here. This fucking town is bass-ackwards and cold as a fish in a glacier. The one group of people I find that wants to give me the time of the fucking day, and they're not good enough for you? What the fuck's wrong with you, Calvin?" Shane rubbed his stomach, all of Deacon's and Kimmy's and even Mikhail's misgivings coming back to burn a hole in there. God, they were right. Nobody wanted him in this job, in this place—he needed to find something else to do.

"Man, I'm just sayin'—they're all queer over there. Except for the Leavens, and there's been rumors. Hell, that little girl had a baby all her own, and then put the father in jail—"

"Because maybe he was a fucktard who got her drunk and date raped her?" Shane was starting to like the word "fucktard." It just seemed to encompass so much of the world that pissed him off.

Calvin shrugged uncomfortably. "But, you know, her brother's queer... maybe she gave off... I don't know. Vibes or something."

Shane took a deep breath, smiled thinly, and said, "You say one more word about that girl and 'vibes', and you'll be pulling your teeth out of the back of your throat for a week. And you know what? Crick is a decorated war veteran, and Deacon has done nothing but worked his ass off to provide for his family—"

"But they're not his family!"

"They are to *him*! And you'll sit here and judge them, and judge me for going over there, and you'll give the drunken little bastards on the football team a free pass because they bang their girlfriends in the back of their cars instead of other boys. I think that's fucked up, and I think you're fucked up, and I think the only place in this town that shouldn't get flushed down the shitter is Deacon's place. And mine, but that's mostly cause the dogs are there. Find someone else to work your testosterone glory hole with you. I don't want any part of it."

There was silence while a line of cars waited not-so-patiently to get past Shane's squad car to get into the little grocery store parking lot. Shane sighed and put the car in drive and pulled away, trying to figure a non-obtrusive way to go back to the station so he could find something else to do besides be in the car with Calvin.

He gave Calvin a glance, and the boy was chewing over the words "testosterone glory hole" to try and figure out if they meant what he thought they did, and Shane fought back a bitter laugh. Maybe he should find a job where people actually spoke words bigger than two syllables.

The silence grew lead wings, and Shane was damned if he'd break it. He was surprised when Calvin did.

"Look," he said softly, "I'm sorry I disrespected your friends. You're right—this town ain't been real nice to Deacon and Crick, and he is a veteran and all. I'll… I'll try not to repeat every fool thing I hear the guys at the bar say, okay? We can still be partners, right?"

Shane sighed. "Why do you want to be my partner, Calvin? You think I'm weird."

Calvin looked at him in surprise, as though he didn't know how Shane would know this extraordinarily top secret little tidbit, and then he had the grace to flush. "You talk funny—but you know, you've got all those dogs?" Calvin had been with Shane a time or two when he'd swung by to check on them, so Shane nodded.

"I've always wanted dogs. If I had any money left over after the new baby, I'd have a shitload of 'em. I don't know—I figure a guy who has dogs can't be all that bad."

Shane puffed out a breath. "Okay. Fine. We'll start with that."

He ended up leaving a dumbassed message on Mikhail's phone. *Hey, Mikhail? I was gonna come by on Thursday, so as not to scare the shit out of you because some big dumb cop is stalking you, but I ended up working on Thursday, so I'll be by next week, I swear. I promised, dammit, and I'll kee—*

And that was when the phone cut him off, and he felt like a first-class asshole, gibbering like a girl.

He told Deacon about Homecoming, and Deacon looked at him sideways from the hay he was shifting and grunted. "Tell Crick's old art teacher 'hey'. She's gonna be there."

"Doing what?" Shane didn't recall the art teachers at his school being all that excited about football.

"Presenting something to the graduates that were in the military. Gonna be some sort of a memorial for that Fitzpatrick kid too." Deacon threw another bale of hay that looked bigger than he was and pulled out the hooks, then hopped into the back of the pickup and started throwing another batch out onto the ground.

"Shouldn't Crick be going to that?" Shane asked, puzzled, and Deacon squinted at him sourly.

"Who says he wants to?"

Shane sucked in a breath. "He was invited, right?"

"Uhm-hm," Deacon said, "with a whole lot of caveats about 'can't guarantee your safety'. Principal always was a fucker. I told him I'd go with him, but he hated high school. He'd be happier at home." Deacon heaved another bale and then stopped and wiped some hay off his cheek. "I'm gonna be a while here. If you want to go help Crick with dinner, you know you're welcome to stay."

"Where's Benny?" Usually she was the one working on dinner, but Shane hadn't seen her around today.

Deacon's quiet expression let a grin slip. "There's a dance teacher at the community center. She and Andrew took Parry Angel there in her little tu-tu and all."

Shane's laugh was the nicest thing he'd felt on his face all day. "She's not even two, Deacon."

That grin grew and became a doting smile. "Yeah, but she's in love with that damned dress."

Shane laughed, shaking his head, and walked inside the house, where Crick had a very different take on why he wasn't showing up for the farce at the football game.

"Yeah, I was asked. That fucker Arreguin making it sound like I was going to need a fucking National Guard to keep my poor gay ass from getting plastered to the scoreboard. I was gonna go, too—just so I could stand up at the podium and tell the whole town to kiss my poor gay white ass…." Crick trailed off and concentrated on chopping onions to add to the chili.

"Why didn't you?" Shane asked curiously, and Crick ducked his chin and looked behind him. Deacon was still outside, shifting hay, but they both knew where Crick was looking.

"He had a court appearance this week—I think he lost three pounds just thinking about it, and he hasn't eaten since." Ah-ha—hence the chili and the butter beans and the cornbread and the pie that Crick had in the oven. They were trying to fatten Deacon up some more.

"He doesn't like being in the public eye," Shane stated, feeling obvious, and Crick shuddered.

"After he graduated, before I shipped out, we'd go to the Homecoming games with Jon and Amy—they'd get up and do the float thing and wave and smile." Crick threw the onions in and ran the water to wash his hands and the board, and then he wiped his eyes on the shoulders of his shirt because the onions were strong.

"Anyway, you know Amy was homecoming queen, and Jon was the king, and Deacon was the valedictorian, and while his friends were doing the Holy Kingship thing, Deacon would stay seated, right next to me, while the crowd lost their fucking minds." Crick sighed and checked on the butterbeans, then got out some sliced almonds and some bacon bits to throw in with them. "It was like he'd never been to high school. He was an all-state quarterback, but not once did he stand when they called for alumni.

"We were the ones who knew he spent two days before giving the valedictorian speech throwing up in a cold sweat in the bathroom. His dad was a cat's whisker from calling the school and having the next guy in line speak up. Deacon told him not to, and he looked cool as a cucumber when he gave the speech, but Jon and Amy passed up a whole lot of parties that night to come back here with me and his dad and make no big deal out of it so he could calm the fuck down. He is that fucking terrified of crowds. The law suits are fucking killing him, and he hasn't complained, not one fucking time."

Shane sighed and put a hand awkwardly on Crick's shoulder. He was surprised when Crick let it stay there.

"He offered to go with me, you know? And I am damned straight not going to tell him that I'll go but he has to stay home—I might as well rip his heart out with a steak knife. But I can't imagine anything more awful for him than to be in the middle of that crowd when they're saying mean shit about me. He can handle it for himself, but not for me. So I'm staying home that night. You say 'hi' to Ms. Thompson for me, would you? She's an awfully nice lady."

Crick turned toward the mudroom then, and Shane heard him rustling around in the soda fridge they kept there, and he waited thoughtfully for Crick to come back. He thought about how sometimes people's greatest sacrifices were the ones they didn't want the world to acknowledge or even to know about. Maybe that's what made them great.

THE freshman game was all right—Levee Oaks won, because they were playing an easy team, and that was okay too. But the Varsity and JV games were every bit as bad as Shane expected them to be.

It was strange—on the outside it looked so very innocent, so very middle-America, but that was never the part Shane saw. He saw the kids sneaking in booze and the adults arriving plastered. He saw the ugly shouting at the refs and the posturing by the students and marked all of the boys who were very possibly going to either get their girlfriends drunk or pressure them into sex.

He saw the excitement, it was true—he even saw the beauty of the sport and those young, healthy bodies doing spectacular things in the name of joy. It just didn't seem as joyful to him with all of the pressure from the crowd. He wondered how Deacon had borne it, and then he watched a wide-receiver make a spectacular catch as he was literally using the guy who'd try to tackle him as a springboard, and he figured that maybe Deacon's brain had shut out the crowd. Maybe, it had been just like showing horses for him—it had been all about the beauty on the inside of the ring, and the rest of the world had faded away.

At halftime at the varsity game, he saw what they meant when Crick and Deacon called their old principal a fucker.

"You're going to use the pre-approved speech, right, Judith?"

Shane and Calvin were leaning up against their patrol car as it was parked out on the track for visibility, and two other guys were leaning up against theirs as it sat behind them. Shane looked away from the group of kids who were trying to sneak in without paying and saw a pretty woman in her early thirties scowling at a squat man in his fifties with a square pale face and steamed-up glasses. The woman wore a swirl of tie-dyed skirts under a brown cardigan that looked hand-knit to ward off the faint chill in the mid-October air. Her dark hair was pinned up at her crown in some way that let it curl around her face, and the scowl didn't look like it belonged there. In fact, Shane thought she probably smiled more often than she scowled.

"Of course, Mark," she said with saccharine sweetness that Shane could hear from where he was standing. Calvin caught his eye and smirked, and Shane thought well, hell—even Calvin knew she was lying. The guy she was talking to didn't seem to have a clue, though.

Batting her eyes, the woman walked up to the field and waited as a couple of students hurriedly set up an impromptu podium, and then to be announced by the guys up in the press box who had been calling the game.

"And now, to present an award to our alumni who have served in the armed forces, Ms. Judith Thompson!"

The cheers and applause were heartfelt, and Shane looked at her with renewed interest. So this was Ms. Thompson. Somehow, Shane had pictured her older.

Her speech started out fairly predictably—she honored the three young men in the crowd to much applause, and had a moment of silence for the boy who didn't come home. Then she smiled gamely at the crowd and rocked Shane's world.

"But those aren't the only boys here who have sacrificed for our country in recent years, are they?" she asked the crowd, and there was a sudden, thoughtful silence. "No, I was there when our esteemed principal offered another soldier—one who was wounded for his country—a chance to come here and be honored. Unfortunately, we had to tell the young man that his safety couldn't be guaranteed."

There was a sudden murmuring then—Shane could spot the people in the crowd who got it first, and then the ones who didn't. He could also spot the folks who got pissed off and the ones who felt guilty. He eyed Crick and Deacon's old teacher with a whole lot of respect.

"I'd like to ask this community how it feels," she continued, "to know that we can't be trusted with the safety of a man who risked his life to protect ours. When we said we couldn't guarantee Carrick Francis, we were talking about protecting him from *you*—from every person in the stands who has spread a rumor or talked ugly about or sabotaged two men who have lived in this community all their lives and have done nothing but good."

From out in the crowd someone shouted, *"Fucking faggots!"* and Ms. Thompson looked in that direction and nodded in grim satisfaction, as though this person had just cleared something up for her.

"And that's what I'm talking about right there, isn't it?" she said calmly, her voice suddenly ringing through the brightly lit darkness, over the uncomfortable silence of those massed bodies at the bleachers. "Here we are, giving thanks for the people who went out and protected our freedoms, but we're unwilling to give our own community members the benefit of being free. So I'm grateful to the young men we're honoring here—I'm so grateful for their service. I just wish we could serve them better by being worth their sacrifice, that's all."

With that, she left the podium—and a very uncertain crowd. There was a smattering of applause, and then it seemed to pick up momentum, but Shane was sure he wasn't the only one who could hear the boos and hisses under the noise as it grew.

Shane jerked his chin at Calvin, and was mildly gratified when Calvin trotted alongside him toward the art teacher as she walked off the football field and down the track toward them.

"Where you guys going?" Mike Williams called from his spot leaning on the other car.

Shane barely spared him a glance. "To do our jobs," he muttered, and beside him he heard Calvin swear.

"Dumb asshole—he thinks she's going to be safe after that?"

"Ballsiest thing I've ever seen," Shane said, and he heard Calvin grunt in the affirmative next to him. The boy rose a few notches in Shane's esteem, and together they walked casually up to the art teacher as she stepped off the field and onto the track and flanked her, one on either side as they made it toward the parked squad cars.

"Hi, gentlemen," she said softly, smiling with such warmth that Shane didn't doubt she was a favorite of the students. "To what do I owe this privilege?"

"Deacon and Crick say 'hi'," Shane told her, and was rewarded by a look of pleased surprise. She had apple cheeks, a wide mouth, and fine smile lines around her brown eyes now that they were up close, and she had put on fresh make-up—understated, but fresh—before she went up in front of the crowd.

"I'm glad they're doing well," she said. There was a crash behind them, and Shane didn't have to look to know a smuggled beer bottle had just made it to the track. Calvin swore.

"I've got it—I saw the fucker, Shane—you get her off the track."

They were to the squad cars by now, and Shane snapped at the two lounging officers who were reacting in slow motion to the beer bottle. "You two may want to make your presence felt, dammit, and you"—this directed at the principal, who was glaring at Ms. Thompson with wide eyes—"you may want to go stand behind her, or this bunch is going to think the school's all excited about gay bashing, and that would be a damned shame, now wouldn't it?"

Mr. Arreguin darted a glance over their shoulder and then took one look at Shane's glare and rabbited over to the podium. As Shane took the art teacher professionally by the arm and led her past the snack bar, he heard the man redirecting the crowd's energy to the marching band. They sucked, Shane thought critically, and then Ms. Thompson directed him to the gym behind the football field, opening a door to the coach's office with keys in a surprisingly steady hand.

"Where are you parked?" Shane asked as he followed her in, watching as she started clicking lights in what looked to be a standard issue P.E. office.

"Other side of the school," she replied with a wry roll of her eyes, and Shane shrugged. The radio at his belt buzzed and he picked it up, answering Calvin's query as to where he was with a terse, "In the coach's office in the gym. If you can pull the squad car around, we can escort the lady to her car."

"Gotcha, Shane—but the guys got some punks in the back of their car. We need to wait until backup comes to get them before I leave the field."

"You gonna be okay?" Shane asked. He couldn't tell from the ambient noise whether or not the crowd had gotten ugly.

"No worries, buddy. Tell Ms. Thompson 'hi' for me—and tell her I didn't grow up to be a fuck-up, would you?"

Shane glanced up to see Ms. Thompson smiling as she heard Calvin, and he arched an eyebrow at her. "I'll tell her, Calvin. Radio when you're on your way. Over."

He clicked off the radio, and the nice teacher lady laughed softly. "Something tells me that the line between fuck-up and Calvin is still sort of thin."

Shane laughed with her. "A thing I ponder more and more thoroughly every day we're partnered," he drawled, and she grinned at him. She said the word "fuck-up" like she was used to saying it, and he liked that about her too.

"So, Officer"—she looked at his name tag—"Perkins...."

"You can call me Shane, Ms. Thompson," he told her, and her grin became even warmer.

"And you can call me Judy, Shane. I was going to ask you how long you've been in town. I know most of the guys by now—they keep a close eye on the school—but I haven't seen you yet."

Shane grimaced. "That's probably because I avoided football duty like the plague," he told her baldly. "But I've been in town since late April."

Judy's look became thoughtful. "It's too bad you weren't just a tad earlier," she said. "I think Deacon could have used a friend like you last February."

Shane nodded. "Yeah—I don't think he's really recovered in some ways. I know Crick would have come here in a heartbeat if that didn't mean that Deacon would have shown up with him."

"Ah, God—they're so good for each other," she said, sitting irreverently on the teacher's desk behind her. She swung her legs and dangled her leather clogs as she sat, and Shane found himself charmed.

"Like wolves or eagles or something," he said, and then he flushed. *Jesus, Shane, try not to be such a psychopath.* But Judith-call-me-Judy Thompson just laughed.

"I concur," she murmured. "I'd say like horses, but I know how horses mate, and that's just not an appealing thought at all."

Shane was so surprised that he choked on his own tongue laughing, and when he looked up, she was blushing.

"I'm sorry," she murmured. "I don't know what pops out of my mouth sometimes."

He grinned at her. "Join the club—my mouth should just be declared a disaster area and closed down."

They laughed quietly, and the next half hour passed pleasantly for both of them. Shane was regretful when Calvin buzzed him to say the squad car was coming around, and he shook his head at Judy, who was looking a little sorry herself.

"Why thank you, Officer. You made being threatened by redneck gay-bashers almost fun tonight. I didn't expect that."

"Are you going to get into too much trouble?" he asked seriously, and she shrugged.

"I've got tenure—and I know how to use it. Hey," she started, and then looked uncomfortable.

He looked at her, surprised. They'd covered everything from books to plays to federal funding in the last half-hour, and he didn't think he made her nervous anymore.

She smiled tentatively anyway. "Look... I'm... I'm still learning how to do this after my divorce, but... I'm not reading this wrong, am I? You, uhm... you do think I'm cute, right?"

He blinked and flushed and looked at his toes. Oh God. He hadn't even realized it but it was true. He'd been *flirting*. All his fine talk about keeping promises, and he'd been *flirting* with this very pretty, very available, very *fun* woman, and now she expected....

"Oh God... I'm so stupid. You're friends with Deacon and Crick, and I didn't want to assume...." She was blathering, embarrassed, and he couldn't let her feel like it was all her fault.

"No, no!" he said, keeping his smile warm. "No—I think you're beautiful, and truth is, I've got an equal opportunity pecker, so that's no worry...."

"Then what is it?" she asked, and then stopped and mouthed "equal opportunity pecker" as though she liked the way it sounded.

"The thing is," he said with another blush, looking away, "I've also got a one-chance heart, and I was... I was sort of giving someone else that chance right now."

To his surprise, Judy Thompson laughed that warm, rich laugh, and then she stood up from the desk and came over and kissed his cheek.

"Do you have a cell phone, Shane Perkins?"

Shane nodded and pulled it out, and she took it from him and started programming in a number.

"The thing is," she echoed as she played with the buttons, "that any man who would claim to have an equal opportunity pecker and a one-chance heart is the sort of man you might want to set yourself on standby for. So here." She handed back the phone. "You take your one chance, and if that doesn't pan out, you give me a call, okay?"

Shane took the phone and looked the place where her name should be, and he couldn't help laughing. It said "just-in-case."

"You won't get mad if I use this to invite you to Deacon's for dinner, will you? Even if my chance pays off? I think the guys would love to see you."

Judy smiled some more, a little sadly as if she already saw that she'd lost, and patted his cheek. "So cute. And such a good guy. I think you're in the wrong profession, Officer—but I'd be happy to come see Deacon and Crick for dinner. And I'd even be happy to meet"—she arched her eyebrows—"her? Him?"

"Him," Shane confirmed.

"I'd be happy to meet him and tell him what a lucky bastard he is."

And that was when Calvin knocked on the door, and their warm little interlude in the coach's office was over.

Chapter 7

Wounded deep in battle, I stand stuffed like some soldier undaunted...

"For You"—Bruce Springsteen

MIKHAIL heard the phone buzz on the desk during his last class and was embarrassed as he tripped over his falling heart in front of the mirror.

He was even more embarrassed when the batch of seven-year-olds who were following his lead interpreted the stumble as a dance step and repeated it. He had no choice but to stop the music and turn to them, laughing when he least felt like doing so, and telling them that they were very clever to follow him, but that he had been the one at fault.

He was not prepared for eleven identical looks of awe.

"But," Lily, his favorite student, whispered, "you *never* make mistakes Teacher Bayul." She had long, curly blonde hair up in two pigtails that fell down around her ears like a lop-eared rabbit, and big brown eyes. He'd never thought about it before, but he did appreciate brown eyes.

Mikhail's laugh was a little more real this time. "Of course I do, *malenkaya* bunny-girl. For instance, I made the mistake of smiling at all of you so now you think practice is over! Now from the top, please, third position!"

All of the students promptly straightened their spines and placed the heels of their right feet against the toes of their left, and although there wasn't a smile on the lot of them, they looked at Mikhail with twinkling eyes. It was a comfortable relationship he had with these children. If he pretended to be stern, they pretended to be well behaved, and since he pretended very well, their lessons were both productive and fun.

In short, he took all of his childhood memories of harsh voices in his ear, heart-leveling criticisms that took his breath, and unkind hands manipulating thin limbs to the point of pain and threw them into the little black box in his mind and started over.

As it turned out, he loved to dance more now when he was teaching children than he had when he had been one, and that was saying something. So that was what he threw himself into on this night, during his last class, when he'd unfortunately allowed himself the hope of throwing himself into Shane's company instead.

It was galling to realize that he'd fallen for that hope. He knew better.

When the class was over, he said goodbye to his students (who said a grave goodbye back) and nodded courteously to their parents, who were probably warmer to him than he deserved. When everybody was gone, he looked heavily at his phone as it sat on the desk in the back of the room and decided he couldn't listen to the message. Not now.

The first message, saying that Shane would be by a week later than he'd thought, came as a pleasant surprise. Mikhail had honestly thought that their last conversation would be all, and if the thought left him a little sad, well, he knew how the world worked.

Shane's second message, saying that he would be by the dance studio after the last class on Wednesday, had been much more confident than the first one. There had been promise in that warm, dry voice, and Mikhail had slipped himself a forbidden dose of hope.

He hadn't known how much of the drug he'd taken until he saw the phone vibrate. It could only be a call bailing—there was no other reason the phone would ring. Mikhail hadn't returned either of the other two messages, why should a man like Shane—a handsome man, one with family and friends—invest any more time in a stray like Mikhail than he already had? It had to be a rejection.

And Mikhail, crashing from the hope, did not have the strength to hear it. With a squaring of his narrow jaw, he stalked up to the stereo and programmed his iPod blindly. Something angry, about betrayed promises... and Pat Benatar thundered through the room.

Mikhail danced angrily. The injury he'd endured when he was younger had healed in the years he'd gone without dancing. Now it ached in the cold and needed a brace if he overexerted it, but for the most part, his knee behaved. This night it served him well. He jumped with perfect execution and as much impetus as he could manage. He leapt, he pounded, he even did a handspring, the pale wood paneling of the dance floor harder on his wrists than it had been in his younger days, but he didn't let that slow him down. His dance was bitter and disappointed and fierce, and inside it he was the calm, grim eye of the hurricane, the Ice Man in action.

And you try to be hard but your heart says try again...

The end of the song roared to a conclusion, and Mikhail, feeling reckless with his body, his means of making a living, went for the spectacular move. Nobody was watching—if he succeeded or failed, nobody would see him make pirouette after pirouette, his eyes focused on the mirror in front of him, his face locked in grim lines, his body pushing, pushing, pushing past the disappointment that came when you let yourself....

Four bars before the song was over, he turned his body hard and whipped his head around to spot his eyes in the mirror.

In the next bar, as his shoulders were already beginning their turn, his eyes actually registered the broad face, the patient brown eyes, gazing at him in the mirror from the glass wall behind him.

The song roared to its conclusion as he stumbled for the second time that night, this time finding himself face to face with Shane through the plate glass window. Shane had been watching him dance with a terrifying admiration.

Mikhail had no idea what his expression was as he sat there on one knee, panting and gazing at Shane through the sweat dripping from his hair, but he knew that before he could stop himself, he whispered, "You came."

Shane's mouth—it was a lean mouth, but it crinkled up on the ends easily—curved in a gentle smile, and it was easy to read his words even with the loud stereo and the sound muffled through the window. "I'm sorry I'm late."

Perhaps next time, it would do to check the phone before dancing yourself into a sweaty mess. Yes, yes, there is always a better way.

Mikhail stood with as much dignity as he could muster and walked to the locked door, pushing it outward and nodding Shane in. Shane walked in and looked around curiously, smiling at the row of toe shoes hanging by ribbons next to the little plaque of every student who had earned a solo and then graduated.

"I'm sorry I'm late," he repeated, not looking at Mikhail. For his part, Mikhail grabbed a clean white towel from the pile and wiped his face and hair, wishing he had a clean shirt or something in his locker. He had come expecting to teach—not to stain his best button-up shirt with sweat.

"I thought you were not coming," he confessed, hoping the towel would mask whatever emotion was left after that cathartic dance.

Shane looked at him in surprise. "Why would you think that? I left you a message."

Mikhail shrugged. "Yes, yes, I know. I did not look at the message, I just assumed…. Why are you late?"

The look on Shane's face said that he well understood why Mikhail might jump to such a conclusion—and then change the subject so abruptly it left them both with whiplash. Shane's sigh was heavy, though, and Mikhail looked at him sharply. Shane caught the look and shrugged.

"I was putting my cat down," he said sheepishly, and Mikhail raised his eyebrows to the sweaty curls hanging on his brow.

"I'm sorry?" He was honestly surprised.

"One of my cats—she was really old when I got her from the shelter, but, you know, I got home from work, and poor Judi Dench was looking like shit. Her kidneys had just closed down for no reason, so I had to put her down." Shane was keeping his face very neutral, and Mikhail had a sudden insight—and he wasn't used to those. This big strong man with the warm, low voice had loved the damned cat.

"I didn't want to wait until I got home tonight—that's not right, you know?"

Mikhail nodded, and his throat worked. "Well, shit," he said, at a loss. "How can I be angry with you for being late? That's not fair of you at all." He turned around and put the towel in the hamper—Anna, his boss, had a cleaning service, and they would be by in the morning to collect the laundry. "I can't even pout over that." He glared at Shane, honestly irritated. "You might have at least had the decency to have a flat tire, or to just be an insensitive bastard, but now? You left a message and have a perfectly good explanation, and now I'm fucked. How am I supposed to reject you now?"

To his relief, Shane's face split into a sweet, good-natured grin. "You're not supposed to reject me—you're supposed to come to dinner with me. That's the rule."

Mikhail found himself blushing as he reached for his jacket from the peg above the desk. "That is not necessary, you know. A ride home would be fine."

"You going to invite me in to watch a movie?" Shane asked brazenly, and now Mikhail was sweating all over again.

"No," he said, shaking his head and avoiding Shane's eyes. "I would, you know—because I have not seen *Up* yet, and we bought it already. But my mother… her health is not good. I would have to prepare her for you, so she would be ready for company. It… it takes a while." He thought painfully of his mother, putting on a nice dress and fixing her turban just so—and then finding out that his companion was a man. She would be disappointed, and he did not think he could bear that.

Shane nodded. "Well, then—you'll have to come with me to dinner. Anywhere you want."

Mikhail sighed. He normally had a great deal of pride, but he had assumed the worst about this nice man, and he felt as though he owed Shane a date at the very least. Besides—he was in charge of meals at home, and he knew for certain that his mother was very tired of his cooking. He allowed himself to reach for a treat—for her, he assured himself.

"Can we get something for my mother?" he asked awkwardly. "She really loves Panda Express, and I think tonight she will be able to keep something down."

Mikhail liked Shane's car immensely. It rumbled when it rode and felt substantial when he sat in it. It was also… intimate. None of the coolness of a modern car, just the warmth of the black leather interior and a seat that seemed to put him in very personal space with the big man next to him.

"So you named your cat Judi Dench?" Mikhail asked as Shane turned left onto Sylvan.

"Yeah—I named them all after movie stars."

Mikhail shrugged. "Well, if they are going to sleep with you anyway, why not, right?"

"Exactly!" Shane said excitedly. He looked Mikhail's way with a great deal of delight, and Mikhail shrugged again. It made sense to him—he liked cats. He understood them. If their apartment complex allowed animals, he and his mother would have had many.

Abruptly Shane sobered. "I just didn't realize this one was as old as she was. She had a real princessy attitude—I liked her. I wasn't sure if I could keep a cat, you know? But the animal shelter knew I was about full up on dogs, and I couldn't seem to stop coming around, so they told me they'd start me off with Judi. Her owner was elderly and passed away first, and there was poor old Judi, just waiting for a pleasant place to pass the time. And then I got her, and she seemed to be so lonely when I left for work, and the rest of them sort of made up her family."

Shane had been driving with certainty as he spoke, and Mikhail realized he knew the area well. He stopped talking, though, and Mikhail saw the blush. He was embarrassed, going on about his cat—which was silly, of course.

"Well," Mikhail said after a moment, feeling graceless, "thank you for coming anyway." Oh, hell. All of Shane's honesty deserved a little on his part, right? "I would have been disappointed if you had been unable to make it."

They were at a stoplight, and Shane turned a grin to him—it was sweet and shining, and Mikhail had to look away. "And now I am done being nice to you," he said, sticking his lip out and knowing he sounded like a brat but unable to stop. "It is like feeding a cat."

Shane's quiet laughter let him know that he was fooling nobody. "Yup," he said as he took a right onto Sunrise with its little mall and happy lamppost advertising. "It's too late, Mickey. You've already fed me once. I'll be back for-fucking-ever."

Mikhail brightened. "So there will be fucking?" He had been half-tempted to give in to Brett's advances again this past weekend, but two things stopped him. One was that Brett cared too much, and Mikhail didn't, so it was no longer just a quickie in the tent to relieve tension.

The other was that… well, that potent drug of hope had been surging in his veins. He found now that it paled to sitting in the rumbling darkness with someone who had gone out of his way to be with him.

Shane made a pained noise. "Not immediately," he said with what sounded like a whimper. "Not tonight, at any rate."

"Why not?" Mikhail looked around. The car wasn't roomy, he thought, but he was pretty sure the seats reclined.

Shane pulled into the parking lot of Panda Express and gave Mikhail a look like he knew exactly what Mikhail was thinking. Mikhail was horrified to find himself blushing. He never blushed over sex—*ever*. He was unapologetic. The Ice Man. Right?

"I just thought," he stammered, wondering where that unsteady voice came from. "You know… you've proved yourself. You are not a one-night stand. We can have sex now."

"Uhm-hum." Shane nodded and reached out a finger to trace Mikhail's jaw. That little touch… just a little, and Mikhail felt his hand tremble on the door catch. "I actually missed dinner," Shane drawled. "I think we should maybe eat food this time out." And with that he rubbed his thumb in the divot on Mikhail's chin and then got out of the car.

Mikhail had to sit for a moment and remember to breathe before he got out himself. He made his way to where Shane was waiting patiently for him, and they went into the restaurant together.

A few minutes later Shane asked, "When is your mother going to get better?" when Mikhail was in the middle of a mouthful of broccoli-beef.

Mikhail made an effort to swallow and then looked carefully at his Styrofoam plate as he said, "February or thereabouts, when she dies."

There was silence, and he risked a look up. Shane was looking at him without pity, even as he mouthed, "I'm sorry," to Mikhail's unspoken question.

Mikhail shrugged. "So is she. She had great plans to see her grandchildren, you understand." He surprised Shane badly—he could see that in the wide eyes and the quirk of his lips.

"Was that something you were going to get right on?" he asked, letting Mikhail choose how to answer.

Mikhail sighed. Apparently he was going to be honest and pitiable this night. It made him cranky. He was not comfortable here, but he felt… *indebted* was the word… to the man who had kept a promise when Mikhail had thought the worst of him.

"It is a game we play," he confessed. From under his brow he eyed the potstickers that Shane had bought for both of them and was not surprised when Shane took two of them and put them on Mikhail's plate. "Thank you," he murmured, dipping them into the hot Szechuan sauce and wishing it was even spicier.

"A game?" The prompt was gentle, and Mikhail finished swallowing before he answered.

"She knows who I am—you cannot be what we have been to each other and not know that. But…." He smiled a little. "I think you may have to be Russian to understand. No one can take care of me like another woman—that is what she thinks. She does not want to leave me alone, so we have a fantasy, you see, where I will find a nice girl—she does not even have to be Russian—and this girl will cook and clean for me and bear me children, and I will not be alone."

Shane nodded and chewed thoughtfully. He ate a lot, but Mikhail thought he might even have gotten thinner since they'd seen each other last. Mikhail sniffed. Stupid man. There was no need for that.

The silence made Mikhail uncomfortable. "You probably think I am unenlightened for America," he said with dignity, and Shane's surprise was gratifying.

"No—not at all." Shane took a sip of soda, still thoughtful. "I just"— and now he looked embarrassed—"I just was thinking about mine and Kimmy's mother. She… she was hardly there, you know? Kimmy talked about rehab and how Mom sent money—it's all she's ever done. We wanted attention, Mom put Kimmy in dance, and that's where she got her attention. Dad wanted perfect little students, and we tried to be just that. There was no worry—there was no 'happy fantasy', unless you were me and Kimmy, in our own rooms, having the happy fantasy that someone gave a shit."

Shane took another bite and nodded, looking studiously out the window into the Target parking lot across the way. "I'm sorry your mom's sick, Mickey, but I gotta say, I'm sort of jealous. You've got someone in your life who doesn't want to leave you all alone. That's a good thing, right?"

Mikhail found that his hands were shaking as he picked up his fork. (He did not do chopsticks.) He nodded dumbly but didn't say anything, just chewed and breathed evenly and tried to think about something, anything, but the man sitting across from him and his painful, important perceptions.

"You are right," he said at last, still looking at his food. "Sometimes empty promises, they are still important. Sometimes the fantasy is as much the love as what is real, yes?" He felt silly. It was... impolitic to talk about emotions like this.

"Exactly," Shane said, nodding earnestly, and Mikhail turned shiny eyes toward him. His face twisted a little, and he fought to swallow. "What?" Shane asked, as though he was afraid he'd gotten something wrong.

Mikhail shook his head. How to explain? Kimmy had told him to take her brother seriously. How could Mikhail have a choice in the matter, when everything he said seemed to be spelling out the things in Mikhail's heart like the voice of God?

"You are right. In fact, you have made me feel better about many things," he said now, but his voice was not as steady as he would have liked, and Shane blushed.

"I'm sorry. I'm prying... I would imagine you're ready to go home now."

"No!" Mikhail actually couldn't believe he'd said that. He felt as though he'd been tricked somehow from giving just a little of his time to not make this nice man feel bad, to wanting this moment to keep going. It was just like the Faire all over again, he thought wretchedly. It was supposed to be a heartbeat. It was not meant to continue—it just wasn't. Nothing good was meant to stay. "I mean," he continued, blushing, "that is not necessary. My mother will need to eat in an hour or so. There is no need to return until then."

Mikhail peeked uncertainly at Shane to see how he would take that. He looked surprised and more than a little pleased. Mikhail nodded, as though something had been decided.

"But maybe we should leave this place. It has no charm at all." Panda Express was his mother's favorite food, but it was loud and cold, and the floor was hard, and he could see Shane agreeing with him.

"There's a Starbucks by the bookstore—feel like coffee?" Shane sounded so eager, and Mikhail looked at him helplessly. It was like the man was Satan himself, come with temptation. *What is the harm? You will frighten him with your honesty, and then this will be the end. There is nothing to bind him to you, not even sex.*

"A very large mocha, with lots of milk," Mikhail said, feeling his back straighten with anticipation, and Shane smiled, his warm eyes crinkling at the edges some more.

"I like caramel myself, but it's a deal." He retrieved his brown bomber jacket and a rather handsome, handmade scarf from the chair behind him. They cleaned up, stowed the food they'd bought for Ylena in the car, and set off across the parking lot.

"I like the scarf," Mikhail said, and he was not just making conversation. The bomber jacket looked expensive—an indulgence, and it did not look as though Shane did that much, in spite of the money he had been gifted with. The scarf was something else—it was not perfect. Some of the edges were uneven, and there were one or two places where the ends were not woven in completely. But it was getting chilly—just a little—in the middle of October, and Mikhail envied it.

Shane smiled shyly and touched the mottled brown wool. "It was a gift from Benny, Crick's little sister. I told her I'd be working the football games, and she told me it got cold and made it for me in about a weekend. It was nice of her—I promised her I'd wear it."

"It looks warm," Mikhail acknowledged with a touch of envy, and before he knew it, the scarf was over his shoulders, tucked in at his neck under his little denim jacket. He hardly had time to protest, and then he couldn't, because it was soft and squishy and had been warmed by Shane's body heat (a little too warm, Mikhail recognized, because the big man looked more comfortable with it off) and it smelled… mmmm….

"You used the oil," Mikhail said dreamily, tucked into the soft wool scarf and the heat and the scent. It was Shane, all of it, and it was wrapped around him, cedar for protection, chamomile for comfort, and big, sweating, sweet-as-chocolate man… oh, God, it was better than heroin, and Mikhail would know.

Shane was blushing. "Yes, well, I figured you gave it to me for a reason, right?"

Mikhail nodded, too caught up in the scarf and the warmth to say anything, but he was flattered. He was more than flattered—he was as enchanted as a child. He was afraid that if he opened his mouth, all of his self-reliance would desert him, and he would be left begging this man to take him home.

Shane talked instead, and Mikhail got to hear about the football game and the brave woman who had stood up for Shane's friends. There was something in Shane's voice, and Mikhail looked at him sharply. "She was pretty, this teacher?"

The way those brown eyes peered at him sideways put Mikhail especially on edge. "Yes, yes she was."

"And single."

"Oh yes."

"Then she must have been crazy," Mikhail snapped without thinking. "Otherwise she would have hit on you."

Shane was fighting a self-satisfied smirk, and Mikhail could have kicked himself. Oh, he had walked into that trap so easily. "Who says she didn't?"

Mikhail clutched the scarf closer and folded his arms tight around his chest. "Well, then, if she wants you, you should date her. She is probably more suited for you. I would imagine she has need of someone to take care of her. I have no such need."

"Of course not." Mikhail couldn't read the expression in Shane's voice. He might possibly be laughing, but he sounded so neutral, Mikhail could not be certain.

"So you will date her?" He felt very noble. This interlude would end, and Mikhail would remember this good smell and be happy that Shane was happy. Mikhail caught himself casting a wistful look at the big man striding beside him. Shane deserved to be happy.

"No," Shane told him, and Mikhail was surprised to feel a strong arm draped over his shoulders. It was not sexual, not really—but it was intimate, and Mikhail made his strides a little closer to Shane's (which was hard because the man was over six feet tall, and that wasn't fair) and adjusted his body position so as to not shake that arm off.

"No?" Fucking hope. It would kill him.

"Nope. I told her I had an equal opportunity pecker and a one-chance heart, and I was giving that heart a chance somewhere else." The smug satisfaction in Shane's voice was almost enough to make Mikhail shrug him off—but not quite.

"Then she was a foolish woman. She should have tried harder."

"She did," Shane told him softly. "Put herself in my phone under 'just-in-case'. I told her that Deacon might want to have her to dinner some night, since she's a friend and all. She seemed to understand."

I wish I did. But Mikhail didn't say it. It stayed quietly in his head until the rest of conversation from that night drowned that little voice right out.

They wandered the bookstore for a few moments, coffee in hand. Mikhail went to the travel section and pulled out a full-colored photo essay on Mexico and sighed at the price. "My mother would love this," he murmured, "but she will love the real thing more."

Shane took the book from him and thumbed through it. "You're going to Mexico?"

"Oh God, I hope so." And then Mikhail truly lost his mind, because he told Shane the whole story, foolish promise and all. "I've made two promises to my mother since she brought us here," he said in the end, as they were walking back through the parking lot. "The first was to stay off the streets, and the second was that I would take her some place to bake herself in the sun before she died." He shook his head. "I swear, were it not for the first promise, I could have worked a weekend and the second promise would be a sure thing."

Shane was so surprised he stumbled on a curb and spit out his coffee. Mikhail looked up at him in horror and wished he could swallow his tongue.

"I was joking!" he said a little desperately, watching as Shane stopped dead and bent over, hands on thighs, and tried to choke through some coffee he'd inhaled.

"Thank God!" Shane managed, but Mikhail kept pounding him on the back anyway. "Ouch, dammit, you're fucking strong!"

"Sorry!" Mikhail stopped pounding on his back immediately, and started massaging between Shane's shoulder blades where he'd been pounding. Shane stopped talking and the quality of his breathing grew more even, and then it grew strained again, and then he straightened abruptly.

"Thanks," he said gruffly, pulling away.

"I have offended you," Mikhail said miserably, watching as Shane took a couple of stiff steps. "See. I am no good with people. You will leave and call the teacher woman, and she will know how to not make you choke on your—" He stopped because Shane had stopped and turned around and was advancing on him with an expression half of exasperation and half of determined good humor.

He walked right up to Mikhail's space, and then into it, until Mikhail's eyes were even with the throbbing pulse in his neck. Then he grabbed Mikhail's hips and pulled them flush with his own, and there against Mikhail's belly was the grand-bitch-mother of all erections, straining through his jeans.

"It's not exactly San Francisco, here, Mickey," Shane rasped, catching his eyes meaningfully. "I didn't think making out in the parking lot was such a great idea."

Mikhail nodded dumbly, thinking that Shane's breath smelled like coffee and his five-o'clock shadow was dark and rough, and that the dent at his clavicles seemed deep and tender, and that his lips looked so strong. Mikhail was trembling as Shane pulled away, and he made no argument when that heavily muscled, casual arm looped around his shoulders and pulled him close to Shane's side. They were quiet—quivering with tension but quiet—until they got back to the car.

Shane started the ignition and said "Where to?" and Mikhail directed him up Sunrise to Auburn, and then left. It was longer than going down Greenback, and he knew this, but he was reluctant for the moment to end any sooner than it had to. He was a selfish bastard sometimes—he knew this also.

"You should tell your mom I'm coming next week," Shane said as they pulled into the apartment complex. "I'll give you a ride home and bring dinner. We can watch *Up*."

"Turn left here," Mikhail directed, so shocked he waited for the last minute to give the direction. "I will see you next week? This complex here. I am on the second floor—apartment number 225."

Shane found an empty space (a miracle unto itself) and put the car in park, turning off the ignition. "Yeah, Mikhail. What—you think I get a hard-on for just anybody? It's been a while; I'd like to see if I remember what to do with that thing."

"How long?" Mikhail asked, looking at him in surprise.

Shane shrugged. "A year and a half, but who's keeping score?"

Mikhail's eyes practically bulged out. "Oh God. A year and a half? I hope you've been relieving yourself, or you'll kill me!"

Shane turned to him, laughing—hard. Mikhail just watched him, his head thrown back, his teeth glinting a little in the pale soda light above the parking lot, and wondered how such a generous man had ended up buying him dinner. Oh God—he wanted this man to come back. He wanted to laugh with him some more, talk with him some more. He was funny and had good stories and would risk irritating his date to put a poor cat out of its misery, and he kept his promises.

His mouth went suddenly dry. "I'm sorry," he said suddenly. "I... I should make you stay away. I... you would be very happy with the teacher woman. I could find you someone else—my boss is Russian, she would make you a very good wife...."

Shane stopped laughing, and his exasperation came back, but this time, instead of saying anything, he grabbed Mikhail by the front of the jacket and hauled him in for a kiss.

Mikhail shut up and opened his mouth. Mmmmm... so good... so very good. Shane's lips were firm, and his tongue tasted like coffee and caramel. One hand was still clutching Mikhail's jacket, but the other was cupping the back of Mikhail's skull, holding his head in place so he could adjust the angle of the kiss and plunder some more. Mikhail whimpered and clutched at Shane's shoulders. They were broad and solid, and Mikhail inched his hands under the bomber jacket so he could feel Shane's warmth seeping through a yellow shirt. Mikhail wanted closer than that. He fumbled with the buttons on the shirt and pulled back, indignant.

"You have a T-shirt on!" He had not pulled back that far, and Shane's face was only inches away—just far enough in the darkness to see his lips curve up in a faint smile.

"Shut up and keep kissing me," he commanded, and Mikhail was helpless. He was fumbling again at the shirt when Shane caught him by surprise and simply pushed his hands up Mikhail's stomach and under his own dress shirt, and they were warm and sensual, and they touched his tender skin with appreciation. Mikhail gasped, heard Shane chuckle, and then Shane's big hands were circling, rubbing the bare skin of his back, sliding down the back of Mikhail's jeans, and Mikhail groaned and tilted his head back.

Shane kissed his chin and then his throat and then the skin on the side of his neck, still warmed by the brown wool scarf. Mikhail turned his head a little, and Shane kissed his way up to his ear, his tongue coming out to play with the little stud he wore, and then he was breathing harshly into the hollow.

"Mikhail?"

"Da?"

"I'm not fucking you in the parking lot in front of your mother's apartment." His voice was unsteady, panting, breathless—and unbelievably firm.

"I hate you very much a lot." To emphasize this, Mikhail grabbed one of Shane's hands and brought it to the front of his own jeans and then arched his aching cock against Shane's palm. Shane squeezed his hand, and Mikhail knew he was watching Mikhail's expression. He let go and shut his eyes, throwing his head back against the car seat, then stayed there for a minute until his breathing evened out.

"I'm not so happy with myself at the moment," he acknowledged, and Mikhail blew out a breath.

"Next week?" he asked uncertainly, and Shane opened his eyes and looked at Mikhail sideways, which did terrible things to a pulse that was thundering as it was.

"You can count on it. I'll bring dinner. What do you want me to cook?"

Mikhail stared back at him with stunned eyes and shook his head with a shrug. "I have no idea. I'll tell Mutti—she will be pleased to have company who is not church people, telling her to repent."

Shane reached out a hand, his head still tilted back, and cupped Mikhail's cheek then rubbed his swollen mouth with a rough thumb. "I promise to behave for your mother, Mikhail—I'll try not to be too weird for her."

Mikhail captured the hand and closed his eyes. "You are not weird," he whispered, and then he grabbed his food from under the seat and got out of the car before he could say anything else embarrassing. When he got to his stairs and up the door, he heard the car start up, and he turned around and waved with an unsteady hand. Shane's hand appeared out the window and waved back, and Mikhail started up the stairs again. It wasn't until he got to the top of the stairs that he realized he still had the scarf around his neck.

The front door of his apartment opened into the kitchen, and he went straight to the shelves for the dishes.

"You are late, *mal'chik*. I was worried."

Yes. She would worry. "I'm sorry, Mutti," he called, putting the cool food into a bowl and setting it into the microwave to warm. "A friend came and took me to eat. I brought you some." He walked into the living room and gave his mother the expected kiss on the cheek.

"A friend, yes? What did you bring me?"

He smiled and turned on the way to his room. "Panda Express," he told her proudly, and was pleased at the way she lit up.

"Oh, it is a very good friend—did he give you that scarf?"

Mikhail grimaced. "He lent it to me—it was a gift for him, he could scarcely gift it back to me, now could he?"

Ylena nodded, her expression catlike. "I suppose not. And yet he buys you food and lets you wear his scarf and maybe buys you coffee, if I smell right?"

Mikhail's slight grin betrayed a lot of things, but then, he could never hide anything from his mother. "Da. But he is not for me." He turned to go.

"Wait—why not?"

Mikhail's expression grew sober, and his lovely, light mood fell with it. "He keeps his promises, Mama, and we both know I do not."

He tried to go then, but he was not fast enough. Her eyes grew bright and she said, "You need to forgive yourself, *mal'chik*."

"Mutti...."

"Nyet!" And she so rarely spoke angrily that he had to stop and walk deliberately back to her to have this out.

"We cannot change the past," he said, cursing his damned voice. It had been running riot all day, and it was time to get it under control.

"We can change the way you look at it!" she retorted. "You were young and desperate, and it was not your fault."

"I said I'd take care of you—"

"Yes!" she snapped. "You were nine years old and promising me you would take care of me! You should have been playing in school, but instead you were dancing to support us both—"

"We both know that school was not as idyllic as it sounds," he said, raw. Not where they had lived before the apartment and the food coupons that dancing had given them.

"I should have known you were hurt!"

"Mutti..."

"Don't 'Mutti' me—we both know I should have. I should have seen the drugs before they ended your career.... I should have seen what you were doing for them before they ended your life...."

"Mutti!" He hated this conversation. He hated it—it was wrong. She had been so young—hell, when he'd been recruited for the ballet in the first place, she'd been scarcely as old as he was now.

"We will have this conversation," she muttered, overriding his protests, "and we will have it my way, and we will have it before it can destroy you anymore for not having it. Why has it never occurred to you, my sweet boy, that I was as much to blame for Olek's death as you were?"

"It was *not* your promise to make!" he shouted. "It was mine! *I* told him I would be back. *I* told him I would never leave him. *I* was the one who lied to him, who did not mention that my mother was trying to get us out of Russia for once and forever—"

"And I was the one who locked you in your room so you could see what the drugs were doing to you!" she shouted back. "I tied you to your bed so you could feel withdrawals, feel it, so you would know why we needed to leave so you could overcome it. I was the one who did not listen to you when you told me your friend was alone and sad. I was the one who did not let you out until it was too late. I am sick and I am dying, and why can you not give me some of the blame, Mikhail? It will sit more lightly on my shoulders when I am dead than it will on yours as you use it to poison your life!"

Mikhail's hand was trembling as he used the heel of it to press against his eyes, but for some reason they would not stop blurring. "I told him I'd be back," he said brokenly. He squeezed his eyes shut again and saw Olek, cold and blue, his flesh long since stiff in the tiny pallet of the back room they'd used to turn tricks and shoot up. The needle was still in his arm—he'd shot a week's worth of stash in one go. Next to him had been the note Mikhail left in Cyrillic: *Gone home to give my mother the rent. No worries. Back in an hour. Don't shoot it all.*

Yes, yes, the fucker had broken that promise and had shot it all, but damn it to fucking hell, Mikhail had broken his promises first.

In the silence between them, the microwave dinged that the food was warm, and he moved mechanically to go get it. He brought it back with a placemat and a fork and set it on the table in front of her, and she caught his hand and pulled him down to her, framing his wet face in her hands and kissing his cheek fiercely.

"I'm sorry your friend died back when you were a lost child, *mal'chik*, but I am not sorry it was not you. Of all the fucking awful things I did as a mother, seeing you grown is the one I will not regret."

Mikhail couldn't look at her. He gave her cheek his own fierce kiss and straightened. He would not speak of Olek again. Poor Olek, who had shown him how to bend over and take it when the loneliness had gotten so bad, and how to shoot up when the pain did not leave the knee because he came back too early to dance on it, and how to turn tricks when they could no longer dance. He'd started life as a sweet boy with red hair and blue eyes and whose one true evil in life had been the same as the heroin that killed him. All of his efforts had been to stop Mikhail's pain in the "now," and he had not known how to stop it for the "later." Well, now it was later, and Mikhail had to live through the pain, and he had done it by being alone, by not being in the position to let anybody down again.

Except his mother.

And now Shane.

"You are a wonderful mother," he said roughly. "When you die, that should not be a weight that sits your shoulders, you understand?"

"And you are a good man. When I am dead, that should not be a thing you worry about, either," she said thickly.

He nodded and made his way heavily to his back bedroom to take off his denim jacket. He took off the scarf as well, but not before he'd buried his nose in its softness for comfort. It still smelled like Shane—right down to the Chinese food and the coffee and the innocence.

He couldn't help it. He held it to his face and breathed it in again and again and used it to blot his cheeks, in spite of how scratchy wool got when you did that. When he was done, he folded it carefully and put it on top of the box, where it sat neatly since it would not fit inside.

He might give it back to Shane when he came back the next week—but only if Shane asked.

Chapter 8

...the house is haunted and the ride gets rough...

"Tunnel of Love"—Bruce Springsteen

THEY sat side by side on the floor of the small apartment with their arms wrapped around their knees and watched *Up*. Shane had tried very hard not to cry like a woman in the first ten minutes, and he had caught Mikhail's wry glance at him, complete with rolled eyes.

Shane had slugged him in the arm and ignored him after that, and they became completely immersed in the children's movie. Mikhail's mother lay stretched out on the couch behind them, just as captivated as they were.

Shane liked her very much—he was sorry she was sick; he would have liked to have known her for a long time.

Dinner had gone well—he'd made that chicken, mayonnaise, and cheese thing with the potato chips on top, and Ylena had been pleased at the gift if not the taste. There was no reason to inform her that the masterpiece had been completed with a maximum of fuss, a destroyed kitchen, and three phone calls to Benny to make sure he was doing it right.

"It's chicken, mayonnaise, and cheese, Shane—add in some pimentos and some almonds, and how hard can it be?"

"I don't know!" Shane had wailed, looking at the mess the frozen chicken thighs had made as they boiled over on his stove. "But I seem to be finding every damned thing to do wrong that is possible to do wrong."

He opened one of the bags of potato chips he'd bought for the project and started munching on it glumly. Deacon had dragged him and Jon an extra mile that morning, and he was starving.

"Look," Benny was saying, "clean up the shit on the stove, because if the water boils away and there's more fat than water, it'll catch fire."

"SHIT!" Because the warning came a little late, and Benny spent some minutes being entertained on the other end of the line as he took a pot lid and beat the fire out.

When he was done and she'd walked him through the rest of the process, she'd said, "Okay, Shane, give. Who is this for?"

Shane was drinking a beer by then—something he rarely did, actually—and eating more potato chips, but he still wasn't relaxed and happy enough to answer that question.

"I'm not telling," he said, knowing it sounded petulant and not being able to change that.

"Jesus, Perkins, what are you, five?"

"It's not that," he muttered, still unable to put a finger on it. "It's just… Benny, I'm not sure this will work out, you know? I don't want to…. You guys are good enough to take me into your home… not random strangers who might not come back."

Benny sighed, and in spite of the fact that he was pretty sure his latest batch of casserole might not suck, he could feel the moment weighing heavier than it had.

"The thing is," the girl on the line said with a great deal of thoughtfulness, "who exactly do you think is going to pick you up if this doesn't work out? It would help if we met the guy, you know?"

Shane grinned and tried to make things a little lighter. "Who says it's a guy?"

Benny laughed. "The girl who lives with two gay men, that's who. Guys don't cook to impress girls—not often, anyway. But I'm pretty sure Crick learned to cook just especially to take care of Deacon."

Shane had to concede that was true.

"Just please," Benny said anxiously, "please tell us if something goes wrong. If he breaks your heart. Deacon almost killed himself grieving when Crick left—we just need some warning if we're going to have to scrape you off the floor, okay?"

Shane couldn't answer that. He just kept thinking about the empty apartment he'd come home to after his real, physical heart had actually stopped on the surgery table. The knowledge that he had a group of people who wanted to be there if he broke his figurative heart made him humble.

"I promise," he told her gruffly, and then he'd asked her if Deacon would want a dog for Christmas, and if he bought the yarn, could she please, please, pretty please make him another wool scarf in blue.

And so far so good. It helped that he arrived not only with the casserole but also with the book Mikhail had eyed for his mother the week before—at least in Ylena's eyes.

Mikhail had glared at him as he'd pulled the book out of the back of the car. Shane had given him a ride home and at Mikhail's glare, he'd given a very cheesy impression of a smile.

"Beware of geeks bearing gifts?" he tried lamely, and that had startled the glare right off the little dancer's face.

"I was just thinking that you are very sly as well as stubborn," Mikhail replied sweetly. "I shall have to remember that when trying to convince you to go away."

The man had been edgy since Shane had picked him up, and Shane was pretty sure that this was the part of the dance where Mikhail was going to try to bolt and run. He'd been waiting for it—he wasn't even surprised that it had come so soon.

"Of course you're going to try to make me go away," Shane sighed, hefting the casserole and the book and shutting his door with his hip. "Where's the fun in courting someone without the constant, terrifying fear of rejection?"

He turned to walk up the stairs then, and Mikhail was suddenly right next to him. "You are just going to leave your car here without setting the alarm? In this neighborhood?"

Shane shrugged. "It's not like I'm going to be here all night. Besides, my hands are full." It wasn't necessarily true—he wasn't *that* clumsy, but Mikhail was already reaching for the keys in his pocket, and Shane liked the excuse of getting that close. It was funny, too, that as Mikhail reached into his jeans and pulled out the clicker, he didn't seem to realize how intimate or familiar the gesture was until the alarm was set and he had to put the keys back in Shane's pocket.

Mikhail froze, his hand right above Shane's pocket, his chest rubbing up against Shane's arm. His eyes were wide and surprised, and his pouty little mouth was drawn up into almost a comic O. Shane smiled gently at him and waited patiently for him to recover himself and put the keys back in the pocket of his jeans. For a moment, the air was so still between them that they both could hear the jangling of the keys in Mikhail's shaking hand, and Shane was a little disappointed but not surprised when they were dropped roughly into his jacket pocket instead.

"It's just a pocket, Mickey," Shane said mildly, and Mikhail turned without looking at him.

"I'm not afraid of you."

"Of course you're not."

"Stupid, insufferable man." Mikhail led the way up the stairs, and Shane followed, their feet echoing on the concrete steps in the corridor.

"I'm the devil."

"I'll fuck six men between now and next Wednesday."

"Well, I had an old girlfriend who did that too." Shane sighed. It would be funnier if it hadn't been true.

Mikhail turned to him, appalled. "How could she! How could anyone! You are not a man someone cheats on!"

Shane just looked at him, holding enough casserole to feed the Bayuls for a week and a book on Cozumel as Mikhail stood in front of the yellow apartment door and defended his honor. It took Mikhail a minute, but his cheeks turned red soon enough, and he looked down, his ice-gray eyes picking out the scuffs on the bomber jacket where Angel Marie had planted her paws right before Shane closed the gate.

"It is a horrible threat," he said quietly. "And obviously an empty one, at this point. I am not a good man. I do not keep my promises. I probably cannot be faithful to one lover—I certainly have never tried, and I've never had anybody expect it of me. But I would not go out and fuck people for spite. Out of weakness, perhaps, but not to hurt you. But I will hurt you. Of that I have no doubt. Perhaps this should be our last date, yes?"

Shane was quiet long enough for Mikhail to lift his eyes and meet Shane's patient, measuring look.

"No."

"No?"

"Did I stutter? This casserole's hot; can we go inside?"

So he made it through dinner and through the movie, and Ylena seemed to like him. She ruffled his hair at the end of *Up*, chuckling quietly as he and Mikhail stayed seated through the credits, which told a story of their own.

"So," Mikhail said when even the soundtrack was done, "what do you think? Does it replace *WALL•E*, or is it a tie?"

Shane grinned at him. "I don't know—I think I'll have to watch a few more times to figure out which one I like best."

"You are welcome to come here to see it again," Ylena said with good humor, "but next time I think Mikhail should cook."

There had been something... off... about the taste of the chicken casserole. It was edible, but apparently the third time was *not* the charm.

"Yeah, really—what can you cook, Mikhail?"

Mikhail blushed. "Nothing Russian," he mumbled. "No *borscht* or breaded cauliflower or fish soup. Mutti cooked until we came here, and then all I wanted was American food. Cheeseburger macaroni, lasagna, chili—I wanted nothing to do with Russian food, and Mutti was right there with me."

"Yes I was," Ylena said mildly, "and I still am. I'm sure your friend won't mind whatever you wish to cook, yes?"

"Me?" Shane smiled, taking Ylena's plate from her as he stood and stretched, "I never turn down free chow." He patted his stomach good-naturedly, and Mikhail elbowed him sharply in the ribs.

"You are not fat."

Shane rolled his eyes. "I'm not underfed, either."

"So, Shane," Ylena interrupted before the argument could escalate, "how long have you lived in the area?"

Shane shrugged. "Eight months." He had tried a transfer to another precinct in L.A. after he'd been okayed for work—he used to have to shower for an hour to get rid of the permafrost on his back from all the icy stares.

"You are a detective?" Ah, yes, here it came—the inevitable parental interrogation. Whether she admitted it or not, mothers had been grilling the romantic prospects of their baby boys since the beginning of time.

"I was going to be," he admitted, "but then I got hurt, and after that I decided it was time to do my job somewhere else."

"You got hurt?" Ylena was instantly concerned, but Mikhail made a little sound, too, and when Shane turned around to take the dishes from his hands, Mikhail's ice-gray eyes were avid on his face for details.

"I got called to sort of a hairy situation, and backup didn't arrive in quite enough time," he said diplomatically.

"How long?" Mikhail asked. "How long before the stinking cowards showed up to get you?"

"Twenty-five minutes," Shane muttered. "Do we have to talk about this again?" He sent Ylena a furtive glance, and Mikhail swallowed and made a bitter face before nodding.

"What made you leave your home?" Ylena prodded, taking in the byplay of the two of them. Shane blushed, even as he started running the water to do the dishes, but he answered with his characteristic honesty.

"Well, I got home from the hospital and my apartment had been vacant for a month, you know? And I realized there wasn't a thing in there—or even on the planet—that would have missed me if I didn't come back. So when I realized that nothing in L.A. was in any way good, I figured I'd make a new start, you know? Some place where I'd have people who would miss me."

"Or six dogs and six cats," Mikhail said, as though finally making the connection.

"Five cats," Shane prompted gently, and in the kitchen, within full view of his mother, Mikhail touched his wrist above the dishwater. It was a gentle touch—comforting and familiar. Shane wanted to kiss him so badly right then his chest actually hurt, but Mikhail moved his fingers and began drying the dishes Shane had been putting in the rack.

The interrogation continued but in a friendly way, and by the time Ylena yawned and excused herself to the couch to rest, Shane had covered his job on the tiny Levee Oaks police force, his property, his attachment to Deacon's family, and his thoughts of the future. He'd answered all of the questions honestly except the last one, because he didn't know mostly, but also because you didn't want to tell your date's mother that you were too weird to be a policeman. It sounded a little frightening, and he'd promised Mikhail he wouldn't frighten her tonight.

"Well, I hope you return," Ylena said before she retired. "I haven't seen Mikhail wear his clubbing clothes in some time, and I am happier to see them on him when he is not clubbing."

"Mutti...." Mikhail muttered, mortified, and Shane looked at the bright teal shirt and tight black pants that Mikhail had been wearing when Shane picked him up. It occurred to Shane that he had been dressed pretty nicely the week before, and he couldn't stop grinning even as he picked up his jacket and asked Mikhail to walk him out.

"Wipe that insufferable look off your face," Mikhail snapped. "For all you know, I plan to go out tonight when you're gone."

"Do you?" Shane asked, watching as Mikhail closed the door behind him. Neither of them made a move to go down the stairs. Instead, they just leaned against opposite walls in the corridor, as though settling down for a casual conversation.

Mikhail shook his head and then looked up hopefully. "You could always come with me." His eyes opened prettily, and Shane felt like an asshole for shaking his head.

"I don't dance, Mickey—I'd be like a two-ton weight around your neck, and where's the fun in that?"

"You don't dance?" Mikhail said it like he'd say, "You don't breathe?" only with more horror.

Shane shrugged, feeling awkward. "I'm sorry—I'm a clumsy asshole. Is that a deal breaker?"

"No," Mikhail muttered, then, "I mean, you're not a clumsy asshole, and it's not a deal breaker." Then the pout left his sulky mouth, and he narrowed his eyes at Shane. "What was their excuse?" he asked, and to anybody else it would have sounded out of the blue, but Shane knew exactly what he was talking about.

"For not coming to back me up?" he asked, and Mikhail nodded. "The message didn't get through dispatch."

"Did it?"

"Well, since I left a message at Internal Affairs before I got out of the car, we had a pretty good case that they were lying." Shane didn't want to remember that night, but at least Mikhail wasn't threatening to fuck somebody else and run.

Of course now he was gasping like a fish, and that wasn't much of an improvement.

"You knew?" he asked, outraged. "You *knew* you were being set up, and you went anyway? Why would you do that? Why wouldn't anyone stop you? Didn't you have a partner?"

Shane shrugged. "I didn't say it was the smartest thing I've ever—"

"*Answer me!*" Mikhail shouted, and Shane shushed him frantically, looking over his shoulder as though he expected Ylena to throw open the door and accuse him of molesting her son.

"She's asleep," Mikhail snapped, "and our neighbor works nights, and the people downstairs are old and can't hear for shit, so you might as well answer me. Why would you walk into that situation without backup or even a partner? You promise me.... God, you have no idea what it is you are promising me, and then you show you have no respect for your own life, and who do you think is going to keep that promise if you are dead?"

Shane held up both hands in surrender. "Okay. Okay. You want the truth about that night? Fine. I'll give you the truth." Oh fuck. This was so fucking embarrassing. "The truth is that my first boyfriend tried to cop a feel in the squad room and we got busted. And instead of saying something smooth and blowing it off like he did, I blushed and said something socially retarded, and the entire department knew about me, and Brandon, fuck his black Teflon heart, walked away without a scratch on his lily white reputation. So I knew it was coming. My entire career, the thing I'd wanted most in the world, was in fucking shambles, my love life had just crashed around my ears, and the guy who was supposed to be my partner—in all senses of the word, mind you—had just sacrificed me to the department to save his own skin. I walked into that ambush because it felt like the last stand of every cowboy movie or knight-in-shining-armor book I'd ever seen. For once I got to play the hero and not the clown, and that night, it was just worth dying for—is that so fucking hard to understand?"

Unlike the first time Mikhail had slapped him, he wasn't expecting this one to crack across his cheek. Damn, the guy moved fucking fast, but not so fast that Shane wasn't able to catch his wrist before his palm cracked across Shane's cheek again.

"What was that for?" he growled, shouldering Mikhail back against the opposite wall.

"Yes, it's hard to understand," Mikhail growled back. "You have this... this magnificent heart, and you just... try to throw it away. How could you do it?"

"I don't know, Mikhail," Shane muttered, not wanting him to feel bad—not for Shane. Not when Shane's life was so good right now. Not when he was so close to happy. "You've been trying throw me away since we met." Shane sighed, and the fight went out of both their bodies. "At least now you know there's worse things than being cheated on, right?"

"You deserve better," Mikhail murmured, and suddenly they weren't confrontational at all. They were in their own world. All of Shane's body heat made a little cocoon in the cold stucco hallway, and Mikhail must have been cold, because he shivered into Shane's shoulders without even trying.

"That's why I'm reaching for you," Shane whispered, nuzzling Mikhail's temple around the tight blonde curls.

"I mean you deserve better than—"

Shane kissed him. It had worked in the past and it didn't fail him now. Mikhail opened his mouth generously, and that was a first, and Shane fell into that sulky mouth like a bird falls into the sky.

His mouth was warm and wet and welcoming, and when Shane pulled back to change the angle of the kiss, Mikhail matched him, tilted his head perfectly, and Shane went in to kiss him again, and again, until Mikhail broke away to pant desperately in the hollow of Shane's shoulder. Shane didn't leave him like that. He moved his lips to Mikhail's ear and around the shell of the outside and to his neck, liking the little whimper and moan that Mikhail made as Shane brushed his teeth down the tender skin of the other man's carotid. Mikhail stood there, quivering, as Shane brushed the button of his shirt open and bent, lips to skin, and planted little kisses along his collarbone, ending at the joining of neck and shoulder and closing his teeth very gently on Mikhail's pulse. The sound of Mikhail's breath catching in his throat was one of the most erotic sounds Shane had ever heard, and when the other man raised his hands to Shane's shoulders, they were shaking.

Abruptly—*very* abruptly—Mikhail's hands went to Shane's belt buckle, and he tried to sink to his knees, right there in the hallway.

Shane pulled him up by the armpits and kissed him again, holding him still with a big hand splayed across Mikhail's chest, near his throat. When the kiss was done, Mikhail tried to pull away again, and Shane whispered, "You're not doing that here."

"Why not?" Mikhail asked stubbornly, resisting. Shane got tired of fighting with him—Shane was bigger and stronger but that didn't mean it wasn't a struggle—and manhandled him until Mikhail was facing the corner of the hallway, one hand up on either wall, panting as Shane locked his hands against Mikhail's chest and plastered his body—raging hard-on and all—against Mikhail's back. Mikhail pushed backward, rubbing his ass against Shane's groin, and Shane groaned into his neck and bit down hard enough to warn.

"Stop that!"

"Why?" Mikhail gritted, doing it again, and Shane, in frustration, pulled Mikhail's shirt up and splayed his hand across the tender skin of a muscle-corded stomach. Mikhail whimpered again—a damned sexy sound—and Shane undid the fly of his black jeans to reach inside. Mikhail's cock was long and not too thick, the smooth skin of it feeling so right in Shane's palm. Mikhail stopped grinding backward and started arching into Shane's hand, and he leaned his head to his arm so he could groan, loudly and passionately, into his own shoulder.

Shane took his other hand—the one not starting a blind stroke over the iron in Mickey's pants—and splayed it against Mikhail's throat, and Mikhail groaned again. He seemed to like that. He liked being manhandled and overpowered. He arched into Shane's hand again, and Shane felt how much.

"This is good," Mikhail panted. "But why am I not sucking you off?"

"Because." Shane released his shaft and moved his hand down under Mikhail's briefs—he just wanted to feel, that was all. He cupped heavy testicles—just for a moment, because they were tender and the position was awkward—but he wanted to feel as much of Mikhail's body as he could

"Ahhh... why be... be...." Shane had started stroking him again, and it sounded as though his brain shorted out for a moment. "Dammit! I'm going to... I'm going to come and...."

Shane kept stroking, burying his nose in Mikhail's neck, stroking the tender flesh of his throat, and memorizing every ridge, every vein of Mikhail's cock as it burgeoned against his hand, growing slick with pre-come. "Then come," Shane whispered in his ear, and Mikhail whimpered again. Bending his head, Mikhail captured Shane's thumb in his mouth and suckled hard as he pushed against the hand on his cock, and Shane heard the groan—felt it, as it started in Mikhail's groin and traveled up through his chest and against Shane's other palm—that signaled a quick and dirty orgasm, right there in the hallway.

Mikhail spurted against his fist, spattering on the front of his jeans and against the inside of his shirt. Shane stroked harder, using the lubrication, grunting in satisfaction as Mikhail spurted again and again and again.

Finally he was done, and Shane buttoned up his fly with shaking fingers. He stood there, arms wrapped around Mikhail's chest, rubbing his cheek against that pale, corkscrew hair. For all its springy curl, it was surprisingly soft.

"That was...." Mikhail was still panting. "That was very nice. But why did you not let me...?"

"Go down on me in public?" Shane asked, panting too. His balls felt positively blue with pressure, and he wasn't sure he could walk. Mikhail leaned his head back against Shane's shoulder, and Shane closed his eyes. It was a trusting gesture—so, so worth it.

"Yes."

"Because that would have been it," Shane murmured, sure of this as he was of nothing else. Mikhail took one of his own hands from the wall and used it to lift Shane's damp hand to his mouth. As they spoke he sucked one finger after another until they were all clean, and Shane wondered if he'd have to turn in his man-card if he came in his pants right then.

"That would have been what?" Mikhail asked, after pulling Shane's index finger out of his mouth and moving to the webbing between it and Shane's thumb.

"That would have been the end. Next week you would have found a reason to blow me off, and you would have stopped returning my calls. I would be in the 'done that' category. You could tell yourself you'd done that, and it wouldn't work, and that was the end."

Mikhail sighed against Shane's palm, which had been thoroughly licked clean, and then he placed a delicate, tender kiss there. His head fell forward, and he turned in Shane's embrace, leaning his cheek against Shane's chest and rubbing against his shirt in the space of his open jacket.

"How do you know that? I hadn't even put it into words."

Shane kissed the top of his head, laughing a little, although it wasn't funny in the least. "Mickey, you've got a sense of honor in you. You figure you put out for me and you've paid me in full for any attention I gave you. It's not that hard to figure out."

Mikhail was quiet. His arms crept around Shane's waist, and he tucked himself into Shane's arms with the rightness of a kitten curling up in a sock basket.

"So how do I pay you back for this?" he asked eventually, and Shane had no choice but to smile. It felt like a victory of sorts.

"Hang with me until you can't stand my company anymore. I'll get on your nerves eventually—you can ditch me then."

The noise Mikhail made sounded like a laugh but wasn't one, either. "You make it very hard for me to ditch you when you make it necessary for me to defend you from yourself."

"Right backatcha, Mickey. Right backatcha."

Chapter 9

I'm begging you to beg me…

"I Want You To Want Me"—Cheap Trick

"ANOTHER Wednesday night, Mikhail?" Anna sat at the desk behind the partition doing accounts as Mikhail took off his jacket and Shane's scarf and prepared for his classes. It was an easy time of year—everything was skill-building. After Christmas would come the hard part, where the students received the new choreography for the big recital in the spring.

"Da," Mikhail muttered, looking down. He was once again wearing his clubbing clothes—this time it was a pair of blue-gray plaid pants and a black shirt. He had nothing else for a date, and, well, it felt nice to dress up for a handsome man.

"He is a nice man?" Anna asked, looking at him gently, and Mikhail sat down on the chair across from the desk and made a business of putting on his soft-soled leather shoes. "Mikhail?" she prompted, and he looked at her and tried not to blush.

"He is the best man. I am waiting for him to see how badly I can fuck up his life so I can wear jeans on Wednesdays again."

"This is what? The sixth time you've worn your good clothes to work? You will need a sweater next week. It is November."

Mikhail blushed. It was true—he had been cold on his walk to work under his thin denim jacket. But he didn't have many good clothes and certainly nothing new. All his money had been going into his fund for his mother's cruise. He shivered—it would be time to count that soon, and he was so very afraid there would not be enough.

"Yes," he muttered. "It is a record. Call the news, they will send a truck, and I will do the camera man behind it, and then the streak will be over."

Anna was looking at him as though he were insane, and he reflected sourly that Shane might actually think that was funny. Except he wouldn't say such a thing to Shane anymore because it was intolerable that Shane would think he had something like that coming.

Mikhail sighed and looked back at Anna. "He is a very nice man— he should be dating a very nice person, and he has chosen me instead. I do not know how to live up to that."

"Be nice back." Anna shrugged. She was older than Shane by ten years or so, but since children didn't seem to be an issue, Mikhail thought this would not bother him. She was plainly pretty, with permed curly hair—most of her beauty came from her enormous vitality and the laugh lines around her eyes. The children adored her, although she took shit from none of them—not even the adorable pudgy little three-year-old redhead who had the rest of the world wrapped around her plump finger. Shane should be dating her, Mikhail thought wretchedly, but then he remembered that she smoked. His mother had quit two years before, when the cancer had been diagnosed, and only recently had the smell gotten out of his clothes.

No. Mikhail could not give Shane away to someone who smoked. There had to be someone else out there who was better for him than Mikhail. Besides—Mikhail was pretty sure she was a lesbian, and that was one too many switches thrown to make that current flow.

"Be nice back," Mikhail repeated now. "Of course. Why didn't I think of that? Now all of my problems are solved."

Anna rolled her eyes at his sarcasm, and shrugged back at him. "The least you could do is see him more than once a week!"

Mikhail looked at her in horror, and she shook her head.

"Look, lubime—it is not my place to butt in, but you've been teaching here for seven years. You walked into my studio and just begged to watch, because American school was so painful and you missed dance so badly. You made no promises, but you showed up, and then you swept the floor, just so you could dance on it. And then I saw you dance, and I made you teach, because something of that *must* be given to the world. You have never been late, you have never been absent, and you have never, not once, given me a reason to distrust you. Why should you be any worse at love than you are at work? If you care about this man even the least little bit as much as you care about dancing, what harm is seeing him more than once a week really going to do?"

I would have to meet his family. I would have to see his home. I would have to picture that maybe, they could belong to me too. I would have to sleep in his bed and imagine myself in his life. I would have to see the hole in my soul that would be left if he finally decides I am too much trouble and finds someone who is not broken.

"The damage cannot be measured in words," he told her, and she laughed as though it were a joke.

Still, when the dance was over and the children had filed out—the last one, Lily, running back to give him a hug that completely enchanted him—he did not try to stop the lifting of his heart when he spotted the familiar black car in the parking lot. Shane was leaning on the trunk, and Mikhail gestured excitedly for him to come into the studio. He did, walking through the door with that shy smile he often had that said he wanted to kiss Mikhail but he wasn't sure if Mikhail would accept it.

Mikhail was so glad to see him that he stood on his toes and touched lips to the big man as soon as the door was shut behind them.

"So, Mickey—what's up?" Shane said, his cheeks coloring in a pleased fashion after the kiss was over. Mikhail took a risk, feathered a touch across Shane's high cheekbone and down his jaw line. He really was a handsome man—his face was more a square than a rectangle, but his eyes had a way of lighting up and tilting at the corners that made him quite beautiful if you knew how to look.

"Take off your shoes," Mikhail ordered. "I want to show you something." He was trying not to be nervous.

He moved to the back of the room where the stereo was and pulled the iPod out of the jack and reprogrammed the mix.

He had a special one just for Shane, put together from listening to his stereo on rides home and trips to the market or to a restaurant to get takeout, and mostly from knowing the man himself. He knew what would

make Shane move. But Shane moved before Mikhail was ready—
suddenly he was at Mikhail's back, holding his hips with familiar hands
and looking over his shoulder.

"Ooh—I like that one," he said as Mikhail scrolled through the list.
Mikhail looked at the Springsteen title and shook his head. "Not for the
first one. We'll do that one second."

There was a bemused pause. "Okay… what are we doing?"

Mikhail turned around, closing his eyes at the warmth radiating from
that broad chest. They had kissed often—long and passionately—and he
knew the feel of Shane's bare chest under his palms. The man had no
vanity; he did not wax or pluck or shave. His chest was unapologetically
hairy, and Mikhail loved it. The hair was not coarse under his palms, and
sometimes, after their dates, he would go to sleep imagining laying his
head on Shane's bare shoulder and simply stroking that heavily muscled,
silk-haired chest like a child would stroke a stuffed animal for comfort.
Even as he closed his eyes and spanned his hands across Shane's pecs
through his shirt, Mikhail knew this was not the time.

He opened his eyes and peered impishly at Shane. "We're dancing."

He was not surprised when his big cop took a horrified step back.
"No," he said miserably. "Mickey—I'm not good at this. I can run pretty
fast, and I'm pretty strong, but I'm not pretty when I move. Not like you—
"

"Bullshit!" Mikhail smiled as he said it to take away the sting. "I see
you—you dance. You pound on the steering wheel, you nod your head in
time. It is all dancing. I'm sure you dance at home, right?"

Shane blushed, and Mikhail had the sudden thought that he'd give
much of his soul to see Shane, alone and unselfconscious, dancing his
heart out in a room full of adoring dogs.

"It's safe there," he said, and for the first time Mikhail saw
uncertainty in those warm brown eyes. He was afraid of being foolish,
even—perhaps especially—in front of Mikhail.

Mikhail was honored beyond words. He tried a smile, but he did not
know what it looked like. "It is safe here," he said softly, and although
Shane smiled gratefully into the pause afterwards, he was still shaking his
head "no" when Mikhail pressed play and turned up the volume.

The opening notes of Cheap Trick thundered through the little dance room. *I waaannnt you to want me. I neeeeeeed you to need me. I'd looooovvvvve you to love me. I'm begging you to beg me....*

Mikhail smiled gamely and held out his hand. The look Shane gave him was miserable and limpid with trust, and Mikhail swore he wouldn't let him down, not in this.

"Here—move your feet like this." He did a simple jazz square, and Shane followed. Mikhail did it again, and Shane followed again. "And now move to the music!"

Shane tried it that way as well. Mikhail turned to face him, executing his move in reverse, and held out his hands. They met palms and laced fingers, swinging their arms at the elbows just like teenagers at a fifties sock-hop, and then Mikhail swung out on one hand and did a spin under Shane's arm, coming back laughing to hold Shane's hips so they could swing their bodies together. Shane's uncertainty was being hammered out of him with each beat—this was Shane's music, his blood absolutely had to thunder in time to it. He had no choice—Mikhail knew this, because it was true of him too. Shane might not think of himself as a dancer, but their hearts both beat to music, of that Mikhail had no doubt.

They swung, they danced, they whirled. Shane stumbled once, but Mikhail caught his hand and kept him upright, and they danced on. Mikhail had set the song on repeat once, so they were breathless and laughing—oh, thank you God, Shane was *laughing*—by the end of it, and Shane leaned forward, hands on thighs and knees bent to catch his breath. He straightened, and Mikhail moved closer, treasuring that wide smile because *he* had put it there. Of the horrible things he knew he was capable of, in this moment *he* had made Shane laugh—and for a moment they simply laughed into each other's eyes.

In that moment, the music changed. The yearning moan of Springsteen's "Worlds Apart" filled the studio, and Mikhail smiled a little, putting his hands on Shane's hips and pulling them flush together.

"Yes—see. We can dance to this too."

They did. Following Mikhail's lead, Shane swiveled his hips sensuously, bending his knees so that their groins met. It was torturous and almost too personal to do with the big picture window showing the inside of the studio. Mikhail turned so his back was at Shane's chest, and his bottom nestled against the cradle of the big man's hips. He placed his hands backward on Shane's thighs, and Shane's hands went over his arms at his waist. Together, they danced in the most elemental way, simply moving to the music as Bruce Springsteen and his lady love wailed about building a bridge of blood to let love give what it gives.

Mikhail caught sight of them—how could he not?—on the mirrored wall to their side. He looked small in Shane's embrace—and sheltered. Protected. There was very little that could come through that wall of muscle and will. Mikhail shivered in the middle of that power. He had spent life on the streets—rapes, beatings at the hands of tricks or other junkies, yes. He'd done that, and as Shane said, he did not need to do it again. But here in this shelter, not even those memories could hurt him. He had to look away, afraid of what could happen to him if he gave in to the promise of that safety.

Shane did not see—he was looking down on Mikhail with such a helpless mixture of yearning and affection that it made Mikhail's chest ache.

The song came to a wistful close, and Mikhail turned his head into Shane's nuzzle at his temple and then turned his body into a yearning, voracious kiss.

Shane's hands came up to frame his face and throat, and Mikhail allowed himself, for that moment, to be sheltered. His self-sufficiency melted, and he kissed back, starving and passionate and tender all at once. His hands trembled as he put them on Shane's shoulders, and Shane pulled him into his heat and his sweat and the tenderness that had been there for the taking all along.

Mikhail found he was being walked backward, maneuvered, and he allowed it, until he found himself in the partitioned office, able to see over the top edges into the dark sky beyond the window but hidden from prying eyes. Shane pulled away long enough to say, "S'okay if we're in here?" and Mikhail nodded dumbly. He probably would have agreed to Shane bending him over the ballet barre and fucking him in front of the mirror, but he needn't have worried. Shane turned and drew the little curtain that Anna put up for when she was really busy and pushed Mikhail back to the overstuffed chair she kept in the back of the cubicle for conferences. He kissed Mikhail again, and when he pulled Mikhail's tongue into his mouth and suckled, Mikhail's knees literally buckled and he fell into the chair bonelessly.

Shane stood there for a minute, grinning, but Mikhail started pulling at his belt buckle and the grin went away. "No," he murmured, and then he sank to his knees in front of the chair and pulled Mikhail down for another kiss.

This time, Shane's hands roamed. They spanned Mikhail's chest, smoothing along the definition of his muscles, kneading at his shoulders, and then rubbing his palms on tiny, pebbled nipples until Mikhail tilted his head back and groaned.

That grin popped out, and Shane unbuttoned his shirt carefully. "You sure do like nice clothes," he murmured. "I'll try not to wreck them."

Mikhail found he couldn't speak. He was busy watching the fine tremble in Shane's hands, the way he was a little desperate as he pushed up Mikhail's T-shirt, and the reverence with which he bent his head and kissed the exact spot where pectoral muscles met sternum. Mikhail sucked in a breath, sure all his nerve endings had just exploded, and Shane worked his way to one of his tender flat nipples. When he sucked that into his mouth and worried the end gently with his teeth, Mikhail found his hands were knotted in Shane's hair, begging him for more, begging him to move, just begging him in general. Shane looked up, gave the nipple a playful lick, and moved from the side to between Mikhail's knees so he could suckle and tease the other side.

"You bastard," Mikhail breathed, arching up. Shane was pretty flat against him, so his groin was grinding up against Shane's stomach, and Shane reached down and pushed against it, squeezing until Mikhail groaned some more.

When Shane started fumbling with his fly, Mikhail thought he should protest.

He gave blowjobs. He did. That was his job, his duty. That was his payment in full. He was good at them—he could make a man come before he realized it was a boy with a mouth around his cock and not a woman.

He did not receive blowjobs. He tried and failed to remember the last time someone had actually made love to him, had run lips over his chest and tickled his abdomen with a stubbled chin, and then Shane pushed against his cock again and he quit thinking. He could only feel, and his overwhelming emotion was gratitude. Oh... oh... oh God... how had he lived his whole life and not been touched like this?

Shane moved down his stomach with kisses, and Mikhail keened in the back of his throat. His hands were in that thick brown hair again, and he massaged Shane's scalp some more because it was all he could do. Shane kissed under the snap to his pants, and he whimpered, and then down the torturous line of his zipper as it was pulled open. He grabbed the waist of the pants in both hands and started to drag them down, and Mikhail just stared at him.

"C'mon, Mickey," Shane said, peering up at him with sloe eyes and impatience. "Help!"

Mikhail arched his hips and let Shane pull his pants down to his ankles and slouched, half naked and vulnerable, on his boss's couch, and watched as Shane put his mouth on his cock for the first time.

Mikhail almost came from the sight of it.

Shane pursed his lips and ran them down the length from crown to ball sac, and then he extended his tongue a little and went back up. Mikhail whimpered as he pulled down the foreskin and played with that sensitive place, the little harp string where the foreskin stretched taut on the underside, and then Shane grasped his shaft and pumped at the same time he engulfed the crown in his mouth.

Mikhail threw his head back and closed his eyes so hard he saw stars. Oh... oh God... he was going to come immediately, and he couldn't... he couldn't... not when it had just started. Oh God, not so soon. He grabbed a wad of tissue from Anna's desk and shoved it into Shane's hand as it rested on the arm of the chair.

"Don't swallow," he commanded, and Shane nodded wordlessly. Then Shane transferred the tissue to his other hand and laced his fingers with Mikhail's, and Mikhail rubbed Shane's cheek with the hand he had free.

Their eyes connected, and Mikhail's grew hot and bright. *He wants to do this. He likes my body. He wants to touch me.* It should not have been a revelation—Mikhail had a nice body, he knew it. Dancing kept him muscular and made him a good fuck. But being a good fuck and having someone look at you with that sort of hunger, touch you with hands that trembled from wanting... God... oh God....

Still keeping eye contact, Shane lowered his head and engulfed Mikhail's cock, pressing on the base with his lips and swallowing the crown in the back of his throat, and Mikhail could no longer watch him, no longer see himself being touched with reverence, no longer see someone's mouth moving on him as though he were precious....

He leaned his head back against the couch and watched the dark slice of sky above the partition and simply felt, and even then it was not sex as he remembered it. Even then he felt Shane's hand sliding up and down his thigh, cupping his testicles, rubbing his base with his thumb. Shane's hair was thick and silky under his fingers, and Shane's music was throbbing behind them as "Worlds Apart" gave way to "The Fuse" and that plaintive, thundering, yearning beat made him ache.

Oh God... you damned stupid man, what have you done to me, that coming in a man's mouth hurts worse than church?

Not, he thought with a gasp and a swallow as Shane's teeth deliberately and tenderly scraped the ridge of his crown, that he had much experience with either of them.

He started to speak softly in Russian, barely aware he was doing it, and a sudden chill on his body made him look down again.

"Look at me," Shane murmured, "look at me."

Oh, God... "The things you ask," he murmured brokenly, but he looked, and Shane took him into his mouth again, and those clever, questing fingers skated the crease of his thigh, slipped between his buttocks, teased his tender opening, and gently—using Shane's spit for lubrication—one of them entered, and Mikhail's world exploded.

He managed to choke out a warning, and Shane pulled away in time and caught his spend in the tissues, pumping him gently until he was all but limp in the wide-palmed, strong hand that stroked him.

Gentle hands wiped him off, pulled up his briefs and his tight plaid pants and fastened them, pulling down his shirt and making him presentable. At the last possible moment, Mikhail looked up from those hands and into Shane's broad, shining face. He reached out a hand and stroked that stubbled cheek, his thumb rubbing along a high cheekbone.

"You look very pleased with yourself," he said after a moment when only the music spoke between them.

"You enjoyed yourself," Shane said smugly, and Mikhail had to smile—he had no choice. The big man's arrogance was rarely seen—and lovely.

"I did." Mikhail couldn't seem to make himself move. "I would like a chance to see you do the same."

"Well, Mickey, that depends on you," Shane said softly. "I'm a big fan of sleepovers."

Mikhail nodded and patted Shane's neck absently. "I would like to…. It is… it is difficult right now, you understand?"

His mother. She had one more round of chemotherapy that the doctor told him quite frankly they would skip if it would not keep her alive and well enough to go on the promised vacation. He did not like to leave her alone, or it was possible he would have given in to Shane's demand of more than a one-night stand weeks ago.

"I definitely understand. I'm not going anywhere." He got easily to his feet for such a big man and held out his hand. Mikhail took it and was hauled into a warm, rough embrace that engulfed his slender body, protecting him once again from anything that could hurt. As Mikhail burrowed into Shane's heat and his broad muscles, he realized that the protection of those arms and that embrace included protection from the terrible emotions that seemed to be shaking him to his bones in the wake of what he could only think of as making love.

It was possibly the first time he could ever apply the term.

They stood there for some time, and it wasn't until Shane rubbed up and down his arms that he realized he was shivering.

"Why the tissues?" Shane asked eventually, and Mikhail couldn't look at him as he replied.

"My last test was in August," he muttered. "I am very careful with condoms, but I will not risk it with you until I am tested again."

Shane dropped a kiss on the top of his head. "That was really thoughtful of you, Mickey."

Mikhail couldn't hear himself praised like that. "It was nothing," he dismissed. "Ninety percent of Russian whores are sick with HIV—if I had not been careful, I would not have lived through life on the streets."

There was a silence, and the song on the iPod changed. Stevie Nicks was singing about being on the edge of seventeen, and Mikhail wondered when he had ever felt as young as he did in this moment. God… let a man make love to you and then remind him you were a whore. What was he thinking? No wonder he had lived his life doing tricks and one-night stands. Dating was terrifying.

"That must have been hard," Shane said, his hands never stopping that calming motion on his arms. "How'd that go over when you were on the job?"

"Sometimes good," Mikhail said softly, knowing Shane wouldn't leave it like that but hoping anyway.

"And sometimes?"

Mikhail shrugged. "I ended up in the hospital once." He opened his mouth and tongued two of his back teeth—they were replaced with stainless-steel crowns. "Knocked out two teeth. When I came home from the hospital, I practically ran my mother over to get back on the street." He'd shoved her into a wall, actually, and the shame of it still stung.

"Why so eager?" There was not the faintest bit of judgment in Shane's voice, and Mikhail should know. He was listening hard for it and missed it when it was not there.

"She used all my drug money to pay the hospital bill." Mikhail laughed without humor. "She also used all the rent money—I had two days to make the rent. She didn't want me to go—I think at that point *she* would have gone out in my place, but…." He found he couldn't look at Shane for this part.

Shane dropped another kiss on the top of his head and simply listened, and that is what allowed him to continue.

"I had someone waiting for me. We worked together, you see—he taught me how to shoot up and how to have sex and how to survive. He had the wallet of the fucker who beat me. We would score, and I could give Mutti the rent—it was a good plan."

And again, that curious, waiting silence. Mikhail gave in completely—he leaned his cheek against Shane's chest and let his words take them where they would.

"What happened to the plan, Mickey?"

"Olek wasn't there," Mikhail said simply. "I was still buzzing from the painkillers in the hospital—I did not need to fix. I left the drugs where we kept our stash and left a note that said I would be back, and I went home. But…." Oh God. "I had shoved my mother into a wall, you see.

And yelled at her for trying to care for me. She's a strong woman, my mother. When I got home, she had two of our neighbors hiding behind the door—they tied me to the bed for two days, so I could feel—*really feel*—what the drugs were doing to me."

"Oh my God!" Shane sounded surprised—shocked, surprised, and a little bit pleased.

Mikhail was startled enough to look up and into his eyes, and all he saw was interest in his life and compassion and kindness. Shane blushed at his scrutiny and mumbled, "You weren't shitting about her being a strong woman, Mickey—that's a ballsy thing to do, you know?"

Mikhail smiled into his eyes a little. "Yes. Cowardice has never been a failing of Ylena's. And she knew—she knew why I'd become addicted, and she knew I was only trying to pay my way after the dance money was gone. She was like you—she did not judge. But she could not let me do what I was doing, either. After two days, when I was sweating and screaming and begging, she gave me a small dose, just enough to take the edge off, and asked me to look at myself." He blushed now furiously. He could remember the stink of his sweat, the smell of his vomit. He'd shit himself during the worst of that, and he could remember that too.

"It was not pretty," he muttered weakly, avoiding Shane's eyes.

Shane took his chin in firm fingers. "I've seen withdrawals, Mickey. They're horrible. I understand, okay?"

"Yes, but I am vain enough that I would like you not to think of me that way, yes?" he snapped, tired of being naked.

"No question," Shane reassured him, and Mikhail went on.

"So Mutti, she talks to me, while I am there in my filth, and she asks me if this is how I want to live and how soon I want to die, and the angels must have had her voice that day because I actually listened. She had been squirreling away money—and damn, she was smart because she didn't tell me where it was—but we had passports and visas and plane tickets, and she'd had a cousin in Brighton who made the arrangements for rehab. All we had to do was get me to survive for two weeks."

Shane's arms shivered around him, and Mikhail apologized. "I'm sorry—this is not a pretty story. I will... we can leave now." And he tried to draw away, tried to pretend this moment wasn't extraordinary. Shane wouldn't let him.

"Finish the story, Mikhail. You're letting me hold you—it's all good."

Mikhail blinked hard. "Of course it's all good. I'm a junkie-whore—what a catch I am!"

"Shut up." It was the first time he'd ever heard Shane sound truly irritated at him. Suddenly Mikhail was being maneuvered again, and Shane flopped, not so bonelessly, onto the big chair with Mikhail splayed against him. They were eye to eye, Mikhail sprawled on his chest, feeling firsthand the depth and power of that mighty body.

Mikhail carefully traced Shane's lean mouth under his fingertips. "You are very handsome," he murmured. "You could have anyone—literally anyone. Why me?"

Shane's smile twisted a little. "You're talking like kittens and yarn again, Mickey—find the end of the yarn and knit me a story. How did your buddy take the news you were leaving?"

An answer without an answer—a code of sorts. He felt more at home in the working of Shane's language than he did in his mother tongue or his adopted language. It gave him the strength to finish.

"He took it very well," Mikhail said, trying for nonchalance. "He had no choice—he was dead."

Shane grunted as though he'd expected this and had just been poised to take the hit. "How'd it happen?"

Mikhail shrugged. He liked this color Shane was wearing—it was a deep red. He'd been looking at it enough, he should know the thread count by now. "I broke my promise to come back; he broke his promise to not shoot all the drugs. He'd been dead for three days—I don't know. Maybe he thought I was not coming back. Maybe he got bored. All I know was that he was dead with a needle in his arm, and Mutti was pulling me out of our little shack in the back of a tenement, and in the middle of that she managed to find the last envelopes of heroin to keep me from losing my mind in the next two weeks. And… and here I am. I am alive. I am happy. And Mutti…."

What was wrong with the world that Mikhail, for all his self-sufficiency, could not finish that sentence? What he said next surprised him as much as anything that night.

"Oh God, Shane. What if I don't have enough money?" This fear had been riding him since June, when the doctors determined that the cancer was terminal. "She found out she was dying, and she said 'Oh Christ, boy. Do I really have to die in winter?' And I... I would do anything, you understand? I said, 'Stop complaining, old woman. If you promise to live through another Christmas, I'll take you someplace warm, just to stop your bitching.'"

Shane's chest shook under him, and Mikhail met his eyes and was reassured by the warmth there. "It was a good promise," Shane told him simply. "I have faith you can keep it."

Mikhail sighed and stood up, tired, suddenly, of baring his soul. "It is more than I have, *lubime*."

Shane took his offered hand and walked out of the cubicle to find his shoes. He put them on while standing, seemingly as eager as Mikhail to get out of the dance studio for the rest of the night.

They walked into the darkness, the last of the fluorescent lighting dying as the door closed behind them, and Shane threw a possessive arm around Mikhail's shoulders. Mikhail thought longingly that he could get used to that sort of attention, especially when they stopped at Shane's car and Shane carefully arranged the scarf so that it was tucked under Mikhail's chin and knotted for warmth. He didn't say a word about the fact that it was his own scarf, and yet he must have noticed.

But that comfort didn't stop Mikhail from lying at Shane's next carefully worded question.

"Mickey?"

"Da?"

"What does 'loobeemee' mean?"

Mikhail could actually taste the fog he sucked into his lungs in a terrible gasp.

"Where did you hear that?" he asked, putting his hands on Shane's biceps to steady himself. He felt his own pulse speed up under the skin of his palms.

"From you—twice, actually." Shane was keeping his voice casual, but the man was not a fool. He was listening very carefully for this answer.

"Twice?" Oh God. His voice was shaking again. Damn this man. Damn this man and damn his kindness and damn his blowjobs and damn the fact that he wasn't stupid and knew an endearment when he heard one, whether or not Mikhail was ready for him to hear it.

"Yes, twice. Once when you were…." The air around Mikhail grew suddenly warmer, and he had to smile. Shane really was innocent. "You know… uhm, excited. And once just a minute ago, when we were on our way out. So, uhm, what does it mean?"

Mikhail swallowed hard and lied. "My friend," he said. "It means 'my friend'."

"Mm-hmm. I'll remember that." The voice was carefully neutral, and Mikhail found himself studying that button on Shane's shirt again. Shane bent and brushed a kiss over his lips then, and Mikhail responded with more force than he thought he had in him. When they were done tasting and tangling and were breathing fiercely into the foggy night again, Shane drew back and opened Mikhail's door, and then got in himself to start the car.

Mikhail wondered if there was a penalty of sorts for lover's lies— especially of the variety he'd just told. Should a star fall from heaven for such a thing? If it did, Mikhail hoped rather fervently that it would crash on his head and leave Shane the hell alone. The poor man loved him— didn't he have enough problems as it was?

"So, uhm, Mickey?" Shane said as they were driving to the apartment. "How is it you don't know how much money you have? Doesn't the bank give you a statement?"

Mikhail blushed in the darkness of the car. "I'm a Russian peasant, cop. Do you really think I keep my money in a bank?"

Puzzled silence. "So where do you keep it?"

And this truth was easy to tell. "Where all Russian peasants keep their money. In their sock drawers."

Shane was still laughing heartily when they pulled into the complex and parked.

Chapter *10*

...let love give what it gives...

"Worlds Apart"—Bruce Springsteen

SHANE had always sucked at lying—he really hoped he could manage it this time. His hand shook a little as he raised it to Mikhail's apartment door to knock, and he waited patiently for it to open. He knew Ylena would be home—he had asked her during the last date night—and he also knew she was moving slowly these days.

He looked around as he waited, the grayness of the foggy day making the light tan walls of the apartment building look a little brighter than they probably did in the sun. It wasn't a bad place, he thought critically—but it didn't have six acres or a passel of dogs, either. He'd been returning home after date night with a deeper and deeper conviction that going home alone was wrong.

He should be going home with Mikhail. It was just as right as anything he'd ever known. He'd lived with girlfriends before, and that had been nice, until his weirdness got to them or their cheating or bitching got to him—he knew about sharing space with people. He knew when it would last for a week and would barely entail an extra toothbrush, and he knew when it would suck a year and a half out of his life that he could never get back. (Okay, that had happened once—she had been the girl who had cheated on him from the get-go. His only excuse had been that he had been barely out of the academy and she'd been able to suck a golf ball through a garden hose. He just hadn't realized how much she'd practiced when he was out of the house.) Brandon had rarely come to his apartment, but Shane had spent a lot of time at Brandon's. Brandon's had been nicer, the bed and the television had been bigger, and Brandon had better beer.

Brandon had also not had anything special or private in his home, like shelves upon shelves of books or concert posters painfully collected from the third grade or, now, fuzzy, psychotic quadrupeds that thought they were human and counted as family.

The doorknob turned, interrupting his thought, and Ylena looked out. She smiled, apparently pleased to see him, and he relaxed. He could do this. It was important.

"Hiya, Ylena—I'm sorry to bother you in the daytime...."

"Not at all, Shane." She backed up and let him into the apartment. The outside might have looked a little brighter in the fog, but the inside looked a little more drab in the light coming in through the sliding glass door at the balcony. There were framed prints on the walls—poor quality but lovingly chosen—and crocheted afghans on the couch and the chairs. But the carpeting was old, and the paint was peeling in the creases, as was the linoleum. The neighborhood was not too bad, but the complex had seen better days.

Still, it was a damned sight better than the high-class pit Shane had left in L.A.

"I'm sorry you are missing Mikhail—he is at work, you know."

"Yeah—I brought him lunch." It was true—and it was all part of his carefully constructed plan. Mikhail had been happy to see him—and a little embarrassed—and had seemed genuinely sorry that he had a room full of preschoolers and was unable to stop and eat with him. "And since I was in the neighborhood, I brought you some too!"

She smiled a little, but he could tell that no food was good food at this point in her illness. Still, she seemed to appreciate the effort. "Well, by all means, I shall eat it," she said graciously. "Would you like to keep me company?"

It was his pleasure. He dished up the Panda Express and brought a bowl to her usual place on the couch. She had pressed pause on the television and he could see that she had been watching a movie on cable. He had to smile.

"One of my favorites," he said. *The Knight's Tale*—it really was.

"I love this movie," she told him, smiling. "You and my son, you have good taste in movies. Is it wrong to spend so much time living in other worlds?"

Shane shook his head. "Nah—I always figured it just made it easier to determine what kind of person you'll be in this one, you know?"

Ylena swallowed a small bite and smiled at him warmly. "Da—I think it is this way with Mikhail too. It is hard to be the person in your dreams in real life, but movies—they give a primer. What is good, what is honorable. I think you and my son take these lessons to heart."

Shane blushed. "That's a nice way to look at it." *Loser. Nerd. Psychopath.* There were definitely worse ways to look at it, and that was the truth. They watched the movie for a while—it was more than halfway over—and when AC/DC belted out the closing credits, Shane attempted his biggest lie to date.

"Hey, Ylena, since I'm here, I was wondering if I could check Mikhail's room for something. My friend's sister knitted me a brown scarf that I lent him—I'd let him keep it, but she's been asking to see it on me, and I sort of need to get it back."

Ylena arched a bald eyebrow at him that let him know he wasn't being that smooth, but he'd been visiting on Wednesday nights for nearly two months now. He had even come the Wednesday night before Thanksgiving, with a little offering of turkey and mashed potatoes (which Benny had walked him through and which had turned out a damned sight better than the chicken casserole). The Bayuls had been eating dinner with Ylena's church the next day, or the compulsion to shove Mikhail in the car and make him eat dinner at Deacon and Crick's would have been overwhelming.

"I think he may have worn it today, but you are welcome to check his room," she said with a smile. "We trust you here, Shane."

Shane smiled back, warmed and relieved. They trusted him. Damn, that felt good. He stood and took the plates to the sink to wash them off and then walked back into the little hallway to Mikhail's room.

It was orderly but not neat. There were piles of clothes in the corner, waiting for the Laundromat, and folded clothes on the bed. The bed itself had a comforter—blue and green plaid—pulled up over piled pillows, but nothing was pleated or smoothed down. Shane liked it. An orderly, self-sufficient mind, but no obsessing over tiny things like pillow creases or folds in comforters.

Where do you keep your money?

Where all Russian peasants keep their money. In my sock drawer.

He was praying that Mickey hadn't been kidding or lying about that.

He was standing in front of the veneered dresser and about to pull out the top drawer, when he noticed the box. It was a large cedar box—the kind that women kept jewelry in—and the kind that someone might keep money in if they didn't trust banks, so he decided to check it first.

He spotted the two-inch tag of yarn first—one of Benny's unwoven ends—carefully clipped and placed in one of the little cubicles in the top of the box. And then he saw everything: the receipt he'd written his number on, the little vial—now half-full—of scented oil. There was a free bookmark from the first time they'd visited the bookstore and a cheap plastic toy leftover from when Shane had taken Benny and Parry Angel to dance lessons once for Deacon. It had been floating around the bottom of the car, and he'd wondered where it had gone. Now he knew.

In the bottom of the box—the bigger compartment—there were pictures. A heartbreakingly young Ylena, holding a brand new infant. A three-year-old boy with a thousand-yard stare, wearing dance shoes. A flyer from a performance, and another, and another. A pair of ballet slippers so small even Parry Angel couldn't have fit in them. Two tickets to a concert, probably, but written in Cyrillic so Shane couldn't tell who was playing.

He closed the top of the box gently, with a shaking hand. A treasure box. Carefully hoarded mementos of a man that claimed not to keep such things. And the smallest moments spent with Shane had a place of honor.

Shane pulled in a shaking breath and firmed up his spine with resolve, then opened up the top drawer of the dresser.

"Have you found it yet?" Ylena called from the front room.

"No—I'm looking in his dresser if that's okay." There was a silence, and then she must have figured he wouldn't have told her this if he had meant to steal something.

"Yes, this is fine." And he continued on. Of course, he'd seen the scarf hanging on the coat peg at the dance studio or this whole thing would be for nothing.

And there it was. Pay dirt. A neat stack of bills, completely out of order, rolled tightly in the corner of the drawer. Excellent. Shit. They *were* out of order. Shit shit shit shit....

Shane reached into his pocket and pulled out a roll of fives, tens, and twenties almost as big as the one in the drawer. With clumsy fingers, he took the bills and shuffled them into Mikhail's roll, trying to make them not stand out too much. He'd washed and dried them six times with brand new jeans and an old pair of tennis shoes—and his washer and dryer had the repair bill to prove it—but they were still a little crisp. He wasn't sure they'd fool Mickey, but at this point he had no choice. The deadline for getting the money in was on Friday, and the ship left on Monday. Mikhail had told him he'd be counting the money tomorrow.

That way, if I do not have enough money, I can panic on you when you get here. How is that for needy—am I a satisfactory fuck buddy now? It had been a mean-spirited thing for the other man to say, and if Shane hadn't been able to read the absolute terror in his voice, he would have been hurt beyond words. But he *had* heard the terror, and he *had* been there for the nakedness of Mikhail's past. Instead of getting angry, he had simply reached a hand across the car and cupped Mikhail's cheek until the tension had left the other man and the shame washed over him. *You should probably at least get some sex out of a person before he says something that shitty to you, shouldn't you?*

I wouldn't complain. Shane's answer had been mild, but the truth was, sex had been the last thing on his mind. He'd been coming up with this crackbrained scheme, and now it might be the undoing of everything. He listened with half an ear for Ylena to decide he was too weird to be trusted in her son's room, and with the rest of his attention he kept shuffling bills into the stack, trying to still the beating of his heart with some comfort. He was sort of committed to this, and what was Mickey going to do? Accuse him of stuffing money in his sock drawer? What kind of psychopathic loser did something like that?

With a gasp he slipped the rubber-band back around the roll and stuffed it back in the drawer. His hands were sweating, and he'd never felt so guilty in his life, but he managed a bit of theater and started talking to Ylena on his way out the door.

"I can't find it in there," he said with a good-natured sigh.

"He might be wearing it," she told him. She hadn't moved from the couch in the hundred or so years he'd been rifling Mikhail's drawer, and Shane could only be grateful. "He will be very sorry to see it go."

Perfect. Excellent. It was like she had read his mind for his next line.

"You know, in that case, don't tell him I was looking for it. Benny will understand—in fact, I think she'll be thrilled that someone liked her work so much. It'll give her an excuse to knit another one for me, right?"

Ylena looked at him levelly, as though she knew exactly what he'd been doing, and nodded with complete serenity. "Yes. I think that would probably be best." She made as though to rise from the couch to see him off, and Shane put her off with a wave of the hand, moving to the couch to kiss her cheek. The first time she had lifted her cheek in farewell, he had been surprised, but now he wouldn't think of leaving without bidding Mikhail's mother goodbye like she was his own.

"You take care of yourself, Ylena—Mikhail's counting on that cruise, you know." She stopped him from moving away by taking his hands and peering up into his face from her place on the couch.

"I am living for him, just so he can give me that. It will make my going so much easier."

Shane nodded, his throat going dry. She had never spoken of dying to him, but apparently neither of them were good at lying. "Your son is going to miss you," he said roughly, and she nodded.

"I kept hoping, you know, that he would find a girl, because girls will take care of boys like men will not, you know?"

Shane blushed. "Yeah. Girls can cook."

And of all things, *that* made her smile, and the smile made him realize how young she had been in the picture, holding Mikhail as an infant—how young she truly was now.

"I do not mind if you cook, Officer Perkins. What I care about is that you seem to see into the heart of my son and find it good. It will, perhaps, be easier to go, knowing that someone like you will be looking out for him."

And now that blush was everywhere. Oh God—he had not been a part of the game Ylena and Mikhail had played, the careful dance between telling her the truth and dashing her hopes that her son would find a home the way she dreamed.

"Ylena, what does 'loobeeamee' mean?" he asked, feeling awkward. But she answered without hesitation.

"It means 'beloved'."

Shane nodded. He'd known Mickey had lied, but he hadn't known the full extent of it. "So, it doesn't mean 'buddy' or 'my friend'?" Just to make sure.

Ylena shook her head, smiling slightly. "No—it means 'love', like, say, a mother to a child, or, perhaps, one lover to another. Where did you hear this word?"

"Mikhail used it."

Her smile widened then, almost shyly. "And he told you it meant 'my friend'?"

"Yeah—I didn't buy it at the time."

"You should not have. My son lied. Why do you think he would do that?" The smile tilted up at the corners, and, like her son, Shane mourned her lost beauty. Oh, this woman would have been a stunner.

"I think he knew it was important," Shane said softly. "He was a little afraid of how much."

"I think you are right, *lubime*," she told him, and her smile faded but not in a bad way. "I think you just keep reminding him how important you are, and one day he might not lie about it. And I will be glad when that day comes—it means that my work is done, and someone else will care for him. I can sleep with no bad dreams."

"No bad dreams, Ylena," Shane murmured and bent down to kiss her cheek again. "I'll see you tomorrow night."

"I look forward to it." She said it with enthusiasm, but before Shane was out the door, she had put her head on the arm of the couch to rest.

SHANE was patrolling in the car the next day when he got the phone call. He hit the button on his earpiece to hear Mikhail's rapid-fire voice, pattering so quickly he might as well have been speaking in Russian.

He pulled off into the liquor store parking lot so he could savor the conversation.

"Mickey, slow down—you're not making any sense!" It was the first time Mikhail had called him since that one, miraculous call the night after they'd met.

"Money, Shane! We have money! I counted, and we have enough for the cruise, and for the better cabin. There is even enough for a new dress for Mutti...." There was a deep breath as he tried to get hold of himself. "We can do it, Shane. We leave next Monday. We'll be back the sixth of January. We're going!"

Shane grinned. "That's awesome, Mickey. Really terrific. I'll miss you at Christmas—I sort of wanted you to meet the family, but that's okay. We can do that when you get back."

There was a sudden silence, as though it had just occurred to him that they would not be together over the holidays. "I... I will miss you too," Mikhail said, and Shane was glad he had pulled over because he could picture that look of sudden revelation the man got when something he'd never thought of just walked up and bit him on the ass. He'd seen it often—when Shane had shown up with food for lunch, the first time he'd arrived in time for their date, when he'd kissed Ylena's cheek the first time. More recently he'd seen it when Mikhail's head had been thrown back and his eyes closed while Shane's mouth was on his cock.

He'd made Mikhail look at him because that expression alone had almost made him come.

"You'll have to take pictures for me," Shane said, and then he heard another stunned silence.

"I did not even think about that. Shit. I shall have to buy a camera...."

"No worries—you can buy those disposable ones, get them processed at the drugstore."

A happy laugh. "Oh God, yes. There. See? You are indispensable. You... you will be there to see us off? I... my mother's church people could give us a ride into San Francisco if you cannot, but I... if you can get the time off, I would...."

Shane wasn't sure what he looked like with that goofy-assed grin on his face at the moment, but the world would have to live with his weirdness. He wouldn't be anyone else in the world. "I'd love to see you off, Mickey—maybe I should borrow another car, though. The GTO isn't as comfy as it might be, and it's a long trip for your mom."

A silence, and it sounded like Mikhail swallowed—hard—into it. "You are a really good man, do you know that? Mutti—she has talked about you for weeks. After you brought her lunch yesterday, she thinks you hang the moon."

"Yeah, just don't tell her about my designs on her son's body—that sort of brings a mother's esteem down a few notches."

Another silence. Then, shyly, "Perhaps I should keep my designs on your body to myself then?"

Shane blushed. "I was hoping you had some of those," he muttered. He'd wanted Mikhail to know how good he could make it in spite of how much like a pinup he was *not.* "Maybe you could, you know, share them with me when you get back, right?"

"I'm looking forward to it," Mikhail said with absolute sincerity.

Shane opened his mouth to say something when his radio crackled. "Shit, Mickey, wait a minute." He hit mute on his phone and listened. Levee Oaks and L street. Shit. Shit shit shit shit shit. Domestic dispute— and who knew which one was stoned on what. Didn't matter—both the Rivas could be fucking insane.

He picked up the radio. "Officer Perkins—responding. Be at the scene in less than five." He started the car and hit the talk button on his phone again. "Mickey, I've gotta go—I'll see you later tonight, okay?"

"Absolutely," Mikhail said. "Be safe."

"Count on it." Shane rang off and his radio buzzed again. "Perkins."

"Perkins, this is Calvin. Dude, that nine-one-one call was pretty intense. Do me a favor, man, and wait for me, would ya?"

"How far out are you?" Shane asked. The only problem with waiting for backup was that Donny and Rachel Rivas had three kids. If the kids were in foster care, fine—let them get some of their meth out on each other while he waited for backup. If one of the kids was involved, well, that was a whole other story.

"I'm out on Elkhorn, just out of the station."

"Well, I'm here. I'll just nose around a little—no door knocking 'til you get here, I promise." Shane signed off and parked the squad car in front of the overgrown lawn. There hadn't been enough rain to green up the valley this winter, and the long, mostly brown weeds seemed to highlight the disrepair the rest of the Rivas house stood in.

Shane got out of the car, slammed the door, and heard a child screaming around the back of the house. Well, shit.

He later gave himself credit. He didn't just go running into that house, half-cocked and ready to shoot. He crept up to the side of the house and looked around the corner and saw one of those things that wake cops up in the middle of the night.

There was Donny Rivas, with his oldest daughter—about seven years old—caught up under the armpits with one arm, a hunting knife in the other hand. He was using the hunting knife to carve slow patterns into the flesh of her upper thigh.

"Now where's the stash, you little shit? It was in the fuckin' house, and now it's fuckin' gone—you're always creeping around—where'd ya fuckin' put it!"

Shane's heart dropped. Well, shit, this was really not a waiting-for-backup situation. It violated every law in the be-a-cop handbook, but he was going to have to step up and do something.

"I didn't I didn't I didn't!" The little girl's wail was terrified, and what she said next was worse. "The baby ate it, I couldn't do nothing, and now she's sick!"

Oh fuck. Oh fuck oh fuck oh fuck. Shane pulled out the radio at his belt, and buzzed Calvin. "Calvin, send an ambulance—there's an overdosing infant on the site."

"Fuck—where are you?"

"Side of the... *fuck!*"

Rachel Rivas was running at him with a kitchen knife, shrieking. He dropped the radio and ducked the clumsy swing, getting a good view of her stringy brown hair and her rotting teeth as she launched herself at him. She swung again, and the knife bounced off the Kevlar he was wearing under his uniform. He took a step back and reached for his extendable billie club at his waist, only to have his elbow connect with a solid body.

Donny Rivas grunted and fell back just as Shane got the club out and knocked the knife out of Rachel's hand. She screamed and fell backward, gibbering, and Shane tried to turn so that his back was toward the house, only to find Donny had him securely around the shoulders with one arm while the other was plunging the knife downward.

The knife found the gap between the Kevlar and Shane's rib cage and ripped through his flesh and grated on his bone. Shane howled and threw his big body back against the house, and he heard Donny groan as his stringy junkie's body was squashed up against the wall. The hand holding the knife was driven further down before Shane threw himself back again and Donny was forced to let go. Shane managed two steps out, away from the both of them as they were panting and whining, their pain magnified by their withdrawal symptoms, and he pulled his gun from his holster and held it out with shaking hands.

"You two," he barked, "calm the fuck down. I'm a fucking cop, you're both under arrest, and there's an ambulance coming for your kid in case you forgot to give a fuck." He had to yell that last part over the sound of the approaching sirens, and he managed to hold the gun up while his blood ran down his side and his vision blackened, until he heard Calvin's voice from the front yard.

"Perkins! Perkins! Where the fuck are you, man?"

"I'm right here!" he called. Breathing was suddenly difficult, and he remembered the feeling of a punctured lung from the last time he'd ended up in the hospital. He heard the sound of Calvin approaching and tried really hard to hold it together.

"Calvin?" he rasped, pulling in a tortured breath, "how many ambulances you got out there?"

"Three," Calvin said, coming up the side of the house. "Oh my God... Shane, you're covered in—" Donny picked that moment to whimper, and Calvin shifted his gun and his focus to the two moaning junkies, writhing on the ground. The knife at Donny's feet was covered in Shane's blood, and Shane's arms were shaking as he tried hard to think.

"Get their weapons," he said, fighting for some more air. "Now, Calvin. Don't have much time."

Calvin jumped to, kicking the knives off and far away from Donny and Rachel's grasp. From inside the house, Shane heard the sounds of policemen and rescue workers and frightened children. Peripherally, he heard backup coming alongside him, but he was focused on Calvin.

"You got this?" he asked, and his voice sounded high—almost casual—and Calvin nodded numbly. "Good," Shane said, feeling wise and calm. And that was when he blacked out.

Chapter 11

I find it hard to tell you, I find it hard to take…

"Mad World"—Gary Jules

LATER, it would hit Mikhail and hit him hard that not once did he think Shane had broken his promise. When he looked outside after class and did not see the car, his first thought was to call and see what the hold up was.

When there was no answer, his stomach went cold, and he told himself he was being foolish and dialed again.

The second time, someone picked up, and there was a hollow sound of corridor echoes behind the voice, which was good because Mikhail did not immediately think of another man in Shane's bedroom. He knew that sound. That was a hospital sound. That was a hospital sound, and the man who answered was not Shane.

"Uh… hello?"

"Shane?" Abruptly Mikhail felt lost. He fought the very real bolt of cowardice that told him to just hang up and walk home and pretend that it was not Wednesday and that Wednesdays had never meant anything beyond the middle of the week, and even that did not mean anything unless he was working a faire on the weekend.

"No, no, he's not out of surgery yet. Who is this?"

Mikhail had not left the dance studio yet, which was good because he sat down on the floor. If he'd been outside he would have sat down on the ground in the poorly lit parking lot next to the dance studio, and he would have been killed.

"This is a friend," he said weakly. "Did you say surgery?"

"Oh God… you didn't know… of course he didn't know, Jeff, you asshole, or he probably wouldn't be calling Shane's phone…." That last part sounded like the man was talking to himself, and Mikhail tried to pull together a question or something intelligent and what he managed was, "You are the Jeff that eats dinner at Deacon's?"

There was a silence, and then the man on the other line said, "And you are the person that Shane won't admit he's dating because he's afraid you'll bolt madly for the hills."

Mikhail swallowed hard. Ouch. And yet, completely the truth. "That would be me," he said, and his voice fell limply into the darkened room he was sitting in. "How… what happened? How badly is he injured? I… oh, God. I cannot get there until tomorrow, the busses don't run that late, and I can't leave my mother alone…." He was blathering. He was thinking out loud. He was panicking. "Fuck," he interrupted himself. "Please, just please tell me he's going to be okay."

There was a digestive silence on the other end of the line. "It's probably going to end well," Jeff said carefully. "The knife—"

"Knife?"

"Yes—he was stabbed from behind—the guy went around his Kevlar with a hunting knife and slid between some ribs and punctured a lung. I think he nicked something else vital, and now it's all about stopping the bleeding and dumping antibiotics into him so he doesn't get an infection. Don't worry about not being here tonight—he probably won't come to until tomorrow. If you could make it then, I'm sure he'd appreciate it."

"Nobody called me," Mikhail said, almost to himself. "Of course nobody called me. Nobody knew about me. Nobody knew about me because I couldn't even tell him I'd see him next week. I kept telling him reasons he wouldn't show. And now he's been hurt and nobody knew to call me…." He was starting to shiver and shiver hard, and he might have gone into shock, right there, just from hearing bad news, if Jeff's voice hadn't cut through the muzz of his head as he sat on the floor.

"Honey… honey… look, sweetheart…. *Motherfucker*! Now snap out of the guilt-death-spiral and fucking listen to me, okay?"

"Da," Mikhail said weakly, and Jeff-the-voice-on-the-other-line started to give him directions.

"First, I want you to go get a jacket or something—you got something to get you warm?"

"Da," Mikhail said, and went to get his jacket and his scarf and put them on. He moved into Anna's cubicle and took the afghan from the back of the chair and wrapped it around him. It wouldn't do much when he walked home, but here in the studio it started to take the shivers away.

"Good. I've got your attention. That's fucking awesome. Now, you're right—we didn't know about you—or how to get hold of you, and that's something you're going to have to fix or live with, right?"

"Da... I mean yes. I understand. I... you understand, last time he was in the hospital, nobody visited. He was there for a month, and nobody visited. I cannot bear to think of him alone there, thinking nobody would come...."

"Christ," Jeff muttered. "Well, now that is something I didn't know, so I guess we're even. No worries—hell, what is your name?"

"Mikhail, but"—and he blushed because there was no reason to throw in this detail except that it felt incredibly important—"Shane calls me Mickey."

"Well, then, I should probably call you Mikhail or he'll bust my teeth out when he can stand. Okay, Mikhail, don't worry. He'll be here in the morning—"

"You are sure?" And oh dear God, did he not sound pathetic, like a child, but he could not help it.

Jeff, whoever he was, had a way of being both gentle and crisp. Vaguely Mikhail wondered if he was a doctor—they could do that too. "Yeah, Mikhail—he's too damned big and too damned tough for this to level him. Now he'll be here tomorrow and the next day, too, and you can make up for not being here tonight. We're all here. Deacon, Crick, Benny, Andrew, Jon, Amy—hell, even the baby is here in the hospital, waiting for him. He's not going to shake us until he tells us all to piss off, and even then he'd better be damned convincing, okay?"

Mikhail could breathe as he couldn't earlier. "Okay," he echoed, the word sounding small and lost as he said it. There were a couple of heartbeats of space between them, and it suddenly occurred to Mikhail that, "Oh God. I shall have to meet Deacon."

"There is a distinct possibility," Jeff said dryly. "But you've been pretty good at ditching out of that one so far."

"You do not understand.... He talks about Deacon like... like a father and a god at the same time.... I am not the man you bring home to a father and a god. I'm the man you hope the father and god never finds out about."

There was an amused, tired snort at the other end of the line. "Jesus, honey—given that résumé, ten years ago I would have been dating you myself."

Ten years ago I was a junkie whore living in Russia, assaulting my mother so I could get back out on the streets. "Ten years ago I was fifteen."

Again that dry, amused sound. "Well, maybe not."

"I don't want to meet Deacon," Mikhail murmured, almost to himself again. "Meeting Deacon means I really will have to live up to something."

"Well, yeah," Jeff said, blowing out a breath. He sounded tired and he sounded worried, and Mikhail had a sudden thought that he should probably not dump his same terrified bullshit on this nice man. "Honey, if you want to be the guy someone calls during an emergency, that sort of comes with the territory."

"Where is he? Which hospital?" Mikhail asked, because he didn't want to think about that right now.

"U.C. Davis," Jeff told him, and then told him the room number. "It's the intensive care unit—but he might be moved tomorrow if he's out of danger."

"Oh God, I hope so," Mikhail muttered. "I will be there tomorrow," he said. "If... if he asks for me, tell him. Tell him I said it was a promise."

"I'll do that. You going to be okay now?" Oh God. Even this man with his dry, amused voice was nice to him.

"Yes. I will go home and make plans to be there tomorrow. I can do that." U.C. Davis Med Center was a two-hour bus ride, and his mother had chemo the next day. He also had classes to teach in the afternoon. He would, indeed, have to make plans to keep this promise.

He rang off numbly, then stood up and managed to make it out of the dance studio without forgetting anything like his shoes or whether or not to lock up.

The walk home was a blur of Christmas lights on wet pavement, and most of it happened in Mikhail's head. He was actually surprised to open the door to his apartment, and it was only his mother's voice, hoarse and weak, that brought him to reality.

"You are late, *lubime*. Is Shane with you?"

Mikhail froze at the door. For a moment he thought that he would not tell his mother. He would tell her that Shane had left him, had bailed, had decided not to pursue the relationship. It would hurt her, but it would not worry her. He opened his mouth to do just that, when he heard his own shaking voice.

"He was injured at work, Mutti. He… he is coming out of surgery. I… they think he will be… okay…." His voice broke, and he was not sure of when he moved across the small apartment, but there he was, his head in his mother's lap as though he were a child and his mother's hands were smoothing through his hair. She whispered to him in Russian for a little while, and then, when he was starting to realize how foolish he felt, she spoke to him crisply.

"Well, call Olga Divacz, then, and she can take me to the doctor's tomorrow. You need to visit him, yes?"

Mikhail looked at his mother and nodded. "Yes. He has many people there already, though. He may not even notice me."

His mother's disgusted expression was reassuring. "Phfaw! Nonsense, *mal'chik*. Your face will be the first one he looks for."

He took a deep breath and sat up completely, wiping his cheeks with the heel of his hand. "Thank you, Mutti. I am afraid I am being very foolish… here. I'll go get us some dinner."

But Ylena didn't let go of his hand. "Don't feel foolish, Mikhail. Please…." He tried to get up. "Please don't feel foolish. You've let this man into your heart—I was afraid you would let no one into your heart, and you've let him in. I… I am pleased."

Mikhail turned to her and tried for his usual arch expression. "Even if he is not a girl who will cook for me?"

Ylena laughed and ruffled his hair. "I am afraid that you are the girl who will cook for him, *mal'chik,* but he is a nice man, so I do not mind so much."

THE next day it took three bus transfers and most of his morning to get from Citrus Heights to Stockton Boulevard in Sacramento, but he did it with his usual self-sufficiency. He was tired and fretful by the time he asked the nurse for directions to the hospital room and pattered his way down the hall. As he neared the room, he passed two men—one of them very tall and the other one extremely beautiful and wearing a cowboy hat—muttering to each other about a damned fucking stubborn man, and Mikhail's heart leapt for no particular reason.

It sounded like Shane.

He found the room number and looked in hesitantly. There was a dark-haired man wearing a very trendy sweater and shiny shoes sitting at the end of the bed and fidgeting with a book in his hand. He was talking irritably to Shane.

"Of course they're pissed," he said, and Mikhail knew him by his voice. "You scare the shit out of all of us, and all you can ask us to do is feed your animals? Come on, man—take them up on the real food, for fuck's sake."

"I'm not hungry," Shane muttered from the hospital bed, "and I don't want to be a bother."

"Oh Jesus—you're worse than Deacon!" Jeff protested with a laugh, and Shane gave a tired smile.

"No one's worse than Deacon." His dark hair was oily and sticking out all over his head, and his fine, broad body was draped in a white gown. There was a bandage wrapped around his chest, and he was unbearably pale. He was beautiful.

"Yeah—you need to just admit you feel like shit and you don't want food. We'd understand that. This 'Don't put yourself out' shit makes us want to strangle you."

"Please?" Shane muttered. "Because the truth is I feel like shit, and I don't think I can eat much more than soup."

Jeff perked up. "Soup! Excellent. I'll go outside and call them so they can send some with Benny!"

"Jeff...."

But Jeff was already heading out the door. He almost brushed completely past Mikhail, but he stopped just in time.

"Hey," he said tentatively, "you wouldn't be...?"

"Yes." Mikhail bobbed his head nervously. "You were very kind yesterday. I should thank you."

"I'm glad you made it, sweet thing," Jeff said crisply. "He's been asking for his cell phone, and I told him you were coming. You caught me by surprise last night—you know we're not supposed to use those things in the hospital."

Mikhail nodded. "Yes. I... thank you again." And still he hesitated there at the doorway. His Shane—except not his, not here. Here he had a family, and they were worried and anxious and in his business. He felt superfluous. Suddenly he felt Jeff's hard, capable hands on his shoulders, shoving him through the door.

Shane looked up and spotted him, and his entire face lit up the drab little room.

"Mickey! You made it!"

Mikhail took three steps to his bedside and found he could summon some mock irritation, because it was a better alternative to falling all over himself to make sure Shane would be all right. "You miserable, irritating man. You make plans with me and then get stabbed? *Stabbed?* It is like you make up bad pastimes just to avoid our date. I'm really very pissed, you realize that, yes?"

He couldn't even look at Shane as he said it. He found he was picking at the coverlet next to Shane's big hand, and as he finished his little speech he saw the big ugly bruises that were there from the IV needle, and he stroked them softly with his thumb, avoiding the needle that was still in his flesh.

Shane grabbed his hand and murmured, "Mickey, I'm going to be fine," but Mikhail still couldn't look him in the face.

"Could they have been any clumsier when they put this in? My mother weighs ninety pounds and gets poison pumped through her veins three times a week. She has less bruising than this."

"Mickey, look at me."

Mikhail shook his head, and Shane sighed.

"Please?"

Mikhail's eyes blurred, but, well, hell. It could be the first thing Shane had actually asked of him, ever, and he was going to turn him down now?

Shane looked tired, and very pale, and his brown eyes seemed half-focused with pain medication, but he was smiling, and Mikhail sighed. "You look like shit," he said, but his voice wobbled and he was not very convincing.

"Well, you look wonderful," Shane said, and his smile widened. "I guess we're about like we always are, right?"

Mikhail shook his head. "No. No we're not. I am... I am not okay. I don't see how you can lay there and smile when... what were you thinking? I don't even know what you were doing when this happened, and I'm still so incredibly angry with you for getting hurt. You cannot... you cannot promise me you will be there and then let this shit happen...."

"Amen to that!" Mikhail turned and saw a skinny young man in a tan policeman's uniform walk in, and he suddenly had a more appropriate focus for his anger.

"And where were you?" he asked bitterly. "He is supposed to have help. You did not just let him get smashed this time, like a pink brick? Because that is intolerable—"

He did not see Shane wince behind him, but he did hear the sucking sound of wind through his teeth and watched as the young man wrinkled his nose and mouthed the words "pink brick" as though he had no idea what Mikhail was talking about. He was still stuck on that when Jeff walked in behind him, having apparently heard everything.

"That's a good question, actually," he said, his voice hard. "Aren't you his partner?"

"Calvin, this is Mikhail and Jeff. Mikhail and Jeff, this is Calvin," Shane said, his voice dry. "And you two, leave the poor kid alone. It wasn't his fault. He was the one who arrived with the cavalry, and I was the dumbshit who just had to get a closer look before he got there. How're those kids, since you're here, Calvin?"

Calvin looked furtively at Mikhail and Jeff in a way that told them he was going to dodge that question if he could.

"Why would you think I wouldn't come and back him up?" Calvin asked, obviously buying time while he figured out "pink brick." "He's a cop, same as me. He just went in for a closer look and it bit him on the... well, in the kidneys, I guess." He smiled a little uncertainly at Shane, and Shane smiled reassuringly back.

"Well, it's not like you people have a great track record where Shane is concerned, you know?" Jeff snapped, and Shane's smile fell, and he made a faint moan in his throat.

Mikhail blinked and watched a truly painful realization cross over young Calvin's face. First he said the words "pink brick" under his breath—then he mouthed "you people."

Then he looked at Mikhail's hand, which had never left Shane's, and took in their obvious proximity.

And then the light bulb went on.

"Oh my God! You all think I... no! I would *never*! I don't care who a guy sleeps with, I'm not going to leave someone with dogs just flapping in the breeze like that!"

"Oh shit," Mikhail said faintly, and then Jeff blinked, and he said "Oh shit," and Shane's helpless, pained chuckle was the only sound in the room.

"Mickey?" he said after a terrible silence had fallen. "Mickey—you wouldn't want to go get me some ice cream with Jeff, would you? I need to talk to Calvin. Just come back in a few, and we can have this conversation all over again."

Mikhail sighed. "I would, but I should probably go."

"You just got here!" Jeff protested, and Mikhail looked at him miserably.

"It takes a long time by bus. I work in three hours—my bus leaves in ten minutes."

Jeff looked at him with surprise and more than a little admiration. "Where do you work, Mikhail? If it means you can stay for a little longer, I'll drop you off myself."

Mikhail smiled gratefully. "That would be wonderful. Thank you." Then he turned to Shane after taking a distrustful glance at the still stunned Calvin.

"I think I have just done a terrible thing, *lubime*. I don't see how I can make it better."

Shane's smile was tired—and sweet. "No worries. Calvin's a big boy. He can take a little bit of truth, can't you, Calvin?"

"I just hope you can," Calvin muttered, and Shane's face fell. He squeezed Mikhail's hand and caught Jeff's eye.

"Guys—go get friendly. Jeff, if you call him any names I'll kick your lily ass."

"Oh honey, why would I pick on your little friend here when you're *such* a better target? Do you want any ice cream, you big weird bastard?"

"He is not weird!" Mikhail said unhappily, and was rewarded with another squeeze of his hand.

Jeff's look at him was surprisingly gentle. "Of course not, baby. My bad. Come on—I could really use some fucking ice cream."

Mikhail turned unhappily to Shane. "I'm sorry," he muttered, and Shane smiled again. That plain, earnest smile was suddenly the most important thing in Mikhail's life. Oh God—to think he might never have seen it again.

"Well, Mickey, since you just outed me to my job, the least you could do is gimme a little kiss before you go." Shane's words were starting to slur, and Mikhail wondered what was so urgent that he had to talk to his cop friend before he fell asleep. That didn't stop him from bending over and running his lips lightly along Shane's, and treasuring the feel of his lean mouth quirking up at the sides.

"We will talk when I get back," he told Shane sincerely, and Shane smiled again, his eyes half closed.

"Best part of my day."

And then Jeff led him by the elbow and was steering him out of the room while Calvin watched them go unhappily. When they cleared the door, Mikhail turned to Jeff and asked why it was so important that they leave the room.

Jeff sighed, and suddenly all traces of the flamboyant flirt who had talked so crisply to Mikhail drained away. The man who was left seemed tired and very, very worried.

"Because I don't think the scene where Shane got hurt went well. From what I understand, Shane was peeking around a corner, getting the lay of the land, when he heard that there was an overdosing infant inside the house. He called for an ambulance and that tipped off the bad guys, and that's when they tried to shish kebob our big, stupid cop."

Mikhail frowned even as he and Jeff made a left, following the arrows to the cafeteria. "Why did he even get out of the car? Should he not have waited for somebody to help before he went in?"

Jeff looked at him and nodded. "Yeah. He knew there were kids there, Mikhail. I don't know what to tell you—I love the guy, but he seems to have more heart than common sense sometimes."

Mikhail looked at him, worried about several things. "He needs someone to make him think of himself first," he said, because this was true. He remembered that day at the Faire—all of that buying. Buying clothes that Mikhail said he should buy, buying presents for the people he loved, buying a shirt for a man he had barely met. Where in all of that was what Shane wanted?

Apparently, you were what Shane wanted.

Mikhail fought the urge to go sprinting back to the hospital room and looked at Jeff instead. "You would not want to…." He remembered all of Shane's stories, about how the two of them had fought like brothers from the very beginning. No, this nice man was not a good match for his Shane. "Never mind."

Jeff's mouth quirked, and some of that flirt was back. "You can't give him away, you know. I'm pretty sure he's yours."

Mikhail's mouth pinched unhappily. "I don't think I know what to do with something that valuable."

Mikhail was surprised by the genderless, comforting arm looping around his shoulder. "Sweetheart, just try not to break it. Deacon gets pissed when we're broken."

They met Calvin coming out of the room when they got back, and Jeff gave him a hard look. The young officer blushed and looked away.

"Shane's a good guy. You... you all don't have to worry. I'm not going to... you know. Tell the world. I wouldn't ever just let him walk into something without backup. Who would do that?"

Jeff scowled at him. "An entire L.A. precinct, apparently. But I'm glad to hear you're not going to go gossip about our friend there. If we hadn't been so worried, you never would have needed to know."

Calvin nodded and then looked thoughtful. "That's not... that's not right," he said, almost to himself. Then he shook his head and told them, "He's... he's sort of upset right now—or he was before he fell asleep. That kid—the one who was overdosing—the kid didn't make it. The one who was getting carved on when Shane got there, she's going to be okay—sort of. I mean, you don't have daddy carving you up like that while your little sister's dying inside the house and actually be 'okay'. But... anyway. Shane didn't take it well. Guess I can't blame him—it was the whole reason he put himself out there."

Mikhail felt the ice cream he'd just eaten congeal in his stomach. "That is several kinds of horrible," he said numbly, and Jeff grunted an affirmative next to him. "Excuse me, I need to...." And he couldn't even finish the sentence. He hurried into the room and saw that Shane's eyes were closed. Little silver drops trembled on his eyelashes in time to his even breathing. Mikhail sighed and pulled up a chair, plopping into it and putting his chin up on the uncomfortable rail.

Jeff came in a few minutes later and laughed softly. "Here, baby—let me fix that for you."

With a minimum of fuss and a practiced hand he dropped the rail on the side, and Mikhail crossed his arms on the mattress next to Shane's head and propped his chin up on his fists.

They were quiet in the room for a moment and then Mikhail said, "Are you a doctor, Jeff-the-friend?"

"No—I'm a physical therapist."

"Why are you not a doctor? You are very good at those things that doctors do," Mikhail mused. Shane's even breathing was soothing, but the quiet in the room unsettled him.

"You know a lot about doctors," Jeff said, sounding amused.

"My mother is dying. I have seen many of them." He said the words automatically—it occurred to him that someday soon, they would no longer be true.

"Wow," Jeff murmured.

"You didn't answer my question." Once again, he was asking for a past he had no right to.

"I tested positive in college," Jeff said softly. "Fewer sharp, pointy things in physical therapy than as an actual doctor. Less time spent in med school when my time might be shorter than the rest of the world's."

Mikhail turned his head in surprise. "So you have a past too. Does your Deacon know?"

Jeff was sitting at the end of the bed under the only available light. He had his book out—a horror/thriller/detective something—but he was looking at Mikhail as though the conversation, even with the intrusive questions, was welcome.

"Yes," he said softly. "I told them both."

"So I am the coward, then?" Mikhail asked, mostly to himself. "And so we both have pasts we may not be so proud of." He had a sudden urge to run out and find this Deacon and confess himself clean and pure, so maybe he would feel like being here, at Shane's bed, was exactly right, instead of a stolen privilege he would have to pay for later.

"Everyone has a past," Jeff said gently.

"Everyone except Shane," Mikhail murmured back. "He has done nothing in his life to be ashamed of." Oh, God. He was so damned tired— he had not slept the night before, and the bus ride had been terrifying. He did not know this part of town at all, and all of his self-sufficiency had been wrung out of him as he realized he was nearly three hours from home, and if his mother's last chemo session did not go well, he had no way to get to the hospital in Roseville to see her. (Sacramento was a terrible place for hospitals, he thought despondently. There were too many scattered across the map like drops of water.)

"I have to agree with you there," Jeff said quietly.

"No—no terrible past." He stroked the tender inside of Shane's hard, solid bicep. The skin was so smooth under his fingers... so terribly vulnerable. "No evil deeds, no crippling regrets. Just a heart as open as the blue sky. Any evil fucker can shoot an arrow into it and make it rain blood."

His eyes closed, and he thought he heard Jeff gasp, but he was too tired to see why. He did not know how long he slept. At some point, he was aware that someone else entered the room and started speaking quietly to Jeff, but by then he was in that state of exhaustion where even though he was semi-aware of his surroundings, he really could not rouse himself to respond to them.

"Hey, Benny—where's Drew? Mmmmm… soup."

"Drew's parking the car, and you're welcome. Do you think Shane'll want some when he wakes up?" It was a girl's voice, but she spoke quietly, and Mikhail thought he would like her if they could talk.

"I hope so," Jeff said quietly. "He's had sort of a day for someone who hasn't moved much since this morning."

"Is that him?" Mikhail felt the urge to move, but he couldn't. Sleep weighed him down and left him a little bit helpless to do anything but listen to this conversation.

"Shane's secret guy? Yeah—that's Mikhail."

"What's he like?" There was some rustling, and Benny pulled back the curtain that separated Shane's side of the room from the other side of the room, which was vacant. Mikhail heard a squeak and assumed she was sitting on the other bed.

"Like?" Jeff sounded amused.

"Yeah—what's he like? I've been trying to teach Shane to cook for a month to impress this guy. What's he like?"

"Skittish as a feral cat. How're the cooking lessons going?"

"Like shit. I had to sneak real food into Shane's house last time because I was afraid he was going to poison the guy. I swear, Shane could fuck up a microwave burrito."

Jeff's tired laugh was suddenly not snarky at all—it was pure affection. "Cooking to impress, hah? Oh, baby, that *is* serious."

"So, do you think he's going to stay?"

Jeff grunted. "I don't know, Shorty. I think he wants to. I even think he's a good kid. But everyone has their damage. He might think he's too damaged to do this right."

Benny made a *hmmm* sound and then said, "We'd better not introduce him to Deacon until we're sure, then."

"You think?"

"Jeff, two men in my life have hurt me. Deacon personally put one of them in jail and the other one in the hospital. He doesn't like it when people hurt us."

"Good point," Jeff said softly. "He wasn't exactly gentle with the guy who was here from the police department last night."

"Yeah, well, if he's the guy who called the house, he was a snide asshole."

"His partner seemed all right." Jeff sighed and leaned back. Mikhail could picture him closing his eyes and stretching out his legs. "I hope so, anyway, since Mikhail and I sort of busted Shane out of the closet right in front of him."

"Oooh... do tell!"

Mikhail's sleep deepened while Jeff was telling the story, and the next thing he knew, Shane's hand was gentle on his shoulder.

"Mickey! Mickey—man, it's time to get up."

Oh hells. "Did I sleep through my visit?" he asked blearily, and Shane stroked a rough finger down the side of his face.

"'Fraid so. But I just woke up, too, so I guess we're even."

Mikhail looked at him unhappily. Close up he looked even worse—and even more dear. "I want to stay," he murmured. "I want to spend the night by your bed. I want... I want to be the man that people will expect to be here."

Shane's mouth quirked. "You are here. That's enough for right now. And you have other promises to keep—don't think I don't know that. Don't think I don't respect that. Tell your mom I said hi, all right?"

Mikhail nodded and leaned forward, pressing his forehead to Shane's. Shane was warm, and a little clammy. Oh God. What did Jeff say? Something about infection?

"I can come back tomorrow. I can maybe cancel my classes—I have never called in sick. Anna will forgive me."

"I can't promise I'll be really charming tomorrow. They took my temperature while you were asleep—apparently I'm going to be sick tomorrow." Shane's grin went a little goofy and lopsided. "'S'gonna be a laugh riot. But I'd love to see you. You have to leave on Monday, but I'd love to see you tomorrow."

"Then I will be here. And the next day too. But after that…." He looked up and around the room, because he needed to make sure Jeff would be there to take him home. Jeff was, and Mikhail nodded. "I want to be that man, Shane. I want to be the man people will call. I want to be the man who is here through night and day. I don't know how to be him, but that's who I want to be."

"You are that man, Mickey. What you're doing for your mom— that's one of those things that makes you him."

"But I have to leave you…." He could not even feel like a child, because the hurt was so acute.

Shane closed his eyes, and before Mikhail could feel bad, he opened them again. "Mickey?"

"Da?"

"I know what loo-bee-mee means."

Mikhail blushed terribly. "Da?"

"Yeah."

"Good. It is good that you know that. I am glad."

"Then give me a kiss and tell me you'll see me tomorrow."

The touch of their lips was sweet and sustaining—but Shane's lips were hot, and as Mikhail straightened he caught the eyes of an anxious nurse who was there with something to pump into Shane's IV.

"I will see you tomorrow, *lubime*. Please believe it." And then Jeff had him by the elbow and was pulling him out of the room before he even had a chance to be introduced to the girl sitting on the hospital bed or the young black man who was leaning against the wall by Shane's head.

The trip to the dance studio was much shorter in Jeff's little Mini-Cooper than the trip to the hospital had been on the bus. Jeff dropped him off with a wave of the hand.

"See you tomorrow, Mikhail—I'll be here around ten, okay?"

Mikhail nodded, supremely grateful. "You have no idea how big a favor it is that you would do this for me. The bus ride… it is very long."

Jeff grimaced. "Yeah—I figure it is. And don't worry—we'll do our best to work you around Crick and Deacon, because I know you're still a little spooked, but Mikhail?"

"Yes?"

Jeff sighed and shifted the car into neutral and took his foot off the brake. "Look, man—if you want to be the guy people call, you've got to *be that guy.* That's all. Just be him. No dodging the scary people in Shane's life—just be the guy in his life, and be the guy in all of it. I can see you've got some shit to take care of right now, but when you get back from wherever you're going, you need to make a decision, okay?"

Mikhail nodded. "Yes," he said quietly. "I will see you tomorrow, Jeff-the-friend. Thank you again."

Jeff nodded as though he'd said more than he had and drove away into the cold traffic making its way through the dark.

Chapter *12*

You did not desert me…

"Brothers in Arms"—Dire Straits

MICKEY brought his laptop and some DVDs the next day, and he sat with Shane through most of the morning and part of the afternoon, watching children's movies and laughing through *WALL•E*, *Up*, and *Lilo and Stitch*. They also talked quietly—and Shane would have liked more of that, except, dammit, his head hurt and his body ached, and his wound throbbed fiercely under the pain medication. More than once he lost his train of thought when they were in the middle of a conversation, and in the middle of *Lilo and Stitch*, he wandered off and came back to find Mikhail's hand fretfully on his forehead.

"You were making noises, *lubime*," Mikhail muttered. "Here, let me call the nurse."

"I'll be fine," Shane muttered, and Mikhail kissed his forehead.

"Of course you will. Where is that fucking red button?"

The nurse came and took his temperature and added something else to his IV and then returned with the doctor, who looked grim. Mikhail asked what the problem was, and the doctor pulled him aside.

When he came back to Shane's side his face looked pinched and miserable, but he patted Shane's hand reassuringly. "Shane, do you remember Deacon's number offhand?"

"It's in my cell phone—right there by the end table."

"Good. I… I am going to call Deacon. The doctor says you are going to be fine, but they are going to need to dose you with some horrible things that will make you sick. Your family needs to know. I will not be here when the worst of it passes, *lubime*. I am sorry—I will come tomorrow, but I do not think you will know I am even here."

Shane took his hand and tried to think beyond the pounding in his head. "I'll know," he muttered. "I'll know."

He was aware of Mikhail searching through his cell phone for numbers and then sighing as he pushed the numbers into the standing phone by the bed. He also heard Mikhail's relief when someone besides Deacon answered.

"Benny, right? You are Benny? We didn't meet yesterday—I'm sorry, I was asleep." Mikhail finished the conversation, and Shane heard the fine edge of panic creep into his voice.

"But Jeff will be here in an hour… oh, Christ… I will not be here when they give him the first dose. Somebody will be, yes?"

Mikhail hung up and laid his chin by Shane's head, as he had the night before.

"I'll be okay," Shane mumbled, and Mikhail smiled faintly.

"I truly do hope so, *mishka*. That is what I am going to tell my mother, and she will be most provoked to find I am lying."

"You don't lie," Shane muttered. "And you are here. I know you are." He closed his eyes then, and for a while there was only Mikhail's cold hand in his hot one, and a broken voice singing something in a language he didn't know.

Mikhail's voice and touch left him, and what followed was a nightmare of heat and cold, of nausea and shaking, body aches, and cramps. He would fall into a fitful sleep to be jerked out of his rest by pain—in his wound, in his head, in his stomach, in his limbs—it didn't matter. Once, he woke up screaming through a raw throat, only to be soothed by a quiet hand and a deep voice.

"That's nice, Deacon. You should sing more often."

There was a quiet laugh, and then hard, competent hands sponged off his forehead, neck, and chest. Shane realized that he'd been screaming because he was hot and freezing cold, and he was freezing cold because he was in the middle of a sponge bath.

"A little personal?" But he was too tired to be embarrassed.

"Nah—I kept my EMT license current, Perkins. Trust me, I'm a pro."

And he was. Shane was too tired to keep his eyes open, but he felt himself being made clean and dressed in another hospital gown. Because it was Deacon, he didn't talk—but because Shane was mostly asleep, he did sing. Shane remembered thinking that it was a wonder of the universe that he knew Deacon who could sing and Mikhail who could dance and his only talent seemed to be installing sound systems that let him yearn to do both things.

His next sleep was easier, and when he woke up, he no longer felt like screaming. He cast bleary eyes around the room and saw Benny and Crick asleep on the bed in the adjoining cubicle and Deacon sprawled out on the chair. He grunted and tried to sit up and remembered he couldn't put his elbow down on the side that had the wound. With a groan he flopped back down on the hospital bed, and Benny swung her legs over the side of her bed and got up.

"Shhh…," she whispered, coming over to the side of his bed. "What do you need?"

"Water?" he rasped. His mouth felt like powdered borax.

Benny nodded and brought him the little pitcher with the straw. He sipped, and then he gulped, and then he was too tired to do either. He fell back against the bed with a sigh.

"Where'd Mikhail go?" he asked, and he watched Benny shake her head.

"Shane, it's Tuesday. He had to leave town yesterday."

Shane closed his eyes. Shit. Shit. And he never got to say goodbye. "Oh, God—I need to call…. What do you mean it's Tuesday?"

Benny let out a tired laugh. "Do you know how much I hate hospitals?" she asked randomly. "Last year me, Deacon, Parry Angel—we were all in the hospital for a week. And then Crick got back, and we spent a week there in Virginia, trying to get him to come home. And you—feels like we've been here all week, you know? And Christmas is in, what? Six days? Damn, Shane. I'm so tired of you guys getting sick. It's horrible. All these men, being my big brothers, and they're all threatening to die on me. It's really starting to piss me off."

Shane blinked at her and tried to put it all together. "I didn't mean to scare you," he muttered.

"Well, you did. You scared us all. Mikhail actually took a bus here the day before he left—he looked like hell. Andrew had to take him home and then he helped him pack because the guy was a wreck. And after all that, he managed to miss Deacon and Crick entirely. By the time he called us when your fever spiked, I don't even think he was trying anymore. He just ended up here when they'd left, and he didn't care. He probably would have walked through the gates of hell and bent over for the devil himself if it meant he didn't have to leave you when you might die on him."

Shane's eyes were closing in spite of himself. "Call him," he muttered. "Call him. Tell him I'm fine."

"I'll text him and tell him you're awake," she said irritably. "But I'm not saying you're fine until you're well enough to feed your own damn dogs. That pony-sized thing keeps trying to lick my face off—you really need to get better, you know?"

"How're the cats?" he asked, smiling a little. He did miss Angel Marie. Hell, he missed them all.

"Feral," Benny sniffed. "And horny. Every time one of us walks in, they all start humping our shoes."

"They're fixed," Shane mumbled, but the conversation was oddly reassuring. It sounded normal, and like home.

"Tell that to the big fuzzy brown one…."

"Orlando Bloom?"

"Yeah, whatever. Last time I was there that damned animal violated my knitting."

Shane lost a battle with a laugh and then whined because it hurt his ribs. "Violated?"

Benny was tired, and she looked older than sixteen. Her outrageously colored orange hair was showing a good inch of plain brown root, and the vestiges of makeup only served to etch her exhaustion into her face more deeply. She had a baby to care for and the three men at The Pulpit (four if you counted their hired man, Patrick), and she'd been pitching in to help him out like the rest of the family, but her eyes still managed to twinkle.

"Let's just say that wool is no longer virgin," she quipped dryly, and Shane's chest shook.

"Benny," he said, too close to sleep to back away now, "I love you like a sister, sweetheart. I'm so sorry you had to go to all this trouble."

The last thing he felt was a kiss on his brow. "I don't mind, dumbshit. Just try not to get hurt again soon. It was rough on us all."

When Shane woke up again, Deacon was there with him, reading a textbook on animal husbandry. "Only you," Shane mumbled. He felt better. For the first time in days, only his wound ached.

Deacon looked up and smiled. He was tired, too, and his hair could use washing, and he'd lost some weight, dammit, but his smile was still amazing. It wasn't the same smile he gave Crick, but it was still lovely.

"Only me what?"

"Only you would be reading a textbook in a hospital room."

Deacon stood up and pulled his chair near the side of the bed. "Yeah, well, only you would scare the shit out of all of us six days before Christmas."

"I'm sorry," Shane said again, and Deacon nodded.

"Apology accepted. The doc says you should be able to come home tomorrow, as long as home is The Pulpit and tomorrow is the day after tomorrow. We're working on that last one. No one gets better in a hospital. Me 'n' Crick can take care of you fine."

Shane smiled with some relief and felt weak tears sliding down the creases of his eyes. No going home to a cold apartment. No four white walls that didn't care. "Thank you," he choked, unable to look at his friend. "I'd love to spend some time at The Pulpit. Sorry you all got stuck with the animals."

Deacon shrugged. "Your cop friend has been doing a lot of that. He does a good job—even brought his son to visit with the cats, which was a pure relief. Horniest goddamned animals I've ever met."

Shane was going to ask him about Mikhail, but Crick and Jon walked in right then, and Crick looked at Shane and said, "Thank God. I thought we were going to have to spend Christmas here—ouch! Jon, would you cut that out? That's my bad side, and I can't hit back."

Jon shook his head mournfully. "Deacon, I know you're trying, but could you try to civilize him a little quicker? I'm not sure we can take this one out in public yet."

"I like him fine," Deacon replied mildly, and Crick scowled at him.

"Are you going to like me when I nag you about eating? Come on— tell Shane buh-bye and let me go feed you."

"Steak?" Deacon said hopefully, and Crick looped his good arm around Deacon's shoulder and kissed his temple.

"Yeah, fine. Steak. Just let's go home, and you can nap after you eat the steak, okay?" Crick looked at Shane and shook his head. "Crazy bastard's been trying to take some online classes this semester—it's not like he has time to sleep as it is."

"Need my AHT license," Deacon mumbled. "Damned vet won't let me give the horses their shots without it. Like I don't know how to give a fucking shot." He looked up then and saw Shane smiling weakly, and smiled back. "We're making Perkins tired," he said, the shyness gone and the authority back. "Jon, you here for the next shift?"

"Yup. Anything to get out of the house while the women are baking."

"Pussy," Crick shot with a little bit of malice in his voice. "Learn to cook like a real man, and they won't drive you out of the house!"

Jon looked down a haughty nose at him. "The reason," he said, "that they drove me out of the house had nothing to do with my cooking."

Deacon smirked. "You were roughhousing with the girls again, weren't you?"

Shane smirked too. Jon's own daughter, Lila, was barely six months old, but Shane had seen him crawling on the floor with her and wrestling with Parry Angel, and he figured Jon could cause enough ruckus to make even his sweet-tempered wife throw him out on his ear.

"I," said Jon with dignity, "was creating a much needed distraction from naptime."

Deacon reached out a hand and smacked his best friend across the side of the head. "You asshole—who do you think is going to have to sing that child to sleep tonight when she's too wound up to go down easy."

"You sing nice, Deacon," Shane mumbled. He was getting sleepy again, but not too sleepy to see Crick and Jon meet amused glances at Deacon's discomfiture.

"You were awake for that? Shit. C'mon, Crick, we'd better go. Everyone needs to be walked, and the stalls don't clean themselves."

The two men left, but not before Deacon gave Shane's hair a tender tousle, like a brother, and Crick shook his hand as it lay limply on the cover at his side. Human touch—unsentimental and highly, highly appreciated.

When they were gone, Shane watched Jon settling down with a book—he was reading a sci-fi epic, and Shane had to smile. Someday, he'd like to get a look at the paperback library that fueled this family. He'd seen bookshelves at The Pulpit but, detective that he was, hadn't looked much closer.

"Jon?" Shane asked before Jon could get too comfortable, and Jon looked up in response. "Could you give me my cell phone? I need to text someone."

Jon looked at him steadily but didn't move. "Your guy knows you're going to live," he said quietly. Jon's pretty-boy looks could hide an unexpectedly serious side, and that was the side of him that Shane was seeing now. "And Deacon still doesn't know about your guy. Which makes this the second biggest secret I've ever kept. Now, are you going to tell me why everyone except Crick is keeping this from Deacon?"

"Why isn't Crick keeping this secret?"

"Same reason I didn't tell Crick about Deacon's drinking when Crick was overseas—which is the first biggest secret I ever kept. Crick does not exactly think before he acts, and if anyone could frighten the raisins out of your guy by hunting him down like a big bloodhound, it would be Crick."

Shane grimaced. "Well, thank you. I'd still like to text him...." He tried to lift his arm up and fell back with a grimace. "I haven't even asked. What in the fuck happened to me?"

"They dosed you with sulfa drugs..."

"I'm allergic to sulfa drugs!"

"We know—but the regular drugs weren't doing it. So they filled you with sulfa drugs to kill the bug, then they filled you with Prednisone to kill the sulfa drugs, and now they're trying to decide which place is going to be less harmful to you, the hospital or The Pulpit."

"The Pulpit," Shane sighed. "Definitely The Pulpit. Please can I text Mikhail? Actually…." Shane wrinkled his nose. "How can *you* text him? His cell phone was shit. I was going to give him a new one before he left…." He didn't have the strength to blush, really, but he felt like the flush would have traveled from his toes to his nose. "I just… I didn't want him to forget about me."

Jon looked at him sympathetically and shook his head. "Man, you don't have to worry about the cell phone. We found it in your pile of Christmas gifts on the couch when we went in to feed the dogs. You had them all labeled and half of them wrapped—I'm telling you, Perkins, considering you had nearly two weeks left, it was just sick. My daughter's going to love the fifty bajillion things you bought for her—and I would, too, but you're making me look bad."

Shane gave it up and blushed. Maybe it would be good for him—wash out all the shit they'd been pumping into his body or something. "I've never shopped for children before," he mumbled. "I didn't have a plan for that phone hooked up or anything…."

"Jeff hooked him up—told him it was part of the present from you or some bullshit. Truth was we felt like crap. He was wrecked, leaving you like that. And…." Jon blew out a breath and shook his head. "It's not like one of us blamed him. Not after we figured out where he was going and why. You know, Shane, I don't know what it is that's got him on the run, but I'm pretty sure the reason we all helped keep him away from Deacon for now is because he's worth the catching, you know? I think he really, really cares about you. I hope you can bring him to dinner soon."

Shane nodded, a rather dreamy smile taking over. "I've wanted to bring him to dinner since we met. Hasn't been a good time. Could you just tell him I'm going to be okay? Tell him I woke up thinking about him? Tell him I understand why he had to go…."

Jon sighed. "Okay, Cyrano." He pulled out his own phone—something elaborate and highly technical—and then started tapping stuff into it, talking slowly as he went. *"He's awake, he misses you, he hopes your trip is wonderful.* How's that?"

"Good… real good. Maybe I can go home tomorrow. That would be good too." Shane was fugue-ing—he could feel it, but he was so tired and so relieved. "Tell him to call me on Christmas, okay?"

Jon looked at him brightly and then grunted, scowling at his complex piece of machinery. "Technical difficulties," he muttered. He typed something furiously onto the keyboard, and Shane fought sleep. There was a buzz from the little thing, and Jon grunted, then typed some more. Shane had actually nodded off before Jon made a happy sound, and he jerked himself awake.

"He got it?" Oh good. True relief flooded his body—he knew it would be okay now.

"Yup. And he promises to call or text you right about now until he gets back."

"Really?" More good news! "Are you sure? He's usually a little cagier than that."

Jon's smile was still bright, and he held up the phone close so Shane could read it through unfocused eyes. *Okay. Will call on Christmas. Tell him I promise.*

And that was all he needed.

HE DIDN'T get to leave the next day—but he did get to leave the day after that, where he felt like a big lump on Deacon's big couch. Everybody assured him he was helping just by playing dolls with Parry Angel while they were running around trying to get Christmas things done, and he chose to believe them. He had to admit that having to sleep for sixteen hours a day was a lot more fun when you nodded off with a baby in your lap.

"Parry is the best baby for that," Benny agreed, running in from the kitchen where she was doing the baking and some of the wrapping. "She can just sit on you and play while you nod off. You're like the best patient ever, can I just say that? Deacon kept trying to get up and feed the horses last year, and Crick was bound and determined to go out and muck the stables before he could barely walk."

Shane was unsure of when laziness had become a virtue, but since all he could seem to do was sleep, he didn't have a lot of time to contemplate the problem.

Of course, he lived for the moments on the phone with Mikhail. His original phone had been destroyed in some bizarre accident involving a hospital gurney and lots and lots of little pieces of plastic. Jon could never really explain how it happened, but fortunately the SIM card remained intact, even if Jon got him a different carrier when he replaced the damned thing out of pocket. Shane felt bad about that—it had been an accident after all. But the phone Jon got him was pretty spiffy and easy to text with, and once or twice a day his phone would buzz, and he would no longer be in Deacon's living room, using oxygen, he'd be someplace new and exciting and beautiful, and he'd be there with Mikhail.

The sunset has not so many colors here, but each color is very sharp. And none of them are brown.

Mutti spends all of her time on deck, wrapped in blankets, holding her face to the sun. She looks very 1930s movie star.

Children in the street call for pesos. I give some, but you cannot fill the ocean with a few drops of sweat.

I think I shall have a book of postcards. All of my pictures are of Mutti, but here is one of me.

The picture had been sent on the phone, and it featured Mikhail looking self-conscious and avoiding the camera with his blue-gray eyes. He was standing on the prow of the vast cruise ship and holding the camera out with his arm, and the sunset that was not brown was behind him. His skin was a pale brown, and his tiny corkscrew curls were washing nearly white with the sun, but the skittish look was pure Mikhail.

Shane spent a long time looking at that picture before he sent back his reply: *You look happy. I'll send you a picture on Christmas—I won't look so much like a mental patient by then.*

Mikhail's reply made him laugh. *You probably are too thin. Eat something, you obnoxious man—no one likes to grope a skeleton.*

So when Christmas Day rolled around, Shane tried not to be too much of a big garden slug. Deacon and Crick still had the big plastic bench in their shower from when Crick could barely stand, and he'd been keeping clean, but Christmas morning—while Crick cleaned up the rubble left when a bunch of grown men tried to spoil a teenager and her baby absolutely rotten—he actually shaved and buttoned up loose jeans and a shirt with a collar and then retired to the living room, thinking maybe he could go home the next day and actually feed his dogs.

When Shane sat down on the couch, feeling more himself than he had for nearly two weeks, Andrew came and handed him a mug of hot chocolate, then sat down next to him.

"You're looking pretty spiffy there, chief. You got a date tonight?"

Shane rolled his eyes. "Trying to look like a productive citizen is all. You know—go home, feed the dogs, pay the bills, find the presents that weren't on the couch and give those out." He'd meant to send Kimmy her present—a big comfy throw for her couch that he'd bought from a craft fair Benny had dragged him to one weekend—but obviously that hadn't happened. He realized with a sudden slash of guilt that he hadn't even told Kimmy he'd been injured and sick. He was going to call her tonight—he'd have to make it sound small so she wouldn't be hurt.

"Deacon doesn't want anything, you know," Andrew said now, and Shane blushed.

"Tough. I got him something anyway. And Crick too. I just hadn't gotten the bags out to organize and wrap and shit." He'd gotten them a Wii, and it was expensive and it came with games, and he didn't give a shit.

"Yeah, well, I appreciate my hat and all, Shane, but you know, you're part of us. I don't think you have to be giving us all presents and shit—I mean, don't worry. It was going to be a lean Christmas, and you've spoiled us all rotten, and Deacon doesn't know how to say thank you for it, but anyone who gives to his girls is pretty much one of his favorite people."

Shane blushed and looked away. "I don't know families," he said awkwardly. "I don't know... limits. I just... I'm so grateful for people, sometimes."

Andrew nodded, patted his back, and stood. "We're grateful for you. Man, our best Christmas present this year is that we're all here. Crick, Deacon—there were times last year we weren't sure either of them were going to make it. And just when we thought it was smooth sailing, you go and get hurt. Just know that, you know. You got the job. The audition's over. You're part of our family now, okay?"

Shane couldn't look at him. Crick wasn't sleeping well—he woke up every night around two a.m., sometimes screaming. Sometimes he just wandered into the living room and sat at Shane's feet and watched television. Deacon was sleeping worse—he would go to bed with Crick, and then get up when Crick fell asleep to do chores or study for his classes or study the finances for, please God, another way to save his home. He was always in bed just in time to comfort Crick when he woke up. Shane was part of the family, but he couldn't help them—not in any real way. Apparently, all he could do was sleep on their couch and make their complicated lives harder and drink in the love that saturated the house like a plant took in water.

"Yeah, well, Merry Christmas to you too." God—what else was he supposed to say?

So it felt surreal that night, as everyone was gathered in the living room, finishing up with dessert, to realize that he was a part of this big group of people. Mostly he was a baby seat, but that was nice too. He found that he liked the little people—they didn't mind if he was weird or awkward, and they certainly didn't mind the puppets or the pretty dresses or the little wooden toys and blocks he'd given them for Christmas, even if they didn't know who'd done the giving.

Still, when the phone in his pocket buzzed, he had Andrew take Parry Angel so he could stand clumsily to pull the thing out of his back pocket.

He was so nervous about talking to Mikhail that his hands were actually shaking.

Jon saw him reaching for the phone and moved close enough to mutter, "Go use Deacon's room. It's quieter."

Shane nodded thanks and pulled out the phone as he was walking down the cool, dark, hallway.

"Heya, Mickey," he said into the quiet.

There was a gasp on the other end of the line, and then Mikhail's voice, uncertain and wobbly.

"You really are going to be okay. That is good. I was starting to think they were pretending to be you, just so I would not jump from the ship."

Shane laughed. "Nah, Mickey, you're tougher than that."

"So you say." Mikhail sounded more sad than amused. "I know I'm not so tough. If I was all that hard, I'd be very, very angry at you, but I'm not."

"I'm sorry I got hurt," Shane said, wincing. "I didn't mean for you to worry."

"Yes, well, I'm still angry about that. In fact, it made me a little crazy there for a moment. But that I can yell at you for. This other thing, I cannot even yell at you for. In fact, I was not even going to tell you I knew, but now I find that I must."

And then he did. And Shane felt even worse.

Chapter *13*

You want it, you take it, you pay the price.

"Prove it All Night"—Bruce Springsteen

THE day Mikhail and his mother left for San Francisco to board the cruise ship was almost surreal in its pain. Mikhail didn't think he could have gotten on board the ship—hell, he didn't think he would have even gotten in the car—were it not for Shane's friends.

Andrew had come into his home and charmed his mother and helped the two of them pack. Benny had sent dinner with him, so there was nothing to do but eat and clean up, and even that Andrew had helped with. Jeff had pressed a new phone into his hand with a plan that included texting from the far ends of the earth and even talking without spending too much of a fortune. It was complete with numbers, including Andrew's, Benny's, Jeff's, and Jon's.

And, of course, Shane's.

So when Mikhail boarded the ship and waved goodbye to his mother's friend who drove them and smiled and laughed for his mother and threw a flower for good luck, he had a perfect device with which to fuck up his life.

He could not help it. He left his mother on the deck, swathed in blankets and sipping a fruit drink and looking as happy as she was bemused. Then he went down to the cabin to check his messages, and to see if this big, stupid man who had made him so happy and who had asked for so little in return was going to live or die.

Benny's text, "*Fever broken. Doing well,*" had him falling to his knees and howling into the fluffy pillow on the little twin bed next to his mother's. And that was when he lost his mind.

He could barely remember dialing Shane's number, but what followed was one of the angriest, most vitriolic rants he could ever remember spewing into the world. He was pretty sure most of it was in Russian and the parts that were in English were too hysterical to make out—he remembered swearing a lot, and he remembered screaming "*Fuck off!*" more than once. He could not help it. All of that worry… oh, oh God, all of that worry. His whole body had been trembling with it. He had told his mother that Shane would be fine and then had lived with the agonizing worry that he would not be, and the tension between the truth and the lie had left him shaking and insane.

He had pulled himself together for his mother—he had to. It wasn't until he'd set her up in bed—an IV of fluids provided by the ship's doctor at her side—and he was alone to hear her breathing in the dark—that the full enormity of what he'd done assaulted him.

Oh, God.

The things he'd said.

He hadn't been able to eat the next day, and while he smiled for his mother and savored the picture of her, under the sun, the thought of the things he said—what he could remember of them—haunted him. How could Shane forgive him for that?

Ylena noticed. "You are too sad, *lubime.* You said he would be fine."

Mikhail shrugged and adjusted her blanket. They were not quite south enough for the wind to not cut deeply if he was not vigilant. "I… I did not behave well with the worry, Mutti. I would be very surprised if he wanted to face me after that.

Ylena waved her hand in denial, and then her eyes turned inexorably to the sun and the blue sky. She seemed to feel an enormous amount of peace out here, her head wrapped in a turban, her eyes protected from the fierceness of the sun. Mikhail found he did not have to protect her from his own problems, her heart was already starting to detach a little from the world and drift to the glory her church had promised her.

Mikhail was only interested in one glorious thing, and his own stupidity had probably removed it from his grasp.

When he got the text from Jon, he had already started wondering when Shane would text and say he never wanted to see Mikhail again.

From Jon—*He's up and he's asking about you.*

Oh God. How to explain? *I left terrible message on his phone. I was insane. He will not want me after I lost my mind.*

From Jon—*WTF? Seriously—how bad could it be?*

Oh please. Don't make him think about it. *I called him horrible names. I was so mad. I worried so much. It hurt so badly.*

Jesus. He could never have imagined feeling so naked in front of a virtual stranger whom he did not love. But Jon and Benny and all of Shane's family had been so very kind. He could not just refuse to respond to Shane's pleas to talk to him after all they had done for him. He owed them. As much as he didn't believe in making promises, he did believe in paying debts, and he owed them this much. He knew it.

Look. I'll take care of it. I promise. You were under stress—everybody gets a free pass to the zoo when they're under stress. He'll never even know the message was there.

As foolish as it was, Mikhail felt hope. *You can do that?*

I promised, didn't I?

A terrible hope reared its head. *How will I face him after that?*

And apparently Jon's patience snapped. *Goddammit, Mikhail, if you don't get on the horn I'm going to helicopter out and haul your scrawny ass off that ship!*

In spite of himself, Mikhail smiled through his panic. Shane had the best friends. *Tough words for a straight boy.*

Damned spiffy. Now tell him you'll text later and talk to him on Christmas. It's all he can talk about and he needs to sleep.

It was a break. A reprieve. Another stolen week or three or five of Shane's good opinion, of being surrounded by that sweet glow that made up Shane Perkins and all of the earnestness and kindness that he carried in his heart.

Okay. Will call on Christmas. Tell him I promised.

And it was like being released from prison. He did not have to experience the wonders of the ship or the blue sky or the clear horizon alone. He could text Shane, and Shane would be there, delighted, happy to hear from him. Another human on the planet to whom Mikhail mattered. As Ylena drifted further and further away from him on a haze of happiness and (thank the gods) bone-baking warmth, Shane's immediacy became Mikhail's lifeline.

It became the thing that made him real.

I am on shore—the roads are dusty and I have a terrible urge to buy the cheap dolls they are selling as we walk the road inland. I need to buy you something.

Only need you.

Talking pretty will not save you from a tacky knick-knack. Mikhail sniffed and spotted a likely place—it had pottery in it, brightly painted, and hand-woven textiles. He walked in and noted that there were women there—all of them working on something. Some were knitting, some were spinning, and in a small area off to the side, some were even throwing pots.

This, he thought happily, was a collective. He liked it. The goods were obviously quality, and the women who made them appeared to be the ones selling them. He was wandering around the store when a man looked over his shoulder at the heavy poncho he was eyeing. It was very expensive, but Mikhail didn't care. He had two gifts for Shane waiting in his apartment—a scarf that Ylena had crocheted at Mikhail's request, to replace the one that he could not bear to part with, and a homemade CD, with the songs Mikhail had put on the playlist with Shane's name on it. He wanted something else. All this time of scrounging his pennies, and he finally wanted to squander a little money on someone.

"That's kind of pricey," the man said, smiling slightly, and Mikhail glanced at him. A few years older than he was, dressed well in a button down and khakis, brown hair, blue eyes, and clean-shaven. Mikhail shrugged and looked for another poncho in an earthy red.

"This is a collective. These women take their profits and feed their families, and they do not work for slave wages. Free hearts make better products." He had read the sign, printed in English. He happened to believe it.

The man shrugged. "Yeah, but there's a place down the street that sells the same thing for less."

Mikhail curled his lip. He had seen that place on the way in. "There is a place right here where children don't have to work for pesos," he said shortly. He decided he wanted more color. Shane wore dark reds and browns—he had brown hair and brown eyes, and he must have known those colors would look good on him, but they were not the only colors that would do so. A rich purple, perhaps, with a warm brown pattern worked into the weave?

He browsed happily and was just about to pick his purchase, when the man spoke again with a conciliatory smile on his face. "Are you aware that you are humming and bouncing on your toes?"

Mikhail blinked at him. Shane had told him he did that when they were at the book store—but Shane had smiled when he said it, and his eyes had crinkled in the corners, and he had looked as though it was an exceedingly charming, wonderful quality. This man looked as though he deserved a prize for perception.

"Yes," he said now. "I've been told I do that." And with that he picked out his purchase and went to have it wrapped. He also bought a blanket for Mutti, and although they both would know that it would be his very soon, for this day it would keep her warm as she sat on the deck under an enormous sunhat and gazed happily at eternity.

He was not prepared for the man to fall in stride next to him on his way back to the ship, nor for him to attempt to strike up a conversation again. Mikhail chatted with him distractedly, and then his pocket buzzed.

Okay, I'm dying to know. How bad is the knick-knack?

Mikhail smiled, and he stopped where he was to text back. *It is so tacky your hundreds of cats won't even bother to break it.*

There was a pause, and Shane's next text had Mikhail making a small moue of sadness. *I miss my cats. I hope there's still five when I get back.*

How many did you want? A dozen?

Wouldn't mind. But that's a lot of cat shit.

Don't expect me to clean it. I don't do windows, either.

Mikhail barely looked up to see that the man had finally left. It didn't matter—he had the company he needed right here in the palm of his hand.

All I'd expect from you is a little bit of time and a lot of skin.

I could do that. I could even give a lot of time.

I can wait.

Mikhail sobered. Shane knew. They both knew. His return home would be… marred. Sad. He would not have any free time until his mother got better, and her recovery would be marked in black.

I do not want to wait. Stolen time is still time. We may only have moments. I will not throw them away.

Maybe we can save them, like candy.

Maybe we can devour them, like steak.

And so on. It wasn't until Mikhail had placed his purchases in his cabin and run up to give his mother her blanket that he realized that the man, the one at the store who would not leave him alone, had been trying to hit on him. He thought for a moment that perhaps he should have gotten the man's name, and then he remembered the man's ungenerous heart. He would not make a suitable match for Shane, and so Mikhail could not be bothered.

So he was in a good mood when he brought Mutti her blanket. She looked at it wonderingly and stroked it.

"So soft, *mal'chik*—what is it made of?"

"Part wool from sheep and part alpaca. They are very soft—this will keep you warm in a blizzard."

Ylena smiled, then looked up at her son and pulled at the brown scarf he'd wrapped around his neck. "We are not in a blizzard here. I know why I feel as though I need more blankets—why are you wearing that when it must be eighty-five degrees?"

Mikhail blushed. "I… I simply grabbed it, out of habit. I…." Well, hell. It was his mother. Who would she tell? "I miss him is all."

Ylena nodded. "Well, yes. I'm surprised you still have it, though. I keep forgetting he said he would not ask for it back that day."

Mikhail frowned and wrapped his hands protectively (had he known it) around the brown wool. "What day?"

"You know—the day before he was hurt. He brought us both lunch? He went into your room to look, and when he did not find it, he said to forget it. He would not take the scarf away, since you liked it so much."

Mikhail blinked. "I did not know he'd been in my room." He tried to think—was there anything embarrassing? Incriminating? Anything that would scare him and drive him away?

The narrow shoulders, cloaked and wrapped even in the heat, lifted in a shrug, and Ylena curled her lip in dismissal. "What? He is going to steal from you? I do not think so. For one thing, you counted the money and there was more than enough. For another, this is Shane. Do not worry yourself, *lubime*. That man would not do a thing in the world that was not to make you happy."

And that was when Mikhail knew.

He sucked in a breath and tried to remember. The bills had been randomly stacked, as he'd kept them, more out of superstition than anything else. There hadn't seemed to be any new ones, or any that seemed out of place. There had been an unusual number of bills that had been *blue* of all things, but since the dyes in the clothes at the Faire often ran, this didn't seem unusual either. But still. Oh God—he had been so worried. So panicked. What if he did not keep his promise? What if this— this lovely interlude with his mother, this time to see her happy and unworried before she left him for good—what if this moment had not been possible?

But it had been possible. It had been possible because Shane had wanted it as badly for Mikhail as Mikhail had wanted it for himself.

For a moment, his pride reared its ugly head. For a moment, he contemplated picking up his phone and leaving a message he could never take back. But his mother reached out a hand and patted his thigh reassuringly, and it occurred to him: she had known. She must have known, or she would not have brought it up.

"You knew," he said quietly.

"I guessed. I did not tell him I guessed, but I did. Your friend does not have a face made for hiding things."

Mikhail had to laugh at that. He pictured very clearly the wonder and wanting that had been transparent on Shane's face that day at the Faire as Mikhail had performed. How could Mikhail not single him out? Grab his hand? Make him a companion for a day and see who this tall, strong man with such a child's heart could be?

The subterfuge must have been agonizing.

"No," he said to his mother now. "He has not a face for hiding things." It was as Mikhail had said in the hospital: Shane had a heart as open as the clear blue sky. Mikhail would be damned if he was the fucker who shot an arrow into that and watched it rain blood—but he couldn't ignore it, either.

When he made his phone call the next day, the rest of the ship— including his mother—were dressed gaily and eating an extraordinarily fattening meal in the dining room. Mikhail had been there for a time, enjoying watching his mother charm people with her still amazing smile and her new red dress and a blonde wig bought special for the occasion. There was no mistaking her illness or the ravages of it, but Ylena kept her face so very proud and pain-free when she was in a crowd. She had made many friends on this trip, as she had sat on deck "dying in style" as she called it, and Mikhail was proud to be able to leave her at the table, surrounded by people who would not leave her alone.

As he was leaving, she had put her hand on his arm and said, "Tell him hello for me, and thank him for me if not for yourself, yes, Mikhail Vasilyovitch?"

"Yes, Mutti."

But of course he would tell Shane "Thank you." He would make it clear that the gift was unnecessary, but he would say "Thank you."

"Were you ever going to tell me?" he asked now, still at loss.

"Wasn't planning on it." Once again Mikhail had an impression of Shane in a darkened room, and he felt a sudden frustration that they could talk on the phone in a dark room but not in person. It felt supremely unfair that some of the best near-sex in his life had happened in a hallway and in the chair at work.

"How could you not?" And this is what bothered Mikhail the most. "You would just… just let me have this thing—this enormous gift—and not tell me it's from you?"

Shane's retort was irritated. "It's not all from me, dammit! You'd made most of the money. It was your dream. It was your promise. It was your goddamned will. I just gave you a hand up the last of the hill. Is that so bad?"

"But I would have asked you!" Oh God. It was the truth. He had thought it—many times—before he counted his bills. He would have hated it, but he would have done it.

"You never would have forgiven me for that," Shane said glumly, and Mikhail caught his breath.

"That is true," he said unhappily. "God help me—that's the truth. I would not have. And this... this, I can forgive. I have no choice." He laughed softly, without humor. "Damn you, Shane—for a man who claims to have no grace, you have managed to waltz with a porcupine until the end of the song."

There was a silence, and Mikhail wondered if he had finally given a metaphor that Shane could not follow, but he needn't have worried.

"Want to dance to another one?"

"Yes." Mikhail swallowed, feeling as though he were looking at the edge of the void. "Yes." He closed his eyes and jumped. "Would you like to hear the tune?"

"Springsteen?" Shane asked hopefully, and Mikhail had to laugh.

"Springsteen is too sad. How about U2?"

"I can live with that. What are the steps?"

"I want to be that man. The one your family calls when you are sick. The one who gets to see your house and the rail you just put on the porch and the big hole your insane dog has dug. I want them to see me at dinner at least once. I...." Oh God. His hands were sweating. He had to stop, or he would rabbit through the corridors of the ship until his heart failed from sheer fright at his own bravery. "I cannot promise tomorrow. I cannot promise next week. But as long as you still call me, as long as I know you will be there every Wednesday to bring me dinner, as long as you look forward to seeing me next, I want to be that man."

Shane's voice shook on the other line. "Okay," he said quietly. "Okay. Abracadabra—you're that guy. Dinner at Deacon's, as soon as you get... as soon as you can. You can meet everybody. Benny can cook for you—she's much better than I am. You're that guy."

"Are you going to be all right?" He didn't sound all right. He sounded strained and stressed. There was a thump that sounded like a large body flopping ass-first on a floor.

"I'm sitting down," Shane muttered. "I'm fine. Jesus, Mickey—I just didn't think you'd ever have that much faith. Merry Christmas, Mikhail. Merry goddamned Christmas."

Mikhail was sitting on the floor of the cabin too. "Merry Christmas to you, too, you persistent, irritating man. Can I give you a blowjob now?"

Shane giggled weakly into the phone. "Man, I might actually be up to phone sex—but I'm in Crick and Deacon's bedroom, and that would just be awkward."

"Da—I am in the cabin I share with Mutti. That might possibly be worse."

"So what do we do now?"

Like Mikhail would know? This was like a butterfly pretending to be a horse. "Maybe you could tell me about your day?"

And that was all Shane needed. "The baby *loved* the things you helped pick out, and so did Benny. She loved that you helped too. I think you really impressed her when I was so out of it. Have you ever watched a little kid open gifts? I don't know how other kids do it, but Parry Angel just rips off the paper and jumps in.... Benny had her make confetti angels like you know, snow angels, when the ripping was done...."

When the conversation was finally over—Shane had needed to go because his phone was beeping—Mikhail stayed seated on the floor of the cabin and rested his head on his knees. He was there when his mother entered, wheeled to her cabin by a newfound friend who had noticed she was growing tired, and he rose to help her from the wheelchair to her bed, where she sat languidly while he attached her IV and settled her in with pillows.

"Did you tell him thank you for me, *lubime*?" she asked while he was taking off her brilliant red shoes.

"Nyet," he replied absently. "You may do so yourself, Mutti, when he comes to pick us up on our return."

"He will be well enough to do that?" she asked excitedly, and Mikhail blinked. Shane had spoken of being cared for at Deacon's ranch, and he had just volunteered to drive a long distance in a week and a half.

"I suppose so—he has promised. I do not think he will break it." And he did not.

"He is having a nice Christmas?" Ylena prodded, and Mikhail finally looked up at her and smiled, catching the hint that he was not being as forthcoming as his mother would like.

"He is having a wonderful Christmas. I think I gave him what he wanted most, Mutti—that is why I am not talking so much. I am still wondering what it is I have done!"

He moved to sit next to her and took her hand automatically. More and more as her body failed her, she had sought the reassurance of human touch.

"What is it you have done?" she asked now, kindly.

"I have made a promise to be important," he admitted. "As long as we will last, I have promised to be important to him." He swallowed. "It is terrifying, you know? I have been important to you, and I am not sure it was always in your best interest to stay that way. I so very much do not want to hurt this man."

Ylena squeezed his hand, her bones brittle and thin beneath his hard fingers. "You will, you know," she told him gently. "Not irreparably. Not intentionally. And certainly not enough to drive him away, unless you try very hard or fail very badly. You need to live with your failings, Mikhail Vasilyovitch. You are a good man, but you are not perfect. Lovers hurt each other—it is in the nature of things. Mothers hurt sons and sons hurt mothers, and then at the end they are together to say goodbye. It is really all we can hope for. It is the best we can do."

"What about lovers, Mutti? Can they be together at the end as well? I was not there for Olek."

Ylena's jaw clenched, and she closed her eyes. "Olek was not really a lover, you know that. He was a boy—you were both boys. You were lost and had each other, but a real lover does not take his beloved down into misery with him because he does not want to go alone. This man will—he already *has*—sent you off alone because he wants to see you happy. This man can be there for you at the end. You just need to make the choice to journey with him."

His mother was very tired, and Mikhail felt badly for keeping her attention for so long. But, he thought selfishly, she would be able to rest forever soon enough, and he so badly had need of her now.

"I am so afraid I cannot do this," he muttered softly. She was already sleeping, but just hearing her even, raspy breathing in reply was enough.

And that terrible fear did not keep Mikhail off the phone or from texting. It did not keep him from celebrating when Shane talked of returning home, weakness and all. It did not keep him from showing his mother pictures of the dogs (frighteningly huge animals) and the cats (infinitely preferable), and the rail to the porch that Shane finished in his spare time while he recovered. It did not stop him from staring in fascination at the pictures of the family—he never had seen Parry Angel in person or Jon's beloved wife and daughter. He saw Jeff wearing a funny party hat for New Year's Eve while bouncing Parry Angel on his lap, and laughed at the mayhem of Jon sitting on the floor between the little girls, helping his daughter with a large plastic top. He recognized Deacon and Crick as the two men he'd passed in the hospital that first day and wondered that he could see the love between them even from the small, grainy photo on his phone.

This was Shane's family, he thought in wonder and dread. They would have to like him too.

He enjoyed the trip—he took many pictures, the kind that would be processed, that he could keep forever. He forgot that it was Shane's money he was spending on the trip, and resumed thinking of it as dream money. He bought souvenirs for Benny, Andrew, Jon, Jeff, and the babies. He talked to his mother often and honestly, content as the boat pulled into the foggy harbor in San Francisco that they had said nearly everything they could say that was important and that she could get on with the business of dying without any of the pain of living to hinder her or weigh down on her heart.

And in the end, as he pushed his mother's wheelchair down the ramp and saw him leaning against a rail, waiting for them with eager eyes, he realized that Shane was all he could see. The man was thinner, and he was pale. He stood with his body cocked, as though he were avoiding pain.

And when he saw Mikhail looking uncertainly at him, his face lit up so brightly it was like the Mexican sun.

His mother patted his hand. "Are you happy to see him, *lubime*?"

He swallowed. For a moment, he could not even answer. "Oh God, yes, Mutti."

"Then lock this machine in a corner and go kiss him. If there was ever a time to forget your mother, it is when someone is looking at you like that."

He did. He locked the wheelchair in place, out of the way, and trotted forward. Shane's eyes grew wide, and his mouth opened in a little O, and he looked so vulnerable and so sturdy, standing at the end of the gangplank, that Mikhail could not help but smile widely. He practically knocked Shane over with his momentum, and as the big man steadied them both and grinned down at him from his impossible height, his laughter warmed the chill fog around them.

"Miss me?" he asked hopefully.

"If I tell you how much, you will be impossible to live with. Shut up and kiss me, you miserable man. I am happy to be home."

Chapter 14

Close your eyes and try to dream.
   "We Belong"—Pat Benatar

MIKHAIL tasted like sunshine and sweet and bitter tea. His mouth was open and his tongue aggressive, and Shane opened his mouth and groaned and kissed harder. Oooohhhh.... Those wiry, hard biceps felt so good under Shane's hands, and his body, small but substantial, was the sweetest weight against Shane's chest. The feel of that compact, strong body under Shane's palms seemed to give him strength, and he needed it because he'd had to lie to Deacon about how good he felt in order to get to borrow Crick's car.

Mikhail wrapped his arms around Shane's middle and squeezed, and about the time Shane couldn't keep in the whimper of pain, Mikhail released him and glared reprovingly.

"You have lost weight. And you are still not healed. I do not know what idiot left you off your leash, but you should have stayed at home."

"And missed that kiss?" Shane gasped. "Not on your life!"

Mikhail's expression sobered, and he held Shane's face between his palms. People were surging around them, and Shane hardly noticed they were there, and it was San Francisco so the two of them kissing didn't attract much attention. It was just the two of them, and it was wonderful— or it would be if Mikhail wasn't looking so very serious all of a sudden.

"It very nearly was on yours, you know."

Shane wrinkled his nose and shrugged. "On my life? It's all good now. I'll live."

Mikhail shook his head and turned away. He held onto Shane's hand but showed Shane his back as he pulled them toward his mother.

"Mikhail…," Shane muttered, unhappy to upset him. He was unprepared for Mikhail to whirl on him, his eyes bright and shiny and his chin quivering.

"You cannot joke about that," he snapped. "Ever. You cannot say 'I lived so it was okay'. It is *still* not okay. It will *never* be okay. You and your stupid impossible job. I will live in fear every day you work, and I will *never* take for granted that you will walk away in one piece. Never again. If you knew, had any *idea* what you put us through…." Mikhail shook his head and yanked his hand back. "If you knew, you would never joke about 'I'll live!' again."

Shane reclaimed his hand. "I'm sorry—I was really surprised how many people got upset this time. I really didn't mean to worry you."

Mikhail's upper lip curled, and his sulky lower lip thrust out. "This time. Pfaw." He spat, and Shane raised his eyebrows, and Mikhail glared back at him as though daring him to do anything about it. "Well, worry us is exactly what you did. You almost destroyed me. I wanted to run away. I left you a terrible message, screaming obscenities in Russian, just so I would not have to care if you lived or died." He shook his head, and his mouth relaxed a little. "I am so very happy to see you well, but if I ever have to leave you again when you are hurt or sick, it will break my heart. You cannot do that again."

"I don't plan to," Shane said shortly.

Mikhail nodded and made a visible effort to get himself together, but he kept hold of Shane's hand. In fact, he clutched it convulsively as they stood in the middle of the crowd. Shane watched his jaw clench and then saw him swallow once or twice, and he wanted to haul him up and hold him and be sweet and soft and all those things, but not here. Not when Mikhail's mother was watching with sympathetic eyes. Not when a thousand people would be there to watch Mikhail come unglued, because he would really hate that.

Finally, he simply turned and tugged Shane after him. "Come. Mutti hides it well, but she is really very tired. We should go home."

In fact, Ylena was more than tired. She was silent in the back of Crick's sedan, and when they made a pit stop in Dixon, she was more than sleeping, she was nearly losing consciousness. Instead of driving to Mikhail's apartment, Shane stayed on I-80 and took her to the hospital in Roseville.

She woke up a little as Shane lifted her up in his arms and carried her through the parking lot into the emergency room. She weighed nothing.

"Look at me," she murmured. "In the arms of a big strong man. All that time I hoped for a handsome prince when Mikhail was a child, and I had to wait for my son's boyfriend to sweep me off my feet."

Shane chuckled gently. "Well, I might have gone for you when I was younger, you know. I had a weakness for femme fatales."

Ylena gave a paper-fragile laugh; her voice, when she spoke, was weak and hoarse. "I was beautiful then. Not so much now."

Shane paused then, to let Mikhail go through the doors first and find them a wheelchair. "Look at him, Ylena," he said, watching Mikhail's brisk movements, the way he was aware, always, of where the two of them were, even as he spoke to hospital officials with the confidence of a lion. He looked up and indicated Shane and his mother, and his eyes—which could be brutally cold, Shane knew from experience—were soft and concerned. "See the way your son looks at you? You are beautiful to him."

Ylena leaned her head against Shane's chest and patted him with a wasted hand. "And so are you, *mal'chik.* So are you."

She was admitted there, given fluids and some pain medication, and the doctor—fortunately *her* doctor was on duty this day—took them both aside out of her hospital room for one of those little chats that Shane could tell Mikhail dreaded.

"You both know this is going to end soon, and it's not going to end well, right?" He was in his early forties and had "family man" plastered all over him. Mikhail seemed to trust him, so Shane did too.

Mikhail's eyebrows arched sardonically. "Since you have been telling her she's dying since June, it would certainly reflect poorly on you if that was not the case," he said dryly, and the doctor managed a smile.

"Fair enough. Mikhail, this could last a while—a couple of weeks. She's very sick, but she's got a tough will, we both know that. She's very reluctant to leave you alone. Have you discussed whether you want to do this here in the hospital or…?"

"I want to take her home," Mikhail said. "We can set up her IV and her pain medication. She has had a nurse who came by once a week, can we still do that?"

The doctor nodded. "It's still going to be hard—you know that, right? She's going to be in pain and slipping in and out. Even if we can get a nurse in for an eight-hour shift every day, you're going to need to be there for the rest of the time."

"You can get a nurse?" Mikhail asked hopefully, and Shane started racking his brains for the contacts he had in case they couldn't.

The doctor consulted the chart in front of him, though, and nodded. "I'm almost positive her insurance covers that. They should also cover a bed—the kind that raises and lowers and has IV racks and some monitors. You'll need a day to get set up, if you still want to do this, and we'll keep her until then."

"I still want to," Mikhail told him, but he was firming up his jaw as though the task daunted him, and Shane reached down and grabbed his hand.

"I don't have much to do for the next few weeks, Mickey. Don't worry. You'll have help." Mikhail gave him a look like a drowning man would give a rope, and the doctor nodded approvingly.

"Excellent," the doctor said. "I'm glad to know it won't just be you."

"My mother's church can help too," Mikhail mumbled. He was clutching Shane's hand hard enough to cut off the circulation, but Shane wasn't going to complain.

"Here," said the doctor. "This should have the insurance information you need to get set up." He handed Mikhail a card with numbers scrawled on it, and for the first time, Shane saw his lion-hearted dancer look a little lost.

"I… I do not know insurance companies," he said almost shyly. "I have no insurance, and Mutti always handled hers."

Shane took the card from him and put it carefully in his wallet, ignoring Mikhail's surprise. "I'm good at that shit, Mickey. No worries. When will she be ready tomorrow, doc?"

The doctor consulted his chart again, not even raising an eyebrow at the way Shane had commandeered the situation. Shane looked mildly back at Mikhail's surprise, and then the two of them turned their attention to the list of instructions that the doctor was handing them and on all that needed to be done.

TWO hours later, Mikhail had unpacked and aired out the small apartment, and Shane was sitting at the little glass-topped kitchen table, rubbing the back of his neck. He'd been on the phone since they had walked in the door, and he thought that finally—*finally*—he'd made all of the preparations necessary to bring an eighty-pound woman home for her last few weeks.

With a sigh he leaned forward, squinted in the poor light from the hanging fixture overhead, and ran through the checklist again. Suddenly, there were two hands—hard, warm, and moist from the shower— massaging his neck and his shoulders, and he groaned in sheer hedonism.

"God, Mickey—that's awesome." He dropped his head forward and was unprepared for Mikhail's sulky mouth to start moving on the base of his neck. He shivered, and a cold ball of excitement began to pulse in the pit of his stomach along with an aching in his groin.

"How is that?" Mikhail whispered in his ear before kissing his way back down Shane's jaw and nibbling on his neck.

"At least one standard deviation above awesome." Mikhail's chuckle brushed the back of his neck, and Shane fought off a hard, quick shudder of desire.

Mikhail moved up and started to work on Shane's other side. "And how is this?"

Shane whimpered. The warm hands on his flesh, Mikhail's pouty, kissy little mouth…. "Amazing," he breathed. And then, while he was still sane—"You're sure you want to do this now? With your mother and all?"

Mikhail wrapped an arm around Shane's chest, and Shane leaned back into him and swallowed. Mikhail wasn't wearing a shirt. The swallowing didn't take. He tried again and moaned a little in the other man's embrace.

"You want I should wait until my mother is dead to find happiness? There is something very wrong with that, don't you think?" For a moment Mikhail rested his cheek against Shane's, and Shane rubbed up against him. "Besides," he added practically, "I have just tested clean after my window period. And I know you are practically a virgin. This could be my only chance to ever have sex *without* a condom, and I am not going to pass that up."

Shane snorted. "I wouldn't count on it being your *only* one," he said with some determination, "but other than that, you're absolutely right. You should be happy now."

He stood then and turned, and Mikhail followed him. Shane looked down into his eyes, their color almost transparent in the soft light, and held Mikhail's face between his palms, then lowered his head for a kiss.

And the two of them exploded.

Mouths tangled, meshed, devoured. Shane's breath came in ragged pants, and his hands came up to Mikhail's bare shoulders, his thumbs resting on Mikhail's collarbones as he backed the smaller man into the hallway wall.

Mikhail grunted and pushed under Shane's sweater and T-shirt. Shane gasped and sucked in his stomach, and Mikhail made a little sound of unhappiness. His hands were rough as he broke off the kiss and tugged Shane's shirts up above his head, dropping them right there on the floor. He pushed on Shane's shoulders, and as Shane backed up, Mikhail surveyed his chest and the scars on his side, over his ribs, that were still raw and red.

His hand came up to caress them, the touch absurdly gentle. He traced the long, uneven rip on Shane's side, the edges ragged with the infection that had almost killed Shane, and then, with shaking fingers, ran a little pathway over the network of even, slicing surgery scars that went everywhere from abdomen to his chest.

Shane captured his hand with a firm grip. "Hey," he murmured. "It's okay. I really am fine."

Mikhail nodded wordlessly and then leaned forward and kissed the bare skin of Shane's shoulder, kissed him again down the centerline, and again along the other side. Shane huffed out air and tilted his head back, wrapping his arms under Mikhail's and across his back as Mikhail continued. He rubbed his hands in Shane's pelt, making delighted sounds, and lowered his head to a flat, plum-colored nipple and sucked hard, then worried the end with his teeth.

"Aahhhhh…," Shane gasped, and Mikhail looked up at him, a smile flirting with his sulky mouth.

"You trust me?" Mikhail whispered huskily, and Shane gaped at him, his eyes having trouble focusing from the whole-body tingle that was buzzing along his skin.

"Trust you?" God, he felt dumb. Mikhail's hand reached into his belt and started to tug. At first Shane thought they were going to crush up against each other again, which made his brain fuzz-crackle because (ohmigod!) Mickey wasn't wearing anything but boxer shorts with little lines on them, and then Mikhail undid the buckle and shoved Shane's jeans and briefs down to his knees, and Shane's brain gave up the fuzz-crackle and just plain exploded.

"Yes," Mikhail muttered, looking at Shane's cock with big eyes and running a pointed pink tongue over his full lower lip. "Trust me. That once will not be enough. That doing this will not mean I have 'done that'." He ripped his eyes way from Shane's lower body and looked earnestly into Shane's eyes. "Do you trust me now, to do this?"

Shane whimpered a little, and Mikhail reached out a hand and danced a flirting little touch along the tender skin of his erection, his fingers teasing the coarse black hair at his groin. "Oh God," he rasped. "Oh geez, Mickey, I really wish you would."

Mikhail's look under his brows went sideways and sly. "Has anyone told you that your cock is enormous?" he asked with a little bit of wonder. He wrapped his hand around Shane and showed that his fingers did not touch his thumb. "This is asking something from someone who has not done this in nearly six months."

Shane gave a laugh that was almost hysterical and tilted his head back. Mikhail kept that warm, strong grip on his dumb-stick and pretty much steered him backward until he was leaning against the other wall, and still stroking, went down on his knees in the carpeted hallway.

Shane looked down at him. Mikhail held his cock straight out and, meeting Shane's eyes, extended that wicked tongue and swiped upward from the slit to the edge of the mushroom head, and Shane closed his eyes and groaned. "Just remember I haven't done this in nearly two years," he hissed. "That there is a loaded weapon in your hand."

Mikhail opened his mouth and hollowed his cheeks, engulfing the head and nothing else, then allowed his lips to close and glide over Shane's most sensitive skin. He pulled back with an audible smack and said, "Then maybe I should clean it before it goes off, hmm?"

His mouth was warm and moist and very skilled. He moved his lips to the base of Shane's cock and then swallowed, taking Shane all in, and the sensation of his throat working on the wide, flat cockhead almost made Shane come right there. Shane made an unintelligible noise and tangled his hand in Mikhail's wildly curly hair, and Mikhail continued to do exactly what he wanted, and what he wanted was to blow Shane's mind.

He pulled back and swirled his tongue around the head and then grabbed the whole of the heavy flesh and, using spit and pre-come as lube, pumped Shane slowly with his hand while his tongue and tiny grazes with his teeth performed miracles at the crown.

And then he moved his other hand up to Shane's ass, and Shane had to work hard to keep his knees from buckling. Mikhail's fingers tickled the edge of Shane's cleft, and Shane adjusted his legs and bent his knees, because he was completely shameless about wanting those tickling fingers to explore even deeper.

Mikhail was shameless about wanting to drive Shane crazy before he did.

First he moved his hand again, taking advantage of Shane's spread legs to insinuate between them and stroke the tender flesh between Shane's entrance and his scrotum and then to gently cup the tenderness of Shane's balls.

And he never stopped the pumping of his other hand or the playing of his tongue and teeth on the head of Shane's straining cock.

When a spit-slick finger toyed with Shane's entrance, Shane threw his head back against the wall hard enough to see stars and tried to form real words. "Gonna come...."

Mikhail looked up from his position on the floor with wicked, avid eyes. "So? You are clean—all those hospital tests, don't tell me you are not..."

Shane choked back a strained laugh. "Wanna fuck!" he practically whined.

Mikhail wrapped his lips around Shane's rampant cock again and thrust forward quickly and then pulled back, while the finger in Shane's ass did the same thing. Shane closed his eyes and tried to count the dots behind them until he felt air on his cock, teasing him still, and he looked down at his lover, the man he'd been trying to seduce since October.

When Mikhail looked up again to speak this time, his face was shiny with spit and pre-come. "Silly man," he said, his eyes heavy lidded and playful. "If you think, after all this time, you will only come once tonight, you have not been paying attention."

And with that he thrust Shane's cock practically down his throat and added another finger into Shane's ass, and Shane pumped come until his knees buckled, and Mikhail had to let go of him so he could slide down the wall.

When his vision cleared, Mikhail had leaned forward to put his head on Shane's shoulder, and he was absorbed in the task of stroking Shane's chest hair. Shane blushed and caught his hand.

"I like," Mikhail murmured softly. "Let me touch."

"Okay. You win. Anyone who can make me come that hard that fast, I guess he gets a few liberties with my body." Shane blinked again, hard, and then realized that he had a bare-chested armful of gay Russian and he wasn't doing anything about it. He brought his hand up to the back of Mikhail's head and buried his fingers in the springy curls to massage Mikhail's scalp. Mickey shivered sensuously and leaned into his touch like a cat.

"You liked?" Mikhail asked, and Shane had to look at his expression to see if he was serious. He was peering at Shane with a surprising shyness—and a true willingness to please.

"Oooooohhh yeah," Shane answered, and then he lowered his face to kiss that shy smile. Mikhail responded and rolled over, taking advantage of Shane's wide chest to sprawl on top of him, grinding his groin up against Shane's thigh. Shane felt his own cock twitch and pulled away from the kiss for long enough to say, "Mickey, any chance we can do this on the bed? I'm getting a bruise on my shoulders from the baseboard."

Mikhail laughed wickedly and popped up off of him with the quickness of the young before extending a hand. Shane ignored it and clambered after him, feeling old and clumsy.

Mikhail rolled his eyes. "I held out a hand—you could not take it?"

"I'm not that decrepit!" Shane protested, bending down to get the clothes he'd kicked his way out of. He figured his shirt and sweater would just stay on the floor of the living room, but a man never knew when he might need his pants.

"You are proud, that's what you are," Mikhail accused, taking the hand that didn't hold the clothes. There was affection in his voice so Shane figured he was kidding. Since their hands were linked anyway, Mikhail started leading them down the hall and into his bedroom.

"I have no pride whatsoever," Shane protested mildly, and Mikhail grunted.

"That is a lie. You have no vanity, that is true, but you have pride." He turned on the light in his room and managed to look self-conscious. "And here you have it. The room of a man who still lives with his mother."

Shane laughed and dumped his clothes on the dresser, next to the treasure box. "You're dating a man who has more cats than most grandmothers. I think we're both safely out of the realm of the cool and popular." He swung around to Mikhail then and pulled the guy into his arms for a kiss. "At least you're pretty and can dance—that puts you at least five steps up on the coolness ladder."

Mikhail peered at him thoughtfully. "Is that why you want me?" he asked, without a trace of playfulness. "Because I am pretty and can dance?"

Shane smiled, remembering the first time he'd seen Mikhail, moving sinuously under the gold October sun. "That's who I wanted when I first saw you," he said now. "And then you grabbed my hand and talked, and... damn. The whole rest of the package... it was like a really pretty Macy's wrapping job on what you wanted most for Christmas as a kid. And you wanted me too." Shane shrugged and blushed and looked away, pretty sure he was never going to get across what that meant to him, that Mikhail had wanted him too.

Mikhail was looking up at him with something like wonder. He didn't answer but pushed himself up on his toes and met Shane's mouth, pulling him down and into the kiss with shaking hands and desperation. Shane answered him back, just as hard and just as wanting. Shane took over this time, turning Mikhail around and steering him toward the bed. His hand spanned Mikhail's neck, his shoulders, his chest. For a moment he let himself play with the small patch of gold chest hair in the center, before he spread his hands and rubbed until he felt tiny nipples pebbling in his palms.

Mikhail grunted when he backed up against the bed—it was the kind with a pedestal and drawers underneath for his clothes, so it didn't move at all—and then pulled away from Shane and tried to turn around.

Shane grunted and caught him by the shoulders and sat him down, then pushed him backward until he was lying down.

"What are we doing?" Mikhail asked, narrowing his eyes with a little bit of irritation, and Shane flopped down on the bed next to him, planting little nibbles on his abdomen and enjoying the hissing sounds Mikhail made as he squirmed beneath Shane's mouth.

"Exploring," Shane said, sticking out his own tongue and teasing a little divot of a navel.

"Exploring?" Mikhail tried to push himself onto his elbows, and Shane stopped him with a flattened palm in the center of his chest. "I don't want to go... ahhh... ahhhh... ahhh..."— because Shane was kissing down his happy trail of golden fur to the elastic on his boxers— "*exploring,*" he finally hissed.

"No?" Shane teased, palming Mickey's erection through his boxers. "No exploring?"

"No, you stupid man!" Mikhail arched against his hand in hunger. "I don't want you to go *exploring,* I want you to go *spelunking*!"

Shane had to stop for a minute to giggle into the soft skin of the smaller man's hard abdomen. "Spelunking? Is that what we're doing?"

It was hard for Mikhail to keep his moue of irritation when he was fighting a battle with his own laughter. "No, it is *not* what we're doing," he said, giggling back. "It is what I'm *waiting* for you to do!"

Shane's giggles died down and he rested his cheek on Mikhail's stomach and looked soberly up his body. "Don't worry, Mickey. I'll make this good for you. I promise."

Mikhail's hand came out and stroked his dark hair away from his eyes. There was something indefinable, something vulnerable, in the other man's face.

"You've already kept that promise about a hundred times over," he said musingly. "I don't see how it can be any better."

Shane grinned evilly, and the moment lightened. He shucked Mickey's boxers down his legs and took that slender cock into his hot mouth. Mikhail gasped, and the moment burned passionate just that quickly.

He tasted so good. A little like soap and a lot like clean skin—spice, sweetness, soft skin, hard strength. Shane tightened his lips against Mikhail's base and sucked hard, loving the surprised gasp he brought out. With some wiggling, he managed to put himself right between Mikhail's legs, and his hands weren't soft or tender as he shoved at the back of Mickey's thighs until his knees were bent and his body, all of it, was splayed out to look at—and to play with.

Mikhail gasped again and came a little. Shane let it trickle out of his mouth and down the crease of the other man's thigh. He skated his fingers on it, rubbing it into the space between the back of the blond, furry testicles and the smooth pucker of his anus, and when Mikhail whimpered and gasped and thrust into his mouth, he knew he was doing it right.

"Please…," Mikhail begged, and if Shane could have grinned, he would have. Mickey wouldn't beg if it wasn't urgent. Gently he thrust one finger in and stretched, and then two. Mikhail sighed and pushed down, begging for more, and Shane's cock perked up under his belly, and he thought he might be able to give just that.

"Mickey, you got something in your drawer for me?"

"Use spit…."

"I'm not fucking you with a fingerful of spit for lube!"

"Fine!" What came next sounded like the sort of Russian that wouldn't be found in any textbooks, and Mikhail wriggled across the bed on his back to root around in the drawer that pulled out under the bed. Shane followed him and kept sucking and kept his fingers right where they had been, and the small bottle of lubricant that hit him on the forehead was thrown with unnecessary force.

"Hey!" Shane protested, even as he took the bottle and snicked the lid, adding a dollop to his fingers and greasing Mikhail's entrance up right.

"I will be nicer to you when *you are fucking me, dammit!*" Mikhail growled back, and Shane laughed sincerely before moving up the bed, dragging his body up Mikhail's, and stopping, finally, when they were face to face. Shane moved his hand and positioned himself right where he needed to be and pushed just enough to let Mikhail know he was serious.

Mikhail took a deep breath and stilled the thrashing of his wiry, athletic body to look up and meet Shane's eyes.

"You don't need to worry," Mikhail murmured, answering something in Shane's expression that he hadn't voiced. "I know this means something."

"Yeah," Shane sighed, and he thrust home.

The tight ring of muscle was relaxed, and Mikhail had enough control not to tighten up, so he slid in so slick it was like he belonged there. Mikhail gasped and arched beneath him, and together they began to move. Shane's body wasn't fully healed, so he had to work hard to not move like he hurt, and that was okay. Mikhail managed "tender speed" for an admirable length of time, with much touching of Shane's face and nuzzling of his neck, and every touch and kiss and stroke sent Shane higher, there was no doubt about that. About the time Shane was as high as he could get and the pain in his side was far less important than the pleasure underneath him, Mikhail started fucking him back. Shane's cock swelled even more, and his hips thrust and pumped, and the man beneath him, the man who fascinated him and set his skin blazing and made everything from his dick to his heart ache and throb with wanting, looked intensely back at him and begged him for more.

Shane gave him everything, hard and fast and deep and long, and Mikhail wrapped his legs around Shane's hips, buried his face into Shane's neck, and groaned, his asshole spasming around Shane's erection as their bodies grew slick with his come. Shane's vision went dark, and he groaned back, surged powerfully forward, and came.

His body kept going, shuddering endlessly, and he wrapped his arms around Mikhail's shoulders and clutched him tighter while the other man stroked his neck and his chest and soothed him until the orgasm passed.

They lay there together for quite some time before Shane slid sideways—he didn't want to crush Mikhail, and he knew he could. Mickey came with him and spent some more time stroking his chest, which was now sweaty and matted, and Shane shook his head.

"Are you sure you wouldn't rather I wax?"

Mikhail wrinkled his nose. "I don't know who told you that was a good idea, but whoever it was should be shot."

"Actually, her exact words were that if I ever took my shirt off in the forest, *I* would be the one who'd be shot, but that's okay. I'd rather listen to you anyway."

Mikhail wrinkled his nose. "Have you had *any* lover who has not left you with scars?" he asked unhappily.

"You," Shane replied promptly. "Do me a favor and don't fuck this up!"

Mikhail didn't laugh. He didn't even crack a smile. "I shall do my best."

They didn't talk anymore about old lovers and promises. They played with each other's skin and kissed random places on each other's bodies and told terrible jokes about the dangers of spelunking without the right equipment. Mikhail touched his scars some more, and Shane told him about the pain honestly, and Shane stroked the ruin on the inside of Mikhail's arms, and Mikhail returned the favor. They kissed a lot without urgency, and then they kissed some more with urgency, and then Mikhail finally got his wish, and Shane was behind him, pounding unmercifully while Mikhail braced himself against the wall and Shane wrapped his arm around Mikhail's chest. They fell asleep a little after that, Shane spooned around his lover protectively, but he jerked awake at around eleven o'clock, aware that as lovely as this was, he couldn't stay.

He got up quietly and used the shower, then came back and gathered his clothes from the various rooms and dressed. Mikhail was still sleeping, and Shane watched him for a moment before kissing his temple and shaking him gently. He looked so young—and so innocent. Shane was pretty sure that neither one of those was a lie.

"Mickey," he muttered now reluctantly. "Mickey, baby, I've got to go."

Mikhail opened his eyes enough to pout. "No," he mumbled sulkily.

"Yes," Shane told him with some gentleness. "I've got to let the dogs in and the cats out and then vice versa. I've got to trade Crick's car in and get the GTO back. I'd love to spend some time with you here—you've got to know that. But I've got shit to take care of, and I can't."

Mikhail sighed and reached a hand up to his cheek. "I have never spent the night with a man," he muttered. "I was looking forward to it."

Shane smiled and kissed him again. He tasted sleepy and used and delicious. "Well, we'll get our chance, I promise. I'll be back tomorrow before they deliver the bed and shit, okay? Then we'll go get your mom."

Mikhail's eyes narrowed a little, and he woke up some more. "Thank you," he muttered. "All the things you do for us—thank you."

"I'd do anything for you, Mickey. Don't ever forget that, okay?"

He stood and Mikhail dropped his hand, and Shane bent down and kissed his cheek one more time and was gone.

Chapter *15*

One more mile is all we have. You got nothing to fear.

"One More Mile"—Tom McRae

MIKHAIL woke up surrounded by Shane's smell and extremely disappointed that Shane was not there instead. Then he heard a firm knock on the door, and as he slid into a pair of sweats to answer it, he thought in panic that it must be the people with the bed and medical supplies and that he had severely overslept.

It turned out to be Shane, looking tired and freshly showered but carrying a box of doughnuts and Starbucks and a small plastic shopping bag and a large one, which he set down on the table. He looked so dear and earnest that Mikhail took the food and coffee from his hands and set them down on the table and then launched himself into the man's arms without warning.

Shane hissed out a breath and then wrapped his arms around Mikhail and held him tight, dropping a kiss onto the top of his head and then hissing again as Mikhail tightened the hug. Mikhail backed up and frowned.

"You hurt yourself last night, yes?"

Shane shrugged. "It was lots of things—the long drive, what we were doing, and the run this morning…."

"Run? We didn't get enough exercise last night?" Mikhail frowned at him some more and sat down, blowing on his coffee and sipping carefully because it was very hot.

"It's my day to go running with Deacon." Shane shrugged again. "Since he was bringing the car by to swap out, I wasn't going to tell him no. Besides. If I didn't go running, he'd know I hurt, and if he knew I hurt, he'd be here and helping before you could run for the hills."

Mikhail sighed and looked unhappily at his coffee. "I will meet him someday—I promised. I will hold to that."

Shane nodded and sat down beside him. "But not today. I know it."

Mikhail smiled gratefully and then felt like shit. Running away? What a little coward he had proven to be. But Shane, sipping his coffee and blinking to try to wake himself up, did not look like he felt like that. "You will nap while I shower, please?"

Shane looked down at himself. He was dressed in jeans and a hooded sweatshirt, and Mikhail could see him calculate how bad he could possibly look when the medical supply company arrived.

"No one will care what you look like but me," Mikhail said briskly, taking Shane's arm and setting his coffee down. "And all I care about is that you do not fall asleep between here and Roseville." It was ludicrous, of course, because Roseville was fifteen minutes away in traffic, but Shane gave him a sleepy, sideways grin and let himself be led back to Mikhail's bed.

He kicked off his tennis shoes and sprawled out there, taking the edge of the blue plaid coverlet under his arms like a child and smiled at Mikhail as he shucked his sweats and got ready to walk across the hall.

"You know I'm only lying here so I can smell us together, right?"

Mikhail turned around and gave him a little kiss on the temple, much as Shane had given him the night before as he was leaving. "Of course you are," he said, and even he knew that his sarcasm had leeched away and he sounded almost sweet.

Mikhail took his shower and dressed, and then brought his coffee and another doughnut into his room, along with a chair so he could sit at his dresser with his laptop while Shane was sleeping. Curiosity had gotten the better of him, and he had checked to see what was in the shopping bags.

The larger one held a hand-knit throw, which he knew had to be from Benny and was probably for his mother. The way their minds worked sometimes, he thought wryly. The other was an iPod—smaller than his but with much, much more memory and a larger screen. Mikhail sighed as he looked at the incriminating white box. Shane had one—it was older than this one, but it also had the biggest cache of memory. Mikhail knew the gift had to be for him.

"Dammit," he muttered, and he saw Shane open one sleepy eye at him.

"Take it," the big man sighed into the cradle of his arms. "This next month is gonna suck so bad. You need something to take you away from all that."

He sighed then and rolled to his other side, hunching his shoulders protectively over his chest, and Mikhail shook his head. First he got out the throw that Shane had brought and used it to drape over his shoulders, since he was lying on top of the comforter and it was still chilly in the apartment. Then he pulled out the iPod and started playing with it, plugging it into the laptop and downloading his entire music list onto it, as well as some of his favorite movies and television shows. It took a while—the laptop was old and slow—but it gave him something to do besides worry before the expected knock came at the door.

When it did he shook Shane gently by the arm and then went out to answer it, and the day really began.

Shane was right. That first day alone was exhausting and painful, and the next few weeks only got worse.

They had to move the furniture around in the front room, setting the bed up along the back wall where the couch once had been and moving the couch to the side, which made the small living room feel like it was made for Barbie dolls and not grown men. When Shane carried Ylena in to put her on the bed, though, she had smiled tiredly and said that now she could watch as many movies as she wanted. They tried to do that for her—there was always one playing on the television for the next couple of weeks, although, after the nurse came and hooked up her pain medication, it seemed sometimes as though that was the best movie of all.

Later, Mikhail would not be sure how Shane managed to pull it off. The man was still recovering himself, and yet he managed to be there when Mikhail could not. He did the grocery shopping, the laundry, and when the month was over, Mikhail realized Shane had paid the bills and nobody noticed. He helped the nurse change Ylena's sheets, sat with her in the afternoons and evenings when there was nobody else, and then left in the evenings to go attend his own household. And he usually gave Mikhail a ride to and from work as well.

Ylena's church people would come and take up the slack, and for them Mikhail was both grateful and resentful. Yes—they were indispensable. But they had always treated Mikhail, with his open sexuality and his painful past, as either something to pity or something to shun. They often tried to proselytize, and Mikhail would simply turn and walk out of the room. He wearied—was already weary—of hearing Ylena defending him as he left. They were even ruder to Shane, and although Mikhail's grounded, even-tempered lover would simply smile and go find something else to do rather than visit with the stiffly postured, exactly dressed women who sat on the couch and visited Ylena, Mikhail's fury at them—at his people in general—grew into a molten lead weight in his stomach during those final weeks of his mother's life.

One night, Shane did not appear to pick him up as promised, and Mikhail trotted home on his own. He was actually grateful for the walk—it gave him a chance to listen to his music and to think about nothing at all—but when he arrived home, he saw the GTO in its usual spot in the parking lot, and was puzzled.

He opened the apartment door, a question on his lips, when his mother looked up from her bed and shushed him. Shane was sitting next to her bed, his head resting on his arm, fast asleep. Next to him was a photo album, wide open, showing Mikhail as a child on stage, where he had grown up.

"He is very tired, *lubime*," Ylena said softly. "He adopted another dog from the shelter, and it has been sick. He's been telling me about vet appointments and cleaning carpets and paperwork for his job and his sick leave. They are having an investigation into his injury. He says he might end up with a censure on his record—can you imagine?"

A part of Mikhail wanted to say, *Yes, I hope they fire him for being an asinine fool who would risk himself like that,* but most of him wanted to go find the people making Shane's life difficult and kick them in the balls.

"I can imagine that he did not tell me because he did not want to worry me," was what Mikhail said instead. He did not realize how hurt he was until the words came out.

Ylena sighed and held out her hand. "That is exactly why he did not tell you."

Mikhail came to her and took her hand. It was the first time she had been lucid in nearly two days. There had been much moaning, when she lost control of her will and the pain took over, and some meandering in Russian. Mikhail heard her call for her father and her mother, both of whom had been dead for some time. It occurred to him that this could be one of the last times he had his mother—truly, his mother—to speak to.

"I think he has come to love you," he told her, and even exhausted and dying, her smile was still alive.

"I think so too. And I him. And that is why I want you both to do something for me."

"You need water, Mutti? Food?" They had been feeding her Cream of Wheat or mashed vegetables if she could keep it down. If truth be known, most of her food and water came to her through the tube in her arm.

"No. I need you two to go away for a day. Tomorrow. Is your day off, yes?"

"Da. But we cannot…."

"Of course you can. I will not die tomorrow. I promise. I will not die the next day. The day after that I cannot promise, but for a day and a night, I want you to be happy. I remember—you used to go out to clubs and be gone for three days. You would come home and be tired and used and empty. I want you to go somewhere and be happy. I want to see you come home with your face flushed because you are full of something you cannot wait to tell me." She indicated the photo album at her hand.

"I never got to see you come home from school excited about something, Mikhail. The closest I have ever seen to this has been the first night you came home after he had taken you to dinner and to the bookstore. Let me see that again."

Mikhail swallowed hard and moved close enough to Shane to brush his coarse, curly dark hair off his brow and away from his eyes. "Is that what you are waiting for?" he asked, hating the question, hating himself for asking it. But it was nearly February, and she was still fighting, still here. So many days she had been lost, in pain, wandering around a past she so obviously wanted to join. The only reason his mother was still here, fighting, was to look after him. He wanted her to be at peace, and if death was that path, well, then, perhaps it was time for Ylena to walk it.

"No," Ylena said softly. "What I am waiting for, I will perhaps never find. But this will be close, yes?"

Mikhail knelt then and laid his head next to Shane's. "For you. And for him. Yes. We will take a day off of worry. I will make him show me his dogs—the new one is very young. He loves it very much—it is his first puppy. I will visit with his cats." He puffed out a small laugh. "I like cats, Mutti. Do you think he will let me adopt one, just for me?"

Ylena's eyes were half closed, but her next word was very, very bright. "Pffaw!" she announced. "He will adopt an entire shelter, just to make you smile."

Later, he would wake Shane up to say be there in the morning and come pick him up, they were having a break. Later he would hold his lover's face in his hands and kiss him and try to tell him all the things in his heart that he could not seem to say these days. Later he would fall asleep on the couch and listen for his mother's heart monitor, the incessant music that had lulled him to sleep each night and which had seemed to instill in him a terrible loathing of techno-pop.

But that would be later. For this moment he would just rub Shane's back through his sweatshirt and feel his mother's fingers in his hair and accept that there were some things you could not change and some things that you should.

SHANE arrived the next morning looking exhausted and happy. He'd brought a movie for Ylena to watch while they were gone and promised to have Mikhail back late that evening, and Ylena insisted it be late the next evening.

"You two have phones. You have numbers. If there is a change, they will call you. For now, go. Be happy. Please."

They left her in the care of her friends and the nurse, but they left reluctantly. Shane wanted to say something, Mikhail could tell. When Mikhail snapped, "If that damned woman dies while we are gone, I shall hire a medium to scold her in the afterlife for a week," Shane had laughed.

"I'll put in for that," he agreed, and they had both met each other's weary eyes and smiled.

Then they had gotten in the GTO, and the world seemed to open beneath their feet.

"Hey, Mickey," Shane said as he was starting the car, "since you've got two days, how about we get out of here?"

Mikhail blinked at him. "Out of here? Where is here?"

Shane waved his hands. "Out of the valley—out of the fucking fog bowl, man!" It had not rained much this year, but the fog had seemed to coat the sun in gray for nearly every day since Mikhail and Ylena's return. Mikhail found he was staring at Shane with wide, shiny eyes. The prospect of being some place with sunshine, some place, any place, far away from his tiny apartment, a place where they could see gold light and blue sky, almost brought him to tears.

"I think that would be amazing," Mikhail said, and he was aware that muscles in his face were starting to ache. They hadn't been used for a while, but he was pretty sure he was using them to smile.

Shane stopped at the grocery store and bought sodas and French bread and salami to make simple sandwiches along with some apples and cookies. They got coffee at the Starbucks next door, hopped in the car, plugged in Shane's iPod, and went.

Mikhail practically hung his head out the window like a dog tasting the wind when they cleared Rocklin on I-80 and the sun began to make an appearance. By the time they had cleared Penryn, Shane had put on the sunglasses hanging from the visor and Mikhail was lying back in the seat, closing his eyes and bathing his face in the sunshine.

He opened his eyes as they started up the hill toward Auburn, and when he saw the sign for Bell Road, he made a connection.

"This is near Grass Valley, is it not?"

"Yeah, why?" Shane replied, startled. They had existed in a pleasant, companionable silence for a little while, and the music—Shane had downloaded the mix CD Mikhail had given him for Christmas—had begun to saturate their bones with movement and a little bit of angry joy. It was a change from the dirge and the gray that had filled them for the past weeks.

"I know people who live there!" Mikhail said excitedly. "The people who give me rides when I work at the faires. Rose and Arlen. They are nice people—they run a horse ranch...." He closed his eyes to remember and then stopped with a smile. "I think it is simply called Arlen Rose. I wonder if we will see signs for their ranch."

Shane took the Bell Road turn off to Highway 49 and said, "I bet we can do better than that. Keep your eye out for a feed store, will you?"

Mikhail was impressed with Shane's wisdom in these things—and the clerk at the feed store knew exactly where to find the Arlen Rose.

As Shane went up Highway 49, Mikhail truly began to see a world beyond the one he lived in. As they neared Grass Valley and Colfax, there were trees—like a forest, only with the promise of a big, forest-dwelling suburb beyond all of the trees. The turn off they took from the highway took them on a terribly winding road, so narrow that once, when they were meeting a car coming toward them, the car had to back up to pull onto the shoulder so that they could pass. Mikhail thought of Arlen and Rose bringing a horse trailer up this road and back every weekend for years, and he actually turned a little pale. They were such nice people, and they seemed to have existed right close to death for such a terribly long time. He said as much to Shane, and Shane had grunted in return, his hands white-knuckled on the wheel.

Eventually though, they saw a sign, brightly painted and nailed to white four-by-fours, sunk hardily into the red clay and decomposed granite of the driveway. Shane pulled off and gave a sigh of relief. The road beyond the sign was nice and wide, and as they pulled off into the driveway to their left—the one with the name of the ranch wrought in an iron arch above their heads—Mikhail saw Rose out in one of the rings, working one of the enormous black-brown draft horses that they trained.

As Shane brought the car to a halt and turned off the music, Mikhail found he was practically leaping out of the car for a chance to stretch and feel some more of that glorious (albeit cold) sunshine on his face. He reached into the car for his hat (another gift from Benny—Mikhail wanted to visit a yarn store just to buy her colors besides dark brown and navy blue) and scarf and waited for Shane to do the same. Shane was wearing the dark green scarf Ylena had made him, and Mikhail wondered at what a fool he was for that to make his throat thick and achy with pride.

Rose looked up and nodded at the two of them as they approached, and they let her work. Mikhail, who knew little of these things (and who was stoically hiding his terror at being near such a large animal) thought she was amazing. Dressed in jeans and a hooded sweatshirt, with leather gloves and boots to protect her feet from the red muck of the pen, she looked younger than her sixty or so years in spite of her gray bun and weathered face. Mostly, she looked happy.

When she was finished and the horse was sweating and done, she patted the creature's nose and offered him a carrot from her pocket. Then she grabbed the bridle firmly and started leading the horse out of the ring.

"Heya, Mikhail—great to see you, boy! What're you doing out in this neck of the woods?" Her voice was crisp but genuinely affectionate, and Mikhail was glad they'd come, horrifying road, terrifying horse, and all.

"Hello, Rose. My friend and I were out driving, and I thought we would look you up. It is okay?"

Rose flashed him a brief smile in welcome. She handed the horse to a boy of about fourteen, who took him into the stable to groom and feed, then took off her gloves and washed her hands at a spigot before drying them on a nearby towel. When she was done, she gave Mikhail an unexpected hug and then offered her hand to Shane.

"I'm Rosie MacAvoy—nice to meet you!"

Shane smiled his open-hearted smile. "Shane Perkins. Nice to meet you back."

"So, Mikhail, what're you doing out here?"

Mikhail and Shane met quiet eyes, and Mikhail shrugged nonchalantly. "Out for a ride. I remembered that you were out here, and it was as good a place to visit as any. How is Arlen? I wanted Shane to meet him too."

Rosie's eyes sharpened, and she looked at Shane again. Then she looked at the two of them together, and then she smiled warmly. "He's at the doctor's right now. He'll be sorry he missed you, boy!" She turned and started walking toward the family-sized ranch house and jerked her chin for Mikhail to follow. "You want cookies? My daughter baked up a bunch of them so Arlen wouldn't give the doctor any grief. Come on in and sit a minute."

They did, following her into a cluttered sort of space full of old tack and business mail on the table and dogs sleeping on the couches. It was the space of people who spent more time outside than they did inside, and Mikhail had to smile as he sat at the kitchen table and Rosie moved a flat of vaccines and veterinary supplies out of his way so she could pour him a glass of milk. It was good that they were not perfect. Perfect places made him uncomfortable, and one look at Shane's comfortable, open smile as Rosie handed him some milk and cookies told him the same thing was true for Shane.

"So," Mikhail said quietly. "Arlen, he is okay?" Mikhail sincerely hoped so. He did not think he could stand the story of one more person dying a slow, painful death at this moment.

Rose eased his fears by waving a hand. "Oh yeah. He injured his back, though—nothing too traumatic, but enough to make us start looking for someone to take over the breaking."

"Do you have someone in mind?" Shane asked eagerly, and Mikhail looked at him, startled. "Because I've got some friends who are damned good at it and could really use the business."

Rosie looked surprised and then bemused. And then Shane started to talk—about Deacon and Crick and the surrogate family he obviously adored, and she began to look more and more intrigued.

"We'd still be boarding," she said slowly, as though feeling her way through the idea, "but really, what we need is someone to spend about a year breaking them and training the riders how to break them. We need someone really patient...."

"Deacon's your man," Shane said confidently, and Rosie shook her head warningly.

"I hope so, Mr. Perkins. These animals are under a lot of stress—the armor clinks, the weight, the crowd, the battle maneuvers. It's a two-man job—it's why you need a trainer and a rider. I mean, I've heard some good things about your friend's ranch—but there's some nasty rumors about the health of the horses...."

"They're bullshit," Shane said abruptly, and Rosie blinked, startled again by Shane at his most socially awkward.

He blushed. "I'm sorry—it's just...." He looked at Mikhail and shrugged. "These guys, this whole family—I showed up on their doorstep to take their statement, you know? Benny's crazy father had just tried to take her baby, Crick had gotten back from Iraq with major injuries about two months before, and Deacon had just been *beaten* by a police officer he had to take to court earlier that spring. Their whole lives should have been falling apart. They should have *hated* me. And they asked me in for coffee instead. They cracked jokes and made each other laugh, and when things got too tough for Deacon to handle, they let him walk out and gave him his space. And then they invited me to Sunday dinner. The town can't handle Deacon and Crick because they both grew up there and they've got baggage, but that's the town's problem. Me? I just spent a week and a half in a hospital, and the family visited me in shifts so I wouldn't have to be alone. I'd lay down and die for these people. Please, Ms. MacAvoy—please, just give them a chance."

A quiet fell over the table, and Rosie looked at Shane with both surprise and, Mikhail was pleased to see, quiet admiration.

"I'll talk to Arlen about it," she said after a moment. "We'd have to see your Deacon in action first, but if Arlen says it's okay, we'll come out and see what he can do. Most of our riders live in Sacramento—the commute is probably shorter for them, and that wouldn't be a hardship. But first we'll have to see what he can do. I don't want to give my friends' horses to someone who won't treat them right, you hear me?"

Shane nodded, a slow, sunshine grin breaking out over his face, and Mikhail looked at him with a combination of pride and bitterness. *I'd lay down and die for these people.* Well. It was good to know the list of things he would die for. Mikhail was just hoping there was enough of his heart to want to live as well.

They left after a little more conversation and an exchange of numbers, and once they were clear of the twisty hairpin turn part of the road, Shane was exuberant on the ride home.

Mikhail didn't realize that he was being taciturn and pissy until one of his abrupt answers brought Shane up short, and a hurt quiet fell over the car.

"I'm sorry," Mikhail said, meaning it.

"What's wrong?"

"I am stupid. It was a figure of speech, that's all." He was muttering partly to himself because he felt foolish and petty, and it made him angry because he was a coward as well.

"I am so confused," Shane muttered, and Mikhail felt it burst out of his mouth before it burst out of his chest.

"You would lay down and die for them, is that not what you said?"

Shane gave him a brief, sideways glance before concentrating on the road. "Yeah. I would. I'd do the same for you, you know."

Mikhail looked blindly into the sun tipped trees. It was late afternoon, and it would be dark soon, and the sunlight was no longer the joy it had been that morning. "Excellent," he said absently.

There was a small gas station on the side of the road, and Shane pulled off into it, apparently to get gas.

"'Kay, Mickey, get out with me, and let's talk while I'm doing this, fair enough?"

"There is nothing to talk about," Mikhail said, curling up his lip. Dammit, he knew he was being pissy, he *knew* he was being unfair, but... ah, gods. Shit fuck damn bloody, bloody, bloody fucking hell. "Fine," he snapped to nothing in particular.

He stood and stretched and then shivered because it was cold up here, especially in the evening before dark, and trotted around the car to where Shane had just started the pump.

"You will die for everybody, wonderful," Mikhail said randomly. "I'd be overwhelmed if you would live for me instead."

Shane raised his eyebrows. "I wasn't planning on going anywhere...."

"Shut up. You say that. But you exhaust yourself caring for my mother, caring for me, and then you put yourself out for your family. You don't ask for a break or tell either one of us to fuck off, you just.... Why can I not be enough?" In a thousand years, Mikhail would not have thought he was capable of that much pettiness. He shook his head. "I am being *so* stupid. I cannot even explain why. Here. I will go sulk in the car, and you can ignore me like a misbehaving child...."

"No no no...." Shane reached out and grabbed his arm and pulled, and Mikhail awkwardly stepped over the gas pump to come stand in front of the man as he leaned up against his car. "*Talk* to me."

"What is there to talk about? I am a petty, jealous asshole, and I am making something out of nothing." In desperation, Mikhail banged his head softly against Shane's collarbone and Shane laughed and— disregarding prying eyes from passersby—wrapped an arm around his waist and pulled him close.

"Here's the thing," he said seriously, and Mikhail looked up into those warm brown eyes with the crinkles at the corners and trusted him to make this better, since Mikhail himself could not.

"The thing is, you had your mother. I know she's not going to be here for long, and that sucks, but you *had* her. When you really needed someone, you had her. If I had done what you did—gone off the deep end as a kid—Mickey? I'd be dead. There was no one to pull me back. No reason to come back. And these people want me. They want me at their table. Hell—they want *you* at their table. Now I know you got tight with Jon, and with Benny and Jeff and Drew. I think you're just freaking out about meeting Deacon because I obviously respect the hell out of the guy. I can't fix that you're freaking out—but I can tell you that you don't need to. Does that help?"

"I'm an asshole," Mikhail said thickly, and Shane laughed and made him lean his head against Shane's hard chest.

"Yes, yes you are. But I love you."

Mikhail sucked in a shocked breath and tried to struggle away and make something of it, but Shane just pressed him closer. "Don't sweat it, Mickey. You'll say it if and when you're ready."

"You have such faith," Mikhail mumbled, and Shane didn't argue with him. They got back into the car, and the silence between them was easier, and the music was a blessing they both needed.

Chapter *16*

Softly you whisper, you're so sincere…

"Open Arms"—Journey

SHANE didn't know how to fix it. He knew Mickey was jealous, he knew Mickey knew it was irrational, and that was just how it was going to have to sit.

At least until Mikhail learned to visit Deacon and know that Deacon was the last person on earth to judge him and find him wanting.

So Shane had to be content to listen to the music and let the coolness of the late afternoon air blow the fog and the dimness of the last three weeks out of their hearts and to know that it would be okay. It had to. Mickey needed things to be okay—and that couldn't happen if they were on their own.

The fog was back by the time they hit Roseville, and it was getting dark by the time he pulled up to the cattle gate in front of his own home. God, the place looked good.

He had missed it these past weeks and had done his best to spend as much good time with the animals as possible. Lots of long walks with the dogs and grooming with the cats, lots of training the puppy and trimming toenails, lots of home improvement and trimming the yard. By the time he got to Mikhail's place to help take care of Ylena, he'd been ready for something a little more sedentary, and by the time he left, he was ready for something less painful. But between both places, he was really ready for some peace.

Work was actually starting to sound like a relief. Of course a good laugh was always helpful too.

When he pulled up to the cattle gate, Shane had Mikhail get out of the GTO to open the gate so he could drive through. Mikhail had just finished closing the thing when Angel Marie came running to give Shane his usual greeting. It was a good thing that Mikhail had already locked the gate, because he took one look at that big-assed dog, screamed like a girl, and sprinted for Shane. Quicker than Shane could have imagined, Mikhail climbed him like a tree as Shane propped himself against the car to keep from toppling over.

"Good Christ, what is that thing!" Mikhail shrieked, his knees digging into Shane's shoulders hard enough to leave bruises. Angel Marie, happy to see a new friend, promptly stood up on her hind legs, put her paws on Shane's shoulders and started licking Shane's face to get him to properly introduce this new friend. Besides laughing so hard his side *literally* ached, Shane had to juggle Mikhail's weight on his shoulders, Angel Marie pushing him backward, and a mouthful of dog spit, all at the same time.

"Mikhail... dammit, Angel... Mikhail... Angel, for chrissakes get down, you big spaz... dammit, Mikhail! Would you stand on the car or something...." And then, because neither of them were giving an inch or a quarter, "Ouch... ouch ouch ouch ouch...." And he fell to one knee. Mikhail vaulted off his shoulders and over the dog like a goddamned Olympic gymnast, and the dog decided that this was a much better position from which to drown him in drool. And then the other dogs all caught up with Angel Marie, and Shane found himself laughing, wincing, and generally overwhelmed by a mass of furry bodies. In desperation, he wrapped an arm over Angel Marie's neck and let the big animal pull him free, and after administering dog noogies all the way around he picked up the first thing he could find (a big piece of rope with knots tied on either end) and pitched it with enough force to land on the roof of the house.

Eagerly barking, the animals took off after the rope-bone, and Shane dragged himself up, panting breathlessly. "Hurry, Mickey—go up to the porch while I get your clothes. We've got about three minutes before they figure that thing's not coming back down and come back for round two!"

Mikhail was still staring at him in horror. "Holy Christ, what was that thing?"

Shane started laughing all over again, leaning against the car in pain and not caring. "That was Angel Marie—you know, my dog? Jesus, Mickey, I showed you pictures."

There was a puzzled whimper from the other side of the house, and Mikhail started trotting to the front door. "The hell you say! That wasn't a dog—that was a furry dragon!"

"Nah," Shane said, chuckling some more as he gathered the groceries and Mikhail's backpack from the car. "And even if it was a dragon, you don't need to worry—he wouldn't eat you."

Mikhail took the porch steps two at a time and stood next to the bench Shane had built, the whole while quivering in anxiety should the dogs return. "He won't eat me? And how do you know that?"

Shane got there with the keys and flashed a playful grin. "Mickey, you know dragons only eat virgins."

Mikhail almost didn't beat the dogs in, he was so busy gaping at Shane with enough indignation to literally slay a dragon.

They got inside and closed the door and were immediately besieged by cats.

Mikhail's reaction to the cats was completely opposite to that of the dogs. He sat down, right there on the white tile of the kitchen floor, and started to pet them as they milled around, rubbing their cheeks and rumps on his hands and knuckles as he crooned to them.

"Oh, yes, you are pretty. There… if I scratch your ass, will you preen for me? Of course you will. Look at that tail…you are a kitty in search for a piece of ass, yes you are…."

Shane dropped all of Mikhail's stuff by the couch and then hurried to the cupboard for several cans of cat food, which he opened and dumped into the bowls. The furry wave receded, leaving Mikhail alone on the floor, staring in bemusement up at Shane.

"Cupboard love," Shane shrugged, offering his hand. Mikhail took it and watched as Shane tightened his expression with his weight. Shane could have kicked himself when Mickey swore and started rooting under Shane's sweatshirt and T-shirt, and then he found the scar and stepped back, stricken.

"You are *bleeding*!" The look of horror on his face was almost too awful to bear.

Shane took a look under his shirts—the scar was still pretty tight, and all of that movement—not to mention a hundred and fifty pounds of terrified Russian on his back—sure enough had managed to pull the skin apart a little. "Would you look at that?" Shane mused. He grinned at Mikhail, hoping to take that awful look off his face. "It was totally worth it," he chuckled. "Man—you screamed like a *girl*. I've never in my life heard someone scream like that!"

Mikhail's face was something to see—he went back and forth from indignation to self-blame, from anger to pissiness, for long enough that Shane was going to try to find another tack to jolly him out of it. Finally he settled on disdain, and Shane figured they were going to be okay.

"If this is your way of attracting virgins for that monster, it's a wonder he hasn't starved to death. Here—let me get some gauze and tape that for you."

"Wait—I was going to shower in a minute, after I started dinner. If it's still bleeding, we can wrap it then."

Mikhail nodded with just enough shakiness to let Shane know he was still not okay. He reached out and grabbed the waist of Mikhail's jeans and hauled him closer as he leaned back on the counter. "Sorry about the dogs, Mickey. I forget—they really are sort of overwhelming."

Mikhail shook his head and laughed, still wobbly. "You really are an extraordinary person, do you know that?"

Shane snorted. "Not so much." In spite of the fact that he loved having Mikhail right there, he started moving restlessly around the kitchen, because the praise made him antsy. "I figured mac 'n' cheese with some hot dogs thrown in, you think?"

Unfortunately, the kitchen really wasn't that big a place—two counters, about five feet apart, one with the stove and the other with the sink. Shane fed the cats in what amounted to the entryway, so whoever walked in the house had to walk through a variety of food and water bowls to get inside. It wasn't an ideal layout, but Shane had never felt crowded until Mikhail stopped him from rooting in the pan cupboard with a quiet hand on his arm.

"First of all, I'll cook, because I have plans for tonight and sitting on your toilet is not one of them." Shane straightened with a pot in his hand and a rather affronted look. His cooking couldn't possibly be *that* bad, could it? Mikhail took the pot and set it on the stove and continued, with a look of determination on his face.

"And second of all, you really are extraordinary. Please—don't blow this off. Don't shrug like it is nothing. You are wonderful. And important. And so, so beautiful. I need you to know that. I am an awful, pissy, jealous, temperamental little man—don't think I don't know it is so. You could be the one person I have ever met to turn this into a good thing. Whatever...." Mikhail stopped for a moment and looked away, and Shane was grateful, because he was sweating from the praise and the careful scrutiny. Mikhail grabbed his chin and made him meet that lovely, intense pair of blue-gray eyes, and Shane started to sweat again.

"Whatever happens, wherever we end up, you remember I said this here and now. You remember that you can't go be a hero without hurting people who care about you. You... dammit, you make better decisions with your body, please. Your absence would leave a hole in the world, and there are not enough furry dragons or horny cats to fill it. You understand?"

Shane tried with a grin, but it sobered at the honest anger he saw burning in Mikhail's eyes. They hadn't talked about this since that day in San Francisco—Shane had thought the subject was closed. "I'll be careful," he said now, pretty sure he could keep that promise, but Mikhail just shook his head.

"God, Shane—you don't understand at all what I am saying. Tell me something—there is a pill box on your counter. Tell me what it is for?"

Shane looked over his shoulder at the little 'weekly calendar pill box' that he'd gotten the last time he'd been to the doctor's. "It's got some vitamins in it and some antibiotics. And some anti-inflammatory meds. And something like Benedryl that knocks me out so I don't take it. And painkillers. Lots and lots of painkillers. I don't like those, either."

He looked back at Mikhail. Mikhail's jaw was clenched and his eyes were narrowed, and he was shaking his head. "Go. Go take your shower. Go take your shower, and I'll make food, and when I think I can do this without kicking you, I'll lecture you like an old Russian mother about why you are a fucking idiot and I should hit you on the head with a frying pan for doing this to me."

"Now come on...."

"I said go!"

Shane did. He'd never really had a mother, but he got the feeling that from Mikhail's perspective, he'd done something for which ass-kicking was seriously involved.

Mikhail tried to talk to him about it as they sat at the little table by the kitchen, eating mac 'n' cheese and green beans with butter, and Shane was still puzzled. Finally, he sighed. "Look, Mickey—I get it. You're worried. If I promise to take all the pills that don't make me throw up, could you give it a rest for a minute and let me hold you? I got a new movie for us... *Cloudy with a Chance of Meatballs.*"

Mikhail perked up, willing to be distracted for the moment, and the evening got infinitely better. The movie was charming, and best of all, Shane watched it propped up in the corner of the couch with Mikhail backed up against him, which was something neither of them had done when they were watching television at Mikhail's. Come to think of it, it was something Shane hadn't been able to do a lot of, period. Brandon hadn't been a cuddler, and he couldn't remember his girlfriends being that excited about watching movies on the couch. Mikhail seemed to be a pro, though, leaning his head against Shane's chest and sitting still and bonelessly while they both became absorbed in the movie. All sorts of tension Shane didn't know he had went sliding out of his body, and sometime after the ending credits, when he handed Mickey the remote to channel surf, and the end of *CSI: New York* (which is what Mickey decided on), he fell asleep.

He woke up to a cool burst of air on his stomach and insistent hands on his sweats, pulling them down past his hips.

"Oh hello," he muttered bemusedly, and then Mikhail took his flaccid cock completely into a hot, moist mouth, and he said it with emphasis. "Oh hel-*lo!*"

Mikhail giggled around him, which really blew his mind, and then he was no longer flaccid, and his mind was still getting blown. Or rather, his cock was getting blown, and his mind had lost enough blood flow to completely check out of the equation. He got too big for Mikhail's mouth, and that eager, fine-boned fist came into play, and Shane threw his head back against the couch cushions and moaned.

Abruptly Mikhail's motions on his body stopped, and Shane opened his eyes and sat up a little to see why. That strong fist started to move again, but Mikhail kept his gaze locked on Shane's. Very deliberately he extended a pointed tongue and licked the purple skin of Shane's cockhead, and Shane's spine vibrated like a plucked guitar string.

"I love doing this," Mikhail murmured. "It used to be a matter of professional pride, you know?" He opened his mouth and hollowed his cheeks, and Shane grunted and whimpered, and Mikhail still never dropped his eyes, even as he came up and released Shane's body with a pop. "I used to just think, 'Hey, at least I am giving good service for payment', and that was good." He did that same move again, and Shane made the same noises with a little more oomph, and Mikhail kept talking.

"And then, when we moved here, and I was doing this because I did not know any other way, it was still an exchange." That little pink tongue, scraping the underside, exploring the slit on the top, playing with the harp string, which was oh-so-tender. "I did this, I did it well, and in return, I did not have to be alone. And I thought it was good."

He lowered his head and moved his fist, and Shane felt his cock bottom out on the back of Mikhail's throat, and then Mikhail swallowed, and Shane fisted his hands through that wild, corkscrew hair and closed his eyes so tight he saw stars. Mikhail pulled back, and the air hit Shane's body, and he opened his eyes again and tried hard to listen seriously to what his lover was telling him.

"But with you," Mikhail continued, licking again, just to tease, "it's different. I could do this all"—lick—"night"—lick—"long"—suck. "Just to hear you make noises. Just to see your face when I do it. Just to taste your come in my throat." He pumped with his fist and engulfed with his mouth, and then his other hand made an end-run, and Shane felt a spit-slippery finger tease his entrance. He groaned and held back, not wanting to come while Mickey was talking to him, but... oh God. Oh God. He needed... he needed....

"Will you, Shane?"

Oh God... what did he need? "Will I what? Jesus... Mickey...." Because that evil finger and its twin were stretching and probing, and that tongue was never not busy, and Shane's brain and his cock were about to part ways for a couple of seconds, and he had the feeling Mikhail really needed him.

"Will. You. Come. For. Me?"

Well, that he could do. "Ohhhh *fuck* yes!"

And he did.

IT WAS not the only orgasm of the night. It was not even the only orgasm of the hour. But it was an important piece to what made up the puzzle of Mikhail's curious mind, and Shane was mulling it over as they lay—in bed, finally—naked, sated, and drifting in and out.

It was different being in Shane's bed.

For one thing, it was bigger—and that was fun. For another, it wasn't a child's bed with a pedestal and drawers underneath, and it seemed that, without a parent in the house, this was a real thing for Mikhail. Since it was the first time Shane had brought someone to his new home, this symbol of the life he wanted to live as opposed to the one he had been living, it was a real thing for Shane too.

For another thing, they had company. As soon as they were done shaking the springs and making noises, the cats all jumped up on the bed, licking the sweat off of their faces and purring as they curled into little limp balls between their legs and settled down for the night. Mikhail crooned to them—Kirsten Dunst, in particular, seemed to have made him her pet, and they spent giddy minutes touching noses while she kneaded the pillow next to his head.

At last, however, Shane had gotten up to let the dogs in, and the cats were satisfied that their new favorite human wasn't going to change sides and go batting for the canine team, and they were lying in bed, naked and warm under the comforter and enjoying the touch of skin on skin. Shane nuzzled the back of Mickey's neck and said, "I think I get it," and Mikhail startled and said, "Wha?"

Shane giggled into the hollow of Mickey's ear. "I get it, you know. I know why you're so afraid of Deacon. The guy's just a guy. He's nothing scary. He's protective of his family, sure, but you've got him built into this scary patriarch guy who's gonna tell you to go away and that you're not good enough for me, and I think I know why."

Mikhail grunted and pulled the cat close enough that she started to lick the sweat off his neck. Shane figured that meant he was listening and soldiered on.

"You know, you had your mother, right, but you didn't have any men around who weren't after your body."

"I had my dance instructor and choreographer," Mikhail said unexpectedly, and Shane felt another puzzle piece in his head.

"What were they like?"

Mikhail let out a humorless chuckle. "Complete bastards."

Yup. That piece fit too. "See? You've got men who are complete bastards, men who are complete users, and nobody to protect you from the bastards and the users. Your mom had her hands full protecting you from yourself. You just expect Deacon to be a bastard or a user—he's not a lover, but he *is* important, and you just don't have another spot to put him in."

"Benny said he was scary," Mikhail protested, and Shane chuckled into Mikhail's shoulder.

"Benny's sixteen years old. She worships him. She *needed* a protector. The day I met her, her dad was trying to take her baby from her because he's a complete crazy asshole fuckhead. She got pregnant in the first place because another asshole fuckhead slipped her a roofie and date-raped her. Don't you see? Benny *needed* Deacon to be the person who was going to keep her safe from these guys, and Deacon lived up to it. So she's going to see him as scary—to other people. But she's still a kid, and we can give her that. You're a grown man, Mickey, and this is getting ridiculous."

Shane kissed his shoulder gently and then along to the side of his neck, and Mikhail kept his eyes determinedly on the cat.

"Why is this important now?" he asked at last.

Shane blew out a sigh. "Because your mom wanted you to stay until tomorrow night. Tomorrow's the first of the month, Mikhail—it's the day the family gathers to see if they're going to be able to stay here in Levee Oaks or if they're going to have to move. The general consensus is, if they move, we're all moving with them. I know it sounds stupid—a bunch of grown people following folks around the state. But this is our family now, and we don't want to let it go."

Mikhail froze beneath him, and Shane could tell the full implication of the words hit him and hit him hard.

"You would move?" he asked, his voice tiny.

Shane kissed a stubborn jaw and wrapped his arm harder around Mikhail's chest, mostly because his body had started to shiver under Shane's embrace. "For you, Mickey, I'd stay. But I'd rather you didn't force me to make that choice."

"You'd stay? For me?" Again that still, small voice. Shane hated it. He wrapped both arms around Mikhail's shoulders and rested his cheek against his hair.

"Did you ever doubt it?"

"I shouldn't have," Mikhail whispered. "I shouldn't have." He took Shane's hands and raised them to his lips, and Shane could swear he felt hot tears falling on their backs, but he wasn't going to make it a thing.

As it turned out, they were late for the gathering anyway. Rosie called just as they were getting into the car, Mikhail's nerves be damned. Shane was jumping up and down, literally bouncing on his toes like a child by the time Mikhail ended the conversation—she was going to give Deacon a chance. Oh God—all that worry, and The Pulpit might get to stay right where it belonged. By the time they'd set up the times and the dates with her, Shane was gunning the motor so he could whip around the block and get them to The Pulpit.

Deacon was standing on the porch, looking so terrified and worried that Shane slipped in the mud in his hurry to get up to him and tell him the good news.

The slow, beatific smile of joy on his face as Shane spilled the details warmed Shane to his toes, and he bolted inside, trying to get to the others before they voted. Yeah, sure, they could go back and vote again, but the results had the potential to break Deacon's heart, and why take that chance?

By the time Shane realized that he'd left Mikhail outside with the object of his deepest fears, Deacon was bolting inside the house like a kid, and Crick was doing a one-handed catch to keep him from sprawling over the kitchen table with enthusiasm. Mikhail came trotting in after him, looking like he would be content to hide in a corner for the rest of the night, when Benny spotted him, let out a squeal, and ran up for a hug.

The look on Mickey's face as that girl hugged him and chattered in his ear like he was the big brother she'd always wanted when she'd been cursed with Crick instead eased something aching in Shane's heart. God, Mikhail really did love Shane's family—he'd probably been missing them since December.

Jon, Andrew, and Jeff came up, too, shaking his hand and looking happy to see him, and for a good ten minutes there was complete chaos and chatter before Amy's voice cut through the excitement.

"Benny! You'd better get in here—I think Parry got into your makeup, darlin', and tried to make up the baby."

Benny hopped back from Mikhail with her best "Oh shit!" look and bolted from the room. Mikhail watched her go in bemusement and then looked up to find Deacon and Crick eyeing him thoughtfully through their own excitement at the possibility of being able to keep their home.

"So," Deacon said, flashing sharp hazel eyes to his friends, "Mikhail—you're not really a stranger to all of us, are you?"

Mikhail blushed. "No—we met while Shane was in the hospital. Everybody was very wonderful—they helped me visit."

Deacon nodded slowly. "How long have you two been dating again?" This time he looked at Shane, and Shane blushed. Yup. It was like having an older brother. One who was younger than he was, but an older brother just the same.

"Since October," Shane mumbled, and Crick said, "Are you shitting me?" and Deacon said, "Hush, Crick," but his voice was soft and a little hurt.

"It was my fault, you see," Mikhail said, trying to smile. It didn't take. "I… you, your family—you were so important to Shane. I… I did not see how I could measure up." He was still standing in the doorway. He hadn't even taken off his hat and his scarf or his jacket.

Deacon nodded and said, "That's not what you said on the porch," and when Mikhail looked up, stricken, Deacon held out a hand and smiled gently. "Never mind, come on in, then—here, Crick—take his jacket and things. Did you want to meet the baby, Mikhail?"

Shane was not surprised when Mikhail turned a look of sheer gratitude on him. "I love babies—I teach dance. The little ones are my favorite!" And then he blushed and looked at his toes as though that much exuberance shamed him.

Shane was on the verge of going to his side and holding his hand just to keep him from bolting or breaking Shane's heart when Deacon said, "Go on down the hall—just follow the noise. I'm sure Benny and Amy will be happy for the help."

Mikhail gave a brilliant smile—the kind that Shane had needed to work hard for—and gave his jacket and things to Crick, then took off for the hall. He passed Shane on the way and reached out to touch his hand before rabbitting away to the safety of the children.

And then Shane was there, alone, facing Deacon.

"He was afraid to meet me?" Deacon asked, completely baffled. "Me? You had a guy for *months* and you kept him secret because he was afraid to meet me?"

Shane found himself blushing terribly. "The thing is, he heard all this stuff about you...."

Deacon glared at him.

"It was all true!" Shane protested. "And it wasn't all from me!"

Andrew spoke up, looking a little embarrassed. "The thing is, when Shane was sick, Mikhail was there in the hospital, and we were trying to tell the guy why he should meet you."

And then it was Jeff's turn. He spoke awkwardly, for Jeff, casting little darting looks to Shane as he did. "Damn—Deacon, you know how scared we were. Well, Mikhail was like six times as scared—and to make matters worse, he had some serious family shit going down.... How is that, Shane?" Jeff asked, looking at Shane with some head-on concern.

And it was Shane's turn to look away. "Not long now," he said roughly. "She literally ordered us out of the house on furlough, I guess. I told her I'd have Mickey back later tonight, and she promised to live that long."

"His mother?" Deacon guessed, and Shane nodded, swallowing past the lump in his throat.

"Yeah. She's good people."

Deacon put a brief hand on his shoulder. "I'm sorry. But Jesus—this is why you should have told us. Look at you—no wonder you look like hell. We could have helped, right?"

Shane shrugged. "It wasn't really my thing to tell, you know, Deacon? Besides—you all just got finished taking care of me and my dogs. And it's not like you didn't have other shit to worry about. I didn't want to, you know, put you out any more than you already have been."

This time Deacon socked him in the shoulder, saying, "You're family, asshole."

Shane rubbed the spot gingerly and blushed and grinned. "Man, that hurt—and you wonder why people think you're scary."

"I'm not scary!" Deacon protested, still a little shocked. He looked up to where Mikhail had come in, Parry Angel's hands firmly entrenched in his. She was looking up at him with wide blue eyes, and he was completely taken by her round little face and guileless smile. She turned away for a moment and waved at her 'Deek-deek' and he waved back while she preened in her tu-tu, having apparently escaped her mother's wrath by simple virtue of overwhelming cuteness.

"See—seriously?" he said, looking up and blushing because all of the men had stopped to watch him completely captured by the little girl. "How scary could I be?"

Crick smirked, having heard him while hanging up Mikhail's things on the peg near the door. "Yeah, baby—you're a killer."

"Fuck you, Crick. I'm not shitting around here. This guy was so freaked out you all had to lie to me about his existence? What have I ever done to deserve that?"

Crick put his hands up in self-defense. "Hey—I didn't know about him, either. Which is a good goddamned thing, because, seriously— Shane? What in the hell were you thinking?"

Shane blushed. "I was thinking if you guys get any louder he's gonna see how fast he can run from Levee Oaks to Citrus Heights. Jesus, people—has it occurred to you that for a guy who lives with his mother, there is too much testosterone in this room?"

Jon and Jeff met eyes and burst out laughing, and Crick eyed them sourly. "You don't get to laugh about this, straight boy," and Jon stuck his tongue out.

"The fuck he doesn't!" Jeff hooted. "Any heterosexual male who is more at ease with his gay friends than with his straight ones gets to laugh about being one of two steers in a room full of queers until he wets his pants. What? What did I say?"

Shane was aware that his own mouth was swinging open, and he looked around to see that everyone else was gaping as well.

Jon held up his hands to ward them off, saying, "Man, that was *him.* I swear...." He stopped, and his chest shook, and then it shook again, and then he slapped his hand over his mouth, and then *Deacon* of all people started to giggle, and then it was all over. Mikhail looked up from where he was showing Parry Angel how to elevé in fifth position, and Shane was so busy giggling that he could only shake his head and mouth "Later!" to his puzzled lover.

Later, he could explain this so it made sense. Later, he could talk about Benny and how much she needed someone who could protect her, and why she made Deacon sound like Wyatt Earp and the Terminator in one little sentence. Later, he could explain that they'd been trying to make Deacon feel better because he'd obviously been a little hurt. But right now, he was going to let Jon lean on him and giggle helplessly while Crick and Deacon did the same, Andrew wiped his eyes, and Jeff smirked in the center of the circle with his hands out, saying, "What? Seriously— it's totally true!" while the rest of them lost their fucking minds.

Chapter 17

No blinding light or tunnels to gates of white…

"I Will Follow You Into the Dark"—Death Cab For Cutie

SHANE tried to explain the laughter in the car as he was taking Mikhail home, but Mikhail was still lost.

"Bulls and queers. It does not sound that funny to me."

A hand reached out in the darkness, and a rough knuckle touched Mikhail's cheek softly. "It wasn't—not really. It was more the timing of it, Mickey. Deacon was hurt, really hurt, and Jeff said something funny at a time when we needed to laugh or that hurt would just keep going. Trust me. The laugh was better than the alternative."

Mikhail sighed and turned as far as the seatbelt would allow. "I'm sorry I hurt your family. You were right, you know. They are very nice. I should have met them when you were sick—all of them, I mean. The babies were delightful."

Shane nodded eagerly, and in the passing streetlamp, Mikhail caught the happy curve of his lean mouth. "Good—I'm so glad, you know? And now, if I ever get hurt again…."

"Shut the fuck up, you fucking asshole." Mikhail was not kidding, not even a little tiny bit, and his brain had shorted out to the extent that he'd been a stutter away from swearing in Russian.

"I'm not saying I will—"

"And I'm saying that if I have to think about that now I cannot function. Please?" To his shame he felt pleading come into his voice. Oh yes—he was so much the Ice Man now, wasn't he? "Please, *lubime*—it has been the loveliest day…." His voice trailed off. It had been, hadn't it? All of it—the trip out of the valley the day before, the moments spent in Shane's arms, the cats purring on him all during the night. He had awakened that morning to find Shane sprawled out on his stomach next to him, a careless arm thrown over Mikhail's stomach as they slept. As he'd opened his eyes in the unfamiliar room, he'd realized that he could never, not once in his life, remember waking up feeling as though nothing could touch him. Perhaps when he'd been younger, before he'd gone into dance, but he could not remember that far.

"Please. Let me just hold on to the day?"

"Of course," Shane said softly, and Mikhail had to close his eyes tight against the knowledge that he really meant it. He really would simply back off and allow Mikhail to appreciate the time they'd had. Mikhail realized that not once had they mentioned his mother—they'd both been thinking about her, but this time really had been stolen.

It had been beautiful.

When they got to the apartment, Shane got out of the car with him, and Mikhail didn't have to ask why. He'd told Ylena that he'd bring Mikhail back, and he was a man of his word. As they got up to the entryway, Shane grabbed Mikhail around the hips and spun him around (easily—he was such a big man!) and searched Mikhail's eyes in the porch light.

"Tell me it was important," he murmured, and Mikhail nodded, wide eyed.

"It was important."

"Tell me it meant as much to you as it did to me," he begged gruffly, and Mikhail didn't have it in him to deny it.

"It meant everything to me, *lubime*. Believe nothing but believe that."

Shane closed his eyes, a sweet expression of savoring and joy washing over his face, and then he opened them and lowered his head to Mikhail's. The kiss was brief and sweet, only the faintest hint of tongues meshing, only the whisper of the passion that they both knew was there. It was a promise and a benediction. It was a reminder that the other was there, even when they weren't allowed the privacy to show it.

They broke off from the kiss, and Mikhail brushed Shane's cheek with his knuckle, liking the way Shane's brown eyes looked beyond deep in the darkness, and then turned to open the door. His mother turned her head as they walked in the door and smiled slightly.

"*Mal'chiki*, so glad you could make it," she murmured, just barely loud enough for them to hear.

Shane moved toward her bed while Mikhail went to drop his stuff in his room, and Mikhail didn't hear what she said to him. There had been a little piece of paper with advertisements in the *Cloudy with a Chance of Meatballs* DVD box that Mikhail had palmed when he opened it. That went into the cedar box, which still, after this time, carried a small item from every date or dinner they'd had. With the pictures from the cruise, the box was getting crowded, but Mikhail still did not trust that these times would not disappear. When he returned to the front room after that, the woman who had been staying with his mother—someone from the church—was standing stiffly as Shane bent his head to his mother's and spoke softly.

The woman spoke in Russian—something to the effect of "I'll be seeing you tomorrow," and then she left without a backward look. It was too bad, Mikhail thought a little sadly. She missed the way Shane smoothed his hand over Ylena's cheek and raised her hand to his lips in a gallant kiss. The woman and her judgment missed the way Ylena smiled at him as though he hung the moon and the stars. She missed the simple love that could spring up between two pure souls.

"I'll be seeing you, Ylena," Shane said now roughly, and that languid hand came up and patted his cheek.

"Do not be counting on it, *lubime*, but I would not be disappointed, either. Drive safely—my son has enough worries."

"Guaranteed, sweetheart." And with that, Shane gave her a kiss on the cheek and turned to go. Mikhail walked him to the door, and Shane bent and kissed him on the forehead—discreet, but also tender. Mikhail adored him for it.

"I'm going running tomorrow, so probably around nine or ten," he said, his hand on the doorknob.

Mikhail nodded, and his heart ached to watch him go. He should say something, he thought miserably. Say something that would make the going easier. Say something that would make him know that dying mother or no dying mother, it was that moment, when Shane walked in the door, that Mikhail would be waiting for in order to start breathing again.

But he could not. He could only capture Shane's other hand and bring it to his lips and give it his own gallant little kiss. He could watch the slow smile spread on the other man's face and see the blush and the way Shane ducked his head in an embarrassed—and probably aroused—goodbye.

The door closed behind him, and Mikhail sighed, and then walked to his mother's bedside and sat down on the chair nearby.

"A good time, *lubime*?" she asked. He set his chin on his hands and looked at her with shining eyes.

"The best, Mutti—would you like to hear about it?"

"Please."

And so he told her, all of it. He told her of getting out of the valley, and the way the red-gold light hit the tops of the evergreens in Grass Valley. He told her about Rosie and Arlen and watching the enormous draft horses getting worked and the power of the animal in the ring. He told her about Shane's gigantic furry dragon, and he blessed the fact that she could still laugh when he described climbing Shane like a piece of gymnastics equipment and crouching there, terrified at the dog's friendly advances.

"But a dog of Shane's would not be vicious!" his mother protested, and Mikhail laughed, embarrassed.

"It was as big as me, Mutti!"

"You are not that tall, *malenkiy mal'chik*."

He took her hand and kissed it then. As though he needed a reminder of *that*!

He continued, and told her of the cats, and of Shane's lovely house. The floors had been hardwood, and Shane had furnished it simply—

leather couches, dark green or blue rugs on the floor, cream colored walls. Shane had been quietly proud, and Mikhail had loved it. "He painted the walls himself and laid the flooring. He did not brag, because that is not his way, but it was a true home, Mutti. He is surprisingly good with making things—wood and whatnot. His porch is well crafted."

This is beautiful, Shane. You do nice work.

I do okay. Nothing to brag about.

But it was, Mikhail thought achingly, telling the story to his mother. It was something to brag about. Everything about the man spoke of fineness and care. Things too good for Mikhail, but he was not going to burden his mother with that now.

And when he was done with that, he moved on to the family.

"So many, Mikhail? It sounds like a church service?"

Mikhail thought about the rowdy group of men and laughed. "No— there were many people though. They… they helped. The little girls—a tiny baby and a toddler—had so much attention, Mutti. The toddler— Parry Angel—she loves to dance. I love to see little ones dance—it always seems as though that was what dance is made for."

His mother stroked his hair. "You were happy when you danced as a child, *lubime*. Sometimes, when I regret all that came after, I console myself with that. When you were a little boy, that joy was like God's holy light. You must promise me to always dance—even if it is simply in your home, with your lover, you must always dance."

Mikhail smiled at her. He couldn't say why, but it felt like absolution for the thing he loved best to do. "I promise, Mutti."

"So these babies, they had mothers?"

And Mikhail told her about tiny, maternal Amy and bouncy, emotional Benny. He told her about Deacon, finally, who had carried such an air of quiet grace around him.

"He was not scary, this family patriarch?" Ylena sounded concerned.

Mikhail shook his head. "No. He was strong—oh, Mutti, the strength in him. You had no idea. His man, Carrick, was a little scary, only because you can see in him that he will do exactly what he wants when he wants. If Crick is angry, you had better duck. But Deacon—he is all power and control and love. They are good people. They are," and it pained him to say it, "they are worthy of being Shane's family. They listened to him—I could see it from across the room. I had met many of them when Shane was sick, but not as a whole. As a whole... they are wonderful, Mutti. I loved being there."

Ylena smiled a little, obviously tired, but she patted his cheek and made him continue. He tried for details—the size of the stable, the jokes he heard Jeff tell. He stayed clear of the one about steers and queers, but he told her about the terrible amount of pink in the room for the baby and the pie Benny had bought for dessert because it was Deacon's favorite. "He is too thin, Mutti. Finally, I see Shane's concern for him—it is frightening to know what a toll worry can take on a strong man."

"Yes, Mikhail. Look at yourself—you have grown lean and tired these last months. Shane has too. Perhaps, when this is over, you can see what joy it will be to have love when there is no worry."

Mikhail blinked. "I had not thought of having Shane when this is over," he muttered.

Ylena smiled as though unsurprised. "You thought that he was what? A short-term blessing? You'd best think again, *lubime*. This is not a short-term man. This is a man with a family. They will do nicely for you."

Mikhail chewed on that for a while, uncertain of what to do with it although it was something he had always known. There were other things to talk about, though, and he told murmured stories of his stolen moments until his voice faltered and he fell asleep, his head pillowed in his hands on the pillow next to his mother.

He startled once in the night—it was Ylena, reaching to turn off the monitor that beeped softly with her heart and breathing. "I cannot sleep with it on, *lubime*. Good night."

When he woke up again, his heartbeat, alone and solitary, was the only noise thundering in the motionless chill of the morning.

WHEN he thought about it later, he would wonder, what would he have done without Shane? Shane would assure him that he would have done just fine, but Mikhail had his doubts.

First he called Shane, and when the phone didn't pick up, he left a message. The text came back within minutes: *Call the coroner, Mickey. The number's on the fridge.* Sure enough, there it was in Shane's writing. Mikhail didn't remember him writing it down, he didn't remember the discussion or the logic of calling the coroner as opposed to an ambulance, but Shane did. It did not matter. Shane was there before the coroner arrived anyway.

He came bounding in, still wearing running shorts (in winter!) and a T-shirt and looking as though Deacon had shoved a sweatshirt over his head out of sheer desperation. Deacon was there, too, Mikhail would remember, looking grave and composed and mostly helping when he could and staying out of the way when he couldn't. He managed to be down in the car, getting Shane's clothes, when Shane took Mikhail aside and spoke seriously.

"Look, Mickey—I can tell you're holding it all together, and you should." Shane looked as though he'd wept already, but he wasn't crying now. "It's going to be a long day, and you can get all that out of your system when this whole thing is over. But right now, I'm going to leave the room for a minute and hold the coroner off when he gets here. I want you to go say goodbye to your mother, okay? It's not gonna work—not in your heart—unless you get it clear that this is the last time you see her when she's gonna really be yours. You got that? You'll believe me on this?"

Mikhail nodded, trusting him, and grabbed his hand tight. For a moment he was afraid he couldn't let go. But Shane let go for him and turned him gently, and Mikhail went to look at the wasted skin and bone on the bed that had once been the bright shining star of his world.

"Goodbye, Mutti," he said softly, feeling silly. He knew she was not in there. Hadn't they said all there was to say? "You gave me a good life, and then you gave it to me again. I will try to do right by you; it is all I can do." He stopped for a moment and wiped his eyes. "Do you really think he'll still want me," he asked, feeling foolish and self-involved, "when he sees what a mess I will be, now that you are gone? I can hear your voice in my head, old woman, telling me that it is true. I've got to hope that you will stay there, because my whole life, the only faith I've had has been in you."

He stopped then before he could go much longer on that subject and bent and kissed her cheek, which was cold under his lips. The beauty, the charm, the intelligence—all of it was gone. Her face was neither happy nor sad, simply still.

But there was no more pain and no more worry and no more self-recrimination, and it was that, at last, that allowed him to let her go.

"Never mind my problems, Mutti. You've done your job. My job is not to make a hash out of it, and that is all. I love you. Do not ever doubt it. Goodbye, *lubime*. Remember your journey. We will compare notes when mine comes due."

There was a thundering up the stairs at that moment, and it was fortunate that Shane made it through the door before the men wearing black windbreakers who carried the gurney. Shane tucked Mikhail under his arm and conversed with the people in black and gave him things to sign and did not expect much more of him as he stood there and trembled, determined that no one should have his tears but him.

And so it was for the next week. Shane dealt with the people from Ylena's church, he dealt with the insurance people, he dealt with the funeral arrangements. Most of them had already been made—much to Mikhail's surprise—while Shane and Ylena had sat together. She had trusted him, and his documents were legal and the money paid.

The one thing Mikhail had to speak out about was the one thing that would outrage everybody except Shane.

"Now, Mr. Bayul, your mother was very ill when she put this caveat into her will. I'm sure nobody expects...." The lawyer—a man from the old country who specialized in serving the Russian community, was very conciliatory—and very surprised at how upset Mikhail was *not* at the bizarre request.

"She expected me to," Mikhail said shortly. "And she was not so ill when she proposed it to me. You did not know this woman—not well. She swore she would haunt me if I did not do this, and I for one believe her."

"But... you'll be... you understand—she wished you to do this on her grave side!" He looked desperately at Shane, who merely shrugged.

"I did know the lady, sir. I'd die before I ignored her last wish."

Mikhail cast him a supremely grateful look, and—disregarding the censure of the lawyer—reached for his hand and squeezed it, and that was the last the matter was debated.

Which is how Shane came to be holding the boom box when Mikhail danced to Tchaikovsky on his mother's grave.

Mikhail was nervous, at first. He looked out at that sea of faces, all of them disapproving, as he stood there in his black dance pants, jazz shoes, and a white dress shirt, and for a moment he tried to make them understand.

"If you knew my mother," he said in Russian, "*really* knew her, you would understand why she would think this is funny and perfect."

He was met with a stony silence. From the back of the crowd, Shane winked and gave a crooked grin. Behind him, Deacon and Crick and the entire family hopped out of a variety of vehicles and made their way toward Shane.

Mikhail switched to English.

"But you will never know her like I knew her. And that is why I must do this." He gave a glance to the gray February sky and hoped the thin sunshine would hold up and the wind would give him a fucking break, and then he signaled Shane.

The opening notes of French horn chorale rolled out, Mikhail assumed fifth position, and the dance began.

He'd started the choreography from the moment his mother had first made the request. He knew better than to think she was kidding, and he'd designed the dance to be done by an expert, a professional, a dancer who could perform miracles.

On that barely sunny day, on a slick platform of plywood, he became that miracle.

His knee held, his muscles exploded, his timing was spot on and every movement, every nuance, every moment of the dance was perfect. *Dance like an angel,* his mother had said, and he had promised he would.

He kept that promise with every atom of his being. When the explosive conclusion rocketed the piece to a close, Mikhail was leaping, twisting and vaulting on his little makeshift stage, sweat flying from his hair and his heart, for the moment free from everything, free from worry, pain, or mourning, and free from constraint. When the final chord died, he fell to the stage on one knee, panting, and looked out over the community that should have been his.

They weren't. His only tie to them ever had been through his mother, and looking at their disapproving faces, he realized that she had effectively cut that tie forever.

But Shane and Shane's family were beaming at him, proud and happy and amazed. They were his family, if only he would take them.

His shining face dropped for a moment to the plywood beneath him, and he wondered if he could.

Chapter 18

Come down on your own and leave your body alone…

"Can't Find My Way Home"—Blind Faith

IT WOULD be, Ylena had told him, like when Mikhail was kicking heroin. First he would push Shane away, and he would do it brutally and he would do it with terrible finality, sure that his pain would be all he needed to exist. And then, in the aftermath, he would be devastated from the loss and sure there was no way to undo what he had done.

"He will push you away when I am gone, *lubime*," she'd assured him that last night, as Mikhail was otherwise occupied. "He will do it horribly, in such a way to cut your heart into little tiny pieces. I know, because I picked the pieces of my own heart up off the floor and stitched them back together and determined to love him in spite of the pain. Can you do the same?"

Shane had quailed for a moment. God. It just seemed like any lover he chose, and he was destined to have his heart stomped on by someone wearing sharp metal cleats.

"I swear," Ylena told him softly when he hesitated, "it will be worth it."

"Of course I can," Shane told her. "I promise—he won't be alone when you're gone."

The next morning, he'd gotten Mikhail's frantically repressed message, *She is not breathing anymore, Shane. She is gone,* and he had known.

It had begun.

Mikhail had seemed grateful for him that week—he said "Thank you" often and sincerely, but Shane had felt it. They had not made love in the dark hours when everybody had gone home. Mikhail had lain still in his arms, staring into the night, preparing himself to separate—Shane could tell. Sometimes, when Shane was dealing with something that Mikhail didn't understand, Shane would look up and see those blue-gray eyes on him, haunted and cold. *I want you, but I can't have you.* Shane longed to just shake him. *Dammit, you* can *have me—you just have to try!*

The day of the funeral—the final rite in the passage of such a strong, kind, amazing woman—Shane saw Mikhail looking at the family that was offering to be his and saw the terrible fear in his expression. *Oh, God—I can't do this. How can they possibly be mine?* Mikhail had dropped his eyes, resolution clear in his face, and Shane sighed.

Deacon looked at him, clearly puzzled. "What in the hell was that? Not the dancing—that was just fine. What was that look he just gave you?"

Shane sighed again. "That was Mickey, getting ready to run like hell."

Deacon grunted. "Oh yeah. You're right. I should know that look by now."

On his other side Crick grunted too. "Damned straight you should. I don't know how you missed it."

"Not missed it," Deacon murmured sourly. "Blocked it out." He turned back to Shane. "What's your plan with this?"

"Well, first I let him break up with me and say all the nasty shit that he's been backing up this last week, so he can tell himself he doesn't deserve me and I'm better off without him."

Deacon winced, his beautiful face sympathetic. "That sounds like fun—and after we scrape you off the floor, then what?"

Shane smiled at him apologetically. "Then I call in the reserves and show him I don't shake that easy."

"Oh God," Crick grumbled. "We get to babysit Shane's boyfriend. Won't that be fun?"

"He likes kids' movies," Shane told him helpfully. "That's a plus."

Crick brightened. He had a weakness for Spongebob that had become a family legend. "Well, now—that I can do."

The funeral ended, and Shane stood dutifully behind Mikhail, but he brushed the smaller man's shoulder once, by accident, and felt Mickey shrink from him. Very carefully, he shored up his heart then, because he'd promised Ylena, and he'd promised Mikhail, for that matter, that no sin would be too horrible for Shane to forgive.

But Mickey had a mouth on him, and Shane was not naïve.

Shane drove them back to the apartment, aware that not everybody else was going home. Deacon and Crick were behind him, finding a parking spot with Crick's nice sedan, and he assumed they were going to hang out and make sure Shane would be all right.

Shane was pretty sure he wouldn't be.

As soon as they walked in the door, Mikhail shrugged carelessly and said, "You do not need to hang around me like a limpet you know. I do have a life of my own. You can go now."

Shane nodded. "Yeah, Mickey—I can. I wanted to be here for you, but it's true. I don't need to stay."

Mikhail narrowed his eyes—a completely unfamiliar expression of contempt crossed his features, and Shane sighed. Here it came. "Well, it's just pathetic, you know. Hanging on to me like a little puppy. She wasn't even your mother."

Ouch. "No, she wasn't. But she was a nice lady, and I liked her. I wanted to help out her son."

"Well, I've been helped. You can go now."

"Sure I can. I'd like to make sure you're all right first. Is that okay?" Shane moved to the refrigerator to make sure he had enough food for the next two weeks. He figured that would be about right—two weeks would do it. There were plenty of casseroles and dishes that Shane and Benny had put in plastic bags and thrown in the freezer for later, and Shane was satisfied they'd do.

"Are you going to eat? You are fat enough—you don't need anything else."

Shane fought the urge to roll his eyes. Yeah, like this was the first time a lover had called him fat. "You're right about that, Mickey. I am too fat. I wasn't going to eat." He shut the refrigerator door and stepped back, hands out. "See."

Mikhail's face crumpled for a moment, almost in tears, as though he couldn't stand to hear Shane malign himself but had nowhere to stand. "What kind of man takes this abuse? You are not a man. You are a ball-less wonder. If I dropped my pants and waved my ass in the air, you probably wouldn't know what to do with it."

Shane's temper pricked for a second, and he took a deep breath. This was tricky, dangerous territory. Here was the place where if Shane lost it, *he* would say the unforgivable thing.

"I'd know what to do with it," he said mildly. "I'd spank it, because its owner is behaving like a child."

"I'm a child because I'm tired of you? Is that it? Well, the whole world must be tired of you... bringing gifts like some pathetic loser... who needs your gifts? Who needs you?"

You do, you fucking moron! "My family does," Shane said quietly. "Are you done? Do you have something else nasty to say? I need to make sure you get this all out of your system before I take off and let you come to your senses."

"Why? Because I'd have to be crazy to let go of a prize like you?" Mikhail was standing in the middle of the room, alone, vulnerable, and, if he'd known it, weeping. It was all Shane could do not to rush him, not to pin him to the ground, not to *make* him accept comfort. But Shane had his pride too. Mikhail's mother had been right. Talking to him when he was like this—when he was determined to tell the world and the people he loved most to fuck off and die—was an exercise in futility.

"I always knew you were too good for me, Mickey." Shane took a chance and walked close enough to wipe his cheek with a thumb. "You could have any man you wanted—why would you pick me?"

Mikhail looked at him, stunned, shell-shocked, not entirely sane. Shane bent his head to those pouty lips and kissed him—soft at first, and then when he responded, hard and angry, because words *did* hurt, and suddenly Mikhail was yanking at his own clothes and at Shane's. With a vicious shove of his pants, he was half naked and he whirled away to bend over the back of the couch.

"Come on, big man. You want me so bad—you put up with my shit. Come get me! Come fuck me! Be like every other fucker on the planet and just do it!"

Shane backed away from his crazy Russian lover and scrubbed his face with both hands. When he spoke he had his temper under control. "I've told you before, not like this."

And with that, he turned around and walked out. Just that simply. He couldn't take any more, and if he tried, he wouldn't be able to come back, he just wouldn't.

He slammed the door so it would sound final, and there in the hallway, wearing his good slacks and funeral suit, he sank to a crouch and leaned his head against the door. On the other side, he heard Mikhail screaming into what was probably a couch cushion and sobbing loud enough to break the window frames.

He didn't know how long he sat there, but suddenly Deacon was at his elbow, pulling him up and walking him down the stairs, and he was wiping his eyes on the shoulder of his trench coat.

"Pretty bad?" Deacon asked softly, putting Shane in the passenger's seat of his own car. Deacon reached out his hands, and Shane turned the keys over without question. Behind them, he saw Crick pulling out and had a second to wonder how hard Crick had needed to work to be able to drive again.

"Bad enough," Shane said shortly and made another pass at his blurring eyes with the heels of his hands.

"So, what's the plan again?"

Shane took a deep breath, one that shuddered in and out, and put his mind where it needed to be. "Send in the reserves."

THE next day found Shane taking on some long neglected tasks in his own home—and not the fun ones, either. When Benny came to visit—she took her own run to Shane's house down the path that Deacon had cut that fall—he was dressed in jeans and a sweatshirt, wearing leather gloves, trimming claws and giving worm medication to the cats.

Benny sat at his little kitchen table and gulped water, shaking her head as Shane wrapped Maura Tierney in an old sheet with amazing quickness, leaving only a furious caramel-and-cream colored head sticking out, glaring at him balefully from blue eyes.

"Why are you doing this again?"

"Worming them? To keep them healthy. I'm trimming their claws to keep *me* healthy." With that he tucked the swaddled cat under his arm and shoved a pill down her throat until she swallowed. A sound came up—a low, bee-swarm growling that threatened to do dire, terrible things to Shane's body: If this ten-pound animal could only get him alone, Shane would know what it would feel like to be kibble.

Shane sighed. Now came the hard part. With some cursing and some struggling, he managed to adjust the cat-mummy wrappings until the cat's head was mostly wrapped (because the fuckers could *bite*) and her front paws were out. Then he tucked her under his arm again and reached for the clippers, being very, very careful not to clip too close, because that would hurt her.

"No, not that," Benny muttered. "I mean, why are you sending us to go watch the guy who just broke your heart into a zillion pieces?"

Maura Tierney growled again, and her back leg got free. Shane swore ripely, and the cat dug that claw into his forearm through his sweatshirt and ripped right up his wrist under his glove. Still swearing—and dripping blood—he managed to reposition the damned sheet and, since the back paw was free, worked on trimming the claws there. Benny was wisely silent until he was done, had the cat under control, and was finishing up with her.

He sighed and set Maura down, leaving her to get out of the wrapping all by herself, and Benny hissed in sympathy, standing up and heading for the cupboard.

"Here—let me dress that for you.... Don't worry!" she said when Shane would have protested. "I'm good at this. Deacon throws his fist through a wall every so many months or so, or sometimes he dislocates his thumb or gets his foot stepped on. Trust me—he's taught me everything he knows."

Shane gave in and settled down to be tended to, but Benny was a sharp kid, and she hadn't forgotten what they were talking about when the cat had tried to slice his wrist like pie.

"So, you didn't answer my question," she said again as he pulled off his leather glove and she dabbed at the deep scratch with cotton and some antibiotic cleaner.

"Why are you doing this for Mickey?"

"Yeah—I mean, I like the guy, but you're ours, and he hurt you. I'm sort of obliged to be pissed off at him, you know?"

Shane had to chuckle—and then wince because she *was* good at her job, and she was cleaning the scratch thoroughly. "Well, you let him know that. But you get pissed off at family all the time, and you don't cut them out of your lives."

"And he's family now?" There was a wealth of skepticism in her voice, and Shane didn't blame her.

"I'm sort of hoping to get him hooked on us," he told her. "We'll be sort of the opposite of drugs—you know, a family high."

Benny scowled some more and concentrated fiercely on her doctoring. "Why do you do this, anyway?" she asked irritably. "I mean, the damned cats take a chunk of you every time."

"Well, yeah—but I'll live. If I didn't suck it up and take care of them, the odds are good they won't."

"But you never get mad. You do this once a month, and you never get mad. How can you never get mad?" Benny looked up at him, her eyes swimming, and they weren't just talking about Maura Tierney and the six-inch slice down his wrist.

Shane bent down—way down, because Benny's dad hadn't been as tall as Crick's, and she was pretty damned short—and kissed her forehead. "They don't mean it," he said quietly. "I can get mad all I want, but they don't mean it. They love me. Sometimes, some creatures, when they get cornered, they forget who loves them and think everybody's the enemy. You don't just leave them alone, cold and afraid, because their instinct takes over and it's wrong. You don't if you give a shit, you know?"

Benny wrapped her arms around his middle in a stealth and attack hug—she was good at them—and he put an arm around her, grateful for it.

"So, you and Andrew will visit tonight, right?"

She laughed a little against his shirt. "We've got a schedule worked out—you said every night for about two weeks, right?"

"Sundays off, of course." Shane nodded, satisfied with the plan. "And you've got the little… you know, whatnots?"

Benny pulled back and shook her head. "Now that's the part I don't understand. Why do you want us to do that?"

Shane looked away and sighed. "I can't really tell you, sweetheart. It's sort of a secret I'm not supposed to know."

Benny stepped back and started packing up the first aid kit. He took it from her, and she rinsed out her water glass and put it in the rack to dry. "Well, I've got shit to do if we're going to be there in time to give him a ride. Do you really think he'll go back to work so soon?"

Shane gave a grim nod. "Honey, he doesn't have any other place to go."

Chapter 19

The consequences that I've rendered. I've gone and fucked things up again.

"It's Been A While"—Staind

THE children were a relief and a blessing. Anna was concerned that he returned so early to the job, but once she saw him, smiling gravely at the children as he always did, she let him be. She had been at the funeral—in fact, she'd been the one Russian soul at the service who had approved—but she wanted to know about the people who had joined the service late.

"They looked like wonderful people. Hell—they were the only ones there that I could maybe stand. Pfaw—not a sense of humor in the rest of them. You would have thought somebody had died."

That managed to get a small smile from Mikhail, but only a small one. "They are wonderful people. But I don't think they'll be seeing me again. Ever." This was right before his last class of the day, and he'd managed not to discuss "the big strapping man with the stereo" or his "American friends," and he was hoping he could put her off with that and that alone.

And then Benny had walked in with Parry Angel in tow, and Anna had welcomed them with open arms, and his plan had gone to shit. It seemed that Parry's dance instructor in Levee Oaks was one of Anna's employees—a thing Mikhail had not known.

"Yes, Bayul—I have my finger in many pies—why so surprised?" Anna smiled so smugly, Mikhail had to wonder if Benny had called her in advance. "And you said you wouldn't see these people again!"

Benny had smiled sweetly at Mikhail, and Parry waved delightedly. "We were just hoping Parry could come and have class here this week with her favorite dancer. She adores Mikhail. Is that all right, Anna?"

Anna caught the undertow of tension, but she grinned toothily at Mikhail and refused to be sucked in.

"That is wonderful, little one. Mikhail will be happy to teach her—yes, I know *mal'chik*—this is not the same age group as you have here. I have seen her dance—she will listen and do her best. That is all you ever ask of them, so worry not."

And with that, Anna took off, and Mikhail was left there, teaching his class with Parry Angel on his hip, giving instructions with him and begging to be let down to whirl with the big girls.

She was charming, and for a moment Mikhail let himself forget what she meant to him and taught class. When it was over, Benny and Andrew lingered—since Andrew had driven, he had come in to watch—and offered Mikhail a ride home.

Mikhail had tried to refuse, but Benny thrust Parry into his arms again, and Parry had leaned her head on his chest and snuggled, and that had been the end. They used the same tactic to walk him up to his apartment, and when he got there, Benny asked to use the bathroom, so he had to let them in.

Benny made him dinner from something in the freezer, sat Parry down in front of cartoons, and Andrew asked him if he needed help taking apart the bed and furniture in Ylena's room so it would be easier to put in storage. Before he knew it, they had spent two hours there, and he had not yet brought himself to say, "I broke up with Shane. You have no business in my home or in my life."

He couldn't. Mikhail would carry the burden of his hideous behavior toward Shane for the rest of his days—he absolutely couldn't make that worse by being a pissy, whiny, horrible bitch to the people Shane loved too.

This would be the end, he told himself, swallowing a lump in his throat. This would be his final goodbye to the man he loved and was too worthless to hold on to. It would be a fitting goodbye—it would show him all of the things that he could have had but did not deserve.

Watching them go was almost (but never could ever be quite) as bad as when Shane had left the day before. When they were gone, he wandered the empty, echoing apartment disconsolately until he found the little barrette, complete with a blue flower and ribbon on it, left over from Parry Angel's hair. With a hard swallow he palmed the barrette carefully and put it in his big cedar box, then lay down in his bed and listened to his iPod playing Shane's songs over and over again until he fell asleep.

He woke up the next morning with gritty eyes and an achy head and refused to admit where he would get such discomforts. He also awoke with the conviction that he would never see Shane or his family ever again.

Mikhail did not count on Jeff being there after work to take him to a Kings' game.

He said no at first, but Jeff rolled his eyes and accused him of being a "fairy princess" and then shoved the ticket in his jacket pocket. He said that Mikhail could either jump in the car and go see the world's worst basketball team lose to the Phoenix Suns, or he could watch that ticket become a useless piece of paper in about an hour, and Mikhail felt as though he had no choice.

He'd never been to a basketball game. Really, what could it hurt?

Later, he would admit that it hurt in a thousand small ways. Jeff told him that Shane had gotten scratched by a cat and that he started work the next day. He said that Shane looked tired and unhappy, and that he wasn't eating or sleeping much. He also said that Mikhail was a dumbass and that he could fix everything if he would just pull his head out of his dumb ass and admit that he gave a shit about the big doofus, and would he please just give him a call?

He said this right before he dropped Mikhail off at his apartment. Mikhail nodded mutely in the face of Jeff's sarcasm, and then took the ticket stub into his room and put it in his cedar box, bemused and wondering exactly who was going to show up the next night.

As it turned out, it was Jon, who commandeered his television to watch another basketball game. The Kings lost again. Jon left some soda in the fridge and urged Mikhail to eat the rest of the chips and pretzels. He also left a game schedule for the next couple months that ended up in Mikhail's treasure box as well.

The next night, it was Crick, wanting to know if Mikhail would go shopping with him to find a frame for a picture he had drawn and was going to present to Deacon in a couple of months. He showed Mikhail his sketchbook, including one of Shane that he left on the coffee table before he left. Mikhail had debated folding it up and putting it in his box or pinning it to his wall. He'd finally decided on his box, because he didn't deserve even that much of Shane, and seeing it on his wall would only remind him of what he'd lost.

Deacon showed up the next day with the pickup truck to take Ylena's furniture into storage for him, since Crick said it wasn't gone yet, and it finally, *finally* dawned on Mikhail that Shane was trying to tell him that he very possibly hadn't lost anything at all.

"Will I see somebody tomorrow night?" he'd asked after they'd dropped the furniture off at a little storage unit near Levee Oaks, and he was terribly confused when Deacon shook his head negatively.

"Tomorrow's Sunday, Mikhail. Family dinner night—you're welcome to come if you like." Deacon slanted a look at him, and Mikhail flushed horribly.

"That would not be a good idea," he murmured, sure that Deacon would get the hint.

"Why, because you'd take one look at him and forget that you're trying to be an island unto yourself?" Deacon asked with a small smile, and Mikhail's blush got even worse.

"I said such horrible things to him, Deacon," he confessed in a small voice. Wasn't that who you were supposed to confess your sins to? The family patriarch? Wasn't this where he was smote down for being a dumb fucker who could not hold on to someone and drove him away deliberately instead?

"You were in pain," Deacon told him softly. He turned the truck into a drive-thru and asked Mikhail if he wanted anything. Mikhail took a soda, and Deacon ordered him a Quarter Pounder with Cheese, and then got himself a chicken sandwich, no mayo. And two Happy Meal toys for Parry.

"Why do I get the big sandwich and you get the chicken with no mayonnaise?" Mikhail asked, bemused.

Deacon shrugged. "Because my daddy died of a heart attack before he was fifty, and Crick has requested that I not do the same if I can at all help it. I eat steak when I can, but I only eat cheese in my salads now, and mayo is a big-bad."

Mikhail went very still. "How old were you?"

Deacon looked at him. "Twenty-two."

"And your mother?"

"She died when I was five."

Mikhail swallowed. "How is it you can stand this? How do you live with all of it?"

Deacon dealt with the girl behind the drive-thru window, who gave him goo-goo eyes which he ignored, then handed Mikhail his burger and soda, taking his own for himself. Mikhail thought he'd forgotten about the question until they got on the road again toward his apartment.

"I had Crick for a couple of years, and then he pushed me away like a dumbshit, and I thought I had no one, and I didn't. I didn't handle it. I spent three months trying to drink myself to death."

Mikhail sucked in a breath. This man? This man had been that fragile? That weak?

"What made you stop?"

Deacon took a bite of his sandwich and steered the enormous vehicle down Elkhorn with one hand. "Two things," he said after he'd swallowed. "The first was that Crick wasn't dead, he was in Iraq, and he begged me to take care of myself, and I just had to. The second was that Benny was here, and she was in trouble, and she needed me not drunk and not a basket case, and you just don't shut that down, you know?"

His family had needed him. "I see," said Mikhail, taking a bite of his own sandwich. It tasted surprisingly good—he had not been eating well lately. They came to a light, and Deacon looked at him sideways as they sat there.

"Crick and I spent a long time trying to apologize. Him for leaving me, me for being weak. You eventually forgive shit like that, if it's worth it. If you're family."

Mikhail made a noise—an involuntary one. It was sort of like a whimper, actually, and he was glad the sound of the engine and the radio covered it up a little.

They didn't say much after that. Deacon seemed to be comfortable in the silence, and Mikhail would look at him as they drove, his lush mouth compressed in a little smile. He really was beautiful—small nose, high cheekbones, pretty green eyes, and that appealing mouth. But he was also, Mikhail was starting to see, very shy. His cheeks had waxed red, even in the darkness, when he'd been talking about himself, about his past, about the things he'd done wrong. He'd opened himself up to Mikhail, a stranger, and it had hurt, but he'd done it because he thought it was important. Because (and here was the "a-ha!" moment he had been putting off all week) his family had asked him to.

Deacon asked him to schlep their takeout trash on his way up to his apartment. When he got there, he realized there was something still in the bag. It was one of the happy meal toys—a tiny stuffed bear wearing a rainbow T-shirt. Mikhail stood holding it for a moment, wondering if Parry would be there again on Monday. He kept it on his counter for all of Sunday, as he sat at the television alone in the darkened apartment, thinking about where he could be, if he'd been brave enough to keep Shane, if he'd been a good enough man to have that sort of goodness in his life.

He took the thing with him when he went to bed and put it in his box. The box was getting crowded, and he spent a moment organizing. He put a rubber band around the pictures and thought he should maybe get an album for them, like the ones Ylena had left him of her pictures. He put the souvenirs of the rest of the family in a bundle next to the pictures, with the tokens of the baby on top of them. He kept his mementos of Shane neatly stacked in the top compartments of the box.

He still had Shane's scarf. He still wore it every day. He pulled out the little vial of oil, half gone now, and dotted a little on the brown wool, now worn comfortably soft and pilling slightly from the use. He went to sleep with it on the pillow next to him so he could smell it and dream that Shane was there.

He didn't, though. He dreamt instead of the look on Shane's face as he said, "I said I'm not doing it like that!" and then walked out the door and out of his life.

He woke up muttering to himself. "You couldn't do me like that? Just once? Just so I could hate you and I would be over this?"

He spent the morning in a pissy mood, cleaning his already clean bathroom and wandering around the apartment restlessly. Now that his mother was gone, he really needed to think about getting a hobby, because work just wasn't filling in the hours, was it?

Still, he looked forward to work. And when Benny and Parry Angel walked in again—this time escorted by Crick—he looked forward to it even more. They spent the evening at his house again, and this time Benny and Crick brought their knitting. Crick muttered something about occupational therapy for his hand and scowled at Mikhail to mention it, and Benny said, "I'm making a new scarf for Shane," while looking pointedly at the brown one that Mikhail couldn't seem to let go of.

"I...." He swallowed and tried to make himself say it. "I... I should probably...." Oh shit. He fought the temptation to grab the thing as it hung over his coat on the peg-board by the door and cuddle it to his chest, and Benny had shaken her head and laughed.

"Don't hurt yourself, Mikhail. He wants you to have it."

And he had to leave it at that.

The next evening it was Jon and Amy, who brought little Lila Lisa, and he got to spend an evening watching cartoons with a bouncing baby on his lap. The evening after that it was Andrew, who said he had some shopping to do at the high-end mall in Lincoln and wanted to know if Mikhail wanted to come. The two of them spent an hour wandering the exclusive corridors of the stores and wondering where all these teenagers seemed to get such an appalling amount of disposable income before Andrew said that he'd probably be better off going to Sunrise Mall right by Mikhail's apartment. They had something at the food court, though, and Andrew bought Benny some sort of expensive bubble bath, and they called it a night.

The evening after that was Crick alone, who could not lie for shit. He simply showed up on Mikhail's doorstep with Chinese takeout and a *Spongebob Squarepants* DVD in his hand and looked hopeful that Mikhail wouldn't just throw him out.

Mikhail let him in with something like resignation, and Crick made himself busy with the DVD at his television with hardly a hello.

Mikhail dished up the takeout—orange chicken and noodles, his favorite—and sat down next to Crick on the couch and handed him his bowl. Crick glowered at him, and Mikhail sighed into the silence.

"How is he?"

"He went back to work."

"I knew that. How is he?"

"Exhausted. He came by after a shift yesterday, and he could hardly fucking move. Deacon took his keys and went and fed the animals, and your guy slept on our couch. Feel better?"

"Not even a little bit."

Mikhail watched the first cartoon numbly, and every now and then cast a sideways look at Crick, who would chuckle under his breath on occasion. Mikhail didn't get the humor at all, and the little yellow character on the screen was starting to annoy him.

"You left Deacon?" he said in the break between cartoons, and Crick looked at him in surprise and then in understanding.

"Dumbest fucking thing I ever did." He held out his arm, scarred and twisted, and then flexed his fingers, straining to increase the range of motion in them. "I'll have the scars to remind me what a dumbshit I was for the rest of my life."

"Why did you do it?" Mikhail asked, afraid to. Deacon—Deacon who was so beautiful and so strong and so (Mikhail knew now) vulnerable. *How could you leave him?*

Crick sighed. "I hate this story," he said randomly. "Deacon tells it more often than I do. I think he's better at it, and since he hates to tell people anything, that's gotta tell you something about how ashamed I am that I was a part of it."

"You do not have to," Mikhail said. He was not good at the social lie. The disappointment was evident in his voice.

Crick snorted. "The fuck I don't. Your big goofy cop friend is breaking his heart over you, and you need to hear it so that shit can stop."

Mikhail shrugged, like hearing that Shane was heartbroken didn't just dig the knife in deeper, and said, "So tell it," like he was not dying to hear.

With an impatient motion of his good hand, Crick paused the DVD and turned to look Mikhail in the face. "Fine. Here's the thing. My whole life, my family, they did nothing but fucking kick me to the fucking curb. My childhood was a game of 'Hit the Mex kid' unless I was with Deacon and his father, and I was so sure, so goddamned sure that I'd done something to deserve it. It was like those moments with Deacon and Parish, that time spent in a family—that was stolen. So I stole the big thing. I stole Deacon's love. And there we were, all cozy and happy, and Deacon opened his mouth to say—and get this, because it was my future on a silver platter *with* the man I'd loved since I was nine—he was going to say, 'You can still go to school *and* we can see each other.' I mean, perfect, right?"

Mikhail nodded his head dumbly, because Crick was talking a mile a minute and there was no room to ask any questions.

"So he gets the first part out—'This doesn't mean you can't go to school' or something close, and then I interrupt for the second part, assume he's dumping me, and run off to join the fucking army before he can break my fucking heart."

Mikhail blinked. "*That's* why you joined the military?" He blinked again, trying to reconcile the sequence of events, and Crick sighed and flopped back on the couch, shaking his head.

"Yeah, don't bother trying to put the two things together. It just doesn't track. It was a dumbshit move, and by the time I came to my senses—and Deacon woke up from a concussion because he wrecked the truck trying to stop me from doing something stupid because the guy knows me like no one else—it was a done deal."

A done deal? Mikhail just stared at him. "And he *forgave* you?"

Crick had liquid brown eyes, much like Shane's, except every so often there was a defensive, angry hardness about them... but not now. "It was the most incredible thing anyone has ever done for me. He forgave me. He forgave himself. He had to, because I needed it. It was that simple. I'll die before I hurt him again."

Mikhail sucked in a breath and nodded. Crick left eventually, but not before Mikhail decided he truly loathed that square yellow thing and his goofy pink friend. He left Mikhail with an extra pair of chopsticks and an unfamiliar tingle in his stomach.

It wasn't until Mikhail had put the chopsticks in the treasure box that he realized what the tingle in his stomach might be.

It sort of felt like hope.

The next night, Jeff came with a jigsaw puzzle that featured a pornographic homoerotic cartoon. One of the men in it was big, broad-chested, with lots of brown hair—everywhere. Mikhail eyed the final results sourly. "Are you trying to get at something?"

"I'm hoping to make you horny enough to stop this shit. Dammit—don't you miss him?"

"Would you miss breathing?" Mikhail snapped. "I said horrible things. He's better off without me."

Jeff waved his hand and sniffed. "Honey, you say horrible things, and he's tailor made to let them roll off his big, hairy back—"

"His back is *not* hairy!"

"Whatever. He's forgiven you. He forgave you before you said them. He's just waiting for you to forgive yourself."

Jeff left a significant piece of the puzzle on the table when he left, and Mikhail rolled his eyes and put it in the box.

Benny and Amy came the next day with both of the children. It was Mikhail's day off—they took him to the zoo and let him push the stroller and talk to the babies and hold them and show them the animals.

It was a lovely day, but Mikhail couldn't help wondering how much better it could have been if Shane had been there. He took the map to the zoo home with him. There was only one place to put it.

The next night was Sunday, and Mikhail watched his door and listened for a knock from family until eight o'clock before he realized that no one was coming. They were all having dinner together, and he was here, alone, because he was a fucking idiot, apparently. It was not because anybody hated him the way he felt he deserved.

But nobody came to pick him up from work the night after that, either. It could have been an oversight, or it could have been the beginning of the end. The beginning of the family forgetting him—the beginning of the end of his chance to be a part of a group of people who actually gave a shit about his existence, period.

He pulled out his phone six times and then put it back and then pulled it out again and then said fuck it and took the coward's way out and dialed Benny's number.

"I'm just making sure the baby is all right," he mumbled, and Benny's rather ragged sigh told him it was probably a good guess.

"She's fine, Mikhail—but thank you for asking. The thing is, it's foaling season around here, and Deacon, Crick, and Andrew are all up to their armpits in afterbirth and placenta and shit. I don't think they've slept in two days. Anyway, since they're needed here, and I don't drive... I'm sorry. I should have called you—I know we weren't locked in stone or anything...."

"No, no, no, little one, it is all good. I was simply worried. Perhaps you and I, we should look into one of those driver's license things, yes?"

Benny's voice suddenly perked up. "Omigod Mikhail, that's like the best idea *ever*. I'm finally old enough, and damn, it sure would give the guys a break. Now that the place is making money, Deacon can afford the insurance—that's why I haven't pestered him before now, you know? Awesome. I'll wait until everybody recovers. But...." And now her voice dropped uncertainly, and he realized how young she really was and what an awkward position she must have been in these last few weeks. "We might not be by for the rest of the week. Don't worry—we won't stop visiting or anything. It's just that we're...."

"No worries, Benny," he said quietly. "I understand, I think. I understand that you are not going away. Now you sound tired, and I hear Parry in the background. Go tend to your family—wish everybody well."

And then he rang off and sat down on the couch and had a full-out, no-shit revelation.

He had a family. Shane or no Shane, he had a family. And they cared. He had a network of friends, of people to turn to, and he had not driven them away.

His hands were shaking when he dialed the next number, and he thanked the gods that he got the voice mail instead of the real person.

"Shane... look. I know I was horrible. I was unforgivable. I do not expect absolution. I just cannot bear for you to live another minute and not know that I am sorry. That's all. You need to know I'm sorry. I will be sorry forever."

He hung up then and sat for a moment, staring at the phone in his hands. He didn't even bother to press the heel of his hands to his eyes or to pretend they weren't blurring and dripping—there was nobody there in the little apartment to see or to care. He got up then and walked into his bedroom and looked—just looked—at his cedar box.

It was getting full. It hit him then that most people, they didn't keep every moment with their loved ones in a cedar box—cedar boxes got full. Most people, they kept those moments in their hearts. Hearts got full and still made room for more memories, more concerts, more moments when someone important held your hand or hugged you or sat and watched a movie just because he or she could.

Maybe, since his cedar box was full, it was time to stop filling it with trinkets and start filling his heart with people instead.

He had just reached out a hand to pick up the little vial and smell Shane for the last time that night when the knock sounded on the door.

It was Shane, wearing his uniform and panting breathlessly from pounding up the stairs, and Mikhail could not stop his heart from leaping when the door swung open and there were those warm brown eyes, blinking earnestly at him.

He tried to school his expression, to not give anything away, but Shane's face split into a grin, and he crowded his way into the apartment, forcing Mikhail back and back and back. "You can't take it back, Mickey—I won't let you!"

"What can't I take back? My apology? I won't take it back—"

"Good, but that's not what I'm talking about."

"Oolf...." Because Mikhail had hit his back on the apartment wall. "What are you talking about?" he asked helplessly, looking up at Shane and drinking him in like water. He looked weary—and tough in his khaki uniform—and irritated and windblown. But mostly, he looked dear and kind, and Mikhail wondered what he'd been pulling into his lungs for the last two weeks, because it certainly hadn't been oxygen—not when air tasted so much purer now that Shane was there.

Mikhail's face was framed by two big, warm, rough hands, and an expression of peace stole across Shane's expression. "The look on your face," he said softly, now that they were there, chest to chest, their hearts pattering against each other in confusion. "You can't take that look back,

Mickey—you meant it. You were glad to see me—you looked at me like you'd never been happier. You can't take that back. I won't fucking let you. You can't."

"I won't," Mikhail whispered gruffly. He closed his eyes and rubbed his nose along a roughly stubbled jaw. "I won't take any of it back. Oh, God, *lubime*, I don't think my heart could beat another minute without you."

Shane kissed him then, thoroughly and without apology and without reserve, and Mikhail returned the kiss eagerly, groaning and reaching for more. His hands found the buttons of Shane's shirt, and suddenly Shane was swearing and backing away.

"God... we can't do that. Not now," he muttered. "Mickey—I'm on shift. Or lunch break is more like it. I... I got your message, and I had to come see you. Now, here." He knew Mikhail's apartment intimately after those weeks with Ylena, and now he went to the little closet in the hall and started rooting around with purpose. He came up with a suitcase that he shoved into Mikhail's hands. "Now go fill that thing up—and get a move on, they know I'm off duty and I've got another hour, but I don't want to leave Calvin without backup. There's only two of us on tonight, and I've got to get back to Levee Oaks, okay?"

Mikhail looked at the suitcase, confused. "Then why are you here? What is this for?"

Shane wrinkled his nose in irritation. "I'm here to take you home, dammit. You're not spending another goddamned night alone. Now would you get a move on?"

A slow smile spread across Mikhail's face, one he could not control and did not want to. "Of course," he said simply, trotting down the hall at record speed. "You do not think I would leave the cats alone with that monster dog of yours if I could help it, do you?"

Chapter 20

And I'd give up forever to touch you.

"Iris"—Goo Goo Dolls

SHANE got home from his shift around six in the morning feeling like he'd been hit by a tractor. They had talked a little in the drive from Citrus Heights to Levee Oaks—Mikhail had nagged him about being too thin and too tired, and Shane had replied mildly that he thought he was too fat, and there had been an electric silence in the car for a moment.

"You must forget that, please." Mikhail's voice had been taut and hurt, and Shane had only been kidding, so he was surprised.

"I was just trying to lighten the mood…."

"Stop it." Mikhail sniffed, and Shane cursed the lack of time because dammit, he wanted to hash this out and get it behind them.

"Okay, I'll—"

"I mean it!" Mikhail snapped. Shane glanced at him and saw his throat working even as the shifting lights passed over his face in the dark. "I said horrible things. I will have to live with that. But you mustn't believe them. You can't. If you believe them or even pretend to remember them, I can't do this. I called you fat because I knew other lovers had done so, and it was easy to drive you away. I didn't believe it. I've never believed it. I've never even thought it. Everything else I said, it was to push you away. I know you know that—but you need to believe it. I cannot face you if you think I look at you and see anything less than the man you are. I am not settling for you, I am reaching for you, and there is a difference, and you are that man."

Shane had nodded and then tried some honesty himself. "I'm not that strong," he apologized. "I... I can do this once. Those things you said—I even saw them coming, and they still hurt. I... you've got to be honest with me, Mickey. You can tell me to leave you alone or that you've got to sleep at your place for a little or that you feel an attack of the nasties coming on and I've got to clear out. But I can't hear that again. I can't *do* that again, okay? If you want me to forget, to truly forget, I...."

He swallowed, because he knew this was the part where he might have to turn the car around and take Mikhail back and the whole thing would be over.

"I need a promise, I guess." Mikhail jerked his head, and Shane sighed and went on. "I just need to know that you won't break up with me like that. Not again. The other way is fine—you know, 'This isn't working, I don't love you anymore, you really are too weird for words, your lack of ambition is killing me'—you know, whatever. But... not that way."

Mikhail made a sound then—sort of a horrified laugh. "My God, your choices in lovers are horrific. Yes. Yes, I will promise never to do that again, if only to keep you from ending up with another horrible person even worse than myself."

Shane had taken a deep, shuddering breath. "Hey, Mickey?" He saw Mikhail turn toward him and wondered if the other man could see the pulse jumping in his throat from nerves and excitement and just sheer stinking joy to have him back in the GTO on the way to his home.

"Da?"

"Just remember that I'm reaching too."

"That you can say that now—"

"Is just proof that my taste is improving."

BUT that was hours ago, and he'd installed Mikhail in his house, kissed him fiercely (and God didn't Shane's blood still boil from the taste of him, the desperate tingle of his fingers as they dug into Shane's arms, the terrible intoxication of having him close and warm and hard in his arms) and then left, signing back on and letting Calvin know his time off register was over even as he pulled out of his driveway.

It had been an interesting night. A bar fight, a couple of domestic moments, a pretty horrible car wreck—all in all, more action than Levee Oaks usually saw in an evening, and Shane was still recovering. He was tired enough to be weak and a little trembly as he opened the gate and drove the GTO across the cattle guard, and it was easy to tiptoe into the house when you were too tired to move with much force. He got to his room and saw Mikhail asleep on his side in Shane's bed with the dark purple and brown coverlet pulled up to his bare shoulders, and he felt good enough to take off his shoes, put his gun in the safe, and undress for a shower.

It was an improvement over falling face down on the bed in his clothes and waking up with a bruise from his gun belt, which had happened a couple of times in the last week.

He had gone back too early—he knew it. But he hadn't wanted to stay at home and worry, fret about Mikhail alone and grieving, contemplate a future without him if his plan should completely blow up in his face.

So he had faked a few responses to his doctor for questions like "How do you feel?" or "Does it hurt when I do this?" and had shown up for work asking for his old assignment. His captain had made noises about the incident, and Shane had looked at him blankly.

"Are you going to write me up?"

"No."

"Fire me?"

"No."

"Send me to some other training that may or may not make me not do the same thing again when there are children in danger?"

"If you haven't learned by now…."

"Then since my doc cleared me, how about I sit down and start the paperwork for shift? I know nobody's got my cruiser. We're all good."

"All good" this night had gotten him a slug in the jaw when he hadn't been paying attention and an elbow in his bad side. Calvin had looked at him in concern as he'd been checking out to go home.

"Jesus, Perkins—you look like hell. I was sort of hoping you took that hour off to sleep, but it's not looking like it."

Shane shrugged. "Had to go pick up Mickey," he said roughly, and Calvin's response had been surprising.

"Oh, thank God," he'd said with a relieved smile. "Damn—I can't say I get where you're coming from there, but if you've got someone to take care of you, I'll be a hell of a lot easier about seeing you back to work."

Shane had thrust out his lip a little, knowing he sounded sulky and not able to stop it. "I take care of *him*," he said, trying to make this clear.

Calvin had raised his eyebrows and smiled gently. Shane wondered when his scrawny, half-grown partner had suddenly grown up—he was almost a real man now, and definitely a friend. "I think you take care of each other—but you can't do that when you're not home. Now go. I can talk to the captain—get tomorrow off for you...."

Shane shook his head and blinked. "He thinks I came back too early to start with."

"You did."

"Yeah, but I like my job."

"Why?" Calvin asked sincerely. They were walking out of the office now and heading for their own cars in the parking lot. "I mean, you're good at it—when you're not doing something to get you hurt—but I don't think you really love it."

"I love helping people," Shane said earnestly, and Calvin had to concede this was the truth.

"You're good at that—getting homeless to shelters, helping the runaways find a place to stay—that kid you got a job for at the mechanic's, he's doing really good. But there are other jobs that do that besides this one. This one is dirty and mean, and you get hurt—and me, I like it. But I don't think it's where your heart is, Perkins. You're a good guy—you got a good heart. But I hate to see it wasted here."

They'd gotten in their cars then and taken off before Shane could protest or argue or even think about what he'd said. But it haunted him now as he stood under the spray of the shower and hoped he'd have the strength to climb into bed and do justice to the good man who was waiting for him there.

The light was on when he got out, and Mikhail was sitting up in bed, surrounded by cats. The bottle of lubricant from his drawer was optimistically out on the end table, and Shane smiled. Geez, he *really* hoped to get some use out of that!

"You look tired, *lubime*," Mikhail said now, concerned. "And you have bruises all over your stomach and your chest." Shane grunted and started rooting through his drawers for his boxers, pulling them out with hands that held a fine tremble, and Mikhail noticed that too. He was up out of bed in a moment, his hands—warm from bed—rubbing over Shane's, which were still soft from the shower. "What is wrong with you? Have you even eaten?"

"Oh yeah," Shane mumbled. "That would have been a good idea."

Mikhail's hand on his shoulder felt soooooo good, so strong and warm, and he held Shane up and sort of steered him to the bed. "Here—you stay here, you silly man. I'll get you something to eat."

Shane mumbled a protest as he took Mikhail's spot in the bed—it was still cozy from his body heat—and then nodded off. He nodded awake—surrounded by purring cats—when Mikhail came in with a bowl of freshly microwaved canned soup and some toast.

The soup was clam chowder, his favorite, and he perked up enough to take the bowl on the towel from Mickey and dig in. The toast gave it some body, and he felt almost alert and happy as he ate.

"You realize there is nothing in your kitchen but cans of cat food, don't you?" Mikhail asked unhappily, and Shane nodded and swallowed.

"I've been on back-to-back eights—you know, eight hours off between two eight-hour shifts? Makes it hard to go shopping—and on your day off, all you want to do is sleep."

"Well, that is a stupid way to run a schedule—you did not do this before you got knifed in the side. Why the change?"

Shane shrugged, not wanting to go into it. He was pretty sure the change had to do with the fact that Deacon's family had been damned obvious at the hospital when he'd been there. "What sucks is that Calvin's signing on for my shifts too," he said, telling it sideways. "It's hard on him—he's got two kids and a wife. He just knows I don't trust anyone else."

Mikhail shook his head silently and took the empty bowl from Shane's hands. "We will go shopping tomorrow, before your shift. I can throw something in your slow cooker, if you have one, and if you can take me to work, there will be food waiting for you when you get home."

Shane smiled, knowing it was the shy sort. "That would be wonderful. I get off around ten—you want me to come get you? Or I could ask nice and have someone get you when you get off."

"I don't want to put anybody out—more than you already have," Mikhail said, with a wry roll of his eyes. "But I would like to see you tomorrow. And the night after. And the night after that." He smiled slyly, and leaned forward, touching a tongue to the corner of Shane's mouth and licking off the little bit of soup still there. There was a mrowr, and Mikhail dislodged Maura Tierney without the slightest blink of conscience so he could lean all the way forward and give Shane a man-in-the-arms full body kiss.

Shane took him up on it, his muscles shuddering as Mikhail's bare chest mashed against his. Damn... just... oh damn... he felt so good.... Their mouths were meshed in an out-and-out tongue tangle, and Shane used one hand to rip back the covers (and dislodge some of the cats) and shark-roll so that Mikhail was underneath him and they could keep kissing.

It was all he seemed to be capable of.

There was a pounding desire to move on to the "more interesting parts" of Mikhail's body, but he was pliant and giving and so, so sweet underneath Shane. Mickey's hands were everywhere—on his face, his neck, his shoulders, digging into his back and urging him closer and closer, and Shane responded by rubbing his body closer, and Mickey answered him by wrapping his legs around Shane's hips and grinding his groin up into Shane's. It was as far as either of them seemed to want to move.

Mickey's hands came up to rub his chest, and he even tried to slip it between the two of them to hold or grab or stroke or something, but that would have meant separating, even a little, and when Shane tried it, Mickey whimpered and pulled him back. Shane tried to move away, too, to kiss his way down Mikhail's chin, down his jaw line, down his neck, with intentions toward parts hard and erect and soon-to-be-known, but Mikhail took his face in both hands and moved him back up to keep kissing as soon as Shane got to his collarbone.

So the kiss went on and on, and their bodies grew aching, turgid, and oh-so-sensitive. Shane's cock—still covered in soft cotton—found a home in the crease of Mickey's thigh, alongside Mikhail's cock, which was leaking pre-come enough to soak through both their boxers. Mikhail thrust up against him, and Shane answered with a thrust of his own, and their lips and tongues kept up the very vital business of never, ever, ever parting.

Suddenly Mickey's thrusts against him got frantic and rhythmic, and Shane's cock was caught on the ridge by something down there, and they just kept grinding, faster and harder and with purpose and... oh God... oh geez... oh....

"Dammit, dammit, dammit...," Shane panted. "Damn, Mickey, I'm gonna...."

"Aaahhhhhhhh...." Mickey groaned beneath him, arching, spasming, and Shane felt the thick wetness coat their boxers, their stomachs, and seep through to his bare skin, and the thought of being covered in Mikhail's come, of having this man—this reserved, cagey, man—come apart in his arms just from a kiss and some dry-humping....

"Come...gonna come gonna come...." Shane squeezed his eyes shut and buried his face in Mikhail's neck and wrenched out a groan as he did exactly what he promised and came and came and came.

They stayed there panting for a bit and finishing up on that long, intense kiss before Mikhail grunted a little from the weight, and it became necessary for Shane to roll off Mikhail and off the bed. Mikhail stayed where he was, shaking his head in bemusement and holding his hand in front of his eyes.

"I can't believe we just did that," Mikhail muttered, and Shane chuckled softly before reaching down and shucking off his lover's boxers, enduring an indignant glare.

"Came from dry humping?" Shane shook his head, wadded the underwear up together, and tossed them in the open hamper at the foot of the bed. "Yeah, well, I haven't done that since high school. That was something."

He moved to the bathroom then and came back with a washcloth, half wet, half dry. Very tenderly, he used it to clean Mikhail up and then himself so he could climb into bed and they could touch each other skin-to-skin without the sticky aftermath. He tossed the washcloth in the hamper and did just that.

"Move over, Mickey—I don't want to fall off the edge." The bed was pretty big, but Mikhail was in the middle of it. Still appearing to be bemused, he scooted over and then turned in Shane's arms so they could hold each other face-to-face.

Shane reached over and turned off the lamp, and Mikhail said, "I've never done that. I've never just... just...." He shuddered in Shane's arms. "My God, *lubime*, the things you do to me. The way you make me feel. I thought I knew about sex—I was a *whore*, for God's sake!"

He was still shuddering, and Shane could do nothing but smooth hands over his shoulders and whisper to him until he stopped. When his breathing had evened out and his body was a tight bundle against Shane's chest, Shane tried to say something intelligent—or at least coherent—to calm him down.

"Mickey, you know, in some places people eat cats."

Mikhail jerked his head back and stared at him with horrified eyes. "What an appalling thing to say!"

"Yeah, I know." Shit. "I'm going somewhere with this, and I'm pretty sure you'll follow. Now see, they eat them, and use their skin for fur and probably make them into gloves and hats for all I know...."

Orlando Bloom had perched on Mikhail's hip as soon as he'd stopped shivering, and Mickey started stroking him protectively. Shane, as tired as he was, fought a smile.

"And?"

"And these people know cats inside and out. They use them for sustenance and warmth and practicality. But you know what?"

Shane knew the exact moment when Mickey caught up with him. His eyes lightened, and a faint, ironic smile touched his sulky little mouth. "What?" he asked softly.

"They don't love them."

Mikhail stopped stroking Orlando and started stroking Shane's chest instead. "You are very wise, *lubime*."

"I try, baby."

And that was about as coherent as he'd get before he fell asleep.

MIKHAIL woke him up after about five hours of sleep, and they went shopping in Natomas for food. Going to the little grocery store in Levee Oaks was right out—besides being incredibly expensive.

They got back and Mikhail made Top Ramen (after starting chili cooking for dinner) and they managed a whole half-hour to talk before Shane took him to work and then clocked in himself. An hour before he got off, Mikhail left a message on his cell phone.

He'd taken a bus and was cheerfully walking from Elkhorn Boulevard to Shane's place, and Shane had heart palpitations for an hour as he answered a domestic call and took in the intoxicated father. The fact that it turned out to be Crick's stepfather (and Benny's father) made things even more complicated—as did the fact that StepBob (as they called him) had vomited blood on the way to the jail and had to be taken to U.C. Med Center, off of Stockton. By the time Shane got to a place where he could even call someone to make sure Mickey got home okay, Mikhail had left a message saying just that, and Shane was on his way home to see him.

"Jesus, Mickey," Shane said as he all but stumbled in, "you can't *do* that!"

"Can't do what?" Mikhail asked, looking from the couch. He was watching a movie, and Shane could see from the pile on the table that he'd brought a box of DVDs from his apartment. The thought warmed him, but darn it, he had a point.

"Can't walk in the dark out here in open field land. Do you know how many drunken psychos there are in this little town?" He headed straight for the kitchen, where something wonderful was cooking, and dished himself up a bowl. Mikhail came in when he was about to crunch a package of crackers into it and took the whole works from him, tutting.

"There's cheese, cornbread, and onions in the refrigerator, please. If I'm going to cook, you need to treat it with respect."

"Cheese?" Shane perked up and opened the fridge to root for the promised condiment. He found it—grated—and some minced chives and the gallon of milk they'd bought. Mikhail took the armload from him and shooed him to the small table where the chili waited on a placemat that Shane hadn't seen in a month.

Shane grunted. "That's a little fancy."

"You are being served by a gay man who, until recently, lived with his mother. There are certain things you need to get used to. Eating at a table is one of them."

"I ate at your house. Your mother sat at the coffee table." But he sat down happily anyway.

"That was when she was sick. Before then, we ate at the table during dinner. Breakfast, lunch, we were on our own. Dinner? It was always placemat and table. For Mutti it was almost a religion."

Shane took a bite of chili and groaned. "I could worship here," he admitted. "But about walking three miles in the dark in Levee Oaks...."

Mikhail shrugged. "I ran wild on the streets in Saint Petersburg when I was a child. What is there here I could not survive?"

Shane scowled. "Just because you could survive it doesn't mean I want it to happen to you. Besides—you were lucky. You were more than lucky—you were like a goddamned miracle. I just don't want my miracle to wind up as material for a *CSI* episode, okay?"

Mikhail crossed his arms and sighed and then moved closer and jerked his pointed chin at Shane's spoon. "Eat your chili so you can go take a shower and we can sleep."

"Mickey...." But he said it through a full mouth, and Mikhail sighed and pinched the bridge of his nose.

Then he gave that snitty little shrug that Shane was coming to treasure. "If you are going to ask for a miracle, I wish you would ask for a better bus system. The one here is vile—that bus took forever, you know."

Shane smiled and rolled his eyes. "I'll make a note of it. But for now, can we try not to let the one miracle I *do* have end up on a crime show?" He sobered. "I've been on a couple of those scenes, you know. If we found you out there, I'd die."

Mikhail put a warm, firm hand on his neck and started to massage. "Fine," he huffed. "Next time I will ask for a ride from the bus stop, how is that?"

Shane felt a little bit of relief and finished up his chili, and Mikhail backed off enough to let him. While he was waiting, he picked up Jensen Ackles and scratched his tummy until the cat rolled over and purred in the cradle of his arms. When he spoke again, he had a rather catlike expression on his own face.

"Shane?"

"Mmmbblff?"

"If the Drunken Psycho of Levee Oaks *did* attack me, do you think he'd make me into a hat, or would he make me into gloves?"

Shane almost choked on his chili, but when he got it down (with a wash of milk to help) he said, "He'd make you into a loincloth with a matching purse, you goofy kid—Jesus, what a thing to say!"

"Yes," Mikhail replied smugly, "but that is because the Drunken Psycho of Levee Oaks does not love me—do you think?"

Shane wiped his mouth on a napkin and grinned at him, making sure the last of the chili was gone from his teeth as he did so. "C'mere, dammit," he demanded, and Mikhail grinned and put the cat down and then did just that.

But the transportation thing continued to be a big, giant pain in the ass. Mickey and Benny started studying together to take the written driver's permit test, but that was a long-term goal, and it didn't stop the short-term inconvenience of getting Mikhail to and from Shane's house when he wanted to be there. (Besides, Mikhail had very shyly admitted that he didn't have much formal schooling—his handwriting, unlike his texting, was rough and nearly illegible, and when he was reading English—as opposed to speaking it—he often stumbled over pronunciation and meaning. *And this is why your miracle barely has a GED, lubime. It is a shame that the best thing about English class was the stories the teacher read us from the book.*)

And Mikhail wanted to be at Shane's place a lot, to Shane's immense gratification. More than once Shane got home, prepared to shower, change, and trek out to Citrus Heights to go get him only to find that Deacon or Crick or even Jeff or Jon had gone for him, but they had lives, too, and Mickey was starting to be embarrassed about coming to rely on their kindness to get into his lover's bed.

"But I do not sleep well in my own bed anymore," he complained peevishly one night when they were talking about it.

Shane had to admit, as little sleep as he was getting thanks to work, he'd be getting even less if Mikhail wasn't there most nights to keep him company.

"You could always just live here," Shane complained another night over the phone. He was frustrated and tired and his day had been shitty, and he had a whole six hours until his next shift and going to get Mikhail and then drop him off just wasn't feasible.

He heard a surprised gasp on the other end of the line and kicked himself, remembering that Mikhail still had a bit of rabbit in him, and then, fuck-it-all, just continued to blunder on.

"I mean, I've got the extra room, and we could put your bed in there since there's just bookshelves in there now, and, you know, you wouldn't have to pay rent and maybe you could save up for a car for work and...." He trailed off, because work would still present a problem and, shit shit shit shit shit, maybe this would be the last fucking straw.

"That would be a solution," Mikhail said cagily from the other end of the line. "I... I will think about it," he promised before ringing off.

Shane hung up and gave a sigh of relief. It had been clumsy of him, but apparently not unforgivable. He was so relieved Mickey hadn't just hung up and bolted for the hills right then that he didn't figure the conversation would have any lasting repercussions until the next night. Mikhail wasn't at his apartment when Shane went to collect him, and his cell phone went straight to voice mail. Shane drove back to Levee Oaks in the rain-pissing dark, nervous and upset—oh Jesus, he'd spooked the guy, hadn't he? He'd taken off for the hills or was hiding under his bed not answering the door or... or... or....

Or he was halfway between the bus stop and Shane's house, sopping wet and carrying a really large package wrapped in blankets as he trotted briskly through their worst storm all year.

Shane pulled over and shoved the door of the GTO open, trying hard to be angry. It was difficult when Mikhail was shivering and blue and wearing one of Shane's hooded sweatshirts over his denim jacket and still dripping water in a gloppy pool all over the inside of the car, but Shane gave it a try anyway.

"What in the fuck…?"

"Yes," Mikhail chattered. "Yes, I broke my promise, but since it is to make a better one, I thought you would let it slide."

Shane reached over and cranked the heater and the defrog to maximum and hoped the fan could work faster than the steam could build on the inside of the windows.

"Mikhail, I beg of you, please have a fucking good explanation for this, dammit…. Man, I checked your apartment and everything! I was freaking the fuck out!"

Mikhail nodded and put his seatbelt on under the big object in his arms. "Yes, I am sorry—my cell phone quit when I was on the bus." He pushed back his hood, and his hair sprang around his head in a corkscrew halo. He was trying to appear suitably chastened, but he seemed to be exuberant instead.

Shane blew out a breath and sighed. "So?" he asked as he pulled the car away. "Are you going to tell me?"

"Tell you what?"

Shane slid his glance sideways, took in Mikhail's smirk and rolled his eyes. Damn, it was hard to stay mad at him. "Okay—tell me what you're doing walking out here when it's pissing down cats and dogs and even the gods are fucking cold… and if you make a crack about Zeus having blue balls, I'm pulling the car over right the fuck here and letting you walk home, dammit!"

Mikhail let out a little giggle, and the smirk widened. "Yes. Yes. That's exactly what I would do. I would walk home! You see? This is me, moving in."

Shane hit a puddle and almost spun out. He recovered, slowed down, and tried to keep his foot steady on the gas pedal as he shot another glance at his crazy Russian boyfriend. "Moving in?"

"Yes." He reminded Shane of one of the cats after they'd escaped from the house, gone hunting and dropped something unspeakable on his porch. "I went home today and looked around, and I realized, the only thing keeping me there was memories of Mutti. She is gone," and for the first time his voice sobered, "but you are here. And you want me to be happy, and I am happy when I am with you. Until you have found someone better, I will be with you, and it really is that simple."

Shane swallowed hard. "Really?" Damn. "That simple?" He took a deep breath and tried to control the giddy, big-doofus smile that wanted to take over his face.

"Da," Mikhail said smugly. "You see, before I went to work today, I looked around. I thought, 'My bed would go well in Shane's guest room, like he said, and my favorite clothes are already there. We can move the rest this weekend.'" He thrust his shoulders forward, and indicated the burden in his arms. "This is the only thing we need, and so I took it. And now I am moved in."

"But work...." Shane didn't have to ask what the thing in his arms was now—even though he wanted a guided tour of it when they got home.

Mikhail nodded, looking very pleased with himself. "Work is taken care of. I asked Anna tonight—she said I could change classes with the girl who teaches at Levee Oaks. She lives in Citrus Heights—it is closer for both of us. If our students really want us, they will commute—that is what Anna said, and I hope she is right. Either way, I will still teach and I will still dance, but I will come to a place with cats who adore me."

"And me," Shane said, bemused by it all.

Mikhail's expression sobered completely. "You are home, *lubime.* I can always find another shitty apartment. Time when you adore me is not always guaranteed."

Shane grunted, trying to find words to tell him that it *was* guaranteed, that Mikhail *didn't* have to worry, but he drove up to the cattle guard, and Mikhail put his burden down on the car floorboards and got out to open the gate. The dogs were huddling in the giant lean-to Shane had built up against the house and outfitted with some old blankets and food and water for days just like this when the weather changed. On a night like this, they were too cold to come out and greet their pet humans, and Shane and Mickey didn't have to worry about being swamped with wet dog.

When they got inside, Mikhail took the cedar box out of its wrappings (there was a layer of trash bags under the sodden blanket— when Shane asked why he didn't put the blankets under the trash bags, he looked embarrassed and said, "Because I am not terribly bright. And now you know"), and put it on Shane's dresser.

"It is heavier now than it used to be," Mikhail admitted, shaking out his cramped arm muscles. He looked slyly at Shane as Shane was trying to strip off his jeans and socks and sopping wet tennis shoes. "I think I have you to thank for that."

Shane grunted and sat down heavily, Mikhail's shoe in his hand. "I didn't want you to forget about us, is all."

Mikhail stepped daintily out of his jeans and boxers, which were pooled around his ankles. "If my precious box were dropped into a well and bombed out of existence, you would still be etched in my heart."

Shane looked up at him from his ungraceful position on the floor. "You always manage to say the nicest things when I'm feeling like the biggest jerkoff. Why is that?"

Mikhail shrugged out of Shane's sweatshirt and then his denim jacket and then the three layers underneath—all were soaked.

"I do not know. Why don't you join me in the shower and fuck me until neither of us care?" He was shivering, but his slightly blue-tinged grin was one hundred percent invitation, and Shane was on his feet and hopping out of his uniform and putting his gun in the closet safe even as Mikhail turned on the water.

As he stepped into the steaming shower and felt his lover's pliant flesh under his hands, he reflected that Mickey had been right. Sometimes, words really were overrated.

Chapter 21

Lost track of how far I've gone… How far I've gone, how high I've climbed

"The Rising"—Bruce Springsteen

MIKHAIL would later wonder on the good fortune they had to bring his bed to the spare room—not that Mikhail ever needed it to sleep in, no, but it did make the room look good, and eventually it would get use.

In the meantime, he was learning that living with Shane was far easier than living without him had ever been. It was so easy, in fact, as to make Mikhail doubt his sanity just a little. What kind of fool turns down a stolen life when it is given to you?

That didn't mean he didn't worry.

Shane's soul-breaking work schedule continued, and the stress of the odd shift times and the lack of sleep were beginning to tell. Mikhail had even called Calvin to ask, shyly and humbly, if there was any reason Calvin knew of why they were being scheduled so badly.

Calvin had sighed into the phone. "Why do you think, Mr. Bayul? It's not like everybody doesn't know you're staying with him. I mean, Shane's a good man and a good cop, but nobody can take this for too long. Hell—I had to take a day off sick leave. I spent the whole day worried that he was going to get sent out on a call and left there."

Mikhail sighed. He hated to ask. He really did. But it had to be done. "And if I was not living here?"

"Don't even think about it," Calvin had growled. "I think you're the only thing keeping him on his feet."

Mikhail had tentatively broached the subject with Shane. "Well, what do you want me to do, Mickey? Quit and let them win?"

"Well, you could... I don't know. Jon and Amy are doing legal work for Deacon...."

Shane shook his head and looked away. He was spending a precious hour off shift picking up the dog crap in the yard, because with six dogs, if it wasn't done daily, the shit would *literally* crawl up the porch.

"They're doing that because Deacon needs to keep the ranch. I don't need this job. They haven't done anything but harass me a little. And I've already gotten the big gay payoff. I don't want any more money. I just want to do a job I'm proud of!" His voice rose at the end, and even Mikhail, with his flash temper, could see that the man was asleep on his feet. He sighed and took the clever dog-crap-picker-upper from Shane's hands.

"Go take your boots off and nap," he said softly. "I'll take this over, and you can dream of some sort of amazing sexual favor to grant me for it later."

Shane's mouth went mutinous for a minute, and Mikhail remembered that yes, this big warm man had his pride, and it should be honored. To stave off the ego-puffing-chest-fluffing turkey moment, Mikhail raised himself on tiptoe and pressed his mouth to Shane's.

Shane closed his eyes and opened his mouth and went boneless in his lover's arms, and Mikhail took the advantage to push him into the house.

"You know," Mikhail said as he tottered through the doorway, "there are other jobs out there that would make you happy."

Shane turned to him with such puzzlement on his face that Mikhail had to rack his brains to make sure he hadn't been speaking in Russian.

"What other job?" he asked, at a complete loss, and Mikhail shook his head in frustration.

"Don't hurt yourself with the thought, big man. We'll talk about it later."

Of course later was always at two in the morning, and they had better things to do with their mouths and their time at two in the morning. More often than not, Mikhail ended up talking to Benny about it, because that's where he went when he was not working and Shane was. The little connecting pathway between their houses was just so easy to traverse, and much of it could be spent accompanied by the dogs, who always loved the run. By necessity, Mikhail had learned the trick to dealing with the dogs. First, he always had something to throw for them on hand. Second, he always had a pocket full of dog treats. More than once, as Angel Marie had been thundering at him like a furry dragon of death, he had thrown the pocketful of dog treats on the ground and climbed whatever was handy to get off the ground and out of the way of the drooling monsters. Of course, more than once they had overtaken him and covered him in wet hair and dog spit, so it was a pretty even-handed battle at the moment.

But when he dodged out of the cattle fence and caught the trail to go to Deacon's, he left the big furry monsters behind and found someone to share the burden for caring for his open-hearted cop.

Benny, surrounded by big protective men, seemed to have a special fondness for the diminutive Mikhail. In spite of their age difference, she related to him as an equal, and he was grateful for the unburdened friendship.

And they both shared the harrowing experience of getting their driver's license.

"I don't even want to ask him to take me," Mikhail told her one Sunday, mournfully. "He would, you know? But he is always so tired— and then we get in the car and he spends the whole time holding on to the oh-shit bar, and then where am I?"

They were sitting on the porch together, watching as Parry Angel— bundled in a jacket because the wind was bitter on this sunny March day—toddled around a big plastic structure that had been set up in the front yard. Benny actually set down the knitting she had on her lap and turned to look at him wryly.

"I didn't know GTOs came with oh-shit bars. Crick's Toyota has a different feature—we call it the hail-Jesus-handle. Do you think they do the same thing?"

Mikhail was forced to laugh too. "I would imagine it's a difference in semantics only. You know, it isn't very good for the morale when they grab that thing. It makes me nervous as soon as his knuckles go white."

Benny snorted. "Oh yeah—all you have are white knuckles. I have a blown eardrum. I sweartagod, I was sitting at an intersection with Crick in the passenger seat, waiting for a chance to go and suddenly he turns and screams, '*What the hell are you waiting for? A sign from GOD?*'" Benny shuddered. "He spooked me so bad, I tried to pull out right then—there was a car coming, and *they* had to swerve into the oncoming lane to avoid us, and basically, I almost killed a shitload of people because Crick's a complete dick." Benny leaned back and covered her face with her hands. "And Deacon had to drive Jeff home the last time he took me."

Mikhail stared at her. "It was that traumatic?"

Benny shook her head. "No—he brought a hip flask. By the time we were done with the lesson, he was plastered."

Mikhail couldn't help it—he started with a smirk and then progressed to a giggle, and by the time Benny had put her knitting down in disgust and gone to get Parry Angel to come in for a snack, he was laughing hard enough to wipe tears from his eyes.

"Oh shut up!" Benny complained as she walked past him, the baby on her hip. Mikhail courteously picked up her knitting and followed her into the house, where she had taken the baby's jacket and rubber boots off and was putting her into the high chair.

"Why does not Deacon take you?" he asked, trying to get back into her good graces. For one thing, snack today involved little yellow crackers, and he loved those.

Benny sighed. "He did—he's good at it. But Crick told me that the last couple times he did, he got home, clapped me on the back and said, "'Good job, Shorty!' and then went and threw up, he was so nervy. I *swear* I am not that bad!"

"I believe it." She was so competent at nearly everything she did—there was no reason to believe this would be any different. "Why do you think it is so hard for everybody?" Poor Benny—her experiences were starting to make Shane's white knuckles and clenched-jaw smile sound like no particular trauma.

Benny sighed and got out a banana with one hand while handing Mikhail the box of crackers with the other. Mikhail smiled happily and started eating the little yellow fish.

"I think it's because they're all first responders—or they have been—you know?"

Mikhail blinked. His spoken English was *very* good, but he was unfamiliar with this term. "First responders?"

"Nana!" interrupted Parry joyfully, and instead of answering Mikhail, Benny turned to her daughter.

"Are you going to eat it this time or just mash it around on your high chair?"

"Nana! Eat nana!"

"You promise?"

"Pwomise!"

Benny's lips quirked upward in a smile, and Mikhail would not put any money on the little girl keeping that promise.

"You were saying?" Mikhail prompted after Parry was quiet. Of course, once she got the banana, she started using it to chase the goldfish across the tray of her high chair. It was a charming activity—but one Mikhail was glad he wasn't responsible for cleaning up.

"A first responder," Benny continued, "is someone who's first on the scene of an accident. Deacon and Crick were EMTs—hell, Crick was an EMT in *Iraq* for chrissakes… they've seen some really hairy shit, you know? I do something stupid in traffic, and suddenly they're seeing me in a pile of twisted metal, wearing my toes as a necklace. Jeff, too—he sees the survival aftermath of shit like that. It's probably why Shane goes all white knuckle on you—although, knowing Shane, he's probably screaming on the inside and smiling and telling you it's all good on the outside, a lot like Deacon. I mean, I know why they do it, it just doesn't make it any easier."

Mikhail looked at her, chewing his child's crackers and feeling extremely stupid. Of course she was right. Poor Shane, imagining the worst of things while Mikhail was merely enjoying the power of his car. He never had let on, either.

"You know," he said, after he'd swallowed a handful of extremely dry goldfish, "maybe we should switch. You know, have Shane teach you and one of your men"—Deacon, please let it be Deacon—"teach me. They would not worry so much about me, and Shane is very good at keeping his worry inside and his voice level. Maybe if we tried it that way, we will both have our driver's licenses before fall."

Benny had turned seventeen in February and would finish her home-study courses in June. She was going away to college in the fall—it was sort of imperative that she get her license, or she wouldn't be able to come home and visit. Mikhail was hoping to be able to drive to the faires starting in April. He and Shane had heard from Kimmy—she had sounded anxious and distracted but not stoned, so they had both told her to come visit them and looked at each other unhappily. They could not help if she did not ask for it, but that didn't mean they did not worry. But Kimmy had told them that Mikhail was welcome to come work with the little troupe. She had implied that Kurt's arm had not healed, but her exact words were, "Kurt's not up to dancing," so that hadn't boded well, either. At any rate, Mikhail had his summer job again and this time at full speed, with a couple of exceptions for the children's recital at Anna's dance studio, and, of course....

"We can do that," Benny said excitedly. "But not before the picnic in three weeks. We've got too much to do."

Mikhail nodded, still unsure as to why this picnic was so extremely important to everyone. "So," he said now, "it is a picnic, with food and dancing and... document signing?"

Benny rolled her eyes. "No, silly—it's a wedding!"

Mikhail shook his head, still confused. "It is a wedding," he said slowly, "but we can't tell Deacon it is a wedding. Even though it is his."

Benny laughed and poured some milk into a pink plastic cup to finish up Parry's snack. "Exactly."

"I am not seeing why we cannot tell Deacon. Shouldn't he know he is getting married?"

"He's been married," Benny said quietly, her face glowing with the romance of it all. "He and Crick have been *together*-together for three years. If they didn't split up when Crick lost his fucking mind and joined the Army, it ain't ever gonna happen. So the paperwork is a common property contract. It's essentially a marriage contract—it says that Crick is entitled to half of everything, just like a married couple. But you're not allowed to get married in California. So since we were having the big picnic to celebrate keeping the ranch and signing the paper and," Benny blushed slyly, "some other things, Crick wanted to say some stuff to Deacon that he thought should have witnesses. You know—since a bunch of us had to pick Deacon up off the floor when he left, he figured we should get to see Deacon get a promise for a happy ending."

Mikhail was stunned. Promises—the ultimate promise. He swallowed, feeling oddly moved. "That's really wonderful," he muttered.

"Yeah," Benny echoed, and then went off into plans about dresses and decorations and Crick's mystery gift for Deacon, and Mikhail was left following her in a haze of wonder, thinking about promises he'd like to make to Shane. He stopped short while washing up the tray for Parry's high chair. Benny had taken the baby back for a quick scrub and a nap, and since he was staying for dinner, he'd offered to clean up for her and get the dinner started, and she'd taken him up on it.

It suddenly occurred to him that with his current plan in place, he couldn't make promises to Shane. He planned to give Shane to someone better when someone better came along.

It had sounded like a good plan at the beginning—Shane was too good a man for him, and that was that. But it was not sounding so good now. Who would take care of Shane the way he would? Who would make him sleep or take care of the furry dragons or love the cats the way Mikhail would?

Who would blow his mind in bed?

Mikhail felt a sudden sense of panic. Nobody—there was nobody out there who would take care of this man the way he could. But he had promised himself… promised that he would not burden Shane with his imperfections, his temper, his damaged, angry soul.

He set the high chair tray back on the high chair and wiped it dry, and thought of the little girl pushing goldfish across the surface with bananas. Some promises, he thought, were made to be broken. He frequently broke his promise to Shane about walking at night—he was not delicate, and he could take care of himself.

But that did not mean he would *ever* break his promise about pushing Shane away using cruelty or by pouring salt into his old wounds again. He'd die first. *That* promise was meant to be kept as no other would be.

The question was, which promise was this one?

Mutti, he thought, *this is where you would say something wise. Something like, "Less self-serving poetry and more Russian practicality,* lubime.*" Something that would make me keep him.*

But his mother had been dead for more than a month, and as much as he enjoyed wordplay and poetry and may even have believed in heaven, he did not believe in ghosts. Even when he heard her voice in his head, he knew it was just memory and wishful thinking telling him that Shane was all he'd ever need in another person to keep him happy.

He could not trust that voice—it was far too close to what his heart said, and his heart was not the most trustworthy of things.

He turned to start chopping up vegetables for dinner—some sort of chicken thing that Benny got out of a book and Mikhail was looking forward to making—and then, because it was Sunday, Jeff came in, and then Jon and Amy with the baby, and then Deacon, Crick, and Andrew called it a day and came in to wash up. Benny and the baby came back from their nap, and suddenly the kitchen and the living room were full of people who gave a shit that he was there, and he could forget about promises for a moment.

He certainly forgot about them after dinner, as he was sitting down and eating banana cream pie and Jeff sidled up to him for a little chat.

"Where's your big goofy boyfriend?"

Mikhail glared at him sideways. "Be nice, or I'll have my big goofy boyfriend knock out your teeth. He would not do it to defend himself, but he'll do it because I ask him to, so watch it."

Jeff laughed delightedly. "Oh, God, honey—you are just so damned cute! But you didn't answer my question. Where is he?"

Mikhail sighed, and his appetite for pie faded. "He is at work. He will swing by around ten to pick me up and to say hi, and then he will go home and fall down where he stands and go to sleep, because he has to be up in seven hours to go to work again."

Jeff swore. "Fuck—dammit all to hell! He's out at work, isn't he?"

Mikhail grimaced. "Calvin said people just sort of assumed after everybody showed up for him when he was hurt. The poor man has his back, you know. Signs up for the same bullshit shifts, rides in the car with him. It is just so… so…."

"So maddening," Jeff muttered. "So not fair. Not for Shane. Man, all that guy wants to do is be a hero."

Mikhail put his chin on his hands glumly. Shane was *his* hero. If they could find another job for him, maybe that could be enough.

Jeff patted his back comfortingly. "That's gotta be rough on the old love life, huh, babycakes?"

Mikhail looked at him sideways and didn't answer. They did okay. Well, more than okay—but yes. He was sure they would be having more sex and happier sex if Shane got some sleep occasionally.

Jeff raised a sardonic eyebrow and waited, arms crossed, shit-eating grin of sympathy fixed firmly on his pretty face, for Mikhail's reply.

Finally the silence got to him and Mikhail said, "I would rather get him to relax and really rest than worry about the sex. With the sex, he has too much to do. It's all work work work for him—I would just like him to get some real sleep."

Jeff wrinkled his nose. "Well, it's not like you can't go down on him—I mean, you're okay doing that, aren't you?"

Mikhail's professional pride was—for lack of a better word—pricked, and he straightened in his seat and gave a disdainful sniff. "I did this for a living, dammit! I gave the best blowjobs for a six-block radius," he proclaimed, and Andrew, who had been drawing near them with his pie to sit down and talk, got big, alarmed eyes and backed away.

"Sorry, guys, this is where I draw the 'straight' line and follow it!"

Mikhail watched him go with reddening cheeks, and Jeff dissolved into giggles next to him. "Oh. My. God. *Please* tell me I can repeat that story. Jesus, that's better than Crick's little talk with his doctor."

Mikhail gave his friend (yes, he was a friend now) a disgusted look. "You may tell whomever you like," he snapped. "By all means, tell the entire world that I worked as a prostitute when I was younger than Benny—take out a Facebook page if you like."

Jeff sobered immediately. "I'm sorry, Mikhail," he said, instantly contrite. "I didn't know—I was being a jerk and I didn't get the first part of what you said. Didn't understand it. Don't worry—the story stays here in Deacon's kitchen, okay?"

A long, shuddering sigh later, and it really was okay. "I am not even mad about that—I don't care who knows it. I just want to make Shane feel better so he can go out and maybe not get stabbed or shot at or slugged in the jaw or kicked or whatever else the world wants to do to him because it is a vicious motherfucker and he is a nice man."

Jeff lowered his voice and gave Mikhail a meaningful look. "Well, you know. Have you thought about 'leading'?"

"Leading what?" Mikhail had a thought about leading Shane about with a collar around certain parts of his body, and then shook it off. Jeff could not possibly be talking about that.

"You know... *leading.* Being on top." Jeff *sounded* confident, but his hand was fiddling with his immaculately coiffed dark hair, so maybe he was a little more nervous than he let on.

"On top of what?" And now he had visions of dancing on the roof.

Jeff scrubbed his face with his hands. "You know, for a man who just confessed to living out on the streets, you should know more about sex than this. Have you thought about taking charge of the whole operation... you know... *taking charge?*"

Mikhail felt like the furrow between his eyebrows was drilling into the bones of his skull. "I speak two languages, and I swear we are both speaking one of them, but I am not understanding what you are saying."

Jeff looked around them, and Mikhail did too. Apparently Andrew's example had stuck because the rest of the family was giving them a wide berth while they huddled together like conspirators at the big wooden kitchen table. "You know, Mikhail... giving instead of receiving? Being the 'penetrator' instead of the 'penetratee'... you know... slipping Shane the hot beef...."

"Oh God. I get it now, and you can shut up, please." Mikhail felt a terrible flush steal up from his toes to his cheekbones, and he had to sit stunned at the table and blink several times before he could actually resume the conversation.

"I, uhm," Jeff said, coloring delicately himself, "I take it you've never been, uhm, in charge?"

Mikhail thrust out his lower lip and squeezed his eyes shut. "If I give you permission to repeat that story, will you drop the subject completely?"

Still, he responded to Jeff's sympathetic squeeze of his shoulder. "Absolutely, honey-doll. What do you want to talk about?"

"How about teaching me to drive?" Mikhail asked cruelly, and he was rewarded when Jeff blanched.

"Oh fuck you. Dammit—now I need a drink!"

Their conversation moved to other things, and they moved on to talk to other people in the room, but still Mikhail mulled it over.

Shane came and got him, coming in for a couple of minutes to say hi to the family, and he looked so tired—his face was drawn and pale, and the lines by his eyes seemed especially deep. Deacon came up to Mikhail while Shane was giving Benny a hug and listening to her talk a mile a minute about their new plan to have him teach her to drive.

"Work giving him a bad time?"

Mikhail just nodded unhappily.

"Well, let us know what we can do...."

"You could always convince him that he does not need to work. Or that he would be better off doing something else. Or that maybe we should just rip out his heart and slow cook it for breakfast. You know— something easy."

Deacon smirked bitterly, and Mikhail felt a little better. Deacon knew—that was someone on their side.

Still, he couldn't help mulling over Jeff's words that night as Shane took them home. He wondered.... Get Shane to shower, rub his back, massage that mass of heavy and tight muscles at his shoulders, move down, down, down....

Just because he'd never done it that way before didn't mean it couldn't work that way, right?

He was starting to get aroused by the thought—*really* aroused, actually. Then Shane pulled up into the driveway, and real life reared its ugly head.

"I'll just pick up the dog crap before I come in, okay?"

Oh fuck. Fuck fuck fuck fuck fuck.

"I got the cat boxes," Mikhail said contritely. "And fed everybody and cleaned the house...." He'd even trimmed their claws before he'd left for Deacon's place that afternoon, but he'd forgotten the dog shit. Lovely.

Shane looked at him gratefully. "No worries, Mickey—thank you for doing all of that stuff—that's awesome. I'm really grateful—you weren't supposed to move in and take over all the shit jobs, you know. My animals weren't supposed to be your problem."

Mikhail smiled at him fondly. "It was not a big deal," he said, meaning it. Then he shrugged. "Besides. The cats are mine."

To his surprise, Shane started laughing, and then, as the car idled in front of the cattle gate, he reached out and planted a big, warm hand on the back of Mikhail's skull and pulled him in for a laughing, happy kiss. Mikhail groaned and sank into the contact of mouth on mouth and spread his hands on Shane's chest and forgot all about who was on top and who was on bottom and just concentrated on tasting him and oh! The smell of him was just making his toes tingle and oh, God, he was sooooooo warm and so right....

Shane pulled back and rested their foreheads together, and the both of them sat panting in the car for a minute. "You know... maybe the dog crap can wait until morning...."

"I'll get it in the morning," Mikhail assured him fervently. "Let me open the gate and go in and start the shower... please?"

"Da," Shane muttered, his lean mouth curving up into a smile, and Mikhail moved as fast as he could.

He did not top that night. Shane wanted him too badly. They soaped each other up in the shower, hands sliding deliciously along wet, slippery skin. Shane stood behind him and pulled his pliant, lithe body back along Shane's solid, hard one, and took the longest, most heavenly time simply running the bath sponge, squishy with suds, from his chin to his thighs and all points in between. Oh, God... especially all points in between.

That warm sponge went away, replaced by Shane's slippery, strong hand on Mikhail's erect cock, and Mikhail could barely stand anymore, he was so high with arousal. He leaned forward, braced his hands against the back wall of the shower and let Shane's hands take over. It was so good... just so damned good to put this man in charge of his happiness. That slippery hand took him at his base and squeezed slowly, arrogantly, to the tip and then back again. Another slippery hand slid behind him, parting the cleft of his buttocks, and a soapy finger slid inside him with almost no friction at all.

Mikhail leaned his head against his arms, then groaned loudly enough to echo, and then began to gibber and beg into the cave created by the tile and his arms.

"Please... oh, please... *mishka*, more... damn, please, more...."

He could only plead like this because he trusted that Shane would do anything to please him.

Shane's cock—engorged, huge, and slick—pressed against his entrance, and Mikhail almost wept as it pushed inside of him. Oh... oh God... this was his favorite thing, the best form of possession, and it was better, so much better, with Shane's broad chest pressed against his back and his big hands, one spanning Mikhail's chest and the other stroking his almost painful erection until he whimpered, not wanting to come, not yet, oh please... let it last, just a little longer... .

But it was almost impossible, especially with Shane's low voice muttering in his ear.

"You like that, Mickey? You like me inside you? You want me to fuck you into the wall?"

"Oh God, yes...." His ass was stretched and pounded, and Shane's body was so big and so fervent that every touch was carnal and tender and... that voice... it was almost like sex squared.

"Gonna just pound you and take you and fuck you... so good... so... so damned... good...."

"Oh please... please...."

Shane had a sturdy rubber matt under their feet, and a handle on the wall, and the hand across Mikhail's chest was suddenly gripping the handle, and his hips were pistoning like a race car and... oh... oh... oh....

"*Gawwwwdddd...*," Shane groaned and bit Mikhail's shoulder, and that edge of pain pushed Mikhail over the cliff and Mikhail poured himself into the shower as Shane poured himself into Mikhail.

When it was done, Mikhail sagged limply. Shane's arm around his chest was the only thing that kept him from falling to his knees. Shane hefted him up and nuzzled his ear and turned off the water and wrapped towels around them and basically cared for him. He reveled in it, allowing himself to be stroked and dried and even powdered, until they both slid—clean and dry and naked—between the sheets of what Mikhail was now thinking of as their bed.

He rolled into Shane's arms and nuzzled the big man's chest until Shane chuckled softly and fell asleep.

Mikhail lay there in the dark for a little time after that, thinking hard. He thought about trust and how much he trusted Shane, and he thought about promises and which ones were made to be broken. He thought about Shane's integrity and his earnestness and all of the things that made this man, this big, sweet, wonderful man so perfect, and how he didn't want to break these things for all the world.

He thought about being cared for and what sorts of responsibilities one took on when one did the caring in return.

It was a lot to think about, and he resolved nothing. But as he lay in the arms of the man he could not imagine leaving, he traced careful fingertips over Shane's shadowed cheeks and had a little faith that maybe these things *could* be resolved, if only he came right back here to Shane's bed every night to chew them over.

Chapter 22

And when I awoke, I was alone; this bird had flown.

"Norwegian Wood"—The Beatles

SHANE thought that the wedding between Crick and Deacon was possibly one of the most beautiful things he'd ever seen—if he didn't count Mikhail sleeping next to him when he woke up in the morning.

He'd been to Promise Rock in the summer—the family had held swimming picnics before, and he liked the little swimming hole with its tall stand of oak trees and big table of rocks from which to jump into the water. Crick and Deacon's wedding was in April, so the water was still high, and the wind was still sweet, and the sun was not too brutal, like it would probably be in May. The sky was pansy blue, and the surrounding fields were a gold-dotted green with splotches of playful orange, but that wasn't the only reason it was beautiful.

The way Deacon and Crick looked at each other as they stood in the midst of their friends was enough to make his heart stop.

"Ask me again, Deacon."

"I love you. Please stay."

"Of course I'll stay. What kind of asshole turns that down?"

For all that Shane didn't know about the two of them, knowing this place was holy to them made it holy to him as well. Promise Rock—the family church.

Their vows spoken, the surrounding group of family and friends gathered at the food table and gave Deacon and Crick a few minutes alone.

Unlike a big, formal wedding, this one was solely about the celebration of love and not about the pictures and the impression the lovers would make on the guests. The guests were more than happy to let the lovers talk quietly to each other while they got their composure.

"Did you see Deacon?" Mikhail murmured to him. "He looked almost as though he expected Crick to say no."

Shane smiled and nuzzled his ear from behind. "You never take anything like that for granted, Mickey. Ask me how I know."

Mikhail turned toward him thoughtfully. "Don't take me for granted, no. But you do trust that I'll be there, yes?" He smiled hopefully, as though Shane's answer was very important to him.

"Yes," Shane answered dutifully. He believed it too, for the most part. But there was still an edge of... of rabbit in Mikhail. Shane couldn't help but remember the qualifier he'd added once—*until you find somebody else.*

Mikhail's eyes narrowed, and he shrugged Shane's arms off. "I'll believe that when you do," he sniffed, and Shane watched him flounce off to talk to Jeff and shook his head.

"He's a bit of a handful, isn't he?"

Shane looked back to the table and saw Judy, who had come to the occasional Sunday dinner since they'd met—but not one that Mikhail had been at, if he remembered correctly.

"Very worth it," he replied, and he was a little too besotted to care that he was staring at his boyfriend with complete and total adoration in his eyes.

Judy threw back her head and laughed, her dark hair curling around her face in a very appealing manner, and her lovely yellow dress blowing around her ankles gracefully. For a second, Shane wondered if Judy would be as much a handful as Mikhail. He doubted it—but then, as pretty as she was, he liked the payoff of holding Mikhail, so it was not something he'd dwell on.

As if reading his thoughts she said, "Well, I think I'm going to have to take myself off 'standby'. Your 'one-chance heart' is obviously very well taken care of."

Shane turned to her sheepishly and shrugged. "He's pretty awesome," he said earnestly, and then he remembered he was trying not to be too much of a psychopath and pulled his social adjustment out of his socks. "How are you doing? Did you bring anybody today?"

She shook her head and rolled her eyes self-deprecatingly. "Nobody I cared about enough to want to see this," she said softly. "It was beautiful, wasn't it? Like a painting or a poem or something?"

"Or a song," Shane said with some enthusiasm. "Something by Springsteen or Journey or Nickelback or something like that."

Instead of laughing—as nearly anyone but Mikhail would do—Judy nodded. "Yes—exactly. I like Death Cab For Cutie myself, and I could almost hear 'Marching Bands of Manhattan' in the background, you know?"

"I was hearing 'Gypsy Biker' myself," Shane confessed, and Crick's old art teacher made a thoughtful "oooh" with her mouth.

"Nice one—or maybe 'Faithfully', by Journey, you think?"

"Or that one they just did on that show with the high school kids…"

"*Glee*?" she interrupted, and Shane nodded, enjoying the conversation a lot. It was the kind of conversation he might have with Mikhail, without all of the sexual tension and the distraction of wanting to get Mickey into bed.

"We love that show!" Shane told her. "Mickey and I don't miss it—you just have to root for those kids, you know? They're so damned lost."

Judy's eyes grew sober. "Tell me about it," she murmured, darting eyes at Crick, and Shane caught the mood shift as well, and he remembered a question he'd had with nobody to ask.

"Hey—if a kid runs away and finds a way to make a living and pay rent and everything, how can they get back in school? What are their options?"

"You know a kid like that?" she asked with some curiosity.

Shane shrugged. "Know several. I got them jobs, places to sleep, that sort of thing, but they need to finish school, move on, you know? They just don't have anyone to help, and they're afraid to go to the school system because that would mean going home, and most of them would rather live on the streets." He thought about Carly, a waif of a girl that he'd set up at the animal shelter, living in the back room and cleaning up animal crap for a minimum wage. She loved it there—but wouldn't she love it more in an apartment with an Animal Health Tech certificate under her belt?

Judy nodded and widened her eyes. "Wow—that's a tall order. Unless the kid's in some sort of shelter, social services usually get involved. It's a lot harder for a minor to be emancipated than people think—and of course, by the time they're old enough to not worry about the system...."

"They're too damned old for the free education," Shane finished grimly, and they both sighed together.

"Now a shelter is a good idea," Deacon muttered, coming up and surprising them. "Shane keeps bringing me muckrakers, and I don't have anywhere to put them. We've already got Andrew sleeping on the couch, and we're thinking about building a mother-in-law cottage in the back of the property just for him so the muckrakers can sleep in that stall. Hi, Ms. Thompson. It was nice of you to come.'

Judy Thompson wrapped her arm around Deacon's waist and gave him a one-armed hug. "It was nice of you to invite me, Deacon. You know, I was never *your* art teacher—you graduated the year before I got there. Why do you keep calling me 'Ms. Thompson'?"

Deacon blushed, and Judy caught Shane's eyes and arched her eyebrows. The man could be so strong—and unbelievably self-effacing.

"That's how Crick knows you," Deacon mumbled, and Judy laughed and said something about Crick's wedding present to Deacon. Shane had seen it, but he hadn't signed the big picture that Crick had drawn featuring everybody's favorite horse-breaker being all of the things they loved him for.

Shane saw that Deacon would never talk to the nice lady if he was there, so he excused himself to go sign the sketch. He stood there looking at the fine detail work—Deacon breaking horses, Deacon asleep on an outstretched arm, Deacon nose to nose with a horse who seemed to adore him, every small sketch centered around a portrait of Deacon that Crick had sketched when Deacon had been maybe eighteen. He'd been still scrawny with adolescence but still beautiful, too, and had all of the strength and the vulnerability that his family had come to treasure.

"It's a beautiful picture," Mickey said, coming up beside him, and Shane took the offered felt-tipped pen and signed his name in the margins, and then gave the pen to Mikhail. Mikhail looked surprised a little, and then made his rough—and embarrassed—scrawl next to Shane's.

"You can see all of Crick's love in it," Shane said, feeling silly, but it was the truth, and he didn't know what else to say. There was something restless in Mikhail, and suddenly, when there had never been any awkwardness between the two of them, there was an awkward moment now.

"Here, guys," Amy said, showing them the two other documents they were there to sign. One was to witness the common law property sharing that Deacon and Crick were doing, and the other was to give Deacon partial custody of Parry Angel. The county had tried to take Parry away from the family while Crick had been in Iraq, and Benny was determined that nobody would ever tell Deacon that he wasn't that baby's family ever again.

Shane signed the next one, then gave the pen to Mickey, and then they repeated the process. Amy heard the silence between the two of them and raised her eyebrows at Shane, and he shrugged back. He had no idea. She shrugged again and jerked her chin to the other side of the table, and she moved off to give them some privacy, baby cradled on her hip as she did her part as the other half of Levins and Levins, the law firm she shared with her husband.

"She cannot have you," Mikhail mumbled, his voice barely audible over the murmur of the wedding guests and shushing of the wind through the oak trees overhead.

"I'm sorry?" Shane was honestly puzzled.

Mikhail shook his head and then grabbed Shane's hands and hauled him around to the other side of Promise Rock, the side uncomfortably in the sun where they were completely alone in the unapologetic April brightness.

"She cannot have you," Mikhail repeated. He was gazing resolutely up at Shane with a stubborn jaw and a furrowed brow and a terrible import in his blue-gray eyes, and Shane had no fucking idea what he was talking about.

"Oooookay," he said, nodding to calm his lover down, "she can't have me."

"I know she's better than I am, but she can't have you."

"She is *not* better than you are, and she still can't have me."

"I'm *serious* here, dammit!" And Mikhail's eyes were suddenly swimming in tears. He'd barely cried at his mother's funeral, had barely shed a tear at her death, and now he was in tears, and Shane was completely unhinged by it. He wrapped his arms around this strong, wiry little man that he loved more than he loved breathing and tried to calm down the trembling that had taken over his self-possessed body.

"I get that you're serious," he muttered. "I don't know what you're serious about, but believe me, Mickey, I'm totally not taking it lightly."

"You don't understand," Mickey muttered against his chest.

"I really don't."

"I was going to give you back."

"You were going to *what*?" And this was surprising enough to have Shane grabbing his arms and thrusting him out and away so Shane could look at his expression again and see if he was *really* serious about what it sounded like he was.

Mikhail nodded back, not the least bit penitent. "You were on loan, you see? Until you found somebody better. I kept thinking, 'Maybe this person will be better. Or maybe this one.' But none of them were good enough, so I got to keep you. And then I broke up and you still wanted me, and I thought there was *nobody* good enough for you, so maybe I would keep you by... by...." He struggled with the next word, and since his accent was thicker as his voice became more clogged, Shane could hardly think of which word he was going to say next.

"Default?" he suggested, helpful and appalled at the same time.

"Yes!" Mikhail nodded, then wiped his eyes on the shoulder of his lovely blue linen shirt. "I got to keep you by default. There was nobody good enough for you, so you could be mine, but...." Mikhail's look was naked and miserable and defiant, and Shane couldn't think of a single way to comfort him without shaking him and asking, *What in the hell were you thinking?*

"She cannot have you!" Mikhail snapped, irritated—probably at the fact that he was crying, because heaven knew it didn't sit easily on him. "She cannot. She is perfect. She is funny, and I heard your conversation and she likes what you do, and you both have good ideas for what you love best and she is even beautiful," he sniffed, a little of his usual disdain coming through, "if you like that sort of thing, but she cannot have you."

His jaw clenched, and his look of determination squared up, and he became fierce and formidable, which was how Shane loved him, so that was okay.

"She cannot have you. You are mine. I don't care how perfect she is for you. You weren't watching her when you spoke, you were watching *me*, and you are *mine*."

And with that he launched himself back into Shane's arms, and all Shane could do was hold onto him bemusedly, and whisper, "Of course I'm yours. Of course I am. Did you think I wanted to be anybody else's? Jesus, Mikhail, you couldn't ditch me if you tried."

Mikhail sniffed and gave that snitty little shrug that Shane adored, then pulled back his head to scowl up into Shane's eyes. "I did try. It didn't take. I've learned my lesson, and I will never try to lose you again."

Something in Shane's heart settled, something realigned itself. This had been the thing holding Mickey back, this had been the thing Shane had doubted. Mikhail hadn't believed it, not until this very moment, that Shane was his and his alone, and that he wouldn't go anywhere— apparently not even if Mickey offered Shane a pretty girl on a silver platter and asked Shane to take her.

They stood there in the April bright sun, just holding each other until the music started on the other side of the rock. Journey's "Open Arms" began to play, and they still held each other, but now they were dancing.

They got home as the sun was setting, after helping everybody (including Crick and Deacon, who had apparently spent all of their sentiment on the ceremony) clean up the "picnic." They'd left the two men sitting on the rock in the twilight with a pickup truck and a bedroll for company—a workingman's honeymoon if ever there was one.

Mikhail closed the cattle gate behind the GTO and said, "I cleaned up the dog shit this morning. There are no more chores to do. Go inside and shower, yes?" as Shane was getting out of the car.

"Come with me?" Shane asked hopefully.

"Nyet." He used the Russian word purposefully—to be cute, Shane could tell.

"Nyet?"

"Nyet. I will take my shower when you are through. I can shower in two minutes—it takes you forever."

"Now *that* is a lie!" Shane denied hotly, but when he got to the shower there was a brand new bath sponge and some sort of special eucalyptus-mint bath soap, and yes. It did take him a good fifteen minutes to finish. He had to admit that at least five minutes of that was just smelling the bath sponge with the soap.

"Hey, Mickey, what is this stuff?" he asked as he wrapped himself in a towel, and Mikhail deftly stepped into the shower and bypassed Shane's groping hand.

"You like?" Mikhail was talking over the water, but he still sounded pleased.

"Yeah… something about it is really turning me on. Where did you get it?"

Mikhail made a pleased sound. "Crick took me shopping last week while you were at work."

Shane opened the shower curtain and looked at him, he was so surprised. "Really? You didn't tell me that!"

Mikhail had just finished soaping his hair, and he blinked through the water and gave a Cheshire-like grin. "Now go grab a towel and lay down on the bed and see what else I've got for you, now that you are clean." Then he smacked Shane's questing hand, because Shane couldn't help himself. Mikhail had a little patch of gold, curly chest hair that fascinated him—and the rest of his stretched, defined, pretty muscles, the ones rippling in his abdomen and his thighs and across his compact chest did the same thing.

"I said go!" Mikhail said, laughing, and Shane sighed and went. He pulled back the covers and shook out a dry towel and laid down on it, pillowing his chin on his hands. He must have nodded off a little, because Mikhail's thighs straddling his nude body came as a surprise. He shifted, and Mikhail put a hand on his back and soothed him.

"No, no… you stay where you are." His hands—hard from the dancing and gymnastics that he did regularly—began to knead Shane's shoulders, and Shane groaned and shuddered.

"Not a problem," he muttered. "Staying. Not moving. God… that's awesome."

He could almost hear Mikhail's purr. "Good. Then that is awesome, and you know my designs on your body are sinful and yet not painful. It is a good start."

Those hands kept working, and Shane's whole body went on "tingle."

"A start…mmmmrrrrrmmmmm… *damn*, Mickey—this is almost better than sex."

There was a stinging slap across his shoulder, and while Shane was saying "Ouch!" Mikhail continued to massage his muscles but this time in a snit. "What a thing to say. Sex with me is *very* good…."

"It's wonderful…."

"Telling me that you get off more from a little back rub…."

"But it's a good back rub…."

There was a snick from a bottle Shane didn't know Mikhail had, and when Mickey's hands touched him next, his hands glided, and now Shane was the one who purred.

"It is a *great* backrub," Mikhail said arrogantly. "But it is not sex. The sex will be better. Trust me."

And those amazing hands kept working on him, and the room filled with the same eucalyptus/mint smell that had been in the shower, and Shane did. Shane trusted him completely. Shane even trusted him as Mikhail scooted back (dragging his erection down the crease of Shane's bottom, don't think Shane didn't notice that) and straddled Shane's thighs, keeping much of his weight on his knees, and then began to massage Shane's backside, flanks, upper thighs, lower back and all.

Shane had to lift himself up to make room for his erection, because it wasn't good to have it all scrunched up like that under his body, and Mikhail chuckled.

"See? Backrub, sex… it can all lead to the same place."

"Right now, it's all leading to… ohh… ohh God…."

Mikhail's thumbs parted the crease of his buttocks and spread him, and the side of his hand slid between, exposing him to the air, and Shane's lazy arousal turned to a hard-on that could drill concrete.

"Jesus…."

"Isn't here. I am." Mikhail had lowered his head, the better to explore, and Shane felt a pointed tongue come out and taste the flesh of his left quarter. There was an experimental smack of tongue and palate, and then Mikhail said, "Oh good—the label was right. I was afraid it would taste horrible, but no. It's a little like mouthwash."

"I didn't know you were planning to lick my… oh…geez…."

Mikhail's hands were busy again, and this time they were even more personal. One of them slipped under Shane and began to fondle, and Shane's testicles became hard and swollen from the gentle rubbing almost immediately. The other hand was busy too. Shane's backside was kneaded some more, and then spread again, and then one experimental finger slipped its way in, and Shane had to grab the coverlet in both hands and groan into the bed.

"Mickey…."

"Yes. Not Jesus."

Shane would have laughed, because the word play was fun and Mikhail was good at it, but he was being stretched, and it burned a little because it had been a while, but it felt good too. Mikhail's other hand fumbled for his cock and started stroking him in the confines between Shane's body and the bed, and Shane raised himself a little on his knees to make room. Mikhail adjusted his position then, straddling his knees and kneeling behind him, and then grabbing Shane around the waist and hauling him up until his face was planted in the mattress and his ass was sticking out in the air. Shane might have been embarrassed then, he might have felt vulnerable, but those hands again, spreading his bottom, and then….

"Ohhh… God, Mickey…."

That pointed little tongue found home, and Shane almost came, and then when he stopped himself, he almost cried it felt so good. And it didn't stop. Shane moaned and gibbered and swore and begged, but that tongue and Mickey's fingers didn't stop, and finally, he pushed himself up on all fours and *pleaded*, "Oh, *please*, Mikhail… *please….*"

"Please what?" Mikhail panted, but he was already behind Shane, pressing down on Shane's shoulder blades until Shane's face was pushed down into the bed again and already positioning himself. Shane felt the little mushroom head right at his entrance, pushing just barely, and Shane wanted it, wanted it *soooo* bad.

"Fuck me… please, oh geez… please please…. *Oh God….*"

And Mikhail was inside him, moving, thrusting, slowly at first and a little uncertainly, and then natural rhythm took over as Shane screamed his pleasure into the pillow in front of him.

"Stroke yourself," Mikhail panted. "I cannot reach and fuck you too…."

His hand flailed for a moment, but every boy knows how to find his cock in the dark, and Shane had himself in hand soon enough. He grabbed and squeezed, and Mikhail thrust, and then Shane stroked, and his skin was a little rough but he couldn't help how fast he pulled and stroked and squeezed and… oh God… oh geez… oh… oh….

"*Auuuuuuuugggghhhhh….*" His climax went on and on and on as he pumped come over his hands and his stomach. His vision went black, and he couldn't seem to stop coming until Mikhail made the same sound and thrust all the way home, deep into his ass, and collapsed over his back.

He felt it. He felt Mikhail's climax, his spend, hot and slick, inside his body, and as he slid flat to the bed and Mikhail rolled off of him and out, he thought that if he had anything left in him, he'd be hard again just from the feel of Mickey's spend trickling down his thighs.

They lay there, breathing hard, for several minutes, and when Shane opened his eyes it was too look into Mikhail's blue-gray ones and smile.

"God."

"I told you, he's not here." But Mickey was blinking as he said it, looking a little bemused.

Shane reached out and stroked the inside of his lover's outstretched arm, needle tracks and all. "I think He is," Shane whispered. "I see Him in everything you do."

Mikhail blinked. "That's blasphemous."

Shane shrugged. "Or holy. What made you decide to…?" If he'd had the energy, he would have blushed.

"Take charge?" Mikhail asked with an arch of his eyebrows.

Shane's grin was about the most energy he could summon. "Yeah. Take charge. You've never wanted to before."

"I've never wanted to *ever*," Mikhail said seriously. "No one has ever trusted me to do that. I have never trusted anyone else to do that to them. I have never trusted myself."

Mikhail's hand came out and brushed Shane's cheekbone in his turn, and Shane's smile softened. "I do trust you," he said. "And I love you. I hope you know that."

"It is the only thing I believe in," Mikhail said seriously. He was the one who moved in for the kiss—but Shane was happy to follow his lead.

Chapter 23

There she sits buddy justa gleaming in the sun, there to greet a working man when his day is done...

"Cadillac Ranch"—Bruce Springsteen

IT WAS a good thing Shane trusted Mickey. Otherwise, a month later (and two weeks after Mikhail had obtained his driver's license, to Benny's immense envy), he could have seriously fucked up their relationship.

But then, pretty much anybody else would have lost his freaking mind, so Shane could be proud. It was almost proof that they were meant to be together.

It all started when Shane got home from work and saw an ancient Chevy van parked in the driveway beyond the cattle gate. The color was hard to decipher, because most of it was in red or gray primer, and Mikhail was standing behind it, gazing fondly at the damned thing while he absently patted Angel Marie's head and the puppy gnawed on his pant-leg.

It had rusted fenders, blacked out windows, and—Shane would put money on it—a blown something-or-whatsis and two or three whajamawhosis that had been taped together for the trip from someone's front lawn to his driveway.

No parent ever looked prouder of a high school graduate than Mickey looked at that rust-nut monstrosity lowering Shane's property value just by not disintegrating into powder.

Shane parked the car and walked up to the love of his life, setting a warm hand on Mickey's shoulder. "Uhm, wow."

Mikhail turned a beaming smile on him. "Isn't she beautiful? I'm going to drive her to the faires, and that way you don't have to worry about me when I work."

Shane's stomach, which just moments ago had been a simple working organ sitting in his abdomen, suddenly became a ten-pound acid pressure cooker, complete with broken glass and rusty nails.

"Uhm, the one this weekend? In Nevada City?" Oh God. That was only four days and sixty miles away.

"Yes!" Mikhail nodded, excited. "Kimmy called—everything is go!"

Shane swallowed. "Awesome, Mickey. It, might, uhm, need a little work before it's street legal, you know that don't you?"

Mikhail's open-eyed gaze at him was as trusting and guileless as the child he had never been. "It shouldn't need too much work. It only died three times on the way over!"

Oh, Jesus. Now Shane knew a parent's pressure to be Santa Claus. "Of course. Absolutely. Excellent. I'll be out to check it over in a minute, okay?"

"Where are you going now? I wanted to show you the inside—it has a bed!"

Shane mentally added "bleach" and "upholstery cleaner" to the terrifying list of things he was going to need for this to turn out okay.

"Give me a second, Mickey—I gotta go inside and change, and I just remembered I need to call Deacon."

It took the full four days to get that thing into working order and four nights of *everyone* working side by side with hanging electric lights and music playing from the garage and grease beneath their fingernails and men   turning   the   air   blue   with   things   like "motherfuckingcocksuckingbitch—die die die die die fucking fucking fucking fucking assfucking *die*!" (This last was Crick, when the engine wouldn't stop turning over even after they'd disconnected the starter. Nobody knew how that happened, but given Crick's bad luck with mechanical things in general, everyone decided it would be best for him to focus on stripping the dark shit from the windows.)

Jeff was the only one who opted out of the whole business. He chose to watch the children in Shane's house instead. Amy and Benny helped

Mikhail rip out the fuzzy purple upholstery and establish a bench seat (complete with seatbelts) that folded back into bed, with some room in the back for another bedroll.

"Good," said Shane, viewing their work. "It's less like a bong and Wesson oil party back here." And of course that was always an improvement.

Calvin joined them on the third day, when even Deacon confessed that the engine block was going to be a challenge, and Amy and Benny retired to the kitchen. They cooked a lot, and Shane would shoo everybody home and come in to a house that smelled like stew and tacos and other things they'd made for the impromptu work party, and, lo and behold, food would appear like magic on the counter. Calvin's two-year-old, Amos, and Parry Angel took an immediate love/hate to each other, and a lot of effort was apparently spent separating the two of them and then allowing them to reunite when they swore they'd be good.

Calvin himself was a little uncertain at first—but once he realized that none of the men working on the car had any interest in him as anything other than a ready pair of hands, he relaxed and actually enjoyed the company. He was a little surprised when Shane told him they didn't do beer, he'd have to settle for soda, but other than that, he was happy to help Deacon bore out the engine and replace the blown head gaskets and rebuild the carburetor. In fact, he told Shane privately that he was a little afraid of Deacon.

"The guy's so quiet—it's like he's Special Forces or something."

Shane didn't tell Calvin that it was just because Deacon didn't talk to strangers—he figured if Calvin hung out enough at his place, he'd figure it out.

On the fourth night, as everybody was working far beyond the call of duty so Mikhail could drive the van to a faire the next morning, Shane came back from the store with Starbucks for everybody as well as a big bag of candy and nuts so folks would stay awake. Mikhail greeted him in the damp spring twilight.

"Here, let me get that." Mikhail reached and grabbed the groceries, and Shane wrestled with the six jumbo-sized coffee/latte/cappuccinos that everybody had ordered.

Shane set the coffee cartons on the top of the GTO and turned to find Mikhail looking at him quietly. It was past eight, and the sky was still that curious purple between blue and black, and a breeze had sprung up off the delta that made Shane shiver in his still-green front yard. There was something unsettling in Mikhail's look.

"You did not tell me," he said softly.

"You're right. I didn't tell you what?" Shane blinked—hard—because he hadn't taken any days off, and he needed that coffee badly.

"Didn't tell me this would be a... a burden to so many people." Mikhail looked unhappily toward the van, sticking out of Shane's garage along with a whole bunch of parts and tools that Shane had not had four days ago. While they were watching, Crick—who was taking the tire off so he could check the brakes, because they were at that stage—slipped his hand from the lug-wrench and skinned the knuckles of his bad hand, letting loose a string of swear words into the night that made the sky about three shades darker. Deacon's voice floated out to them.

"Goddammit, Carrick—let me see that. Fuck. Fuck fuck fuck fuck. Here—let's go inside—Shane's got the antiseptic and shit in the kitchen..."

"Deacon, it's a scrape...."

"And we'll need a bandage and we've got to scrub the grease out...."

"Deacon, I'm not made out of glass...."

"Just shut up and go inside, dammit. If we put a bandage on it, you can fix that goddamned tire!"

"Sir yes sir!" Crick snapped, saluting sharply.

Andrew stuck his head out from under the van where he was doing something with the chassis and snickered. "Shut up, Lieu, and go inside and let him doctor you. He's the second best mechanic we've got, and we don't want him distracted."

"Second?" Deacon asked, a little affronted.

"Shane's the first," Calvin said, standing up from his place by the front of the engine. "I mean, I knew he restored the GTO, but, damn—I didn't realize he was like a fucking genius with the things."

"Shit." Shane blushed and then he realized he hadn't responded to Mikhail's unasked question. "You were so proud, Mickey. I just didn't want to take that away from you—and look. It'll be ready for tomorrow, right? Jon and Amy said they'd follow you up and make sure it went okay. They're looking forward to seeing the Faire."

Mikhail stood on his toes and pressed his lips to Shane's, and Shane was surprised enough to open his mouth and kiss him back, groaning because there hadn't been much time for the two of them in the past week, and it felt so good to hold him.

"Don't make it small," Mikhail whispered against him, dropping the grocery bags on the ground and wiggling closer. "Don't make light of it. You do that all the time—you create miracles, do wonderful things, and then act as though anyone else would do the same. Nobody would do the things for me that you have done. It is huge. It is bigger than the world. You and your family have done the impossible, just for me. How could I not love you?"

Shane leaned back against the car in surprise. "Really? You do?"

Mikhail stepped back and shook his head in irritation. "And how could I not have said it until now? You do miracles for me, and I can't even say three simple words. No wonder no one has worked miracles for me before; I don't deserve th—"

Because Shane shut that up right quick. They had to stop kissing eventually, because the coffee was getting cold, but Shane kept the words tight in his heart for the rest of the night. For the rest of the weekend, actually, because Shane worked, and he couldn't go see Mikhail and Kimmy at the Faire.

It was hard watching him drive away in the now-working *purple* van. Mickey was going to paint it pink and call it "The Queermobile," but Calvin said, "Oh yeah—and our own police department will egg your house and TeePee your lawn.

Mikhail had been pretty upset, and Shane had sent Calvin a quelling look, saying, "Don't you let my job rule your life, Mickey. You paint the damned thing any color you like."

Mikhail had sulked. "Yes, your damned job—they never can tolerate a purple brick, can they?" And then he'd looked up, a rather unholy gleam in his eye.

"No," Shane said flatly.

"Oh yes."

"Mickey...."

"You said I should paint it any color I like. So I am going to name it after you."

Ten cans of purple primer later, (and one can of black) it was a big purple van with "The Purple Brick" freehanded on the side. Crick did the freehanding, and Deacon said it looked a damned sight better than the water tower. Crick turned red and said, "Fuck you, Deacon," and then Deacon had smirked, and, well, it had been three in the morning by then and pretty much everyone had laughed their asses of.

Six hours later, Mikhail left. He called two hours after to let Shane know he'd arrived on time, and Jon had called shortly thereafter to let him know that Mickey wasn't a bad driver and they could quit their worrying. Since Jon and Shane had finally taken over teaching Benny to drive, Shane figured he could trust Jon's judgment and relaxed just a smidge.

Of course, he relaxed even more when Mickey pulled into Deacon's driveway in time for Sunday dinner. Mikhail spent the evening eating Benny's pot roast and telling stories about the Nevada City Celtic Cross and how beautiful Shane's sister had been when they danced. Shane was glad to hear that Kimmy could still dance, but he heard the undertone of the story. Mikhail had caught his eyes and shrugged—she was still in trouble and still wouldn't ask for help, and that sucked. But Mickey was home and that rocked, and he was exuberant and thrilled to be independent and doing something he loved—truly loved—and Shane's chest swelled and his throat ached to see his lover that happy. His cock ached too, so when they got home, Shane stripped him naked, and took him hard and fast, bent over the bed.

Mikhail came so hard he couldn't talk for ten minutes, and when he was coherent, Shane manhandled him into bed, kissed him urgently, and said, "Now *that's* how much I missed you!" and Mickey had grinned and shrugged, and said, "Not so much then?"

Shane did it again, and he was satisfied.

And he got told "I love you" every night, and he really started to believe it.

Which was why, when he got his ribs busted hauling StepBob and his friends into jail for a drunk and disorderly three days later, he was surprised when Deacon came into the hospital room without Mickey.

"You got the Vicodin?" Shane asked, because Deacon had been going to stop by the pharmacy and get Shane's pain meds, and damn, his side was *really* beginning to hurt. Deacon nodded and cracked the seal on a water, handed him a pill, and let him wash everything down.

"Where's Mickey?" He'd really wanted to see him—and he'd gotten spoiled that way.

"Funny you should mention that," Deacon said, when he was sure Shane had swallowed the Vicodin. "'Cause I asked Benny that same question when the station called us."

Shane made a mental note to put Mikhail on his list of emergency contacts—he'd be hurt if he wasn't. "And what did Benny say?"

"She said that he was on the way to Monterey with Crick."

Shane tried to leap to his feet, but his ribs caught his breath in a blinding flash of pain, and he fell back down. "Monterey? What in the fuck…?"

"Seems your sister called when I was at the feed store? Something about needing to move right now? Anyway, I got home to an empty house just in time for the station to call to say you'd gotten the shit kicked out of you."

"Somebody had a lead pipe," Shane grunted, his brain trying to process this particular disaster.

Deacon grunted, too, and fingered a faint scar at his hairline. "I know that pipe," he muttered.

Oh Jesus. If Kimmy had called, things must have gotten dire with Kurt. "Oh shit… my flaky sister just left her coked-up douchebag boyfriend." Shane stood up this time and walked unsteadily to the door, waiting for his vision to come back when the Vicodin kicked in. "And Mickey and Crick went to help her? Oh, Jesus. The tempers those two have, I don't see how this could possibly get any worse."

He stopped and gripped the doorframe, and suddenly Deacon was at his side, a hand on his bad elbow to help him keep upright. "Jeff was home when Mickey called. He went with them."

"Oh fuck...." And he tried to hobble faster.

"Don't you have to fill out some paperwork to leave?" Deacon asked, but he didn't slow down when Shane said, "Who the fuck cares!"

It took them an hour before they were on their way—for one thing, they had to go get Shane's car from the station house because Deacon's truck didn't go faster than fifty miles an hour on the freeway. Shane was breathing hard, and his skin was clammy as Deacon belted him in, and Deacon shoved two different painkillers at him with a big bottle of water before taking his keys and going to the other side to drive.

"Take them," Deacon grunted as Shane stared at the pills dumbly.

"But...."

"Trust me—they'll work with the Vicodin. I wouldn't steer you wrong here, and it's gonna be a long fucking trip."

Shane did as he asked and closed his eyes almost immediately in relief. Deacon was rarely wrong. "God... there's no way we can catch up with them, is there?"

Deacon shrugged and turned the ignition. Something boyish and delighted crossed his normally reserved, pretty face when he stepped on the gas. "We won't be too far behind. I've seen your boyfriend drive—he pretty much hits sixty and putters there for a bit." Using one hand on the wheel and a bit of panache, Deacon whipped the car out of the parking lot and onto the closest road to the freeway. "I've only driven her in the city. How fast does this thing go?"

Shane grunted, wishing he could laugh. "I opened her up between L.A. and Las Vegas—I pegged the speedo, but I don't know how much faster it went after that."

The sound Deacon made in his throat then was predatory and gleeful, and if Shane hadn't been stoned on painkillers, he would have been positively wonderstruck that Deacon could sound so deliciously evil. "I don't think we'll get a chance to go faster than one hundred and forty," he said thoughtfully, passing two cars legally and grinning just a little. "But we can always hope."

Shane fell asleep about five minutes later, but since they got to Monterey in two and a half hours, he always figured that was a blessing.

God knows what he might have pulled watching Deacon whip his car through traffic to make that kind of time.

Shane didn't know how to get to Kimmy's house, but apparently Deacon had that covered too. When he came to, groggy from the painkillers and still in pain (oh the fucking injustice!), Deacon was on the hands-free with Benny. Apparently she fed Kimmy's address into the computer and got directions, and Deacon followed them. They drove through a neighborhood of pretty two-story homes, narrowly built together with postage stamp lawns. Deacon swore, and Shane blinked and focused, and there was The Purple Brick sitting outrageously in front of this nice bohemian neighborhood, and there were their people on the lawn with what looked like a yard sale. And even as they pulled up and took in the scene, there was Kurt, swinging a haymaker at Crick's lame side, connecting solidly with his jaw.

"Oh *fuck* no!" The car came to a screeching halt, and Shane was thrown up against the seatbelt with enough force to bring tears to his eyes, and before he'd even cleared them, Deacon was out of the car and *vaulting* over the hood.

Shane scrambled awkwardly for the seatbelt and got out of the car as fast as his body would allow. Mikhail was crouched by Kimmy, and Jeff was on her other side, wiping her face with a wet towel.

"Okay, honey, now how're you feeling?"

"Stoned," Kimmy slurred. "Fucking bastard… I swear I didn't do it on purpose. Swear. Mikhail, I swear. I did some at Christmas 'cause I was so lonely, but I kept clean since. I did. I swear…."

"We hear you, cow-woman," Mikhail said brusquely. His hand in Kimmy's hair was all tenderness, though, and Shane realized with a lump in his throat that Mickey loved his sister too. "Now shut up and let the pretty man ask you questions. He's like a doctor without the sharp objects, and he wants to make sure your heart won't explode, because that would be bad form."

"Absolutely," Shane grunted, moving over to them. "We make this drive out here, and you're not around to take back?"

Kimmy looked up at him through swimming eyes, and Shane realized her face was dusted with cocaine and her nose was bleeding—a lot.

"Shaney…." She started to cry. "Jesus, Shaney. I was leaving him. I swear I was. You said you'd be home, and I was going to go home. But we were out here, and that fucker shoved my face in a bowl full of coke… said it was the only way to keep me here…."

"Jesus…." Shane's heart started thundering in his throat—and his broken ribs—and he looked at Jeff, who had finished getting most of the drugs out of her hair and was taking her pulse.

"She's running really fast," Jeff said quietly. "But she's still talking, and she's not passing out."

"You want to take the GTO and get her to the doc's?" Shane asked, and Jeff shook his head.

"If she's going to blow a brain gasket, it's going to happen between here and the hospital, wherever that may be. Usually with coke, something like that happens immediately. We got it off her body—if we can keep her calm, her blood pressure should drop pretty soon. Don't want to freak out the old blood pressure, do we, Shane's sister?"

"You're really nice," Kimmy mumbled. "And you're so pretty."

"You know how this story ends, sweetheart," Jeff said kindly, and she gave a grunt and rested her head on Mikhail's shoulder.

"You're gayer than an Easter parade," she giggled, and Jeff smoothed back her hair and smiled.

"Yup. Sorry, baby—you're the victim of a five-queer intervention."

There was a howl, and they all looked up then in time to see Deacon—who had been fighting gamely the entire time—kick Kurt's shin and then level him with a connect to the jaw.

"Jesus," Crick snarled, wrapping his good arm around Deacon's waist and hauling with obvious effort. "Someone come here and help me with him, dammit!"

Deacon was trying to go in for the kill, and Shane stood awkwardly to his feet and trotted as quickly as he could to Deacon's side. He was the biggest and the strongest, and of all of them, had the best chance of helping Crick.

"C'mon, man," he muttered without much conviction, "you don't want the cops to show. They're all assholes, you know that."

Deacon didn't hear him—he was swearing steadily, and every now and then he'd struggle out of Crick's one-armed control and get in a good kick, and they could hear Kurt grunt as it hit home. Deacon had gotten an arm free from Crick's restraint, too, and his elbow thrust toward Shane's ribs. Shane sucked in a hiss, anticipating some pain, and Deacon went limp in Crick's arms.

"Jesus, did I get ya?"

Shane took a step backward and shook his head, pulling the arm that was shielding his side even tighter. "Nope. But if I'd known it was that easy to get your attention, I would have faked it from the other side of the lawn."

They all took a breath and then looked down at Kurt, who was struggling to get up.

"You fuckers," he wheezed—his nose looked pretty broken. "You queer fuckers. I'll fuck you all up, dammit. You're all pussies, all of you!"

Crick grunted and let go of Deacon, then sank down to a crouch and put his good hand on the flat of Kurt's chest. "Now we both know I was winning before Deacon got here," he said conversationally, and Kurt's flinch told him it was true. "And now that Deacon's here, it would be in your best interest to just lay down and recover here. Nobody on this lawn would particularly care if you stopped breathing. You just don't want us to hurry that along, now would you?"

"Fuck you!" Kurt spat, and Crick dodged, and Deacon kicked him. He fell back with a whimper, and the three of them turned around and went back to Kimmy to make sure she was okay.

"We were moving her shit into the van," Crick explained as they stood there, waiting to see what Jeff had to say. "Kimmy was near the door, and Kurt got home from somewhere—he started screaming at her, about being just as...." Crick looked at Kimmy and flushed, and Shane could hear Crick, the world's most tactless human being, editing his narrative to spare Kimmy's feelings. He swallowed and continued, "being just as bad as he was. Then he... damn—he had like three dimebags in a baggie, and he just grabbed her by the throat and started shoving them in her face. You got here right after that—I'm sorry, Deacon—I swear, the guy had it coming...."

Deacon heard the story and his eyes got wide, and abruptly he turned around, and Crick caught him around the waist again.

"I'm gonna kill him," he snarled. "I'm gonna fucking kill him. I'm gonna rip out his lungs through his asshole after I shove *a motherfucking cannon up it and blow his brains out....*"

"Deacon! Deacon! Calm down!"

Crick went in for the body block, and Shane just stared at them, aware that there was something bigger than just this moment going on.

"Someone did something like that to Deacon," Jeff said quietly, catching Shane's attention. "I think we'd better let them work this out on their own. It doesn't look like douche-bag's life is in danger for the moment, and I'd like to get the fuck out of here before your people get here."

Shane blinked. "My people?" Deacon was looking bitterly at Kurt, and Crick was holding both of Deacon's hands against his broad chest, talking earnestly to him. It did look like they had it well under control, so Shane gathered himself up with a wince and tried to find something he could drag off the lawn without too much effort.

"Cops, big man. We don't want the cops here. This was peaceful until about two minutes before you two drove up. I figure we've got about fifteen minutes to get the really conspicuous vehicles off the lawn and get the fuck out of Dodge, right?"

"Please?" Kimmy begged, weeping onto the knees of her jeans. "Please, Shaney? Can we just go? You promised me home. I want to go home."

Shane grunted and dropped to a crouch again, closing his eyes against the stars in his vision. He reached out and stroked her long, pretty hair, remembering how beautiful she'd been, dancing and free under the sun. "Yeah, baby. Me and Mickey will take you home. You'll like it. Mickey's been buying place mats and matching towels and shit."

Mikhail's hand moved, rested atop Shane's, and Shane grasped his fingers and squeezed. "We even have a spare bed for you, you know? But first let's get you into the GTO—you'll have to sit in the back, okay, sweetheart? We've got some blankets here, we can make you comfy.

Mikhail hopped up, Jeff helped Kimmy to her feet, and Shane gathered himself for the big hoist. Mikhail's hand appeared in front of him, and he took it gratefully. When they'd hauled him to his feet, he looked at his lover, who looked back at him with concern.

"You are not mad?" Mikhail asked, and Shane shook his head.

"I wish you'd called me, Mickey, but no. I'm not mad. You called the family, and that's what counts, you know?"

"I didn't want to bother you," Mikhail whispered. He reached out his hands and pulled up Shane's T-shirt to see the padding underneath. "I didn't want to bother you because your fucking job has been sucking the life out of you, and I wanted this to be no big deal. But you had to come get us anyway, and look at you. You are injured. You miserable man, what does it take for you to go a year without getting stabbed or shot or… what is this?"

Shane grunted a laugh. "Getting beaten with a lead pipe."

"It is not funny," Mikhail snarled bitterly. "It is *not* funny, and I am *not* laughing. You—go sit in front of your car. This is why Deacon was driving, is not?"

Shane nodded, and Mikhail sniffed.

"Well, good for him. The van is not comfortable for you—any idiot can see it. I…."

"Crick can drive the van," Jeff said behind them. He'd put Kimmy in the back of the car and had come out to pick up the clothes next to the suitcases that had been broken open in the melee. "Kimmy's really disoriented—she needs someone she knows nearby. Since Shane has to sit in the front of the car, Mikhail, you're nominated."

Shane nodded, and Mikhail helped him to go sit down, muttering to himself in Russian as they walked. His hands were tender as he settled Shane, and Shane had to admit that the cracked ribs felt like a big flaming wreck of flesh and bone. He wondered when he got his next pain med and then felt like a total pussy. It wasn't like he hadn't done this before.

Mikhail bent then and kissed his temple. "I love you, big man. I love you so much I can't believe the world turned before we met. But you and me, we are going to have a big, ugly, yelling, snarling, Russian-bear fight about your fucking job and how much I want you to quit. Be prepared. It will not break us up, and I am not drawing a line in the sand, and I am not going to push you away, but I *will* be heard, do you understand me?"

"Tomorrow?" Shane begged pathetically, and Mikhail took pity on him and kissed him again. This time on the lips.

"The day after, at the very least."

"Good," Kimmy muttered from the back. "Because the thing that made up my mind was Kurt giving your address to Brandon today on the phone. Shaney, I think he's going to come see you tomorrow about some money."

Shane closed his eyes and leaned his head back against the headrest. "Fuck," he muttered.

"Not until you are healed," Mikhail said shortly, and then he trotted off to finish cleaning up the lawn.

Kimmy chuckled blearily. "I like him even better as a brother-in-law," she said. "And if I wasn't so coked up, I'd probably be able to give him shit about it."

"You okay?" Shane asked now, concerned. Too many people, he thought in a haze. So many people to worry about. And now he had a knock-down drag-out Russian-bear fight to worry about. God, when did he get his painkillers again?

"You taking me home, Shaney?"

"Yeah, baby. Like I said, you'll love it."

"Then I'm fine. Believe me on that. I'm just fine." They sat there then, listening to Shane's family move her stuff from the yard into the van, and Shane realized he could hear and smell the sea.

"It's beautiful here," he said, a little bit of awe in his voice. His eyes were closed, but he was wondering how she could stand to move when the air smelled like ocean and yarrow.

"Nothing's beautiful when you're not safe," Kimmy said, and they didn't say much else after that.

The trip home was actually sort of funny—they kept pumping Shane *full* of drugs while checking to make sure Kimmy was getting *empty* of them. But eventually they *did* get home, and Deacon and Mikhail helped Shane lie down on top of his covers with his torso propped up by pillows.

Deacon took another look at Shane's ribs to make sure the tape job held and ruffled Shane's hair as he tilted his head back in the bliss of being in a semi-comfortable position.

"Sorry to get you into all this," Shane mumbled, and Deacon chuckled back at him. His knuckles were still bloody, and he looked like a very dangerous man.

"You're our family, Perkins. I'm proud you and Mikhail called on us, that's all. Tell your sister to come visit when she feels better, okay?"

So much for danger, Shane thought. And then Mikhail came in with his last painkiller for the night and sat with him until he was asleep.

Chapter 24

Anyone perfect must be lying. Anything easy has its cost.

"Falling For The First Time"—Bare Naked Ladies

MIKHAIL waited until Shane was sleeping to fall apart a little. He had not been afraid of Kurt—he knew the type from the streets, and as small as he was, he could hold his own in a fight. No, he'd been afraid for Kimmy and then for Crick and then for Deacon, because Deacon was a terrifyingly fierce fighter, and he could have easily beaten Kurt into meat, and that would have been bad.

And then he'd seen Shane, pale, holding his body like it hurt, and obviously trying to keep it together. *He'd* been worried. *He'd* been afraid. And *he'd* been hurt, and Mikhail almost couldn't stand it. Not Shane. Not his beautiful lover, who gave his heart and everything else to make Mikhail's world wonderful. *Dammit*, he wanted to shout, *leave him the hell alone!*

Now, watching him sleep, Mikhail simply held his hand and kissed it. He didn't swear, didn't make insane phone calls or rail at Shane's sleeping body. He just held that hand to his lips and treasured the softly beating pulse.

Eventually, though, he remembered Kimmy, stoned and woozy and probably feeling very much alone. He got up and went into Kimmy's room, noting vaguely that it was barely seven o'clock at night. He'd called in to work, and he would have the next two nights off as well. Then there was the weekend, and he and Kimmy would have to make a decision about how they wanted *that* to go. They were dancers—the show really *did* go on.

But Mikhail was part of a family now, and he wasn't sure he wanted to go on if the other half of his heart was hurt or upset or about to be confronted by his horrible ex-boyfriend and yet another person to just hurt Shane and walk away as though that sort of thing didn't have consequences.

Oh, God. All of the things Shane blew off—all of the small things that simply hurt his soul, and he assumed he would heal from. If he would not defend himself, it was Mikhail's job to defend him. There was just no other way.

"How are you doing, cow-woman?" he asked her, and she gave him a bemused smile from his bed, surrounded by a riot of color and texture and one of the cats. She'd brought a lot of her blankets—many of them hand-woven or hand-knitted by friends and all of them bright with color and soft to touch—and Mikhail had a moment to wonder if Kimmy didn't surround herself with these things in the same way Shane surrounded himself with cats and dogs: things to keep his heart warm when it had nearly frozen to death in childhood. Given that Mikhail had carried his own heart around in a big wooden box until very recently, he didn't have a single word with which to criticize.

"I am still stoned, and I'm a little wired, and I think I'm starving," she said honestly, and he grinned. You never had to worry where you stood with Kimmy—she was very good at telling you.

"Well, then, come into the kitchen. I will warm you up some leftovers, and we can eat them on the couch in front of the television. We have movies—your choice."

Kimmy sat herself up a little. "Does Shane still like children's movies? Because I just got *Coraline*, and I haven't seen it yet."

They cuddled very chastely on the couch. Mikhail found comfort just from her presence, and he knew he was helping to keep her calm when the drugs were trying to make her climb the walls. They watched the movie without the 3-D glasses (because Kimmy said that was just too weird on as much blow as she'd just done) and Mikhail was impressed.

"Very… very lovely," he said at the end. "I particularly love the part about if a person is too good to be true, they are not real."

Kimmy sighed. In the past half hour Mikhail had literally felt her blood pressure drop as the last of the drugs burned their way out of her system. "Unless you're Shane," she murmured.

"Even Shane has his damnable irritating blind spots," Mikhail retorted acidly, and Kimmy shifted in his arms a little and made an effort to wake up before she slipped into the drug crash.

"What happened to him?"

"This time? This time he was beaten by a lead pipe. Or rather by a redneck motherfucker who was holding a lead pipe. Deacon said his ribs were cracked—Shane actually left the hospital against orders to come riding to our rescue." Mikhail shook his head. "Miserable, obstinate, irritating...."

"This time?" Kimmy interrupted. She sounded tired and puzzled, and Mikhail made an effort to pull himself out of his own anger.

"Yes—this time. As opposed to last time."

"He called at Christmas—said he'd been sick. You don't get sick on the job, do you?"

Mikhail looked away. "Jesus," he muttered. Yes. It was true—real people were not perfect. Not even his beloved Shane.

"Mikhail?" Kimmy scrambled out of his arms, where she'd rested for the movie, and onto her knees. "Mikhail—what happened to him?"

Mikhail sighed. "Yes. Yes he was sick. He was sick after a knife wound got so infected they had to pump him full of shit he was allergic to so they could stop him from going septic." Mikhail shivered. "I... I had to leave, you see, before we knew he would live. Worst week of my fucking life—and that includes the week my mother died and I broke up with him because I am a selfish, cowardly asshole."

Kimmy put her face in her hands as she was kneeling on the couch. "Oh shit... Mikhail—why wouldn't he tell me?"

Mikhail stood up and moved to the end of the couch to comfort her. "He didn't want you to worry, little one...."

Kimmy sniffed disdainfully in an oddly familiar way. "What happened to cow-woman?" she asked. "I liked that better."

Mikhail laughed and kissed her hair. "Very well—I shall call you cow-woman. He didn't want you to worry. He is always okay, you see. He always expects the worst and is happy when it turns out better than that.

He always assumes the world will shit on his head, so he wears his good cheer and graciousness like an umbrella and simply shakes it off."

Kimmy gave a frustrated groan in his arms. "Gaaawwwdd... that is so *like* him." She sighed and burrowed further into Mikhail's arms—he was her brother as much as Shane was now, Mikhail mused. "Brandon called, spewing something about Shane's money. I told him to fuck off... but Kurt. No, that asshole *had* to get some back, you know? Backhanded me"—she fingered the bruise to her cheek, one of many—"called me a whore, and grabbed the phone, and they started making plans. That's when I grabbed my stuff and went. Called you from the lawn. I just...." She had been rambling and now looked up at him, her face bleak. "I could take it for myself, you know? But I'd be damned if I let my brother get it in the teeth."

Mikhail snorted. "Oh, cow-woman—the things you do not see. You are just like him. You just swear more."

Kimmy frowned at him, a line between her eyes, and Mikhail shook his head and just took her to bed, tucking her in with her pretty blankets and Orlando Bloom and Kirsten Dunst, both of whom were kitty-sluts and *would* sleep with anyone who wasn't having sex or wrestling around in bed.

Then he went and showered and slid into bed next to Shane. Shane wasn't sleeping well—for a man who was so stoic when he was awake, he often muttered or moaned in his sleep when he was hurt. Mikhail knew this from when he'd been in the hospital. This time was different, though. This time he knew to take Shane's hand, knew to stroke the inside of his wrist and to whisper to him—in Russian, now, since Shane was sleeping—and to tell him that Mikhail would not leave. Not this time. Not when he'd promised.

When he woke up, Shane was in the shower, and Mikhail sat up in bed in time to see him struggling into his underwear using one hand to hold the boxer shorts and one hand to balance himself on the dresser. Mikhail tutted and stood irritably, taking the boxer shorts from him and holding them out so Shane could step in. Then he did the same thing for Shane's sweats and his T-shirt, and then he set out a pair of leather moccasins he'd found in Shane's closet that had never been worn because the stubborn man would rather go barefoot, even in the winter, and made Shane step into those too.

Shane grinned at him crookedly. "You know, for a man who was so determined to be alone, you have a lot of mothering skills that would have gone completely to waste."

Mikhail returned his grin with a scowl. "You want to see how much like my mother I am? You just wait until the big fight we're going to have."

"Now I thought I got an extra day!" Shane protested, and he tried to hold his hands up and then winced because it hurt and he hadn't had his pain meds yet, and Mikhail's scowl got worse.

"That depends on my temper, big man—and right now, it's on a spiderweb."

Shane's face fell a little, and some of his playfulness faded. "You weren't a little happy to see us yesterday?" he asked plaintively, and Mikhail relented.

"I was overjoyed to see you—yes. The help was very much appreciated." Very gingerly, Mikhail moved in and put his arms around Shane's waist and leaned his head on Shane's chest. He fit so very nicely—never in his life had he been so happy to be short until he saw how well he fit in Shane's arms. "I would be very sorry to never see you again, you understand? This big hairy fight we're going to have—it all hinges on that. Just you remember that when we're fighting."

Shane sighed and dropped a kiss on the top of Mikhail's head. He started to say something, then changed his mind and started to say something else, and then sighed again.

"Maybe we should talk about something else if we're going to postpone this," he said at last, and Mikhail already had a plan.

"Let's talk about getting something in your stomach so you can have your pain medication, how is that?"

"Aces," Shane replied dryly, and so the big hairy fight was postponed for exactly one hour and eighteen minutes. Mikhail knew because he looked at the clock—it was nine in the morning. He was wondering when the promised assholes would arrive and tangle things up even more than they already were.

All he wanted was hot cereal, which irritated Mikhail, too, because it was just putting oatmeal in the microwave, but Kimmy woke up and went hunting for eggs, so Mikhail worked out some stress making them omelets. Shane didn't even look at the omelets, which meant he was feeling worse than he let on, and that put Mikhail in a deeper funk.

The phone rang as Shane was slipping the last of his oatmeal to the dogs, who had not yet been let out, and Mikhail answered. It was Calvin.

"How is he?"

"He is in pain," Mikhail muttered. "What happened?"

"Not his fault, Mikhail—I swear. We were arresting Bob Coats on a D 'n' D, and this fucker just comes hauling ass out of nowhere with the pipe—neither of us saw him; he was hiding in the garage and apparently even drunker than Bob. He knew Shane—knew who he was, at least—started screaming about how faggots were going to ruin the American way." Calvin blew out a breath. "Dumb motherfucker. Anyway, Shane took him out pretty neatly, you know? But the guy got some whacks in too. All this backup outside, and Shane's almost taken out by some sneaky bastard with a lead pipe—it's a good thing he can duck!"

Mikhail closed his eyes and felt ill. "Thanks for that," he said sickly. "Did you want to talk to him?"

"Yeah—he's in some trouble for leaving the hospital early. Wanted to give him the heads-up."

Mikhail handed over the phone and listened grimly as Shane shrugged off the irritation of his captain. "Yeah, well, it was a family emergency.... No, my sister. She's here with me now.... Yeah, well, the trip to Monterey sucked. Hangover's almost as bad.... Okay, go ahead and tell him to kiss my ass. My med leave is six weeks—I know, asked the doctor. I'll have my paperwork in tomorrow." Big sigh. "Yeah—I know that means I have to go back in to the hospital." Wince. "Make that the day after tomorrow, would ya? Not the smartest fucking thing I've ever done." Pause. "Yeah, it was worth it. They needed me."

Mikhail, who was listening, heard that last and felt some of his blinding, sick anger dissipate. Aha. A weapon. The perfect weapon. He met Kimmy's eyes across the room and could see her thinking the same thing.

Shane finished talking, and Mikhail took the phone silently from him, then picked the cereal bowl off the ground and took them both into the kitchen. He came back with Shane's pain meds and some milk, which Shane downed obediently, and went about introducing Kimmy to the dogs and to their routine.

"Out in the morning, and in when we come in—or in the evening, or they bark and the neighbors complain," Mikhail told her.

"What about the cats?" she asked. Orlando Bloom had made her his personal pet, and her fingers tightened in his fur. She didn't want to let him go.

"The cats mostly stay inside," Mikhail said. "Especially since the dogs are outside in the day. Besides—there are coyotes out there, and Shane says they like a little pussy when no one's watching, so it's best they stay inside." Shane's exact words, actually, and Mikhail smiled a little. Oh, yes. His lover was very good with the wordplay. It was a thing they would enjoy for many years to come.

He turned to Shane then and saw that the milk was gone. "How is your side?" he asked pleasantly, and Shane smiled.

"Better, thank you. I'll be able to clean up dog crap in no time!"

Mikhail nodded civilly and pulled out a chair across from him, sitting on the edge of it and leaning forward earnestly. "Good. But first, a more difficult chore. When are you quitting your fucking job?"

Shane's eyes widened. "Yeah, this really *is* a big hairy fight, isn't it?"

"He's got a point, Shaney," Kimmy said, getting off the club chair and letting the cat plop to the floor. "You don't need to work, and dammit—you're getting hurt all the time."

Shane tried to pull up a shoulder in a shrug, and then winced and stopped. "You both know it's a part of the job."

"No," Mikhail denied. "There are risks, and then there is you. You put yourself out on the line when you don't need to. And it's not your risk to take anymore. It's ours. And it's unacceptable."

Shane wrinkled his nose a little, obviously unsure what to do with out and out rebellion. "Mickey—you knew this about me when you signed on—you knew who I was…."

"I *do* know who you are. You are a good man. You are kind, and you are strong, and you are brave…." Mikhail had to look away. "So brave." He turned around to face his lover again and to be brave himself. "But you are *not* this job. This is *not* what makes your heart beat in your chest, this is *not* what gets you up in the morning."

Shane's crooked grin almost did him in. "Well, yeah, Mickey—but I don't see anyone paying me to make love to you all day, do you?"

"Why do you even need money?" Kimmy exploded, and Mikhail was grateful because this was not a subject he could broach in comfort. "Shane, man—you've got a seven figure insurance settlement, just sitting in the bank making *more goddamned money*! And that's probably *half* of what's in your fucking trust by now, do you know that? Why you got to do *this* job, *this* motherfucker of a fucking job, and one that you don't even love… I will never fucking know!"

Shane looked away from his sister, looked away from Mikhail. "I didn't know I still had the trust," he said by way of explanation.

"Did you think they just disbanded it?" Kimmy asked, surprised. "It's a fucking tax shelter—Hadley told me so herself!"

"Who's Hadley?" Mikhail asked, distracted for a moment.

"Our mother," Shane and Kimmy answered in tandem, and Mikhail looked quickly back and forth between them and saw for the first time that yes, they were really twins.

"So it's not the money," Mikhail pursued, trying to get back on track. "It's not the money, it's not the love…."

"I wouldn't say it's *all* not the money," Shane admitted unwillingly. "I… I've sort of got this plan, you know? To donate the money for a shelter—you know, for all those kids on the streets who don't know how to go home." Shane's brown eyes met Mikhail's with pure, shining intentions. "You know—kids like you might have been, if your mother hadn't been a goddamned miracle, right?"

Mikhail's heart sort of stuttered in his chest. Christ. What a fucking wretched man, making him go all soft like this when he was trying so assiduously to be a hard-line asshole about this entire subject.

"Anyway—I figured if I spent all the money there, my job would still be, you know, my *job*. I'd be, uhm, needed and shit." Shane pulled himself up and gained some of his resolution back, and Mikhail cursed him even further to hell because his jaw was set with such simple pride.

"Needed?" Mikhail found some bitterness after all. "You are needed *here*, damn you. You want to be *needed*, just look at your sister! She needed you and you came through—"

"*You* came through!" Shane retorted. He tried to stand up with the force of his emotion, but his body was *so* not going there, and Mikhail smirked grimly when he had to sit down again. "And I'm damned grateful for it," Shane amended, "but I'm her big brother. I'm her family, that's what I'm *supposed* to do for her—"

"Now we both know that's a *lie*!" Kimmy snapped. "We grew up where it didn't have to be that way, Shaney. You grew up, and you changed your life so that it did. You wanted your life to mean something—and it does! Now you've got big fucking piles of money to do whatever you've ever wanted to do—"

"Big fucking piles of money do *not* make me a hero!" Shane roared back, angry with her as perhaps he could not be with Mikhail, and don't think Mikhail wasn't grateful for it, either.

"A hero?" Mikhail said now, remembering something and feeling ill again. *I didn't want to be a fool anymore. I wanted to be a hero.* "Is *that* this is about? Being a *hero*?"

Shane turned at the fury burning through Mikhail's voice, met his eyes, and flushed. "I don't think I'm a hero," he muttered, but Mikhail didn't buy it.

"No—no you don't. That's the fucking problem. You've got this thing in your head that thinks you can only be a hero when you're *dead*!"

"*That's not true*!" Shane snapped. "That's not true! I just want my life to mean something, dammit!" He looked from Kimmy to Mikhail again, his eyes puckering and a terrible, heartbreaking grimace on his broad, handsome face. "Don't you get it? Either of you?" He shrugged and muttered to himself.

"No. Of course you don't get it. Look at you. Both of you. You move, and it's poetry. You stand up in a crowd of people, and you make them see something beautiful. And I... I walk into a bar fight and say 'Everybody calm down!' and I get shit thrown at me. I am *not* the guy that people take seriously. I am *not* the guy that gives something to the world just by being beautiful. I'm just me, and I'm awkward and fucking weird. But if I'm just me, I want to be doing something important—don't you get it? I want my life to *mean* something. I don't just want to sit on my big piles of money and use up space. I don't want to let the word roll down my big piles of money onto the world below me. I want....” He stopped and dashed his eyes furiously and tried to laugh it off as he said it.

“You’re right. I want to be a hero. Preferably the live kind, though, but still.”

There was a terrible quiet in the kitchen then, as Mikhail and Kimmy both struggled with the words to tell him how wrong he was about all of it. Kimmy was openly crying—but of course she was, Mikhail sniffed. She was a girl. She could do that. Bitch.

“I can’t talk to him,” she sniffled. “Dammit... I... I just don’t have any fucking words, Shaney. How the best guy on the fucking planet could be so wrong about something so huge....”

Shane couldn’t move, but Mikhail could. Mikhail got down on his knees and took Shane’s hands in his own, because he found he had no pride here. No pride at all.

“God... God... don’t you see, *lubime*? Don’t you see at all? You *are* a hero. You’re *our* hero. You’re Benny’s hero. You’re a hero to every poor kid you’ve ever helped on the streets. You’re my hero. You see weird and awkward? I see wonderful. I... I am damaged, God help me. I am damaged and bitchy and a pain in the ass, and you have literally re-made the world around me to keep me happy. And you have made a life from a place where there was no life. You surround yourself with joy and with love, and you try to give that gift to every lost soul or furry dragon or beat-up alley cat you meet, and you don’t think this is a miracle?” Mikhail pressed the heels of his hands against his eyes and tried to stop what was blurring his vision, but it didn’t work.

“Look at me,” he demanded. “Look at me. I didn’t even cry at my mother’s funeral. The only person on the planet who can break my heart like this is you, you bastard, and you don’t even know you are doing it. You are perfect. You are beautiful. You want to be a hero? You make that shelter, and you be a part of it. *You* be the counselor, *you* be the teacher. I’ll help. Kimmy will help. You spend your life trying to fix the damaged and make them whole again—that is what makes you get up in the morning. That is what makes your heart beat. *That* is where you are a hero. Please... God, please, *lubime*—we need you so badly. The world needs you so badly. Please don’t go throwing away your beautiful life to be something you already are.”

Shane was looking at him—looking like he heard them, at least, if not like he was planning to concede—when the dogs suddenly all stood up and whuffed. There was a clanging outside—a car was on the cattle guard—and someone was undoing the unlocked chain to let themselves in.

"Shit," Shane muttered, pressing his palm to his own eyes. "I never thought seeing Brandon would lighten up the atmosphere."

Mikhail stood up, his body suddenly tense and springy. "I will go meet him," he said grimly. Oh yes. Just let him go meet this man who left Shane to the wolves and now wanted the flesh left over.

"No," Shane muttered, pressing himself up on the tabletop. "I'm the one with the history, Mickey. And he's a cop—we can't just go assaulting the guy out of nowhere, okay?"

Shane didn't look at him—didn't look at *either* of them—as he made his steady, painful way toward the door. "Keep the dogs in, could ya, Kim?" he asked politely, and Kimmy muttered, "Fucking moron," but she was standing and moving toward the door like she was going to block the furry bodies for him, so Mikhail took that as a yes.

He helped her, and after Shane got out to the porch, they both wiggled out the shut door to the sound of baying, puzzled dogs who needed to crap and to eat the stranger (probably in that exact order.)

But that was okay. The dogs might have needed to be kept inside, but Mikhail and Kimmy were *damned* if they were going to miss this.

Shane had stopped at the porch railing as a very beautiful man closed the cattle guard, leaving the white Hyundai two-door idling outside of it. Kurt was at the wheel, looking like shit, and Shane saluted him smartly, leaving only a crucial finger extended.

The man got closer, and Mikhail blinked, his eyes getting round. "Shit," he muttered, trying to put this into perspective. "He's much prettier than me!"

"Don't sweat it," Kimmy reassured him. "I think he's prettier than *me*! Jesus, Shaney—this is your ex-boyfriend?"

Shane turned and looked at them both, his smile going a little crooked as he heard them. "Yeah. Emphasis on ex, right Mickey?"

Mikhail swallowed. "Thanks for that," he muttered.

"Don't worry, guys—he's only prettier than one of you," Shane said with a smirk and then started walking down the porch, keeping a tight hand on the rail. "Brandon, you sack of shit, what the fuck are you doing on my lawn?"

"He was talking about you, you know," Kimmy said softly, and Mikhail rolled his eyes.

"That's what he wants you to think." But neither of them cared about that, not really. What they cared about was how much damage this pretty poison could do to Shane before he got kicked off their property. Brandon smiled cheerfully and tried to hug Shane, looking hurt and sad when Shane backed out of his embrace like a tomcat with its ruff up.

"Cow-woman?" Mickey said speculatively, "Could you do us a favor?"

"What do you want?"

"Go back inside and get our phone. Deacon is the first number on it."

"The action hero?"

"That is the one. He'll be here in less than five minutes."

Brandon said something jovial and familiar and then tried to clap Shane on the arm. Shane moved away from him so quickly he pulled at his ribs again and winced, and Brandon's voice could be heard clearly, from the middle of the big yard.

"Jesus, Shane—you're still damned clumsy, aren't you."

"Five minutes?" Kimmy said doubtfully, her eyes narrowing.

"Yes," Mikhail told her decisively. "And hurry. You're going to need to pull me off this asshole in less than three."

Kimmy hustled inside again, and Mikhail watched warily as Shane continued to back away from this very pretty man as though he had scabies and gangrene and syphilis, all wrapped into one.

Chapter 25

I don't see what anyone can see in anyone else but you...

"Anyone Else But You"—Kimye Dawson

BRANDON looked awesome. Tan, lithe, young. He was Shane's age, but he just didn't seem to carry the years the same way. Nope, nothing touched Brandon Ashford.

But Shane was so past the time when Brandon Ashford could touch him.

"Man, don't even fucking try it," Shane snapped when Brandon tried to go in for the hug.

"Whatsa matter, Shane—you're not happy to see me?"

Shane rolled his eyes. "I thought I made it pretty clear that I wouldn't be the last time we talked."

Brandon shrugged and tried to look sheepish. "Yeah—about that. You know, you're right. I *should* have visited you in the hospital. I just felt so bad, you know? And I didn't want anybody to think, you know"—winsome smile—"that I was, like...."

"Gayer than me?"

Oh look. Now he was being bashful. "Well, we both like guys, don't we, Shane?"

Shane nodded like he was talking to a second grader. "Yeah, Brand, that's right. But I don't like *you* anymore, so why don't you go away?"

"You're looking good, Shane!" Brandon eyed him critically. "You've lost some weight—looks good on you, man. Start waxing that chest, and you'll be ready for Showtime!"

Shane looked down at his chest, where his thin gray T-shirt puckered a little from the chest hair underneath. His face washed with heat—Mikhail really seemed to like it. "I repeat: What in the fuck are you doing on my lawn?"

"Shane, man—don't be like that. I mean, after all we were to each other...."

"Yeah—you screwed me over in a lot of different ways, didn't you?"

"Is that any way to talk to the guy who took your cherry?"

Brandon tried to clap him on the arm, and Shane dodged him again, completely repulsed.

"Jesus, Brandon, I bet you say that to all the sixteen-year-old girls. What do you want?" Ouch. Dodging Brandon was not as easy now as it had been that first month when Brand was talking him into bed. Shane's arms went up to his ribs in defense, but his glare at Brandon was no less potent.

Finally convinced that the "so glad to see you" thing wasn't working, Brandon went back to the charm. "Did you get hurt again? Jesus, Shane, you were always so fucking clumsy! Anyway, I had a little trouble with the ol' L.A.P.D.—we had to part ways, you know?"

"Who'd you do in the locker room now?" Shane asked, and knew he scored a direct hit when Brandon grinned.

"Man, she was a *sweet* piece," Brand told him eagerly. "Sweetest ass you've ever seen, and there I was, riding it, and your old friend walks in, and, well, next thing you know, we're *both* out on our asses. And my family's not talking to me after that, and... you know, I just need a little bit of cash to get back on my feet, and I thought of you!"

Shane raised a hand to his mouth and stroked his chin, feeling the two-day stubble he'd left because he hadn't felt like shaving. For a second, he actually thought about giving Brandon the money just to get the fucker off his lawn. Then he saw Brandon's smug look and the waste of flesh who'd driven the car, and he almost snarled. He'd be damned if he played the fool *ever* again, just because he'd rather eat nails than have Brandon Ashford pat him on the arm.

"The cash is going somewhere," Shane said truthfully. Mikhail and Kimmy had liked the idea so very much—he now had a plan for his big piles of money, and he wasn't going to sully it for this fucker. "I'm going to build a teen shelter, and I'll need it—all of it—so you're just going to have to learn to work for a living, aren't you, Brandon?"

Brandon sneered, and for a minute, he didn't look so pretty anymore. "Like you? Man—I couldn't believe it when your sister's boyfriend told me you were still on the job. What kind of asshole works—and works as a cop!—when he's got a thousand things he could be doing? Like getting his brains fucked out someplace better than here." Brand's disdainful look took in the yard—all the mud from the winter was drying into hard-pan, and Shane and Mikhail had been keeping it watered so it didn't turn into a fire hazard. They'd paid to have the weeds whacked on the rest of the property, so that at least was trim. There weren't any star thistles, so the property simply looked on the verge of being scorched and brown, but the dog crap hadn't been cleaned up in two days, and that was always unpleasant. The house was in good shape—recently painted, modest and small. Shane thought the porch had held up to the winter well—the stain, at least, had kept the wood bright.

But best of all was Mikhail, standing on the porch and staring at Brandon with hard, bright eyes. God—how could Shane have ever thought Brandon was beautiful? How could he have ever looked at that empty heart and thought it was worth a risk?

"This is my home," Shane said simply. "This is my family. You show up after two years to shit on my family, and you want me to give you money? Jesus, Brandon, if you think I'm that much of a chump, I'm surprised you ever wanted to sleep with me at all!"

Brandon gave him a disgusted look. "You're hung like a fucking horse, Shane—why *wouldn't* I want to sleep with you? You're the one who gets all hung up on shit like 'respect' and 'family'—man, if you hadn't been so weird about that shit in the first place, you never would have gotten blackballed!"

And that's when Mikhail came sailing over the porch, fist first, like a compact tornado of muscle and fury, right into Brandon's perfect nose.

"He is not WEIRD!"

Brandon went over backward with one hundred and fifty pounds of Russian rage battering at his perfect face, and Shane was helpless to stop him.

"Kimmy—dammit—come here!"

"Fuck, no." Shane looked up, and his sister was standing, arms crossed, enjoying the show. But Brandon was not helpless—his fist came out and caught Mikhail on the nose, and then they were standing in the middle of Shane's yard, beating each other like prize fighters.

"Kimmy, he's going to get hurt!"

Shane thought about it—thought about getting behind Mikhail and hoisting him bodily up and out of Brandon's reach, turning his back on Brandon and letting his fists fall where they would. It would probably bust his ribs through his lung, but it would be worth it to keep Mickey safe. Of course, right about the time he reached that conclusion, Mikhail landed a solid whack to the jaw. Brandon's head snapped sideways, and his knees buckled, and Shane's small, wiry lover was hopping up and down, crowing with glee.

"Take that!" he shouted, turning his head to spit blood. "You useless fucker! You get the fuck out of here, and you leave this man alone!"

"Shabe," Brandon pleaded through his swelling nose, "helb be!"

Shane recoiled. "Man, you want help, get up off my lawn, get in your fucking car, and drive to the doctor's office your damned self! And Brandon, I swear"—because Brandon was hauling himself up off the ground and glaring at Mikhail like he was going to launch a sneaky, dirty attack—"you touch him again, and I'll shove my hand up your ass and use your face as a pooper-scooper, do you hear me?"

Brandon turned toward him in outrage, and Shane ignored him, moving gingerly into Mikhail's space and making a little gesture for Mikhail to come closer.

"C'mere, baby—he got your nose."

Mikhail spat blood again and grinned, looking barbaric and savage and brutal. Shane wondered if it was wrong to be turned on by him right now, at this moment, and then decided he didn't care. His rescuer. His knight in shining armor. Damn—he'd never known he needed one.

"He will not touch you again," Mikhail said, and then he peered around Shane's shoulder and spat again. "You hear that, *mudak*! Not yours. Mine. Touch him again, and I'll knock out your teeth and put them in my treasure box like a fucking necklace."

Shane found he was smiling a little, although he shouldn't be. Mikhail's knuckles were bruised and bloody, and Shane hated to see him hurt—but Shane loved to see him happy, too, and beating Brandon into a pulp seemed to have done that for him in a big way.

"We need to let him get back in his car," Shane said softly, and then louder so Kimmy could hear, "and if he doesn't turn around at the count of five, Kimmy's gonna let the dogs out and Angel Marie's going to eat your face, dammit!"

Brandon scrambled for the gate just as the pounding of hooves made everybody look up.

Deacon and Crick had arrived. Before he could sweep in, Brandon had scrambled out of the yard and had clanged the cattle gate between him and the reinforcements. Deacon slid off the horse and came to stand near Shane and Mikhail, curling his lip and looking in the direction of the cattle gate.

He said, "Who's the asshole covered in dog shit?" at about the same moment Kurt screamed, "Oh my God! Don't get in my car like that, dammit!" and they all snickered openly. Then Kurt saw Deacon, and his bruised eyes got wide over his taped and swollen nose. "Get the fuck in here! If the little one beat you, that fucker will rip you to shreds!"

Shane was holding back laughter because it hurt, but Crick had tied off the horse and was cracking up behind them. "Oh my God... we're some sort of gay enforcement squad!" and then Deacon was *really* laughing, turning to Crick and hanging on to him while the case of the snickers took over his whole body.

Brandon started stripping off his designer jeans and expensive purple shirt. "You think this is real fucking funny, Perkins!" he called.

"Jesus, who wouldn't?" Shane fought for breath.

"Well, good for you! You'll think it's fucking hilarious when I call your captain and tell him about you getting boned by a guy in the locker room! Bet he doesn't know that's why you left L.A., is it!"

Shane snarled, some of the laughter gone. "That's not why I left L.A., asshole! That's why I got fucking shot down in an alleyway without backup, and since you're the one who was trying to talk me into boning, I think what's hilarious is that you're bringing it up now!"

Deacon stopped laughing, and both he and Crick looked at him, their faces screwed up into one of those grimaces people use when they're trying to make things fit. Then Deacon looked at Mikhail, who was still hopping on his toes and looking like he might rush Brandon again for the hell of it.

"Jesus," Deacon muttered, "did *your* taste improve!"

Shane shrugged, a little embarrassed now. Brandon seemed so transparent—so empty. He couldn't believe he'd ever fallen for that. Now, he just had to get it off his property. He started to move forward, and suddenly Mikhail was on his bad side, helping him to move, and Deacon was at his shoulder. Crick was really tall with a chest like a tractor, so he was sort of fun to have around too.

"Brandon," he said, as Brandon grabbed the plastic bag Kurt had offered and shoved his clothes inside it, "I'm already out at the station here. And they fucked with me—but I lived, so you know what? Do your worst. But before you show up at the station house, you might want to ask Kurt here how much blow he's got stashed in the car, because I'll be calling my captain and telling him you're coming."

Brandon looked up and blanched. "You've got fucking *what*?"

"Yeah," Kimmy called before Kurt could reply, "and he's got it stashed in at least six places—you'll never be able to find it all!"

"Shut up, bitch!" Kurt screamed, before Brandon reached into the car and grabbed him by the throat.

"*You've got fucking WHAT?*" he demanded, and Kurt sneered back.

"I've got a fucking naked queer in my car until we can get back to the hotel, that's what I've fucking got! And it doesn't look like you've got any fucking money, either!"

Kurt talked a good game, but he was backing up against the window and looking nervously at Brandon—Brandon was bloody and angry and a little bit dangerous, but not as dangerous as Deacon or Crick or Mikhail.

Shane raised his eyebrows. "Yeah. You guys have a fun ride home. Kurt, I'd wear a rubber if he's going to pay for gas with blowjobs. You don't know where that's been."

They stood there until Brand shoved his clothes in the trunk and then got in the car to let Kurt peel out and drive him away.

Shane took a deep breath—which was harder than it sounded—and called out, "Kimmy, darlin', could you let out the fucking dogs before they shit in the kitchen?"

"Yeah, Shaney," she said back, and Mikhail said, "Dammit, Deacon, keep holding him up!" while he ran interference to keep the dogs from knocking Shane on his ass.

Eventually Shane was settled on the couch, figuring he'd done his good deed for the day, and Kimmy had seen Crick and Deacon out after offering them soda and some breakfast. They took her up on it, and Shane lay there, listening to their easy conversation and figuring his life had gotten really, really good in the last year, hadn't it? Kimmy was a little depressed to be surrounded by so many pretty gay men, but as she said wryly to Deacon, it was probably a good idea that she stay away from the straight ones for a while until her life was straightened out on its own.

Mikhail came out from cleaning up in time to tell Crick and Deacon thank you and offer them some carrots for the horse. It was nice of him, since just seeing the damned horse tethered to the porch had caused him to utter a little squeak and vault his way up the porch instead of taking the stairs near the big animal. But finally it was just the three of them in the house again. Mickey sat next to him on the couch, and Kimmy took the club chair that sat kitty-corner. Shane took Mikhail's battered hands in his and stroked the scraped knuckles.

"That was pretty fucking awesome," he said happily, looking at Mikhail's smug expression.

Mikhail preened. "Well, yes. See what happens when you choose a better man?"

"I never doubted it," Shane murmured, and Mikhail squeezed his hand.

"I did," he said seriously. "Which is why I'm so determined to not let you go."

Shane had been reclining, closing his eyes and fighting the sleep that came with the painkillers and the trip the day before and the adrenaline bleed now that the confrontation was over. Now he turned his head and looked Mikhail in the eye.

"Social work isn't safe," he said quietly. "I could still get shot or stabbed or beaten if I start haunting the streets, looking for kids to save. You know that, right? You're tough, Mickey—you know how you got that way. It's not going to be any safer for me."

Mikhail shook his head. "It will be. It will. It will be safer because you will be going in on your own terms. It will be safer because you will not be working odd shifts or sent to neighborhoods you do not want to go into. It will be safer because you will believe in what you are doing. And still—I know it is not perfect, Shane. I know it will be hard. But you will be happy. You will be happy, and maybe, if you are happy, it will be easier to duck, you think?"

Shane nodded. "You know, that's twice in two days I did everything I could possibly do to avoid calling the police. I guess I don't want to be a part of that anymore." Wow. That big hairy fight, and now, after watching Mikhail come to his rescue like his guardian angel, wasn't it so easy to say? He didn't have to be a hero anymore. He had his own personal hero to defend him. Wasn't that miracle enough?

Mikhail smiled then, shyly. "You are a part of us instead. It will suffice?"

"Mikhail?" Shane asked dreamily. Now that the hairy fight was resolved, he really was going to fall asleep right there on the couch. His side was throbbing to a dull tide, but that was forgotten with the feel of Mickey's rough hand in his own.

"Yes, *lubime*?"

"Where do you learn all those big words?"

"Movies, big man. Same place you learned how to be a hero."

"Mmm. You never did tell me what your favorite movie is."

"*The Incredibles.* What did you think it would be? Now go to sleep—when you wake up, you will call up and quit your job, and then cow-woman and I will jump up and down and scream like children since you can't."

"Love you, Mikhail."

"Love you, Shane."

And that was how he quit his job.

IT WASN'T easy. He had to go back to school, and don't think *that* wasn't a mindfuck, but it was sort of fun too. He took social work classes and legal classes—and a few units of English literature, since, hey, he was there anyway and he loved it.

Kimmy called their mother, and she reluctantly gave up title to Shane's trust (since he was supposed to have claimed it when he turned twenty-one) and Shane had—literally—enough money to establish a shelter, build it from scratch, and run it for many years. They planned on it becoming self-sufficient on generated income since it would be the kind of place that taught job skills as well as living skills—but Shane had a course in grant-writing in his future, he knew that too. He also had enough money to support his family with no worries for pretty much ever—which was a simple relief, and that was the truth.

Kimmy took some of those classes with Shane, figuring, in her words, "There's no rehab counselor like an old addict," and Shane was so proud of her—of them—jumping into this together like the twins they'd never really been.

Mikhail did not take those classes. He figured he would be helping to run the place enough, he would let Shane and Kimmy do the paperwork, and he would do what he was best at: dance and listen. He was really, Shane often told him, the best sort of listener.

They bought the vacant field next to The Pulpit, and Deacon, for one, was very relieved. For one thing, developing the land meant having someone level all the weed growth on the property, and that helped keep the snakes from living there, which also kept the snakes from migrating onto Deacon's property, and that was a concern.

But mostly Deacon was happy because his muckrakers would have a place to live, and Shane would have easy access for a place to employ the kids in his shelter. Between the lot of them, they spent long nights discussing how the shelter should be built and how to make sure everybody had their own room and how to make the living room central to it, so everybody could sit and eat and be safe.

Between them all, the simplest, most obvious name for the place was Promise House.

It was a beautiful dream—Shane just couldn't believe how many people shared this beautiful dream, how many of them wanted it to come true.

Kimmy and Mikhail bought out Kurt's portion of the dance troupe, and Brett joined them, and the dance went on after all. It kept them busy, but when school started in September, Shane was unable to go see them perform as often as he liked. Sometimes, though, he brought his schoolbooks and did his homework with Kimmy during the downtime. This meant that every now and then, he could put on the clothes Mikhail had helped him pick out one giddy, golden October day the year before and go watch them dance.

They still took his breath away. They were the most beautiful things in his life.

One Sunday evening, Mikhail pulled The Purple Brick into the driveway, and an hour later, they were lying on their stomachs in front of one of the drawers in the pedestal bed that used to be Mikhail's. Shane and Mikhail had their chins propped on their hands, and Kimmy was hanging upside down over the edge of her mattress.

They were watching the miracle of birth.

One of Shane's "rescue-ees" had called Shane from the shelter in tears because her favorite cat had yet to find a home and was going to be put down. Mikhail had taken one look at the tiny-boned, pregnant feline with the long black and white hair, called her Angelina Jolie, and elected to make her his.

"I'd call her Britney Spears," he'd said disdainfully, "but Angelina can pump out children and still maintain a little class."

When they'd arrived home from the faire, they found that Angelina had made herself at home in Kimmy's sock drawer and was in the process of squeezing out some babies.

They were all fascinated. A little grossed out—especially when Angelina started licking the afterbirth off the icky thing she'd just produced—but fascinated. Eventually, she was done squeezing them out, and there was an eclectic line of four kittens nursing and a tired Angelina, still licking the nearest one occasionally, just for form.

"Hmm...," murmured Mikhail, pushing himself up to take a better look at the kittens. He was on his elbows with his feet raised above his knees and crossed at the ankles. He looked like a teenaged girl at a slumber party, but Shane wasn't going to complain. He was also still wearing his faire clothes, and Shane didn't have to be at class until ten the next morning. He figured there was still some time for some hot, costumed sex, especially since Kimmy had fallen asleep and was curled up on the mattress above them, snoring gently.

"She *has* been a kitty slut." Mikhail turned to him, nodding vigorously. "Look at her—there isn't a single tuxedo kitten in the bunch." He grinned indulgently. "Well, it is a good thing you went out and had your fun, Angelina, yes it is. You will be fixed before you can shake your ass again, and won't that be a surprise?"

Shane chuckled. "Go ahead and kill a girl's dreams," he muttered, and one of Mikhail's shoulders lifted in that snitty little shrug that could still make Shane's abdomen clench.

"She will live. It will be especially nice to have her not screeching for hot tomcat loving all over the neighborhood, I think we will both agree. Do you think I could touch one?" he asked abruptly, and Shane nodded.

"Yes, but only because you're her favorite. Here—stick out your finger to her, and wait to see if she'll rub her cheek on it."

"Ahh... the introduction." Mikhail did what Shane said, and the cat rubbed her nose and then her cheek repeatedly on it, until she finally settled back, purring.

"Yeah—and now your finger smells like her, so it won't freak her out when you touch her babies. Go ahead—one finger."

Gingerly, Mikhail extended that finger—fine-boned and long and tan—and stroked the top of a fuzzy, ginger colored head. The expression on his face was one of careful awe. He finished and tucked his elbows back under his body, and they continued to watch the new family in the happy quiet.

"You do know a lot about making strays feel at home, don't you, big man?" Mikhail murmured into the peace.

Shane shrugged—it wasn't nearly as graceful—and then flattened his arms and tucked his chin into his hands. "You just have to let them feel powerful," he said, thinking hard. "If they feel like they have options, most of them will take the option to like you."

Mikhail lay flat, too, and turned serious blue-gray eyes to him. "I did," he said with a faint smile, and Shane bristled.

"You weren't a stray," he muttered. "You were… are… like a big jungle cat. I just… I took one look at you, and damn. I just wanted to run with you, that's all. Even if you clawed my heart out."

"I almost did," Mickey told him gently, and Shane's returning smile was whole and adoring.

"Yeah, but the results were so worth it."

Mikhail blinked rapidly and swallowed hard, but he didn't look away. "We should make promises," he said, and in this perfect, quiet moment, it didn't sound abrupt at all.

"Promises? I thought we already did."

"No—in front of friends and family. You know—a wedding, I guess, if two men may have such a thing. Maybe Deacon and Crick would let us use the same place."

"A wedding?" Shane liked the idea. He liked it very much—even when it made him blush. A lot. "Think we could dress up? You know, like this?" Mikhail looked so very much himself in his Ren Faire outfit. Shane was enchanted by the thought of him in front of their family and friends the same way Shane saw him.

The look on Mikhail's face was priceless, though. "If we wanted to break the gay-o-meter, why yes. Sure, *lubime*, we can dress like this." He shook his head in bemusement. "But we should do it."

"When?" Shane asked, warming to the idea.

"In February," Mikhail said decisively. "It will be cold—and maybe that alone will keep us out of costume"—he rolled his eyes—"but," and now his voice dropped, and he looked melancholy for a moment, "but, maybe, if we have it in February, and play Tchaikovsky, Mutti will hear. Maybe she will visit and watch. She really did love you, you know."

"I loved her," Shane admitted painfully. Mikhail's mother had been a miracle, just like her son. "I think that's an awesome idea, Mickey. I'd love to marry you."

"Make promises," Mikhail amended. "Marriage is for the sentimental."

"And we're not sentimental in the least," Shane told him gravely, smiling.

"Stop that, you irritating man. I can hear your smugness from here."

Shane scooted closer then so his body was warmed with Mikhail's heat and raised himself up on his elbows again, leaning in to kiss Mikhail's cheek. He was pleasantly surprised when Mikhail turned his head and they met lips instead, and the familiar taste of his lover flooded him, and he sighed and fell into the kiss. They pulled apart for a minute and resumed their watch on the new family.

"We can keep a kitten?" Mikhail asked happily.

"Buddy, you're the one who cleans the cat boxes."

"Yes, *mishka*, I am. You are right. We will keep one."

"Mickey, what does *mishka* mean? You've been calling me that for months."

Mikhail's look at him was sly and predatory—just like the jungle cat Shane had mentioned. "If you are very nice to me in bed, I just may tell you."

Shane grinned and stood up to go shower, lowering his hand to help Mickey up. He came up and popped happily into Shane's arms.

"I am always very nice to you in bed," Shane assured him, and Mikhail's smile became serious.

"You are always very nice to me, period, my beloved. I am so glad I found you."

Shane blushed. "Yeah. Me too—can we go have sex now?"

Mickey's grin was open and free and perfect. "Absolutely."

They were walking quietly to the bedroom when he added, "Love you, Shane."

"Love you too, Mickey."

It was really the only promise they needed.

AMY LANE teaches high school English, mothers four children, and writes the occasional book. When she's not begging students to sit-the-hell-down or taxiing kids to soccer/dance/karate—oh my! she can be found catching emergency naps, grocery shopping, or hiding in the bathroom, trying to read without interruption. She will never be found cooking, cleaning, or doing domestic chores, but she has been known to knit up an emergency hat/blanket/pair of socks for any occasion whatsoever or sometimes for no reason at all. She writes in the shower, while commuting, while her classes are doing bookwork, or while she's wandering the neighborhood at night pretending to exercise and has learned from necessity to type like the wind. She lives in a spider-infested and crumbling house in a shoddy suburb and counts on her beloved mate, Mack, to keep her tethered to reality—which he does while keeping her cell phone charged as a bonus. She's been married for twenty plus years and still believes in Twu Wuv, with a capital Twu and a capital Wuv, and she doesn't see any reason at all for that to change.

Visit Amy's web site at http://www.greenshill.com. You can e-mail her at amylane@greenshill.com.

Revisit Levee Oaks with AMY LANE

Carrick Francis has spent most of his life jumping into trouble with both feet. The only thing saving him from prison or worse is his absolute devotion to Deacon Winters. Deacon was Crick's sanity and salvation during a miserable, abusive childhood, and Crick would do anything to stay with him forever. So when Deacon's father dies, Crick puts his college plans on hold to help Deacon as Deacon has helped him.

Deacon's greatest wish is to see Crick escape his memories and the town they grew up in so Crick can enjoy a shining future. But after two years of growing feelings and temptation, the painfully shy Deacon finally succumbs to Crick's determined advances and admits he sees himself as part of Crick's life.

It nearly destroys Deacon when he discovers Crick has been waiting for him to push him away, just like Crick's family did in the past. When Crick's knack for volatile decisions lands him far away from home, Deacon is left, shell-shocked and alone, struggling to reforge his heart in a world where love with Crick is a promise, but by no means a certainty.

http://www.dreamspinnerpress.com

Contemporary Romance from DREAMSPINNER PRESS

http://www.dreamspinnerpress.com